SYLVANOR

THE SECRET OF UNDER HOLLOW

ERIC J. WEISSER

Connex Media, LLC

Sylvanor
The Secret of Under Hollow
All Rights Reserved.
Copyright © 2014 Eric J. Weisser
v6.0

Cover Photo © 2014 Eric J. Weisser. All rights reserved. Cover Art by Nichole Cardiff.

Connex Media, LLC

ISBN: 978-0-578-14308-8

Library of Congress Control Number: 2014940312

PRINTED IN THE UNITED STATES OF AMERICA

*This book is dedicated to all those who dare not just to dream,
but who dare to make their dreams a reality.*

I would like to extend a very heartfelt thank you to all of my Kickstarter subscribers who pledged to make this book a reality:

Annette Ada, Jason Allen, Mary Bicz, Cathy Callicut, Jacob Carson, Monica and Kenny Clark, Steve Cypert, Carol and John Denil, Shane and Lori Denil, Buppie Dee, Christopher Doyle, Sunshine Freisleben, Jessica Garcia, Anne and Andy Gimenez, Steve and Nancy Goldberg, Louis and Karie Goldberg, Keith Hall, Judy and Gage Hunt, Megan Leonard, Robin Maras, Veronika Maronyan, Jenifer and Sheri McGuire-Neva, Janet O'Pella, Bonnie Marie Ratner, Philda Todzaniso, Marcie Turner, Megan and Yossi Turner-Tabakh, Stephen Vander Meulen, Barbara Vargas, Marsha and Raul Vargas, Kristian Weinholtz, Patricia Weisser, and Alexa, Joel, and Jack Young

Thank you very much to Rob Carrillo
for editing this fantastic adventure.
To Nicole Cardiff for the amazing cover art.
And to Judith Hunt for the wonderful map of the realm.

And a very special thank you to my fiancé, Jace Vargas, for all of his love and support, without whom this book would never have risen from Under Hollow to see the light of day.

Please like us on facebook at:
www.facebook.com/sylvanor.books
and on twitter:
@SylvanorBooks

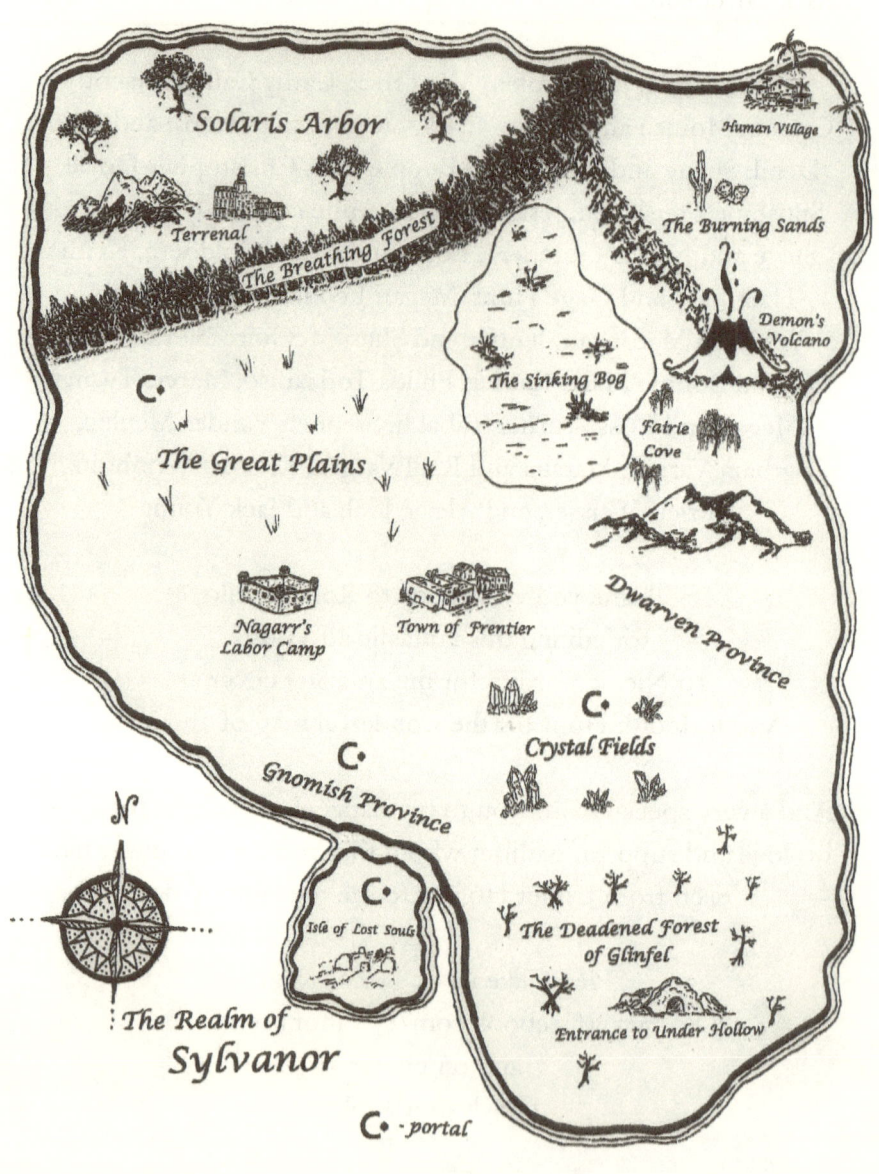

Solaris Arbor

Terrenal

The Breathing Forest

Human Village

The Burning Sands

Demon's Volcano

The Sinking Bog

Fairie Cove

The Great Plains

Dwarven Province

Nagarr's Labor Camp

Town of Frentier

Crystal Fields

Gnomish Province

N

Isle of Lost Souls

The Deadened Forest of Glinfel

Entrance to Under Hollow

The Realm of
Sylvanor

C• ·portal

Prologue

Placing her gray hand upon the large amber-colored globe, Valeria, Queen of the Dark Elves, gently closed her eyes and took in a slow, deep breath. Her eyes rolled back in her head and her eyelids began to flutter. The orb vibrated beneath her touch and she could feel its energy pulsate throughout her body. The energy of the sphere was coursing through her veins and it was as if she was no longer an individual, but a part of time itself.

With a slight hum, the globe glowed softly in its center, the glow reaching outward until its light filled the chamber. The Queen, basking in its radiance, looked more like a goddess now than a mere mortal. Truly, she was a woman of power and more than a force with which to be reckoned.

The brilliant light soon died down and was now contained within the globe. Valeria slowly opened her eyes, careful to make sure that the light was doused just enough so as to avoid hurting her extremely light-sensitive eyes. She marveled at its beauty and wonder, looking upon it as if for the first time.

Careful not to release her touch, she slowly and rhythmically waved her hand across its surface. The light inside the globe moved like water beneath her fingertips, and the Queen's shadow flickered and danced on the wall, as if illuminated by candlelight. The air in the chamber was still and yet her hair thrashed wildly, whipping her in the face. She leaned her head back and opened her eyes wide.

Inside the globe, thick black smoke was swirling like a vortex. As it dissipated, glowing red eyes appeared. They belonged to the Demon Lord Voltanis, who could be seen walking on the soil in the world of the living, out of the depths of the planes of Hell. He marched with legions of dragons soaring through the air under his command. Together, they laid waste to the mortal world. Under his cunning leadership, the dragons charred entire villages and settlements. One by one, the continents fell, their inhabitants not strong enough to repel the demon-led attacks.

Queen Valeria watched history unfold before her eyes with a stern, emotionless face. Mere handfuls of inhabitants of each continent barely escaped their homelands and made it to the realm of Sylvanor. It was there that they made their stand; gnomes, fairies, orcs, elves, and dwarves set aside their differences to become one allied force. The greatest among them joined together and forged the most powerful protective spell ever conjured. Soon, the entire realm would be shrouded in an invisible barrier that would prevent their enemies from entering…but it would also prohibit anyone from leaving.

The Demon Lord's dragon followers were condemned to die on their own charred lands with little food and water. Voltanis, however, discovered a portal that would bypass the magical barrier and take him directly into the heart of Sylvanor. He unleashed his fury upon village after village, bent on destroying the last continent and turning it into his newest plane of Hell.

After much of the realm lay in ruins, Voltanis met his fate at the hands of the most powerful of Sylvanor's heroes and was sent back to his domain; the portal through which he traveled was sealed for all eternity. The races united in celebration, but peace was short-lived. As the immigrants to Sylvanor grew and flourished, the realm soon fell victim to a new problem: overcrowding. Trapped on Sylvanor by their own barrier spell, the races began to fight among themselves, claiming various territories and setting up borders around their self-declared provinces. The territorial struggles soon escalated to all-out war when the dark elves refused to give up their underground lair, Under Hollow.

Closing all but one of the entrances with smaller versions of the gigantic protective spell, Under Hollow became a virtual stronghold. Realizing that their new defensive spells were much less powerful than the one that surrounded Sylvanor and would weaken with time, the dark elves created a new portal that would allow them to find a new home, a place where they could live without fear of extinction.

The Queen shook her head in disgust at the image of her kind leaving Under Hollow. "I care not about the achievements of Fenrik," she said of her rival with a jealous tone. "I wish to see *my* conquests and accomplishments."

The globe grew darker but soon returned with its unique imagery of the realm's history. Queen Valeria was now seen in the globe, leading her people into battle and turning the tide of the realm's war in the favor of the dark elves. On her side was a new, mysterious race of humanoid dragons that were just as deadly as the dragons in the first Great War; however, their smaller, reconfigured frame made them even more efficient killing machines. With this new army at her command, she attacked the dwellers above ground, committing genocide on all races that weren't dark elven. Even their light elf cousins were not spared from the onslaught.

The provinces fell quickly, and those who were left alive were enslaved in labor camps to perform menial tasks for the Dark Elf Empire. Solaris Arbor, the light elf province, was the only land that did not fall to the Queen's terrible power. A surrounding territory known as the Breathing Forest, a beautiful, dense forest through which only the pure of heart could pass, provided complete protection to Solaris Arbor.

The globe settled its image on the Breathing Forest and on the peaceful land of light elves that lay beyond it. She squinted, sneering at the land that would not fall to her. She ran her hand lightly across the globe one final time and the image of Solaris Arbor shimmered beneath her touch. "Soon," she stated with a twisted grin, "you will be mine."

Chapter I

———⟨∘⟩⟨∘⟩⟨∘⟩———

The Heart of the Enemy

The rain fell hard in Under Hollow. The barrage of rain-drops made the large leaves of the Cocil trees bob and dance. The huge rubbery trees whipped in the cold wind, caus-ing several of their branches to occasionally tap and scratch the rooftop of the carriage. The screeching sound went through Aldara like fingernails grating down a piece of slate.

Looking out of the carriage window and into the forest, past the swaying Cocil trees, she spotted the occasional blink-ing of small yellow lights. *Dracal*, thought Aldara. Servants of evil, the Dracal are beasts that are humanoid in form, while possessing the awesome powers of dragons. Breaths of fire, acid, lightning, or gas spit from their mouths in battle, while their huge, leathery wings allowed them to fly in groups over entire villages, destroying them within minutes. The images of the burning houses and the memory of the stench of burning flesh brought Aldara out of her daydream.

Just how could it be raining in Under Hollow? she pondered.

The land of Under Hollow exists underneath the deadened forest of Glinfel. It is not exposed to the sky. Looking out the window, she saw plants she had never seen before. There were flowers as large as dwarves, and vines longer and thicker than any rope she had ever seen. The brilliant colors of these plants were toned down by a wash of eerie dark blue light. Craning her neck, she looked skyward. They were passing under a huge blue force field dome. Aldara believed, from previous attempts to enter Under Hollow, that the force fields would not let any object through them. She had assumed, at least until now, that only light could pass through the magical domes. The rain now smacking her in the face proved her wrong.

So, it looks as if at least water and light can penetrate the domes. Interesting, Aldara thought as she pulled her head back into the carriage and tugged on her hood to bring it down, once again, over much of her face.

She glanced around the inside of the carriage at her fellow passengers. She knew that they were all elders from Solaris Arbor who once held seats on the High Council of the land, but she did not know why they were here. She only knew that stealing one of the councilmen's robes and posing as one of them would be the only way she would finally enter Under Hollow. She had tried for many seasons to enter Under Hollow, always without success. But now she was here, deep inside the strange, magical land of the dark elves. There *had* to be answers down here somewhere. Perhaps they were out there in the forest or hidden in the Overlord's castle. Either way, she had to uncover them if there would be any hope of saving the land of Sylvanor from the Overlord's tyrannical grip.

The Overlord had not been seen since the Dark Occupation

began. *Had he resided in the castle of Under Hollow all this time, letting the Queen do his dirty work while he sat on his throne, enjoying the luxuries of power?* So many questions must be answered. At last, here was the opportunity for Aldara to answer them.

Looking around at the hooded councilmen, she tried, as nonchalantly as possible, to quietly turn the handle of the carriage door. If she could open the door, run into the forest, and hide among the fauna in the storm, she might not be discovered. She might even find a way to penetrate the force field domes, enabling her to come back with an army of troops to liberate the land of Sylvanor. Finally, she would not only be accepted among the various races of the realm, but also be worshipped as a hero.

Stupid, she thought. She had no idea what creatures inhabited the dark forest. For that matter, she didn't even know where in Under Hollow she was. Letting go of the door handle, she sat back and let out a brief sigh. She was now a prisoner of sorts, stuck in the carriage and along for the ride, unable to exit until it came to the stop where the elders would depart. *Just where was their final destination? Why were they even here in the first place, going of their own free will into the heart of the enemy?* All of these questions had her head pounding, craving answers. *Clear your mind, Aldara*, she ordered herself. *Remember your studies. The quiet mind discovers all things.*

As Aldara slipped into a meditative state, her thoughts began to wander back to her childhood. Growing up had not been easy. Her light elf foster parents provided her with a loving home—a sanctuary in which she was surrounded with encouragement and love. The outside world, however, was very different. Most of the light elven children feared her dark elf side, masking their fear with cruelty. She was picked on, bullied, and often spat upon by her classmates. She had but one true friend who had often showed her kindness, and she loved him with all her heart. A part of Aldara died the day she realized that he was developing feelings for his fairie friend. Their friendship drifted, but she continued to love him from afar, never revealing her feelings. She often fantasized that he would one day return those feelings and marry her.

Underneath her cloak, her shoulders slumped as her thoughts traveled to her foster parents. Aldara was told that they were friends of her biological parents who had taken her in after an angry mob of fanatical humans, fearing that the half-breed was a bad omen of things to come, attacked their home. Aldara understood that her biological mother and father had given their lives to protect her as her foster parents carried her into the safety of the night.

Her posture straightened as she recalled her last memory of her foster father, beaming during her lessons, telling her how proud he was that she could pick up magic so easily. She flashed an unconscious smile under her hood that quickly vanished. It was the last time anyone had ever said that they were proud of her.

Sadly, her foster parents had also perished...not at the hands of an angry mob, but under the tyrannical fist of the dark elf Overlord during the taking of Sylvanor. She wished they were still alive to give her the love and guidance she now so desperately needed. Maybe then she would feel more confident about what she was doing. Maybe she would actually *know* what she was doing. Teaching herself the lost arts of the ancients was not an easy thing to do; few artifacts and stories were to be found about the ways of magic when the two races of elves had been one. But now was her chance to observe the black magic of the dark elves. Now she had a chance to learn about the forces that dwelled in Under Hollow. To fully understand the power of the light, one must completely comprehend the power of the dark.

I must be mentally prepared to absorb all that I can while I'm down here, she instructed herself. Hoping that this would be her last thought until they reached their destination, Aldara sat back in the carriage and slowly closed her eyes. Folding her hands with index fingers pointing outward, she began, once again, to meditate.

In what seemed like only a few moments, the carriage jerked to a stop. Aldara snapped out of her meditation when she heard the elegant language of the dark elf mixed with the beastly grunting of the Dracal, shouting all around her. She opened her eyes and saw several figures standing outside the carriage. She turned her gaze to the elders seated around her, noticing that their posture remained the same as it had been a few hours ago. *Were they still lost in meditation? Perhaps they were too old to complete their journey. A few hours' ride must have seemed like years to them.* A smile curled Aldara's lips. No matter how hard she tried to respect the elders, she always somehow found a way to laugh at their expense.

The door to the carriage creaked as it opened. "Kindly exit and follow my lead," said a dark-cloaked figure in a soft, broken version of the light elf language. From her position in the carriage, Aldara could not make out any details about him.

The elders slowly rose to a crouching stance, careful not to hit their heads on the roof of the carriage, and exited one by one. Aldara grabbed the hood of her cloak and pulled it tight over her face. She must make them believe that she is one of the elders or her cover would be blown. Imagining the horrors that would be bestowed upon her if she were discovered, she took a deep breath, rose cautiously from her seat, and followed the elders outside.

Stepping out of the carriage, she found her group surrounded by a dozen Dracal and a handful of dark elves in their traditional dark violet body-length robes. Aldara caught herself staring at the terrifying sight of the Dracal. She had never been this close to one before. They stood before her—towering over her—her own height reaching only to their shoulder blades. They wore no armor; their thick, scaly skin was all they needed to protect themselves from weapons. She cocked her head to glance at the large leathery wings folded behind them. There was something not quite right about their eyes. The brilliant yellow glow that emanated from them was unlike anything she had ever seen. In fact, their whole species had never been seen in any of the realms until the Overlord came into power. *Where had they come from?*

Clear your mind, Aldara. Pay attention to your surroundings and they will provide the answers you need. Aldara closed her eyes and took a deep breath.

Just then, an unexpected voice from the darkness said, "Good evening and thank you for coming. The Overlord will be most pleased you made the journey under such harsh weather conditions. I am Commander Zelgot, in charge of the Dracal army, and I will be your escort through the courtyard to the portal inside the castle."

Aldara opened her eyes and gazed upon the Commander.

He was not dressed like the other dark elves. Instead of a robe, he wore the polished silver armor of a warrior. A tall, handsome man with typical dark elf features, he had jet-black hair and dark blue eyes that seemed to almost glow. He was a proud man, as well he should be. His name was known and feared throughout the entire realm of Sylvanor.

So this is the bastard that captured my friends all those months ago, she thought as she sneered at Zelgot from under her hood. A brief flash of her childhood love washed over her. *Were he and his friends still alive? Were they taken to one of the 'death camps' that existed in the world above?* She often wondered if fleeing the scene of their capture to 'fight another day' was the right thing to do; now that she was in Under Hollow, so close to discovering its secrets and power, she knew she had done the right thing. Perhaps Aldara could use the knowledge she was about to gain to free them all.

Her focus returned to the events around her and to their captor, who was standing directly in front of her. The thought of standing so close to him made Aldara want to spit on that handsome face of his. Anger was quick to rise in Aldara; she often reacted suddenly and without thinking. This had caused trouble for her far more times than she could count. But this time, she *must* control her anger. Her secrecy and her plan depended on it.

"This way, please." Zelgot extended his hand and ushered the group toward the castle entrance. "I know you must be tired but the walk is not far." The Commander walked up to Aldara and leaned down, trying to peer inside her hood, but saw nothing but blackness. "I hope you had a chance to rest on your journey?" he asked her. Aldara slowly nodded and continued to walk with the rest of the group, remembering to walk slightly hunched over, imitating those who were much, much older than she.

It was difficult to take in all of her surroundings with her hood pulled so tightly over her head, but there was no way to remedy that situation. Aldara opened all of her other senses as best she could. The moist, warm, humid air stuck to her skin. The sweet fragrance of the huge flowering plants that seemed to be everywhere clashed with the foul stench of the Dracal. *They smelled like they hadn't had a bath in their lives*, she thought as the stench caused her to cough softly. The sound of their heavy breathing and grunting disgusted her as well. They were true beasts, whose sole purpose in life was to serve the Overlord without question, never offering an opinion or thought of their own.

The courtyard was huge and beautiful. Upon entering, everything could be seen much more easily than out on the path. Torches lined the walls, lighting immaculately carved stone and wooden benches. A magnificent fountain spewed streams of water high into the air before they fell into a foamy pool. Beautiful figures were carved into the fountain as well as magical symbols of luck and prosperity. Aldara was able to make out most of them, but she again found that her knowledge of the dark arts was too limited to fully assist her in translating all of the words and symbols on the fountain. The grounds were also well kept. The grass was not over-grown and all of the bushes were neatly trimmed. Indeed, the dark elves were proud of their homeland. She knew they were a proud race, but she had no idea just how deep that pride would go.

"The torches on the walls are provided mostly for your group. We know how important proper lighting can be to you dwellers above ground." The tone in Commander Zelgot's voice was that of both sarcasm and bitterness, yet he was smooth and charming at the same time. It was no wonder he was able to rise quickly in the ranks and serve directly under the Queen.

"Please wait here a moment while we raise the gates to the inner chamber," Zelgot kindly asked the group of elders. He then turned and shouted a command in his native language to the control tower above. All waited in anticipation as a shadowy figure up in the left tower nodded affirmatively and left the window. A few seconds later, a loud rumbling was heard, and the huge, thick iron gates slowly began to rise. It was a thundering sound. The screeching of the pulleys mixed with the grunting of the Dracal pulling the ropes and wires through them sent a shiver down Aldara's spine. Even the elders, who had not moved aside from walking, winced as the gates were opened.

Another shiver came over Aldara. This one was different. It seemed to have come from inside her. They were being watched. She shifted her focus to one of the tallest structures of the castle, a large circular structure covered by a glass dome that mimicked the force field domes that let the sunlight into Under Hollow. Her gaze fell to one of the windows on the side of the structure. There was a figure standing in the window. Aldara couldn't make out much more than the shadow of the figure but the silhouette was all she needed to see: long, flowing robes and the unmistakable neckpiece that jutted out and up from the shoulders, imitating elf ears.

There was no mistaking Queen Valeria. Even though she was far above them in another building, just gazing in her direction overwhelmed Aldara.

She figured the Queen must have been watching them from the time they entered the courtyard, standing in the window, motionless. But as the gates lifted fully and the large wooden doors behind them began to open, the Queen slowly walked away from the window.

Aldara's attention was brought back to the wooden doors' opening when a warm breeze swept out from inside the castle and past their group. The warmth was a comforting feeling and Aldara found herself anxious to get inside.

"If you'll follow me, the way to the portal is not far. Fear not, honored guests, for your journey is almost at an end." Zelgot was clearly a diplomat who truly loved his position. So much pride and ego ran through his veins; Aldara took note of this weakness for future reference.

The group entered the main hall of the castle. It was a huge multi-story room. Sconces were lit all around the room and huge tapestries were hung over the cold stone walls, making the room quite comfortable. Sitting on benches in the main hall were small groups of dark elves dressed in flowing violet cloaks. They were either buried in their books or engaged in soft conversation. Whatever it was they were doing, each of them paused and looked up at the group. They inspected the group of elders up and down and then went back to their conversations, some now with smirks on their faces.

The large wooden doors were slammed shut behind them, and the sound of the gates being lowered could be heard through the doors. Somehow, Aldara didn't feel as comfortable as she had moments before. Thinking that perhaps this wasn't the best of ideas after all, her heart began to race.

Taking a closer look at the wall coverings, she noticed that the tapestries were from lands conquered long ago, each from a different province above ground. The Dwarven province, the Gnomish province, they were all there. In fact, the only province that had not been captured by the Overlord's dark army was Solaris Arbor, land of the light elves, the province that existed on the other side of the Breathing Forest. There was room on the wall for one more tapestry, one more province to fall. *The flag of Solaris Arbor will not fill the empty space on the wall;* she promised herself that much. Aldara's hands began to sweat as she longed for the safety of her homeland. She could feel the anxiety building within her as her fear mixed with a growing hatred.

You can't back out now, Aldara. Even if you wanted to, there is no way out. You have to see this through. Maybe next time, you'll actually think more carefully before you do something so reckless. Her inner voice was no consolation to her. And she knew that everything it was saying to her was true. She was now in way over her head. *What is this portal they speak of? Where does it lead? Is it the same portal the Overlord and his minions fled through all those years ago? If so, why is it still open? Oh, clear your head and focus, Aldara. You can't afford any distractions now.*

The elders were marched through the center of the great hall. As they were being led through it, Aldara noticed the runes and ancient text on some of the books being read by the dark elves. They were spell books! In Aldara's mind, if she could get her hands on one of those books, her journey here would be a complete success.

Aldara could not afford to blow her cover by staring at the books. She continued to face forward with her head down as they exited the great hall and were led down several long corridors. There were too many to remember and each one looked the same. She lost her bearings in the labyrinth of hallways and was now lost inside the castle with the others, unable to retrace her steps. The realization of having only one true way out did not sit well with her, but she was vastly improving in her ability to control her fear.

The hallway opened up into a large room. This room was much brighter than any other room in the castle. Aldara kept her head bowed, continuing to imitate the elders as best as she could. Using what vision she had through the opening of her hood, she noticed there were several dark elves lining their path, and the foul stench of the Dracal told her that the dark elves were not alone. But there was something else. A cold feeling washed over her, but she dared not lift her head to investigate. She must now rely on her other senses.

"The portal is just down these stairs. If you'll follow me and watch your step." Zelgot's voice sounded even more confident than before, more proud.

Queen Valeria reached the bottom of the tower's staircase just in time to see the group of elders enter the room. One by one they entered, slowly walking, heads bowed, and arms folded. A smile curled the Queen's crimson lips. *At last, the elders are here. Everything is finally falling into place.* She snarled slightly at the thought that she would have been at this point a long time ago if she had been in command. The war would have been over much sooner and the power and glory would be hers alone, not the Overlord's.

The Queen watched as the group of elders started down the stone stairwell. Just then, something caught her eye. Something was not right. The Queen, not saying a word, simply lifted her finger and pointed to Aldara.

Aldara felt two sets of hands grab her arms and escort her out of the line. She looked up and saw that she was in the custody of two dark elves, their icy blue eyes staring into her. She had done her best to mimic the movements of the elders. Why was she being singled out? She started to struggle, to set herself free of the dark elves' grasp, but she knew it was hopeless. She watched helplessly as the last elder disappeared down the stairwell, followed by the sound of electricity and swooshing air, accompanied by flickering blue lights from somewhere below.

That is where I need to go, thought Aldara. So close to finding out the truth. So close to finding out what's going on, but now captured, literally yards away from her objective.

"Bring her to me." Queen Valeria's voice was calm and cool, like a midwinter's night.

The dark elves no longer needed to grab her and force her along. Aldara was now walking calmly toward the Queen, trying to stir as much confidence as she could. If she was going to die, it was not going to be as a coward.

The Queen is beautiful, Aldara thought. Long, pointed ears extended from her jet-black hair. Her hair flowed down in waves and curled around her deep crimson lips. Her black gown was made of a heavy velvet material that was trimmed with violet, perfectly accenting her dark gray skin. Around her neck was a circular medallion of pure silver, about the size of a coin, with a crescent moon in the middle and two wings spanning either side of the circle.

The Queen's hand reached out and tore the hood back from Aldara's face. The admiration was mutual and a look of surprise, even shock, came over the Queen's face. "My, my. What do we have here?" she asked rhetorically in her cool voice.

Aldara had the pale skin of a light elf but her hair was as black as the Queen's, with the exception of a gray streak that fell to the right of her face. A ring of gold in her right nostril was a stark contrast to her pale, pasty skin. Her young eyes were met by the Queen's aged eyes. Aldara was indeed young. Merely in her forties, she was a child compared to the elders, who were approaching two hundred.

"You are a mixed breed. A hybrid of light and dark elf," stated Queen Valeria.

"Yes, Your Majesty." Aldara was taken aback by the Queen's statement. She was quite surprised Valeria was even speaking to her at all. Knowing the Queen's hatred of anyone that wasn't dark elf, Aldara expected to be executed immediately.

"How interesting. How...perfect." A sneer lingered on the Queen's lips and her eyes tightened just a fraction.

"Perfect, Your Majesty? I don't understa—"

"What is your name, child?" the Queen coldly interrupted. The words cut like ice through Aldara's body.

Aldara backed up a step, only to find herself leaning against one of the dark elves who had brought her before the Queen. She regained her balance quickly. "Aldara," she replied.

The Queen kept her eyes focused on Aldara, never looking away, as if trying to read her soul. "Tell me, young Aldara, why are you here? Why did you find the need to infiltrate Under

Hollow and find your way into my castle?" She paused and looked around the room. "No, let me take a guess, shall I?" Her cool tone now turned to that of sarcasm. "No one has ever understood you your entire life. You had to constantly prove yourself to everyone around you. Infiltrating the council and posing as an elder to sneak into Under Hollow to discover its secrets to take back home with you would be the ultimate in proving yourself to the dwellers above. Am I right?"

Aldara's mouth, although cracking slightly, seemed to drop to the floor. She was fascinated, but also annoyed, that the Queen could know so much about her. Was the Queen reading her mind? "How do you know of all this? What magic are you using to probe inside my head?" She thought of denying it, but she could think of no excuse that would not blatantly insult the Queen's intelligence.

"No magic is needed to read into your past, child." Laughter started to pour from the Queen's lips. "It must not have been easy growing up half light and half dark elf, your friends never knowing what side you are on…your compassion to help struggling against your compulsion to delve into the dark arts forbidden to you in the world up above."

Aldara may have been improving on controlling her fear, but her anger was the emotion that still prevailed over any other; it was now surging to the surface. Is her life so open and obvious that she appeared to be nothing more than a laughable joke? "I am not a child. And it appears that you don't know everything about me. To even think that I would like to become anything like you sickens me." Aldara's voice was rising higher than even she was conscious of. "You have no love of the craft of magic! Your love is for yourself and the power that comes with slaughtering millions of countless beings to obtain it." Aldara stood solemnly, ready to die where she stood for making such blasphemous remarks to the face of evil itself.

"Dear, sweet child," began the Queen, keeping her composure. If she was angry, Queen Valeria did not let it show. She was a true master of emotion. "It is clear to me that you have much to learn about what is really going on and what has been going on all along up above. You came here seeking answers to these questions. I will provide the answers you seek."

A trick. It must be a trick. Surely, the Queen would not openly divulge information of her plans to an outsider from above ground. It could not be that simple, but Aldara would play her game. Just how far could she take this? Aldara despised the way the Queen kept her composure and remained in complete control of her emotions. This word game had become nothing more to Aldara than a match to break the Queen. She knew she was going to die; she might as well get in a few good insults before it happened.

"You do not believe me," stated Valeria. "What can I do to prove to you that I have a desire to give you truthful answers and earn your trust?"

"Why would you want to earn *my* trust?" Aldara paused, folded her arms, and looked directly into the Queen's eyes. "Okay. Let's start with the elders. Why have they journeyed all the way across Sylvanor, through Under Hollow to your castle, and then through a portal that leads to who knows where?" Aldara found that she was getting a little too cocky, but because she was sure that the Queen would kill her anyway, she let her demeanor continue.

The Queen's right eyebrow rose. She looked at Aldara for

a few moments and then began to speak. "The elders are here to bring peace between our two peoples. They are here so both sides can come to an agreement and end the conflict that has plagued our worlds."

"A conflict that was started by the Overlord!" snapped Aldara.

"Read your history, my dear. The light elves of Solaris Arbor sided with the outsiders who found refuge in Sylvanor. We were forced to live down here in Under Hollow for our own safety because the outsiders and the citizens of Solaris Arbor were ignorant to our ways; they did not approve of the use of what they called the 'dark arts'. Their ignorance was the cause of it all. We are simply reclaiming that which was taken from us. The land that was ours." The Queen walked away from Aldara toward the window she had been looking through when Aldara first arrived. She turned her head to look back at the young half-breed. "That, my child, is the truth that has been hidden from you."

"I don't believe you." The words flowed so freely from Aldara's lips. If only she could believe them. "The council, the light elves, have built a life around making peace and living a peaceful existence with all the other races of the realms."

"A peaceful existence on *their* terms. I don't expect you to discard everything you've been told and take me at my word. I can see it's going to take much more effort for you to believe me." The Queen actually sounded sincere.

"For starters, you can dismantle the 'death camps' you have set up throughout Sylvanor. Release those you hold captive," demanded Aldara in a tone that was almost commanding.

Queen Valeria let out a sigh and walked back to Aldara.

"My sweet child, how little you know. How misinformed you are." Moving in closer to Aldara, she placed her right hand on Aldara's cheek. "You and I are the same. Light and dark elves, we are all one and it pains me to see any one of us suffer." As Valeria's face moved closer to Aldara, she rested her left hand on Aldara's opposing cheek. Gently, the Queen's lips met Aldara's in a soft, gentle kiss that lasted a few moments.

Opening her eyes, Aldara retreated slowly, ending the kiss. Her eyes fluttered from surprise and embarrassment.

"These 'death camps' of which you speak are nothing more than detention centers and labor camps. They detain those who cannot be controlled by other means and at the same time allow them to help bring our worlds together," Valeria said as she regained her composure.

"Bring our worlds together?" Recovering from the kiss, Aldara still had a hint of sarcasm in her voice.

"Yes. They mine for the missing globes that help enlighten us all. Surely, you must be aware of them." The Queen gestured to a globe in the corner of the room.

Aldara's eyes lit up as she walked toward the globe. "Yes, of course. Everyone knows about them."

This particular globe was about two feet in diameter and nestled in a stand of gold. The globes hold special powers said to have been responsible for the dawning of all magic. When touched, the globes activate and perform the tasks they were designed to perform. Each orb is precious and extremely rare.

Enlightening Aldara with more information, the Queen came to stand beside her. "The globe here is called the Globe of History. It contains the chronicles of the entire realm. Everything significant since the globe was created has been recorded. Its work is never done."

Aldara reached toward the globe to rest her hand on its surface. The globe began to glow, turning from complete blackness to a brilliant white light. Aldara put her left hand in front of her eyes and the globe's light became more subdued, fading to a soft yellow. Placing her hand back down at her side, Aldara gazed into the globe while still resting her right hand on its surface. Images slowly appeared, faint at first, then clearer. She began to see them so clearly, she felt as if she was looking at the realm through a large window.

The Queen quickly grabbed Aldara's hand and removed it from its resting place on the globe, causing it to fade back to its blackened state. "Be careful, Aldara. You have not been trained properly on how to handle the globe. Its powers are strange and you could find yourself forever lost in them if you are not careful."

Aldara looked at the Queen and nodded as if she fully understood. "Where are the other globes?" Aldara asked with fascination.

"I assume the council in Solaris Arbor has a few of its own. What powers they possess, I am not certain," replied the Queen.

"The Globe of Power and the Globe of Future-Foretold are said to be lost in the City of the Ancients," stated Aldara. She suddenly felt a sense of importance, as if she was one up on the Queen.

Queen Valeria started to laugh and waved her hand in front of her face. "I am forced to believe the Lost City of the Ancients doesn't exist. The city and the wealth of magical information said to be contained therein are nothing more than a myth. I myself have spent many years looking for it, turning Under Hollow inside out as well as using the labor camps above to try to find it. All we ever came up with was dirt."

Aldara frowned. She supposed that what the Queen was saying had to be true. If the Queen had found the Lost City of the Ancients, her power would be ten times what it was now. "And what of the other globes? Has all your mining and searching ever turned up one of them?" The curiosity was eating away at her now.

"Actually, yes, in one of our camps. They just uncovered one of them yesterday. I am leaving here soon so I can inspect it myself and bring it back here. These globes are delicate. I do not entrust them to anyone." Valeria looked at Aldara as if looking for something inside her.

Aldara bowed her head, not allowing the Queen to probe the windows to her soul. "I see," replied Aldara. She could sense that the conversation was all but over and she could not help but wonder what was to become of her.

"Aldara." The Queen gently grabbed Aldara's chin and lifted her head. "Would you like to come with me?"

"*Me* come with *you*? To a death camp, err, labor camp, to evaluate a globe?" Aldara was stunned by the question and was wondering why she hadn't fainted upon hearing it.

"That's right," the Queen smiled. "You came here for answers and I told you I would give them to you. You will soon discover that the truth is not one-sided, but a much bigger picture."

Still in shock from the Queen's question, Aldara regained her composure. "Yes. I would like very much to accompany you on your journey."

"Good. Then it is settled. We will leave as soon as I change my attire." The Queen motioned to the dark elves who had pulled Aldara away from the line. "See that she is cleaned up and given proper clothes to wear. When she is ready, take her down to my carriage." Valeria turned to Aldara. "Don't be frightened, child. Go with them. They will take good care of you."

Aldara looked at the Queen, then at the two dark elves. A faint smile crossed Aldara's lips. *I'm getting out of this alive after all,* she thought. Aldara nodded in agreement as she was ushered out of the room by the Queen's royal servants.

"You can come out from the shadows now, Fenrik." The Queen turned to the curtains that were closed on the other side of the room. "I know you've been standing there the whole time. Don't you ever get bored with spying on me?" Her question seemed to have been spoken to the air.

The curtains rustled as a withered old hand emerged from them, followed by the rest of an old body.

Fenrik was an old dark elf. His growth stunted, he was no taller than a dwarf. His hair was gray with age and his long pointed ears now drooped a bit. His spectacles were pulled to the end of his nose as he emerged from the shadows. He was holding his precious, tiny Globe of Communication that he never seemed to be without.

"Never would I dream of spying on you, Your Highness," wheezed Fenrik. "I merely report that which I see to the Overlord per his command. I mean no disrespect to you, your greatness."

"No. Of course not," the Queen replied frigidly.

She hated Fenrik. Over the years she had done everything she could think of, aside from killing him herself, to get him out of her way. The only reason he was alive and well was that he reported directly to her husband, the Overlord. Fenrik was ordered to remain on Sylvanor to watch over her. She despised the way the Overlord did not fully trust her, and she was constantly taking it out on Fenrik.

"Do you think it's wise to take on this young stranger as your apprentice? She's half light elf! Some would call that treason." Fenrik disliked the Queen as well, and he too took every opportunity to discredit her in front of the Overlord.

"How could you become so old, yet remain as naive as the child that just walked out of here?" Queen Valeria's voice remained cool, which thrust her insults further into Fenrik's heart. "I have no desire for her to become my apprentice, you fool. She is half light elf. I am simply curious about her."

"I beg your pardon, Your Majesty, but the Overlord does not share your curiosity. He wants only to destroy them." Fenrik seemed too comfortable with his words. He knew he was untouchable and that he could say virtually anything he liked to the Queen.

The Queen looked down at the globe in Fenrik's left hand. She eyed it carefully to make sure it was still dark. Fenrik had, in the past, used the globe to capture a few of their conversations in various attempts to discredit her.

"The Overlord is relying too much on the negotiations with the elders. He is much too confident in his ability to trick them into granting him passage through the Breathing Forest. His plan is taking far too much time. Should it fail, it would cost us precious time and resources. I am simply providing him with an alternative plan should his not succeed." Queen Valeria's voice did not sound particularly reassuring to Fenrik.

"The Overlord must be notified of this at once." Fenrik's grip strengthened around his globe.

"I would expect nothing less from you, Fenrik." A smile found its way to the Queen's lips when she saw Fenrik frown after her comment. She loved to treat him as the tattletale child he was.

"It would be wise of you to remain in the palace until you have full approval from the Overlord on this matter, Your Highness."

"There is no time, Fenrik." The Queen walked to the room's exit. "I must tend to this globe that was uncovered in one of our camps. I must retrieve it before it falls into enemy hands. Now run along and make your reports to the Overlord. I must prepare for my journey and do not have time for you any longer." Queen Valeria exited the chamber, her black gown flowing behind her.

"This time, Your Majesty, you have thankfully gone too far." Aware that he was now talking to himself, old Fenrik tightened his grip on the globe and it began to glow.

****

Aldara sat waiting in the Queen's transport. The carriage was unlike any other she had seen in her life. Having no wheels, it hovered silently above the ground. It was painted black with violet trim and polished to perfection, no scratches blemishing its surface.

Guiding the carriage were four horse-like beasts. Solid black in color with long manes of silver, their flaming hooves appeared to dance on air. The flames were small and they licked the ground gently. Surely, they would flare up when running. The creatures truly were an ominous sight to behold.

Inside, the carriage was more comfortable than any sleeping quarters Aldara had ever seen. The two large seats that faced each other were more like little beds, plush and comfortable. Each contained half a dozen red satin pillows.

Aldara clutched at the clasp holding her cape together. It was circular with blue diamonds decorating its border. In the center was a crescent moon made of silver. It was one of the most beautiful pieces of jewelry she had ever seen. She sat back in her comfortable chair and grinned. She couldn't help but dream of what it must be like to have so much power, luxury, and respect from your people.

One day, thought Aldara. *I will have all of this. I won't be questioned, feared, or hated anymore by those around me. One day, I will have the respect of the people of both Solaris Arbor and Under Hollow.*

She sat back and looked out the window at the wetness on the flowers and plants of the forest from the dew and the early storm. The sweet smell of the flower nectar made her hungry. If only there were food in the carriage. She'd give almost anything for a bite to eat. Just then and without warning, the carriage door opened. Queen Valeria stood in the doorway and smiled gently at Aldara.

"My dear child, you must be hungry. Here, I brought you some fruits that grow on the trees down here in Under Hollow. They will surely be the most delicious you have ever tasted." The Queen offered the basket of fruit to Aldara.

Aldara was stunned once again by Queen Valeria. *How does she always just know?* she pondered. Aldara accepted the fruit basket from the Queen's hand and rummaged through it. The fruit she picked out was yellow, egg-shaped, and soft to the touch. She put it to her lips and took a bite out of it. The texture was so soft, she almost didn't need to chew it; it seemed to melt in her mouth. Juice dripping from her chin, Aldara wiped her mouth with her cloak.

Queen Valeria looked at her and smiled. "Quin-Ti. They are also my favorite. Delicious, aren't they?" she asked.

Aldara nodded her head in agreement and kept eating. She hadn't eaten in almost a day and she was famished. She was careful, however, of the speed at which she was eating. She didn't want to appear *too* rude at the Queen's generous hospitality.

"Thank you, Your Highness. This is most kind of you and very appreciated," Aldara's tone was genuine. She lifted her head from her snack to look upon Valeria. The Queen was no longer dressed in her throne room gown, but in black leather, complete with leather boots on her feet and dark gloves on her hands. The only accessory familiar to Aldara was the winged neckpiece the Queen wore.

Resting next to Queen Valeria was a long staff of pure silver with a small globe about six inches in diameter clasped to the end of it.

"Nice staff," Aldara said admiringly. "What sort of globe is attached to the end of it?"

"It is a Globe of Imprisonment," replied the Queen.

Aldara's eyes widened. "How does it work?"

"Perhaps you will see. We will be entering somewhat hostile territory. We must be prepared for whatever will happen." The Queen leaned her head against one of the pillows, never taking her eyes from Aldara.

"It is always good to be prepared," Aldara sighed a bit. What a stupid response that was. She was out of her league and she knew it. She was, after all, only a child, sitting across from the enemy talking about subjects with which she had little experience.

"Be careful not too eat too many of those. They will upset your stomach," Queen Valeria advised.

"I've had enough anyway. Thank you very much. They were very delicious," responded Aldara.

"Now, you just sit back and get some sleep. The voyage ahead of us is very long and you need your rest. I will awaken you when we get there." The Queen had an almost motherly tone in her voice, which, unknown to Aldara, carried a hidden magical tone of suggestion.

"Yes, I could use some rest." Aldara leaned against the side of the carriage, unable to fight the sleepiness that was overtaking her. "It's been a most…interesting day."

The Queen smiled, "Yes, it has. For both of us."

The Queen watched as Aldara closed her eyes. She eyed Aldara up and down until her breathing became soft and regular. A wicked smile curled the lips of Queen Valeria. She then waved her hand in the air. The carriage elevated slightly and moved forward. The horse-like beasts that propelled the carriage seemed to gallop on the air, the flames on their hooves now roared like a well-kept fire. The gallop soon quickened in pace and the carriage sped off into the night at a speed no other creature could match.

Chapter II

———⟨ℳℴ⟩———

A Light in the Darkness

The yellowish light that illuminated the cavern was beginning to dim, causing the shadows of the mineworkers to dance vigorously on the walls. That is, everyone's shadow except Ayku's, whose shadow merely fluttered. She was getting tired; her wings of light were flickering like that of a firefly near death. The light from her body was also pulsating as her luminescent powers began to falter. Choking on the dust that filled the air of the cavern, she flung her head quickly to the side, flipping her long, soil-covered blonde hair out of her face. She hung, as if being crucified, from the cavern wall. She was bound by magical energy bindings and her daily suffering was great. Wondering how much more she could take before she gave up the will to live was a constant thought in her head. Perhaps it wouldn't be so bad after all if one of her dark elf captors electrocuted her with a bolt of lightning or just simply disintegrated her.

No. I will not make it that easy for them. I will find a way out of here. WE will find a way out of here, she demanded of herself. Ayku had a funny way of receiving rushes of energy and positive thoughts when things seemed their darkest. If only she could shrink, she could fly away and seek help, but the magical bindings prevented her from doing so. There had to be another way.

She lifted her head and looked out into the cavern. It was a sight so disgusting to her and yet, being here every day for months on end, it was now all that she knew. Torches lined the rocky walls, but their light was washed out by the bright light emanating from Ayku's body. At times, she would feel sick to her stomach from the powerful sulfurous smell of the Drylin crystals. They were beautiful to look at, but when unearthed and smashed by the prisoners during their mining duties, they unleashed a powerful stench known to sicken every species in the realm. It easily overpowered the foul odor for which the Dracal were famous.

Dracal filled the cavern with their tyrannical whips in hand, not hesitating to use them if they noticed a prisoner pausing briefly to catch his breath. A few dark elves were scattered in the cavern as well, giving the Dracal orders for what seemed the simplest of tasks. As powerful as the Dracal were, their intelligence seemed to be extremely limited.

Responsible for nothing other than providing light while hanging captive from the cavern walls, Ayku had nothing to do but observe, to watch her friends suffer…but she was also watching the behavior patterns of her enemy, knowledge that would surely help her if she were to ever escape. Sometimes, she noticed that a dark elf would borrow one of the Dracal's whips and lash a prisoner for the sheer fun of it, especially those prisoners that were light elven in race.

Her gaze turned to her dear friend Tye. Tye was a light elf and a mere boy of thirty-eight (an adolescent, in elf years). Seeing the beads of sweat slide down his pale skin and his blonde hair flop in front of his eyes as he swung his pickaxe would normally make her heart flutter, but there was nothing appealing about seeing him work so hard for someone else, especially the enemy. His innocence was quickly being taken from him as he was forced to become a slave of the Overlord. The bitterness of war was taking its toll on him and yet, as Ayku watched his eyes while he swung his pickaxe at the rock, she still saw the boy she had known when times were different. The boy with whom she had fallen in love.

Working beside Tye, as always, was Gusseus. A close friend to Tye's parents at the time of their deaths, Gusseus vowed to take Tye under his wing and care for him, to see that his fate would not be that of his parents.

Gusseus was a slave by choice. When Tye was captured, he surrendered so he could continue to keep watch over his adopted son.

Gusseus was a dwarf whose height only barely approached Tye's waist. A faint smile appeared on Ayku's lips when memories of the dwarf scolding Tye for his immature behavior flashed in her mind. Gusseus's short, stout body seemed to tremble when his temper flared up. Underneath his bushy beard, his bulbous cheeks would turn a bright shade of red when he got upset, which was usual behavior for him. Despite his temper, he was a kind and gentle dwarf. Approaching middle age, he had a lifetime of experience to offer Tye, if only Tye would listen. But now, there was little that Gusseus could offer his son but a friendly face. At least he could be there to keep his spirits up and to help him think of a way to escape.

The dwarf swung his pickaxe at a much slower pace than his adopted son. Still, his pace was steady. He knew that if they were ever to escape, they would need both strength and mental discipline. As he kept his swings steady, his thoughts focused on ways to escape, his senses open to everything around him while he waited for his window of opportunity.

Ayku saw his lips pucker, and then close, out of a lifelong habit, before his shoulders slumped with a sigh. Dwarves were known for whistling songs when they worked, but his previous attempts at whistling had left him with scars from a Dracal's whip that would last the rest of his life.

There were many other slaves of various races working in the cavern. Dwarves, gnomes, and light elves—if you were not of the dark elf persuasion, you would, at one time or another, feel the wrath of the Overlord. Looking around the cavern, Ayku saw the familiar faces she had seen every day since she had been here, yet she didn't actually *know* any of them. When work detail ended, they were marched to their respective barracks for a scrap of food and a night's sleep, never allowed to socialize with anyone from the other holding areas.

Ayku felt somewhat guilty that she wasn't down there digging with all of the other prisoners, who worked so hard each day. But her suffering was equally as great; she stretched her illuminating powers to the limit each day while shackled to the wall and unable to move.

The crack of a whip, followed by a scream, echoed throughout the cavern. This happened multiple times a day; usually, Ayku closed her eyes and tried to block out the sounds of pain, but this time she tilted her head to the left and saw that a gnome had fallen to the floor and was being whipped by a Dracal. The Dracal whipped him repeatedly, not giving the gnome a chance to rise back to his feet. After several lashings, the beastly soldier paused its whipping and looked at one of the dark elves, awaiting instructions on what to do next.

The beaten gnome lay on the floor with blood dripping from his lips; he watched in agony and fear as the scattered dark elves came together and quietly discussed his fate. Whispering was heard from the robed figures as they gathered in a circle. At this point, all mining activity had come to a halt and all eyes were on the dark elves' whispering circle.

"What is going on here?" a cold voice echoed throughout the cavern.

The dark elves broke their chatty circle and looked to the far end of the cavern. One of the dark elves lowered his hood. His skin was dark gray and his hair was jet black. It was indeed a rare moment when any of the prisoners had the 'privilege' of gazing directly upon a dark elf. They preferred to keep their faces hidden while among the lower species, but they also followed proper protocol in the chain of command.

"Captain Nagarr, we did not hear you enter," the dark elf stated.

"Obviously." The Captain was not dressed like the other dark elves. He was dressed in a suit of bronze armor that reflected the light Ayku provided and a decorative sword hung by his side. Born of the few dark elves that were not blessed with the gift of magical ability, Captain Nagarr took on the role of a military man under the control of Commander Zelgot. He was assigned by Zelgot to command the labor camp and see that the mining process flowed smoothly, like clockwork, for the Queen.

Nagarr walked down the makeshift steps into the cavern, accompanied by four Dracal. He had a pompous walk and power absolute in the labor camp, which he flaunted as frequently as he breathed. He walked down the stairs as if he were a god, with his Dracal minions marching behind him. When he reached the end of the stairs, he looked to his right and saw the tattered gnome lying on the ground. Nagarr put his hands on his hips and looked toward the group of dark elves.

"He was tiring in his work, Captain. We were just discussing a new way to motivate him," the dark elf stated, offering an explanation before Nagarr asked for one.

There was an unspoken tension between the dark elf spell casters and those dark elves that were military, born without the gift of magic. The spell casters looked down on the military dark elves, considering them to be inferior, and the military elves responded to this by developing egos the size of Under Hollow for their brilliant tactics in capturing the realm. But the bickering ended there; the spell casters needed the military elves, and vice versa.

"Your debate on which spell would be most effective to motivate the prisoners is an inefficient use of time and resources. I shall deal with this." Nagarr looked down at the gnome once more and clapped his hands together, just once, but it echoed half a dozen times throughout the cavern.

The Dracal responded to his command by lifting the prisoner off the floor. "Take him to the dais against the east wall," ordered Nagarr.

"No, please! All I needed was some rest! I've gotten all that

I need! I am ready to return to work! I'm ready to dig!" the gnome pleaded as the Dracal dragged him across the cavern. Holding him by his underarms, two Dracal threw him against the rock wall.

"Bind him," Nagarr ordered one of the dark elves.

The dark elf who had removed his hood walked slowly over to the gnome. He raised his hands in the air and started to roll his hands over and under each other in a circular motion. He spoke the words "Quinn Mitokk" and a purple glow began to encompass the area of his hands. His hands began to move more quickly, as if they were spinning the light. The purple glow grew in intensity until it was almost white. The dark elf then rolled his hands out so his right hand was above his left, and his fingers pointed towards the gnome's left arm.

The ball of whitish purple light shot from the dark elf's hands, wrapped itself around the gnome's left wrist, and fused itself to the wall. The gnome watched in horror as this act was repeated on his right arm and then on both of his ankles.

Watching from across the room, Ayku gasped. This is what was done to her each morning. Seeing it done to someone else made her realize just how horrible it was. She could not bear to watch what has happening to the gnome any longer. She put her head down and shut her eyes tight, wishing she could do the same with her ears.

The gnome struggled to free himself of the bindings but it was no use. There was no way he could break free. He could now do nothing but watch, helplessly, what was happening to him.

Captain Nagarr signaled for the dark elf to step away and again clapped his hands at one of the Dracal. "Make it quick."

The Dracal stepped up onto the dais and looked the gnome in the eye without any sense of remorse or pity. "No! Please! I beg you!" the gnome pleaded for his life. He watched Nagarr raise his hand, then lower it sharply as if he didn't hear the gnome's plea for mercy.

The Dracal leaned forward slightly, its red, thick, scaly body armor shining coldly in the glow of Ayku's fairie light. Smoke poured from its nostrils. There was a brief flicker of flame that jutted out from its mouth, followed by a continuous stream of fire. The flames engulfed the gnome. A terrifying scream came from the gnome and filled the cavern. The prisoners winced at the sight and turned their heads. The smell of burning hair and flesh was everywhere, filling the lungs of everyone.

A few seconds later, the Dracal stopped. The flame of the Dracal was much more powerful than any other fire in the realm. It could burn entire villages in minutes, making the task of ending one gnome's life an extremely easy one. Bits of burning flesh on smoldering bone were all that was left of the gnome. The beast backed away, emotionless, at the sight of his work.

The dark elf once again walked up onto the dais and raised his hands. "Mitokk Soo," he whispered. The energy bindings that held his bones to the wall dissipated. Upon hitting the floor, the gnome's bones turned to dust.

Just then, the light in the cavern began to flicker more intensely. Captain Nagarr looked over at Ayku and saw tears streaming down her face. Curiously annoyed at her wavering powers, he approached her. "You will return this cavern to its proper lighting now," he commanded.

"I can't," Ayku could barely speak the words.

Nagarr took the back of his hand and smacked her across the face, drawing blood from the corner of her mouth. "Those are words I just do not believe in."

Ayku paused slightly, letting the blood drain from her mouth and roll down her chin. "My powers are weakening. I cannot use them much longer." The look of hatred in her eyes for Nagarr was intense.

Raising an eyebrow along with his right hand, Nagarr looked at the fire-breathing Dracal. The Dracal took a step closer to Ayku.

Watching from across the cavern, Tye tightened his grip on the pickaxe and also took a step forward. Gusseus grabbed his arm. "No, lad. This not be tha time," he said to Tye in a low voice. "You'll be doomin' us all."

Looking at Ayku, Nagarr waved his hand at the Dracal and dismissed him. "No. There is only time for one execution today." He turned to the huddled group of dark elves. "Take her down and return all of them to their barracks. It is time for their rest. They will need to recharge their strength for tomorrow." He then looked back at the prisoners. "Remember what you saw here today. Do not let it happen again tomorrow." He snapped his fingers and his Dracal minions followed him through the cavern and up the stairs.

Ayku watched him leave, then spit the remaining blood from her mouth onto the cavern floor.

****

The large cracks in the barrack walls let in a constant spray of rainwater that drenched Tye's legs. He lay shivering in his makeshift bed of straw with his eyes wide open, staring blankly at the wall. Letting out a disgusted sigh, he threw his rain-soaked woolen blanket to the side.

"Ayk? Ayku, are you awake?" Tye's whisper was so faint, he could barely hear it himself. He turned to face her. It was too dark to see her, but he could tell she was close to him by the faint purple glow of the energy bindings that held her wrists and ankles together, preventing her from changing shape. Tye wondered if they were any more comfortable than the steel shackles that he and all of the other prisoners had around their ankles.

Ayku rolled over to face Tye. She was perfectly dry, because her bed was toward the middle of the room. Tye insisted on sleeping near the wall so he could take the brunt of the storm. That was one of the things Ayku found most endearing about him. Although he was sometimes thoughtless and a little too carefree with his actions, he had a heart so pure it was worth more to her than all the gold in Sylvanor. "With what happened today, how *could* I sleep?" The vision of the gnome begging for his life as he was being dragged across the floor and up onto the dais returned to her mind. "We didn't even know his name," her words choked on tears.

"We can't stay here much longer. Sooner or later, they will kill us—if we don't die from exhaustion first. We need to find a way out of here. There has to be a way." Tye could hear her sobbing in the darkness and he reached out his hand to hold hers. It clumsily brushed against her waist and thigh. "Sorry."

Ayku let out a small giggle between her sobs and wondered just how much Tye was blushing now. Whenever it came to showing any kind of affection, Tye would always start to blush and end up putting his head down while making a stupid joke to change the subject. Letting her curiosity get the better of her, she raised her hand in the air and a small circle of dim light appeared around his face. Sure enough, he was a lovely shade of red. Laughter now washed away Ayku's tears; she enjoyed embarrassing her friend.

"Cut that out!" Tye scolded her with a smirk.

His voice rose just a little too much, waking another member of the barracks. "Shut up over there and turn out that damned light before the Dracal come and beat us all."

Tye turned his head around and saw a silhouetted figure rise slightly in its bed. The moonlight shining through the cracks wasn't enough to see who it was but it didn't matter. He knew this time that he was in the wrong and that everyone, including himself and Ayku, needed their rest for the backbreaking work tomorrow. He turned his head back around to face her and shrugged. She smiled back and waved her hand. The dim light vanished, returning the room to its darkened state.

Just as they laid their heads down on their straw pillows, the door to the barracks swung open and slammed against the wall with a loud thud. Torchlight filled the doorway and the prisoners sat up quickly in their beds to see the terrifying faces of two Dracal. Their eyes were glowing their eerie yellow color and their midnight blue body armor glowed in the torchlight.

"Now you've done it. This is the last time you get any of us into trouble, elf. Tomorrow, you'll have my pickaxe in your head," the figure from across the room blurted out. Still hidden by shadows, Tye was becoming a little more concerned about who he was so he could avoid him the next day in the cavern.

The Dracal gave the figure across the room a glance and moved to stand on each side of the doorway. As soon as they were in position, a man was thrown into the barracks. He was airborne from the force of the Dracal's throw for a few feet before he fell directly on the young light elf. Tye lay underneath the new prisoner, his face pressed into the ground by the prisoner's elbow. He struggled immediately to break free, but he didn't have the strength to do so.

"You're the first of your kind in this camp." Captain Nagarr now stood in the doorway. A scar on his right cheek seemed to twist when he sneered and it made him seem even more sinister. He stood with his hands on his hips, completely dry from the rain. Ayku looked beyond him to see a Dracal holding a huge Cocil tree leaf over his head. "Every creature has a breaking point. I'm curious to see just where that breaking point is on a *human*."

The human, his wrists and ankles in chains like the rest of the prisoners, wriggled his way off of the light elf and tried to stand. He was quickly kicked in the stomach and knocked back down onto Tye a second time.

"A fighting spirit. That's good. Anger is energy. You will need all you can get, for tomorrow you'll be working in the caverns for me." Nagarr snapped his fingers and turned from the doorway. The two Dracal followed and slammed the door shut behind them. The prisoners could hear them bolting the door from the outside and then there was silence.

"Would you please get *off* me now?" Tye was more than a little agitated to have the human's elbow still in his face.

The newcomer lunged himself forward past Tye's feet and rested his back on the barrack wall. "Sorry, friend. I hope I didn't hurt you too much," he apologized.

"Hurt me?! You weigh a ton, but it takes much more than

that to hu—" Tye's words were cut off when a soft white glow appeared over the human's body.

The human had shoulder-length brown hair that was dripping wet, as was his moustache. His face and feet were cut and bleeding. His clothes were ripped and tattered and Ayku could make out his muscle definition underneath them. She had seen a few humans before in her lifetime and this was by far the strongest looking of them all. Surely, he had put up a worthy fight against the Dracal.

"It's true! You are a human!" exclaimed Ayku. She sat up and gave him her full attention. She also smiled slightly when she saw Tye throw a glance in her direction before putting his head down, pretending not to care.

"Yeah, I'm human. My name is Eldin." Eldin put his hand in front of his eyes to adjust to the light Ayku cast on him. The light wasn't particularly bright and his eyes adjusted after a few seconds. "Are you the only fairie in this camp?"

A quizzical look popped onto Ayku's face. "Yes, I am. I haven't seen my people in months." Newcomers to the camp always made Ayku suspicious. Spending more time in labor camps than she cared to remember made her suspicious of everything.

Eldin sat up against the wall and rolled his head around on his shoulders. He tried to do the same with his arms but the steel bands on his wrists made his efforts to stretch seem clumsy. "Then you must be Ayku."

Ayku blinked at him and Tye leaned forward, positioning himself between the two. "How do you know her name?" Tye tried to deepen his voice to appear more threatening to the muscular human.

Eldin looked at Tye and started to laugh. "Easy there, junior. I'm a friend. I've come here to help you." He eyed Tye up and down as if to study him. He smiled again and turned his attention back to Ayku. "I was sent here by a Winged Angel named Wyndle. She claims to be a friend of yours and sought out my help to rescue you."

Ayku gasped. "Tye! Wyndle's alive! Thank the Gods she made it out alive!" Ayku was truly ruled by her emotions. The news of hearing of her friend's well-being filled her heart with joy.

Tye smiled as well. Wyndle had been a childhood friend of his since his parents died. The vision of their first meeting flashed quickly in his mind; he had been sobbing while playing his flute near a stream one day, soon after his parents were murdered, when Wyndle stumbled into him. Winged Angels are generally forbidden to interact with any other race in the realm. Their job is to keep the karmic balance of all things without interacting, but when Wyndle saw the young light elf sobbing, she couldn't help but come to his aid and explain as best as she could the process of life and death. They formed a close friendship and because of this, she was banned from her own realm and deemed 'disharmonious'.

"If that's true, where is she? Where's Wyndle now?" Tye's disbelief in Eldin's story was obvious in his tone of voice.

"Oh, she's here. She's busy gathering what we will need to escape and telling all the other prisoners when to be ready." Eldin was getting a little annoyed with Tye. He was used to the disciplined life of a warrior. Realizing that he was here to rescue children and rely on them to watch *his* back made him uneasy at best. "Where's the dwarf?" Eldin looked around, remembering Wyndle mentioning a dwarf that was always at Tye's side.

"Gusseus is in a different set of barracks," Tye replied, still eyeing Eldin in disbelief. "If what you are saying is true, why are you here? Why are you helping us escape? What's in it for you?"

"Look, Tyelander, I'm no different than any of you. I'm fighting this war against the Overlord too. This angel said she found out something about the Dracal that could possibly help turn the tide. In case you hadn't noticed, we're losing this war big time. Since very few people ever see a Winged Angel, much less speak with one, I took her at her word and came to free you." Eldin, still sore, rubbed his shoulders to try to relieve some of the pain.

"First off, the name's Tye!" Tye snapped. The only time he heard his full name called out was usually when he had gotten himself into trouble and was being scolded by Gusseus. He didn't like hearing it then, and he certainly didn't like hearing it on the lips of a stranger. "Second, if she discovered something about the Dracal, why didn't she just fly straight to Solaris Arbor and tell the elders?"

"She insisted that we free you and your little friends first before the dark elves kill you." Eldin laid his body on the ground and tried without success to make himself comfortable. He shut his eyes, then opened them slowly and looked at Ayku. "Douse the light, honey, or they'll be coming back to douse it for you."

Ayku shook her head in agreement and waved her hand. The soft white glow disappeared around Eldin, and Ayku laid her head back down against her straw pillow.

"If Wyndle were here, she would have come to say hi to me in person," Tye wouldn't let his questioning go.

"No more questions, junior. We have a plan and it must be followed to the letter. Now shut up and go to sleep. You'll need all the rest you can get for the next few days." The tone in Eldin's voice was enough to keep Tye quiet.

Tye lay on his side, staring out of one of the cracks in the barracks at the rainfall. The spray of rainwater splashed his body. How could he fall asleep knowing that Wyndle was out there trying to help him and his friends escape? Would this really be one of their last nights here? Tye tried to clear his head of questions and calm himself and, for the first time in months, he shut his eyes with a smile on his face.

****

Captain Nagarr stood at the entranceway of the cavern, looking down at his slaves. Being in charge of a labor camp, especially this one, was beginning to bore him. He had been in charge of the camp since it was first established, about ten months ago. There was nothing glorious about the job, no great victories to brag about, and no rewards. How could the Queen see his true brilliance if he were stuck in labor camps for most of his life? He sighed and put his hands on his hips, as if to announce to everyone in the cavern that he had arrived to make his personal morning inspection.

"I do so hate the sunlight," Nagarr complained as he stepped into the cavern. He started to remove the dark visors that protected his light-sensitive eyes but stopped when he remembered Ayku, the fairie bound to the far cavern wall. When it was this early in the morning, she glowed brilliantly. Nagarr hated fairies with a passion. He despised their power over light. Destroying a whole colony of them a year prior was one of his proudest moments.

He watched Ayku on the wall and his brow rose slightly. This was the first time that he could remember that she wasn't struggling. She hung there on the wall, appearing almost content. How dare one of his prisoners have a look of contentment on her face? He started off down the makeshift rocky stairs at a hurried pace and then remembered his place. He slowed to a comfortable stride. He would appear stronger and more confident that way. His stride carried him slowly across the cavern. He gave each prisoner a glance as he walked by them, pausing to watch the human. "Ahhh, I see you are fitting in nicely. That's always such a pleasure to see."

Eldin slapped his pickaxe with such fury down at the rock, imagining it was Nagarr's head. He raised the pickaxe up again and held it in the air. Glancing around, he saw three Dracal standing near Nagarr. His eyes met his captor's in a chilling stare.

"Well, come on. Put your back into it." Captain Nagarr folded his arms and smiled, knowing he was untouchable.

Eldin swung the pickaxe down again at the rock, splitting it in all directions. In the flying debris, he could have sworn he saw bits of wood unearthed with the rock and dirt.

"That's what I like to see. I may just yet discount some of the things I've heard about you humans." Nagarr didn't wait for a response. He was done playing his game with the human. Every so often, he would goad one of the prisoners into a fight, just so he could have the joy of executing them—especially if he secretly found them to be a potential threat. He turned away from Eldin and continued his pompous stride toward Ayku.

Gusseus swung his pickaxe at the rock with a force less great than Eldin's. "Yer well disciplined. I thought fer sure we were goin' ta lose ya, laddie."

Eldin rested his pickaxe on his shoulders briefly. "I know when to fight, dwarf. The captain will get his. Like everything else, it's just a matter of time." Eldin's thoughts of escape and giving Captain Nagarr what was coming to him brought his attention to Tye, who was working about thirty feet away from him. He watched the young elf swing his pickaxe. It wobbled slightly in the air when he raised it. He had to brace himself every time he brought the pickaxe up to stop himself from falling over. Eldin watched as Tye brought the pickaxe down to hit the rock. The rock remained undamaged. It took Tye a long time to break through new rock, and Eldin wondered why Nagarr hadn't killed him a long time ago. "You know, dwarf, I'm really beginning to wonder why I'm here. I mean, look at him. The boy can hardly swing a pickaxe, let alone a sword. I should be finding warriors to fight by my side, not children." He brought his pickaxe crashing down on the rock. The rock crumbled and more pieces of wood flew out.

"He's just a boy. He's got ta learn ta fight. He's got ta learn discipline. If Wyndle brought ya here and went through all this trouble, it mus' be fer a reason. Give him a chance and tha boy will surprise ya." Gusseus stopped swinging his pickaxe and looked down at what Eldin was trying to free his pickaxe from. "Looks like ya found somethin', laddie." The dwarf looked over at one of the Dracal, who was advancing on them while raising his whip. Gusseus quickly pointed to Eldin's find and then looked over at Nagarr.

Captain Nagarr had just reached Ayku. He stood before her for a few moments, hands on his hips, not saying a word. Ayku met his stare and remained silent as well. Nagarr placed his hand under her chin and squeezed both of her cheeks roughly.

"Something is different about you. You're up to something." Nagarr removed his hand from Ayku's face and checked the energy bindings on her wrists that held her to the wall. "I grow tired of you," he scowled. "Your kind sickens me. It will be a great pleasure when I close this camp in a few days to find the rest of your people and exterminate them."

Ayku narrowed her eyes at him and in an instant, the light that her body was providing doubled in intensity. Captain Nagarr turned his head away from her and raised his hand in front of his eyes. The blast of light from Ayku was too bright, even for the dark visor that usually protected his eyes from anything brighter than candlelight. He raised his hand to smack her when he felt a tug on his belt. He grabbed it and looked down to see what it was. Just then, a Dracal bumped him from behind. Nagarr fell forward slightly.

"Watch where you are going." Nagarr still had his hand in the air for his would-be slap to Ayku. His hand had now made a fist. He looked at the Dracal, considering. Even though he commanded them and seemed to control them, he thought twice about striking one. He was a coward at heart.

The Dracal pointed over at Gusseus and Eldin and grunted. Captain Nagarr raised an eyebrow and followed the Dracal's pointing finger. He saw the two slaves moving rock with their hands and exposing a large wooden box. "They found something. It's about time." He took a step towards his new-found treasure then glanced briefly back at Ayku. "Perhaps I can continue with the extermination of your race sooner than I thought, Fairie."

Ayku ignored Nagarr's comment and watched him walk away from her. Surely, she would have been dead by now if they hadn't found that box. She looked over at Tye, who was watching her. They exchanged smiles and then both turned their attention to what Eldin had found.

Gusseus and Eldin had removed all the rocks and dirt from the top of the wooden box. They were digging their fingers into the side of the box to lift it out of the dirt when Captain Nagarr approached them. "Get that box out of there *now*. And be quick about it." There was no need for Nagarr to give such orders, but he constantly felt the need to be in control of every situation around him. He never wanted anyone to forget that he was in charge, not even for a moment.

The two slaves managed to work the box free of the dirt and rock and slammed it on the ground, hoping to land it on Nagarr's foot. The Captain stepped back quickly to avoid the wooden box and flashed an angry look at Eldin. At this time, the dark elf spell casters huddled around the box. Nagarr could almost see their mouths watering. "Stand aside," the Captain commanded as he drew his sword. He swung at the rusty lock and struck it dead center. Swirls of blue electricity licked their way out of the lock and traveled up Nagarr's sword and throughout his body. They encompassed him for only an instant and Nagarr fell to the floor. Gasping and clutching his chest, he slowly got to his feet.

"The box can only be opened by those deserving or by a spell caster." The dark elf looked at Nagarr as he struggled to stand. "Move aside and I will open it for you." The spell caster slowly removed his hood but kept his visor over his eyes to shield them from Ayku's powerful light. He pointed at the box and quickly jerked his hand over so his palm was facing up. The lock on the box moved quickly, unlocked, and fell off into the dirt. The spell caster moved closer to the box.

Captain Nagarr pushed him away. "I'll take it from here." Without a thank you to the spell caster, he put his hands on the box lid and slowly opened it.

The inside of the box was lined with plush red velvet, untouched and completely free of the dirt in which it was buried for so long. In the center of the box was a globe about three inches in diameter. It was a dark golden color. It shone in the fairie light and everyone looked at it in awe.

Captain Nagarr saw it as nothing more than a reward to come from the Queen, as his ticket out of the camp and back to the glory of the battlefield. "Finally. Close the box up and place it in my quarters." He looked at the spell casters. "Be careful with it, and no one touches it. It is for the Queen's hands only."

The spell caster shut the lid of the box and the others helped him pick it up and carry it out of the cavern. Devoting their lives to the study of magic left them with little or no time to work on developing their physical bodies. They struggled with the box and with each step, it seemed like they would drop it.

"You two," Nagarr pointed to two Dracal, "help them." Satisfied with his finding, he looked around the cavern as if to gaze upon it for the last time. Then he looked over at Ayku hanging on the wall. He walked over to her with what seemed to be almost a spring in his stride. "When the spell casters return, they will take you down and return all of you to the barracks. From there, you will all be transported to another labor camp." He leaned in closer to Ayku. "Except for you, my dear. I will have the pleasure of executing you before I depart for Under Hollow."

Ayku's eyes widened. "I'm glad I can help you feel like a man."

Captain Nagarr looked at her and smiled. "I would cut your heart out right now if I didn't have to contact the Queen before the next storm hits. However, I will go to bed happily knowing that tomorrow will be the last day you will ever see." He turned from Ayku and waved to a Dracal. "Return them to their barracks. There is no more work for them to do here today."

Nagarr walked across the cavern and climbed up the steps. From there, he would go to his barracks and use his Globe of Communication to contact the Queen and inform her of his great find.

****

The door to the barracks slammed shut and was locked from the outside. Ayku sat in her straw bed, rubbing her wrists. This is the first time since they had come to the labor camp that they had time to rest and do nothing. That had all forgotten what it was like to sit and rest. It was a nice feeling and they savored every moment of it.

"Where's Wyndle? Captain Nagarr said he was going to kill me tomorrow. If we're going to try anything, it has to be soon." Ayku just didn't fear for herself, she also feared for her friends. She looked over them one by one, gazing at their cuts and bruises. They were all so battered; even if they did have a plan, they were surely too weak to pull it off.

"I hope she was able to steal some keys so we can get out of these chains. I'm tired of having my ankles and wrists hurt along with everything else." Tye could do his share of whining, that was for sure.

Eldin looked over at Tye and Ayku. "Maybe she decided this wasn't worth it. Maybe she found a group of fighters that could actually *help* her," he said sarcastically. Eldin was now receiving sour looks from everyone. Just then, a key fell at his feet. He looked up, and silhouetted in the beams of sunlight shining through the cracks of the wood was a small winged figure, about six inches in height, hovering in the air.

"Wyndle!" Tye had such an excited tone in his voice. It had been so long since he had seen his childhood friend that he could barely contain his excitement.

Wyndle put her hands together and gently bit her lower lip. She was truly beautiful. Her jet-black hair barely touched her shoulders and her black eyes opened wide when she saw Tye. Flapping gently behind her was her beautiful set of wings, fairly large and feathery in nature. But even through her wide smile, there was sadness in her eyes. She had given up everything for her friendship with Tye and for her compassion for all the dwellers of the realm. She could never go home because of it. Disrupting the karmic balance of things was against their most strict rule and even through she hadn't really broken it, just befriending anyone in the realm was enough to keep her from going home, forever.

"It's so good to see you!" Wyndle flew close to Tye and gave him a gentle kiss on the cheek. While kissing his cheek, she noticed cuts on his face made by debris earlier that day in the mine. She touched his face and ran her hand along his wounds, healing them instantly.

"I sure did miss you, Wynd. We both did," Tye gestured to Ayku.

"I missed all of you as well, but we can catch up later. We have to act fast if we are going to be ready. I must use my time here to heal all of your wounds. I've got to hit all three barracks before the morning." As she spoke to the group, she was tending to Tye's injuries. Wyndle flew down to his ankles. "Eldin, unlock his chains so I can heal the cuts those bindings have caused."

Eldin leaned forward and unlocked the steel clasps on Tye's legs. "What of our weapons and a means to escape? Are they in place?"

Wyndle looked in shock at Tye's ankle. The steel bindings had cut his skin and it was all raw. Dried blood covered his wounds and his skin was starting to turn color. "It's a wonder you could walk at all," she commented. She laid her hands on his ankle and the blood slowly disappeared. His skin turned back into its normal pasty, pale color. She did the same to his other ankle and then flew over to Eldin.

"Everything is ready. Dragging the swords took me longer than expected. I had to get creative with that one, but they are in the spot we agreed upon." She tended to Eldin's wounds while they chatted about their plans.

"You've done well, little angel. I must admit I had my doubts as to whether you could pull it off, with you being, you know, as small as you are. I thought we'd have to improvise a lot more." Eldin realized just after he said it that he had just inserted his foot into his mouth.

Wyndle ran her hands along his back, freeing his muscles from the pain of his morning work and freeing his joints of all their stiffness. "Never let the size of a girl fool you, human," she replied with a smile.

Eldin gave her a nod of respect and Wyndle smiled. He stood up and stretched. "Amazing. I had no idea your people had such great healing powers," he stated.

"I'm not surprised. Little is known about my people to the dwellers of the realm. They stay in hiding while 'keeping the balance'. I'm really the first to interact with anyone." Wyndle looked over at Tye and he put his head down. He always felt guilty, knowing that he was the reason she would never see her home again.

"Keeping the balance? Is that what they call it? Is their idea of letting the realm fall to the Overlord and having millions of innocent lives destroyed 'keeping the balance'? You seem decent and you have a willingness to help, but as for your people…" Eldin stopped there and shook his head.

"My people cannot interfere with affairs in the realm. They must let all situations unfold naturally, even the most horrible ones. Only when someone uses unnatural forces to shift the balance will they interfere." Wyndle didn't truly understand her people, so she could easily sympathize with what Eldin was saying. She could see that to outsiders (as she was now one herself) how her people could be considered cruel and heartless at times.

"The Queen and the dark elves have used magic in their

efforts to conquer the land. Magic is unnatural. Why didn't your people interfere then?" Eldin knew there was no time for questions, but he needed answers to the ones he was asking. He was entitled to them.

"You are human and for you, magic is unnatural. But for the dark elves, it is as natural to them as seeing or hearing is to you." Wyndle flew up in front of Eldin so she could look at him in his face. "It gets complicated, but I would be happy to tell you all about it once we're away from here," she offered as Eldin gave her a nod of agreement.

Wyndle flew over to Ayku and tended to the cuts and bruises on her body. "This is all I can do for you now, Ayku. We cannot take your energy bindings off. You will have to wait until they dissipate them to put new ones on you. That will be your chance to change your size."

"I understand. Thank you, Wyndle." Ayku rolled her head on her shoulders while Wyndle released its tension.

When she finished, she flew over to the other two prisoners who were quietly watching all of what was going on. She healed their wounds as well. It must be a combined effort of everyone if their escape was going to be successful.

Eldin went around the room and put everyone's steel bindings back on their ankles and wrists. He kept them loose and unlocked. They were merely for decoration now, in case the Dracal decided to drop in for an inspection.

Wyndle flew over to the large crack in the wall from which she had entered. "I've got to heal Gusseus and the members of the other barracks. Sleep well, all of you. You'll need your full strength, for tomorrow morning we escape." She gave a wink to Tye and squeezed her tiny angelic body through the crack.

Tye hurried to the crack and peered through. He watched as Wyndle flew unnoticed through the camp and into one of the other barracks.

Chapter III

—⚬⚬⚬—

The Best Laid Plans

The sun was high in the sky. The brilliant yellow ball cast a perfectly clear day. Without a cloud in the sky to obscure it, the sunshine illuminated everything. The landscape was a combination of mud and clay, but here and there large flowery plants could be seen. The flowers on these plants were as wide as a gnome is tall and were of various brilliant colors. They became almost fluorescent in the sunlight. It was truly a beautiful sight to behold, unless of course, you were a dark elf. Living underground for generations in Under Hollow, the dark elves' eyes had grown accustomed to the soft blue light of its force field domes. When a dark elf would surface, forgetting his visor could be a mistake that would take his eyesight if he were exposed to the long hours of Sylvanor's daylight.

The dark elves' visors were constructed of obsidian. When obsidian was cut paper thin, it became virtually transparent. The see-through material was then fitted into a pewter-like frame and worn snug against the eyes. They weren't balanced on the end of the nose like reading glasses, rather, the frames extended along the sides of the head and fit tightly between the head and the huge ears of the dark elf. The frames were heavy and uncomfortable, but it was a small price to pay to be able to travel about the outside world in full daylight without risking blindness.

Captain Nagarr stood, arms folded, wearing such a visor. He was dressed in his full military fatigues. His decorative medals were polished to perfection and sparkled in the bright sunlight. His boots were shined and his uniform looked like it had been ironed with him in it, fitting his body perfectly without a wrinkle. He stood in the shade of a large Cocil leaf that was held by one of his Dracal soldiers. If he was going to have to stand out in the sun and heat, he may as well be as comfortable as he could be.

Queen Valeria was expected to arrive any moment to inspect Nagarr's finding. He knew how important the globes were to the Queen and he was sure to be well-rewarded for finding one. The globes, scarce to begin with, had been scattered so widely throughout the realm of Sylvanor that finding them is an extreme rarity. Nagarr had found the Queen's treasure in just ten months since taking over as commander of the labor camp. It would be another victory to add to his list, another medal to be pinned on his uniform. Smiling at the thought of another ego boost, he looked at the two dark elves lined up on his left and then to the other two on his right. He flashed a pompous smile at them, as if to remind them just how important the military was—that it has a place alongside, if not more important than, the spell casters.

"We are so going to miss working by your side, Captain."

The smirk was concealed under the thick heavy hood of the spell caster, but there was no hiding his sarcasm. "It has been a true learning experience for us all." The other three spell casters nodded their heads in agreement.

"Splendid. I'm glad you had a chance to learn something." Nagarr replied. He was too pompous and arrogant to understand sarcasm or to even believe that anyone would use it toward him. He leaned in to try to get a glimpse of the spell caster's expression. One of the things that bothered Nagarr the most about the spell casters is that they were always shrouded in mystery. With their hoods up most the time, they were awkward and even somewhat intimidating.

The spell caster turned his head from Captain Nagarr and continued to look forward, not moving, to mock Nagarr's military stance. As the Captain returned to his perfect standing posture, he noticed a tiny black speck on the horizon. "The Queen approaches," he said as he squinted into the distance. The talkative spell caster leaned forward, trying to get a better view. Seeing nothing more than the same speck Nagarr was seeing, he raised his hands slowly in the air. The heavy sleeves of his robe slid down his arm, freeing his hands.

The spell caster began to move his hands in a clockwise circular pattern, his hands occasionally overlapping themselves. The air in front of him began to waver and distort, like the heat on the horizon. His hands moved faster and the more quickly they moved, the more stable the air in front of him became. The black speck grew tenfold in size. The spell caster suddenly stopped moving his hands and rested them at his sides. In front of him hovered a circle two feet in diameter. His magnification spell was completed; the image was now clear. It was four horse-like creatures prancing on the air. Their hooves appeared to be on fire. They were all joined together by ropes and harnesses and were pulling a black carriage.

"Indeed." The spell caster didn't bother to look at Nagarr when he made his announcement. Instead, he waved his hand in the air and the magnifying circle of air disappeared.

Captain Nagarr glanced at him, annoyed that he was not given an opportunity to see for himself. He returned his gaze to the black speck to let time do his magnifying for him.

The speck naturally grew in size as it approached. Nagarr could now see details of the carriage that was pulled by the majestic beasts, their silver manes bobbing and dancing with each ethereal step. The gallop of the beasts turned into a slower prance. The roaring flames shooting out from their hooves began to die.

The carriage was amazingly polished. It looked as if it had just pulled out from its holding chamber. It seemed to repel the dust that was churned up by the gentle breeze caused by its motion. The carriage's windows were made of the same thin obsidian material as the visors and were too dark to see inside. But Nagarr had no need to view its occupants; he knew that the only person in all of Sylvanor to travel within it was the Queen. Even Commander Zelgot was forbidden to borrow her prized transport.

As Captain Nagarr watched the carriage approach, he signaled to his Dracal warrior to no longer provide shade for him with the Cocil leaf. He did not want it to look to the Queen as though he was weak and could not tolerate the heat of Sylvanor's scorching sun.

The galloping of the horses came to a halt and the carriage

stopped before them. The dancing fires on the hooves of the carriage beasts were now just flickering flames that licked the ground as if to taste it. The carriage lowered itself so it was only an inch or two above the ground.

Captain Nagarr now stood at full attention, arms at his sides. He cleared his throat and nervously swallowed a mouthful of air.

The carriage sat hovering above the ground for only a few seconds, but for Nagarr, those seconds seemed like hours. The door to the carriage slowly opened. A leg appeared from behind the door and was gently lowered to the ground. The Captain recognized to whom it belonged immediately. Queen Valeria was wearing the fatigues for which she was famous; few had the chance to see her dressed in the royal gowns she wore in the palace. Most dark elves, as well as all of the inhabitants above ground, had only seen her this way. Knee-high shiny black boots covered her feet. Her body suit consisted of all black leather, which was cut low in her bosom, exposing her cleavage, yet leaving plenty to anyone's imagination whose gaze fell upon it. Her winged clasp now held a cape, which was draped over her right shoulder. On her hands, she wore shiny black gloves that were made of the same material as her boots. They covered most of her arms and ended at her elbow.

The Queen lowered her thin silver staff to the ground for support as she lowered her other leg. One of the dark elves came to her aid and took her hand. She now stood in front of Captain Nagarr. She looked at her elf assistant and thanked him while pushing her visor up on her nose until her eyelashes were brushing against it.

"Queen Valeria, it is an honor and a privilege to see you

again," Nagarr had a tone in his voice that was honest and true.

The Queen nodded at him and looked up into the sky. "The sun is high and it is much too hot. I wish to get indoors as quickly as possible." She looked back at Nagarr, then over to the four Dracal that were guarding the gates into the labor camp. "You should have kept the shade on you."

Captain Nagarr was caught in a major embarrassment. Was the Queen watching him the entire time her carriage was pulling up? Nagarr smiled and extended his hand toward the gates. "This way, Your Highness."

"One moment." Queen Valeria turned from Nagarr and took a step back to the carriage, lifting her hand toward the door. "Watch your step, Aldara." The Queen's motherly voice had returned.

Aldara placed her hand in the Queen's and exited the carriage. She stood by Valeria's side. Her light gray cape touched the ground, her face well-hidden from the sunlight by her baggy hood. Her body craned forward for a moment, trying to stretch as nonchalantly as she could. Sleeping twelve or so hours in the carriage had made her neck a little stiff and she rolled her head on her shoulders.

"Your Majesty, I did not know you were bringing one of your aides with you. Had I known, I would have had a second room prepared," apologized Nagarr. The thought of not anticipating the Queen's company made him uneasy and he hoped his error wouldn't carry over, in the Queen's mind, to his judgment on the battlefield.

The heat was already getting to Aldara. Feeling a bead of sweat slide down her neck was enough to tell her she was now overdressed. She raised both of her hands at the same time, and in one motion, flipped her hood off of her head and down her back.

Captain Nagarr's eyes widened as he looked upon Aldara. Her pale skin and her black hair with the gray streak were a perplexing surprise to him. She was not wearing any visors; because she did not spend her life underground like the dark elves, she had no use for them. He had never seen a mixed breed before. Most of them had been extinguished or had mysteriously disappeared many years ago. *Why was she with the Queen?* Valeria treated her like one of her own, but knowing the Queen's views on the superior purity of the dark elven race, Nagarr couldn't help but question it. He took a more alert stance and looked at the Queen.

"You will treat her as a guest. She will receive the same treatment as I. Do you understand?" Queen Valeria smiled at the Captain but her tone was sincere. She placed her hand on Aldara's back and gently pushed her forward. "As for our rooms, we won't be needing them. We will not be staying that long. I have come only to retrieve the globe and take it back to Under Hollow."

"Of course. You will find the globe to be in excellent shape, Your Highness. It rests in its box, locked up in my quarters." Captain Nagarr extended his hand once more to the gates of the labor camp.

The Queen guided Aldara off in the direction of the gates. Behind Aldara were the Queen and Nagarr walking side by side, followed by the four dark spell casters. Aldara looked at the entranceway; the iron gates were as tall as the large stone walls that surrounded the camp.

As they approached the gates, Aldara eyed the Dracal up

and down. Each of them was a different color. She had never seen all four species together at the same time. Surely, they were here now by Nagarr's design, to impress the Queen. They were all the same in general physical appearance, tall with large, thick leathery wings folded in; however, the color of the scaly body armor was different on each of them. One was a dark crimson red, another an electric blue, the third an emerald green, and the last a dark yellow, almost gold, color. The most commonly encountered Dracal were the red. They would fly low into unsuspecting villages and set buildings ablaze with their fiery breath. She had heard stories of blue Dracal swiftly claiming victory on the battlefield by shooting bolts of lightning from their mouths at their enemies. Aldara had never personally seen the other two species and didn't especially want to get to know them any better.

The Dracal stood aside and pushed open the huge gates to the complex. Aldara looked to her left and then to her right and quickly came to the conclusion that the gates were the only way in or out of the stone-walled labor camp. As the group passed by the Dracal into the grounds of the labor camp, Aldara could smell their stench. It was bad enough in the castle of Under Hollow, but up here in the heat of the sun, it was overpowering. An exaggerated cough sprang from her lips as she passed by them, as if giving them a hint to bathe.

Once through the entrance, Aldara turned around and noticed the yellow Dracal closing the gates behind them. A dark elf soldier approached them and reached into his shoulder bag. He pulled out a steel key and locked the gates. He flashed a look of annoyance at Aldara and swiftly put the key back into his bag.

If that's the only way in or out of this place, then that's the guy I'm going to have to kill to get out of here. Thoughts of escape were already racing through her mind. She had learned so much about the dark elves on this trip. If she were to escape and put any of this knowledge to use, it would have to be here—today—for her fate would surely be sealed if she were to return with the Queen to Under Hollow. Thinking it best not to stare at the gatekeeper too long, she turned her head back around and gave the labor camp the once-over.

She looked at the huge piles of dirt and rock to her left. She could see an entranceway that led down into the ground. Two blue Dracal guarded the entrance to the mine. Behind the piles of dirt, Aldara could see the wall that spanned the entire perimeter of the complex. It was a jagged stone wall with wire and bits of sharpened steel woven together on top of it. She followed the wall from the left of the complex around to her right. Just as she suspected, the wall fully encompassed the camp and there truly was only one way in or out.

To her right, she saw three buildings of equal size and one that was slightly smaller. She could tell by the foul smell of urine and manure what the smaller building was used for. She quickened her pace to get out of the wind's way that was carrying the smell to her.

The other three buildings were constructed of wood. Aldara could tell by the cracks in the walls and the small holes in the roofs that they were built in a hurry and without care. They could only be the barracks where the slaves rested when their work shifts were over. Aldara started to tremble under her robes. She had almost become a slave with her friends when they were captured in the city of Frentier. Caught up in the whirlwind of war, her friends were taken prisoner and sent away to work in a camp like this one. Aldara barely escaped with her life. That was ten months ago. She couldn't help but ponder the fate of her friends. *Were they even still alive?* Suddenly, the feeling of loneliness overcame her as she realized just how alone she really was.

Aldara could hear the chatter of Captain Nagarr and the Queen behind her. She tuned in for a moment to hear him asking her about her journey to the camp and other trivial matters. Finding the discussion of no value, she focused once again on the camp. If she was to try to escape, she had to know the area as well as she could.

In the far corner of the complex was a round building approximately three stories in height. Aldara wondered how she could have missed it. It was a large stone structure that was crafted with considerably more care than the barracks. Surely, this was where they were headed. Aldara slowed her pace to let the Captain lead the way. The Queen looked at her and smiled. *She smiles too much*, Aldara pondered. *Anyone that smiles that much is hiding a frown of some kind.*

Aldara looked skyward, at the uppermost floor of the building. It had a stone balcony that wrapped around the structure. There were no windows on the first floor and only a few to be seen on the second floor. One could logically assume that Captain Nagarr watched the activities of the camp from the balcony, raised above everyone else—like an egomaniac would. Aldara had only known Nagarr for a few moments, but she knew his type. She had seen it many times over in the past few months.

Bundles of hay were stacked around the stone building

along with piles of hay thrown freely on the ground. *Must be where the Dracal sleep,* Aldara thought, making mental notes of everything. She was getting quite good at it. Finally, her nightly meditations were paying off.

With a quiet mind, she could absorb everything around her. She saw no Dracal around the hay bundles. She glanced over at the barracks and didn't see any there either. So far, her count was up to six: four walking with them and two guarding the mining entrance. She also made a mental count of the four spell casters that were with them as well as the gatekeeper. In total, eleven bodies to sneak past, plus Nagarr and the Queen. Fewer than she had thought. With the Dracal as powerful as they were, there really wasn't a need for more. Aldara quickly began mentally planning her escape.

"Ah, here we are." Nagarr came to a stop outside the wooden door to what had been home for him for the past months. He fumbled in his pockets and pulled out a bronze key. "I'm sure you will find the lighting inside much more suitable, Your Highness." He threw a non-caring glance at Aldara. "It may be a little too dark for *your* eyes, though." Without waiting for a response from her, Nagarr opened the door to his shelter.

"After you, child," the Queen insisted as she put her hand on Aldara's back and nudged her forward.

Aldara flashed one more glance around the camp. If only she had more time to study it. If she were to escape, she needed a diversion. *Calm. Keep calm,* she thought, while remembering her mental exercises. Taking a deep breath, she entered the building.

It didn't take long for Aldara to see that the building had been constructed in a hurry. It was not at all as lavish as the

Queen's castle, not by a long shot. The stone walls were chipped and laid unevenly. Cracks ran through the walls like veins where sconces were nailed into them. Narrow beams of sunlight could be seen entering small cracks between the stones of the wall. Aldara couldn't help but wonder how the building was standing at all. *Looked nice from the outside,* she thought. Only two of the sconces were lit. Any more would have made the room even hotter than it already was. It was a rather boring room to look at. There were no elaborate tapestries, no portraits hanging on the wall, just an old wooden table in the center of the room with a few chairs around it. This was probably where Captain Nagarr held his briefings each day.

"My quarters are on the third floor. Follow me, Your Highness." Captain Nagarr gestured to the stone stairwell on the right side of the building. It hugged the round wall in a half spiral fashion. Light was pouring down the staircase from a window on the second floor.

The Queen followed Nagarr up the staircase. She wasn't at all interested in his command center. She had one thing on her mind and one thing only: the globe. She wondered what secrets the globe would hold. Would it give her the power to destroy the Breathing Forest so she could at last vanquish the light elves? As excited as she was, she kept her composure and didn't let it show.

Aldara climbed the stairs after the Queen, followed by two spell casters. The rest of the welcome party remained outside. When she reached the top of the stairs, she stopped to look outside the window. She looked down at the camp. *I need a higher view. I must get out to that balcony.* Although thoughts of escape were running through her mind, she couldn't help but think about the Queen's kindness to her. What if she was telling the truth? What if Aldara had only heard one side of history?

The two spell casters walked by her, pausing to glance at her. She caught the hint and looked out at the camp once more. The Queen *had* to have been telling the truth. No one as sweet and kind as she appeared to be would inflict such pain and suffering on anyone. She certainly wouldn't put them in these labor camps. *But what if the stories she heard were false? What if the laborers weren't slaves but volunteers, working to bring the realm together? No.* She had seen the horror of the Dracal. She had almost been a victim of them herself. *Why would the Queen be treating her with such kindness? What was she planning?* The more Aldara thought about the subject, the more confused and unsure she became about everything. She closed her eyes, took a deep breath, and turned from the window.

A few feet down the hall, Aldara rejoined the group just as they were entering a large room. The room took up the entire floor, minus the small hallway that connected the two stairwells.

"These are the quarters of my men. I thought you might like a brief tour of the entire facility before placing your attention on the globe, Your Highness. I have worked very hard at building this mining facility up. You can see how much I've accomplished in such a short amount of time." Captain Nagarr stood in the middle of the room with his arms open, bragging about his accomplishments, as usual.

"You have done well, Nagarr. Commander Zelgot will be proud of your achievements. If this globe turns out to be what I hope it is, a promotion will be in your future." The Queen looked at Nagarr and leaned against her long silver staff, which had her Globe of Imprisonment encased at the top. She was quite aware of how pompous Nagarr could be, but he was still a dark elf, and she held a respect for all dark elves. Indeed, she loved her people very much.

Aldara entered after the two spell casters. It was a cozy room. There were no tapestries on the walls; the elves pre-ferred to let the cool wind blow in through the cracks in the walls as well as through the two windows. Their beds were very plush and there were five in total. *There was even one extra for the gatekeeper*, Aldara thought, not forgetting her previous count of the camp's controllers. The beds were covered with red velvet (far too hot to use in the summer nights of Sylvanor, they were obviously laid neatly on the beds for the Queen's benefit). Red satin pillows were propped up just so against the large wooden frame. Aldara took a few steps over to one of the beds and rested her hand on it. She pushed down gently and felt that the mattress was full of feathers. It was truly one of the most comfortable beds she had ever seen or felt. She lifted her gaze and noticed that the Queen was watching her. She paused her conversation with Captain Nagarr and gave her a sympathetic smile. *Am I that obviously poor?* Aldara questioned silently. She removed her hand from the bed and looked around the room.

Her eyes fell on the table alongside the bed next to the door, and to the book placed upon the table. The book was thick and the cover was dark gray and appeared to be made of leather. Aldara couldn't see the binding. It must have been bound on the inside. Such a binding was rare and costly. On the front cover of the book was a crescent moon connected to an eye, the same symbol that was printed on the flags outside the camp, the symbol of the dark elf empire. Underneath the symbol were some runes. They were embossed and written in dark violet. A spell book! Aldara's eyes widened, but thankfully, she was aware of her quickly changing expression and just as quickly returned it to its normal curious state.

Aldara turned from the table and turned her attention toward her fingernails as if to say she had seen enough, was no longer impressed, and was getting a little bored. She returned her hand to the bed and started to push on it once again, feigning a piqued interest in its comfortable feel.

"While all this is charming and your camp impressive, Captain, I wish to see my prize. Judging by your description, it sounds like a Globe of Direction. I'm hoping it will point me to the home of the Winged Angels. Like Solaris Arbor, their land remains untouched by our hands. They are the only race capable of stopping us, should they discover our secret. They must be dealt with swiftly," the Queen paused and looked over at Aldara, regretting that she had revealed so much information in front of her, then she continued, "I am anxious to get it safely back to Under Hollow." The Queen's stance became more upright, showing Nagarr that she was ready to leave the room.

"I understand, Your Highness. If you follow me once more, my chambers are on the next floor." Captain Nagarr left the room. The Queen gave Aldara another smile and left behind the Captain.

Aldara stretched out her hand towards the doorway. "After you," she addressed the two spell casters, wishing she could see their expressions under their hoods. She was a half-breed and a mystery to them, but she had arrived with the Queen, so they had no reason to distrust her completely. At least, she hoped they wouldn't.

The two spell casters nodded at Aldara and exited the room to walk side by side behind the Queen. Aldara smiled, waiting until they were out of view in the hallway to reach out for the spell book. She didn't expect it to be so heavy and quickly grabbed it with her other hand. It felt smooth to her touch and as much as she wanted to open it and learn its secrets, there was no time. She opened her cape and shoved the book inside her concealed shoulder bag.

Aldara was quite the little thief. While the elves back in the Queen's castle helped her change into different attire from the elder robes she was wearing, she managed to grab a shoulder bag and hide it under her cape when she was changing. Now, she let the cape fall back down over the bag, and she exited the room. She entered the narrow hallway to find everyone ascending the second stairwell. Valeria stopped and looked back at her. "Is everything alright, Aldara?" she asked with motherly compassion.

Aldara was quick to reply, "Yes, Your Majesty. I just felt a little faint. It is very warm in here."

"Indeed. We shan't be here much longer, child. Soon, we will be on our way back to Under Hollow and the comforts of my castle." The Queen turned from her and continued on her way up the stairs.

Aldara joined the procession behind the two spell casters that followed Queen Valeria. *I cannot be taken back to Under Hollow. I've learned so much and I have a dark spell book. Going back there now, I would surely live the life of a prisoner.* Aldara was starting to see through the Queen's sweetness. As close as Valeria was to seducing her, Aldara was no fool. She was starting to put it all together—the constant watching of the Queen, the gentle pushes when she wanted her to move in a given direction. Suddenly, Aldara grasped the full gravity of her situation and a feeling of complete fear washed over her. How could she have been such a fool? Was she so blinded by her quest for knowledge and power that she allowed herself to be played so well by the Queen? Cursing herself, her shoulders slumped. It would take a miracle for her to escape.

Aldara reached the top of the stairwell and was now standing on the balcony she had sought to reach ever since she had entered the complex. She didn't waste any time in moving to the edge to look down at the camp. She had only seconds to take it all in and finish planning her escape. She looked down at the three barracks and at the bundles of hay near them. A smile appeared on her lips when she noticed the Dracal spread throughout the camp. Her escape had to be now or never. She looked over at the stairwell and adjusted her bag under her cape.

"Aldara." The sound of the Queen's voice startled her and Aldara jumped a little. "I know the camps can seem a little depressing and can be startling to the eyes of a child. But come inside. We are about to activate the globe." The Queen took her eyes from Aldara only to look at the stairwell. She thoughtfully turned them back to Aldara and it was as if she was looking inside her. "We wouldn't want you to get lost either, now—would we."

"No, not at all, Your Highness." Aldara walked toward her. "You must be so excited about the globe." Aldara tried in vain to change the subject, to turn the Queen's attention toward her obsession and away from herself.

"Yes. I am, child." The Queen, once again, put her hand on Aldara's back and guided her inside the room.

Captain Nagarr's quarters were very comfortable. Aldara's eyes focused immediately on the painted portrait of himself that was hanging on the wall. His bed resembled those of the spell casters, only his was big enough for two. Throw rugs of the highest quality lined his floor and his clothes were no doubt folded with military precision in the dresser against the wall near his bed.

"Here you are, Your Highness." Nagarr set the wooden box down on one of his expensive rugs in front of Queen Valeria.

Queen Valeria looked down at the box. It was small and could easily be cradled in one's arms. The lock was bent and the upper corner of the box was smashed and had large splinters jutting out of it. The Queen looked at Nagarr and narrowed her eyes in dissatisfaction. "Obviously, you weren't paying attention when I told you to take the utmost care in mining these globes."

Captain Nagarr took a deep breath, taken aback by the Queen's remark. The pompous smile soon returned to his face. "Rest assured, Your Highness, the globe is in perfect order. I inspected it myself."

The Queen looked Nagarr directly in the eye. "Has it been activated?" she asked him coldly.

"No, Your Majesty. No one has touched it but me, and as you know, I do not possess the magical ability needed to activate one. It has remained locked in this box in these quarters awaiting your arrival." Nagarr could see the look of concern in the Queen's face.

The Queen closed her eyes for only a moment and twirled

her finger once in the air. The lock opened and fell to the floor. She broke her stare from Captain Nagarr and turned her head down to the box. She raised her hand in the air and the lid to the box creaked opened.

Inside the box, resting snugly in its niche and surrounded by red velvet, was the globe. It was dark gold in color and there it sat, waiting to be activated.

The Queen reached down and lifted the globe out of the box. A smile appeared on her lips and she seemed to forget all about being upset with Nagarr. Her grip tightened around the globe. Nothing happened. Valeria closed her eyes for a moment and tried again. The globe remained dark. She looked at Nagarr, her eyes narrowed and her face became flushed. She looked back at the globe and squeezed it one more time. The grip she had on it turned her knuckles white. Still, nothing happened. The Queen looked at Nagarr with nothing but anger in her eyes now. She turned toward Aldara and nonchalantly tossed the globe to her. "Here you are, child. It appears to be worth nothing. Take it as a souvenir of this worthless journey."

Aldara caught the globe and held it in her hand. She watched as the Queen turned her attention to Captain Nagarr. The two spell casting dark elves looked at each other, folded their arms, and put their heads down. The hoods over their faces made them appear to be looking down at the ground, but their eyes were raised to the Queen and Nagarr. They weren't about to miss any of *this* conversation.

Seeing everyone else involved in the inquisition, Aldara cautiously turned around and made her way to the doorway of the room. She continued to hold the globe in her hand and tightened her grip. To her amazement, the globe started to glow, dimly at first, but becoming brighter in its intensity. Aldara could see faint images emerge in the globe and she felt a tingle in her hand. She realized that if the Queen saw what was happening, the globe would fall back into her hands, so Aldara released her grip on the globe and it reverted back into its blackened state. Very slowly and carefully, so as to not attract attention, she placed the globe under her cape, inside her shoulder bag.

"I swear to you, Your Highness, the globe was sealed in the box the moment after it was discovered." The Captain was now trembling. His arrogance had quickly faded, to be replaced by the coward within him.

"Then it must have been damaged by those who unearthed it. Just who found the globe?" The Queen's grip tightened around her staff and her voice was colder than any of Sylvanor's winters.

"A dwarf and a human." The prisoners raced through his mind as he struggled to remember. Then Ayku entered his thoughts. Using his anger toward her to help replace his fear and shift the blame, he continued, "And... a fairie."

Aldara had reached the door and was about to make a run for it when she heard Nagarr mention the slaves. A dwarf and a fairie? Not many fairies had been captured by the dark elves; they are known to kill fairies on sight. The dark elves' hatred for them, due to their love for and manipulation of light, was known throughout the land. Aldara stopped where she was and turned to look back at her captors.

"Round up the prisoners and prepare to move them to the next labor camp. Except those you mentioned." The Queen's voice, although still cold, was full of anger.

"Yes, Your Majesty. What am I to do with the slaves responsible for damaging the globe?" Captain Nagarr was doing his best to shift all of the blame away from him as quickly as possible.

The Queen's eyes narrowed once more at Nagarr. "Execute them immediately."

****

The energy bindings on Ayku's wrists and ankles were now glowing faintly with a dark violet color. She could stretch her wrists apart more easily now, and she could twist and turn them in complete half circles. A nervous excitement swept over her, drowning her in its anxiousness. She looked over at Tye, who was crouched on the side of the room, peering out through one of the cracks in the wall. Ayku then looked over at Eldin and raised her wrists to him. She stretched her arms back and forth in a playful manner and the bindings pulled like taffy. "They've never let them get this weak before." She continued to play with her wrists while at the same time turning her ankles. "Tye, what's going on now?"

Tye was bobbing his head from side to side, trying to get a better look at what was going on outside through the crack. "I can't make out who they are, but it looks like someone important is here. There's a lot of legs out there walkin' into Nagarr's quarters," he answered Ayku without taking his eyes off of the crack for a second.

Eldin spent most of the morning stretching his muscles, knowing he would be needing them for a fight. He was a trained soldier, and it was automatically built into his mind to always be ready for any given situation that could arise, planned or otherwise. "How many did you count, junior?" he asked the light elf, while grabbing his own right arm and pulling it behind his head while holding onto its elbow.

Tye shrugged while still holding his gaze through the crack. "Count? I dunno. I wasn't counting. I was trying to see who they were. They're gone now. They went into his building, except for the Dracal and two of the spell casters."

Eldin sighed and shook his head. His voice rose a bit above what it was before. "What do you mean, you weren't countin'? We have to know how many came into the camp to adjust our plan." Eldin quickly moved over to the crack, peered through it, and saw nothing. He looked at Tye. "Amateurs," he said under his breath as he stood up and continued with his stretching. "It'll be a miracle if we get out of here alive, even with all of that angel's help," this time his voice was louder. He looked at Tye and then over at Ayku, who was still bouncing her wrists around in all directions. "This had all better be worth it."

Tye stood up and moved over to Eldin. "I'm sorry if saving our lives put you out so much! You complain more than my grandmother! I hope you fight as well as you whine." His voice was raised as he puffed his body up. He tried his best to look as tough as he could to show Eldin that these 'amateurs' were more than capable of escaping the camp.

Eldin grabbed Tye by the shirt and threw him down on his makeshift straw bed, tearing his shirt in the process. "You want a further demonstration, junior?"

"Let's go, knight." Tye wasn't about to be pushed around by anyone, especially not in front of Ayku. He had suffered enough humiliation in the camp already. He didn't need more. He put his hand down on the bed to brace himself. While standing up, he felt a pricking on his hand. He lifted it out of the straw to see a cut in his palm. Blood trickled off his hand and dripped onto the hay, making it a dark crimson color. "What the—" He carefully put his hand back into the straw and felt something cold and metallic. He pulled it out and saw that it was a small dagger about six inches in length. It was lightweight for its size, obviously a knife of poor quality, but it was as sharp as any knight's two-handed sword.

"Oh good, you found the knife." Wyndle deftly slipped through the crack in the wall. No one had seen her struggling; they were all too wrapped up in their argument to help her. "I hid one in everyone's bed last night after I was done healing them." She noticed that Eldin was looking for his. "It would have taken me too long to carry knives that were better quality, they get so heavy. These will have to do. Use these to help make your way to the hay piles on the side of Nagarr's structure."

Tye tightened his grip on the knife and looked over at Eldin, who had found his knife and was looking it over. "What's at the hay piles?" Tye asked curiously.

"Our weapons," Eldin butted into the conversation. "We gathered them outside the camp before I was captured and the angel used the Scroll of Levitation I had from when my men raided a dark elf caravan a few weeks ago to levitate them over the wall and hide them in the hay."

Ayku looked at her knife and set it back down on the floor. She had never used a weapon in her life and she wasn't about to start now. She had her own methods of dealing with the enemy. Her fairie glamour was all she ever needed. "Didn't the Dracal or Nagarr see these weapons float over the wall and down to the ground?"

"The whole thing was timed. She used the scroll when I was captured and brought into the camp. All their attention was on me. So much for dark elf efficiency," Eldin chuckled and thought to himself that maybe the plan would work after all. "I thought I explained it to you last night."

Wyndle shook her head. She flew over to Tye and laid her hand in his. She ran her hand slowly down his palm and his cut disappeared. "I let the other two barracks in on our plan this morning. I came here last because I thought you might have done it," she looked over at Eldin.

"So much for human efficiency." Tye's lips turned upward in a sarcastic smile.

Eldin looked at Tye, started to open his mouth, and then turned from him to lay out their escape plan to Ayku. "We must make our way to the hay piles and get our weapons first thing. Then we have to get in Nagarr's quarters and make our way to the top," Eldin turned to Wyndle, "Are the horses in place? Or are we gonna have to run a few miles?"

"They are in place, waiting on the other side of the wall. I thought we'd have to skip that part of the plan, but no one saw. They were all too busy fussing over the Queen's arrival." Wyndle was hovering around each of them in turn, double-checking for any cuts and bruises she may have missed the night before.

"The Queen? She's here?" Eldin's posture became perfect and he held his knife as if he were about to slit Valeria's throat. "Our priorities must change then. We have to kill her, no matter the cost. Even if it means all of our lives."

Wyndle quickly flew over to the battle ready knight. "No, Eldin. We must stick to the plan. Too much is at stake. There will be another time to confront the Queen; right now, we must get out of here and head for Solaris Arbor. I need Tye to assist me in convincing the elders that I need their help."

Tye got a quizzical look on his face, "Help with what?"

"My bindings!" The bindings on Ayku's wrists and ankles were now turning black and weakening. She closed her eyes and her body began to pulse with a mild light yellow glow. She sat for a moment, enjoying the feeling of what was to happen next, and in an instant, her body shrank in size. She was now the size of Wyndle. A smile appeared on her face as she flew in front of Tye. "Freedom has never felt this good!" She ended her excited exclamation by giving Tye a kiss on the nose.

Wyndle cocked her head to the side and flew over to the crack in the wall that faced Nagarr's quarters. She saw Nagarr come out of the structure and snap his fingers at the Dracal. He gave an order to the green Dracal and pointed at the barracks. A chill flowed down Wyndle's back and she flapped her feathery wings to keep herself afloat. She saw the other Dracal go to the other barracks, two for each building. "Ayku, we don't have much time. Fly out and over to the hay stacks. Start digging the weapons from the loose hay on the ground. Everyone will need them quickly."

Ayku nodded and squeezed through the splintered opening in the wall. She darted to the barrack rooftop and looked around. The Dracal had their attention on the barracks. She looked over at Nagarr's quarters and saw Nagarr standing in the doorway. His stare was fixed on the barracks where her friends were, his hand on his sword. Ayku wondered why he was acting so peculiar. *Did he somehow know what they were planning?* She couldn't afford to entertain any thoughts except for getting to the hay piles. She saw Nagarr turn his head and snap his fingers at the two blue Dracal guarding the entrance to the mine. She could hear him giving them orders to go to the barracks on the far end of the camp, the one where Gusseus was. Ayku took this opportunity to fly from her barrack rooftop to the piles of hay as quickly as she could. As she reached the hay piles, she looked back and saw that a green Dracal had reached the door to her friends' chambers and had started to undo the lock.

Tye, Eldin, and the quiet gnome in the far end of the room were all undoing shackles on their feet. So far, everything was going according to plan. The gnome jumped to his feet, dagger in hand, and moved to stand on one side of the doorway. Eldin and Tye stood on the opposite side of the doorway and waited for the Dracal to finish undoing the lock. Wyndle hovered in the air in the middle of the room and bit her lip in anticipation, knowing that their fate lay in the approaching seconds of time's mercy.

Chapter IV

Winged Doves Will Fly

The lock was heard falling to the ground outside with a thud. The Dracal swung the door open in its usual rude way. The emerald green Dracal took a step inside the barrack and saw Wyndle floating in the air before it. Its head tilted to the side in puzzlement as it stood trying to figure out who and what she was. It didn't take long to discover that it didn't actually *care* who she was. It had its orders and, as always, it was going to carry them out without question.

The Dracal started to open its mouth when it felt a deep, sharp pain in its leg. It looked down to its right leg and saw that the gnome had dug his weapon deep, all the way to the hilt, and was now trying to pull it out. The dagger was held fast under the Dracal's body armor; had the gnome had any time to think, he would have wondered how he penetrated the armor with such a small blade in the first place.

Looking down at the gnome, the Dracal wasted no time in vanquishing its attacker. The beast opened its mouth wide and a cloud of yellow gas rose from its throat, thrust out of its mouth and propelled through the air at its attacker. It was a thick gas that smelled of sulfur. It covered the gnome instantly.

Wyndle gasped and threw up her hands. The air around her hands became jagged and twisted, like heat on the horizon. Wyndle had never killed anyone or anything in her life before. That was the creed of her people. Being the keepers of karmic law in the land, they must never take a creature's life or even have any part in it. She, however, could not sit back and watch as her friends suffered. Her self-made force field leapt from her hands and encompassed the gnome, but it was too late. The gnome had fallen to the floor and was twitching on the ground, still gasping for breath.

Eldin thrust his blade into the Dracal's neck. The force of the thrust was so powerful that the Dracal was knocked off balance. It struggled to keep its footing as it turned to Eldin. The beast's nostrils flared and it took in a deep breath. Eldin recognized that the Dracal was recharging its breath weapon. He had seen it many times before.

Tye lunged toward the beast and stabbed its belly, the only soft part of the Dracal's body. The skin there was leathery, but not protected by thick, scaly armor. Tye held onto his blade and started to twist his dagger around to open the wound more.

Blood was now flowing from the Dracal's stomach like a crimson fountain. The humanoid dragon looked down at Tye and gave him a backhand, sending the elf through the air across the barracks.

Not caring that Tye's blade was still in its belly, the Dracal turned its head back toward Eldin and opened its mouth. Wyndle, being much quicker with her hands this time, threw up a protective force field around the knight's body. The poison was hurriedly coughed out of the Dracal and struck harmlessly at the force field that surrounded Eldin. The gas seemed to linger in the air. The Dracal blinked its eyes wildly, producing tears to wash away the stinging sensation the gas left behind before it drifted out of the open door.

The Dracal turned its head in bewilderment and attempted to backhand Eldin. The beast's hand struck the force field; it felt like it punched a brick wall. The Dracal let out a scream of pain that was surely enough to alert the entire camp that something was happening in their barracks.

Tye rolled over and tried, as quickly as he could, to stand on his feet. While rising on his toes, he saw Ayku's dagger lying on her straw bed. He grabbed the dagger and held it tight in his hand. He then leaped toward the Dracal and plunged the small weapon into the side of its face.

The Dracal raised its head and let out an ear-piercing cry. It turned its head to the side and lowered its line of vision onto Tye. It swung at its new opponent with its hands open, its claws extended. Tye, being the nimble elf that he was, took a leap backward, avoiding the beast's attempt to slash him with its claws.

Eldin stepped out of Wyndle's protective force field, taking full advantage of the beast's distraction, and grabbed its head. Placing his hands on either side of the Dracal's face, he quickly jerked it to the left until he heard a snap. The Dracal's arms fell limply to its sides and Eldin let go of its head, while throwing its body to the floor. It fell to the ground with a thud.

Wyndle closed her hands and her force field disappeared. She darted toward the gnome, but realized he was already dead. He was dead within seconds of being consumed by the Dracal's poisonous cloud. She looked at the Dracal as its eyes flickered and went black. She then turned to Tye, saying "This is what it's all about, Tye. The Dracal...there's just something that's not right about them."

Tye took his dagger out of the Dracal's belly and wiped its blood off the blade and onto his pants. "What do you mean, Wynd?"

Eldin pulled at the beast's neck as hard as he could to retrieve his dagger, but the cheaply-made blade broke off in its neck. "You two, shut up and get moving. There'll be time for more talk later. We've got to get out of here!" He pulled Tye toward the doorway. "Head for the hay stacks; it's our only chance of getting out of here." He pointed quickly at Wyndle, "Keep an eye on him, honey."

They exited the barracks to see the entire labor camp in chaos. Indeed, the uprising had begun, and not only in the building where they were kept, but also in the other barracks as well. Blue Dracal could be seen in the distance, shooting lightning from their mouths. The daggers would do little good against these mighty beasts. They needed more time. They needed *more* chaos in the camp. But most importantly, they had to escape before the Queen became involved. Eldin looked skyward at the Captain's quarters.

****

"It would seem the Captain has an insurrection on his hands." The Queen looked down from the balcony at the disarray below her. "Come, child. Witness the power of my forces and how they are used to crush all those who oppose me."

Aldara looked on in horror, both at the Queen and at the killing below. The look on the Queen's face was that of pure hatred, and for the first time, Aldara realized it was the look of pure evil as well.

Valeria moved to the edge of the balcony and rested her hands on its stone railing. "Haven't they learned by now that everything, including the air they breathe, belongs to the dark elves?" Realizing that she was getting swept away in the heat of the moment, she turned her head to look at Aldara.

The young half-breed's eyes were wide open in shock. Aldara was helpless. She could not help the slaves, for that would mean certain death for her. She struggled to hold back the tears of pain and helplessness and turned her gaze from the battlefield below to the stone floor of the balcony.

The Queen moved closer and put her arms around Aldara. "Come, child. Perhaps this isn't for your eyes after all. It was my intention to show you the truth about what is happening, not to subject you to unhappy workers who feel they must use violence as a means of release." The Queen was struggling with her words now. She now knew that letting Aldara see the horror below was a mistake. She was not supposed to see the ugly truth of the camps, but Valeria was swept up in a grand display of her own ego. Nothing she could do could make it up to Aldara; nothing could regain her trust. "Come, we will go below to the dark elves' sleeping quarters."

Aldara held her ground. It was time to escape from the Queen. If only there was a way to get away from her for only a moment—she might then have a chance. She no longer needed to worry about the soldiers below; they were all too busy fighting for their lives. "Give me a moment. I'm not feeling very well, suddenly," she lied to the Queen, in the hope of buying a little time while she thought of a new escape plan.

"Very well." Queen Valeria threw one more glance back down at the camp. "I'm sure Captain Nagarr will have the situation resolved in no time."

****

Ayku returned to full size and wildly tossed the piles of hay about. Wyndle had done a good job of hiding their weapons…maybe a little *too* good. It seemed like she had been digging forever before she started to see steel shining in the midday sun. She started to uncover swords, battle axes, and a larger item that she thought was a shield. She grabbed the shield and raised it out of the hay pile when she noticed that the sun was suddenly being blocked out. She turned her head and saw a silhouetted figure with its hand on the hilt of its sword, ready to draw.

"I would love to know how this orchestrated escape attempt got organized in my camp." Captain Nagarr stood over Ayku. His words were cold and angry. They had all caused him such embarrassment in front of the Queen, especially the fairie. "I would also like to know how it is that you are all in such good health. You will explain this to me now, and I may let you and your friends live."

Ayku rose to her feet. She was no longer afraid of Nagarr. Sure, he had his sword and he was physically larger than her, but she was no longer helplessly shackled to a wall. Her fairie powers were now fully available to her and she intended to use them. "A little glamour will enlighten you, Nagarr." With that, she put her right hand to her lips and blew a kiss full of fairie dust at the Captain, followed by a wink. The dust sprinkled all over his face, sticking to him like moistened glitter.

Captain Nagarr found that his vision was changing. Not just his sight, but his mind as well. He looked at Ayku to see that was now glowing beautifully. Her fair skin and her rich full lips made her the most beautiful creature Nagarr had ever laid eyes on. He stood dumbfounded as he gazed upon her beauty.

"Now, you are just going to stand there and be a good boy while I get these weapons together for my friends. You are to do nothing but stand and admire that which you hate the most. You will love me. You will love a fairie." Ayku was a firm believer in poetic justice and this was a classic example of that.

"Yes. You are beautiful. So very beautiful." Nagarr looked and sounded like a zombie, caught up in Ayku's charm. He stared at her without blinking for a few moments until his head started to twitch. The twitching turned into a brief shake, and when he recovered, so too did the look of hatred in his eyes.

Ayku stumbled and backed up a step. She should have gotten out of that corner when she had the chance. How could she have forgotten that elves have a natural resistance to charm spells? Before she could finish her thought, the Captain backhanded her across the face. The force of his backhand was powerful enough to send her to the ground. He quickly drew his sword. "Your life ends here and now, fairie." He raised his sword into the air just as Eldin's fist struck him in the face. Captain Nagarr lost his balance and fell to the ground.

"You were always curious about humans." Eldin looked down at Nagarr, who held his sword protectively in front of him while rising to his feet, "Let me put an end to your curiosity, elf." Eldin stood above him ready to fight with his bare hands.

How brave, Ayku thought, *but also how stupid.* She quickly cleared the hay from a sword, picked it up and handed it to Eldin.

"Eldin, let me help you!" Tye approached the hay stacks, panting to catch his breath.

Eldin assumed a defensive posture with his sword ready when Nagarr rose to his feet. "This is my fight, junior. Help Ayku distribute those weapons before the Dracal kill them all. I'll join you after I finish killing Nagarr," he said as he flashed an intimidating smile at the dark elf captain.

The Captain swung his sword at Eldin's smile; it was blocked by the human's blade. After the block, Eldin swung his sword at Nagarr's waist. In response, Nagarr raised his sword in the air and parried in a clockwise motion, successfully blocking Eldin's blow.

****

Gusseus was the only slave left alive in his barracks. At his feet lay three dead gnomes and one dead blue Dracal. Scorch marks lined the walls, which were smoking like the bodies on the ground. Pulling the dagger out of his victim's eye socket, the dwarf made his way out of the barracks as fast as he could and started his trek to the hay piles. He could see Tye and Ayku already distributing weapons to any slave who was lucky enough to reach the stacks of hay. To his left, he saw four gnomes on top of a blue Dracal, repeatedly stabbing it in its underbelly. The Dracal stood up, blood running from its stomach. It tossed the gnomes off of him like they were rag dolls.

The Dracal opened its mouth and a bolt of lightning rose

out of its throat and shot toward a gnome. The gnome avoided the purplish light by jumping and rolling behind a watering barrel. The bolt of lightning struck the barrel with a thunderous crash, sending splinters everywhere.

The gnome sat behind what was left of the barrel, expecting another blast of lightning. Nothing came. He peeked around the splintered wood to see the Dracal lying on the ground, its head a few feet from its body. Standing next to the body was a tall orc. He was a prisoner of the third barrack and didn't speak to anyone the entire time he had been imprisoned there. Every encounter with him had been an unpleasant one, but now—as he held the sword that Ayku had given him and stood over the lifeless body of their mutual enemy—he became the most pleasant sight the gnome had ever seen.

Gusseus stopped running and shouted to the orc, "Follow me! We mus' be makin' our way ta Nagarr's quarters!" Gusseus took a moment to catch his breath between words.

The orc, without saying a word, pointed to the front gate. He ran toward it and the four gnomes followed.

Gusseus could see the gatekeeper and a blue Dracal guarding the gate, remaining at their post. "It's tha wrong way! You won't be makin' it, lads!" Gusseus knew his words were in vain, but he did not have time to debate the situation any longer. He turned to continue toward the haystacks when he felt a burning sensation in his side. It knocked him, backward, to the ground. He shook his head and looked up to see a dark elf standing a few feet in front of him. The elf's hands were raised in the air and glowing green. The green light grew in intensity and shot forth from the dark elf's fingertips. The energy split apart and took the form of three energy-like darts. Gusseus quickly rolled to his side and the darts buried themselves into the ground, leaving no trace of where they struck.

The spell caster seemed unaffected by missing his target and raised his hands a second time. This time, his hands were raised as if he were holding a ball or cupping the air. A gentle breeze picked up and gathered in the dark elf's hands. It blackened in color as it grew in power and the dark elf arched his back as if he were ready to throw the ball at Gusseus. Just then, the breeze stopped and the ball quickly disappeared. The elf's arms fell limp to his sides and he fell flat on his face. Gusseus lifted his head and saw an arrow sticking out of the elf's back. He looked past the elf and saw Tye standing with his bow drawn.

"Nice shootin', laddie," said Gusseus, expressing his gratitude as he moved closer to the haystacks. It was only then that he heard the clanking metal of the sword fight between Eldin and Captain Nagarr.

The Captain and Eldin had been fighting for quite some time. They appeared to be equal in fighting ability, but each was driven by different desires: Eldin, the drive for freedom, and Nagarr, the drive to show off his fighting skills for his Queen.

The clanking sound of the duel was heard everywhere, making it very difficult for Nagarr to concentrate. There should never be the sound of weapons striking each other. The only sound that should be heard throughout the camp was the breath of the Dracal and the sizzling flesh of its victims. Why was that not so?

Nagarr knew that his career was now over. Even if he were to regain control of the labor camp, the Queen was a witness to everything that had transpired. His name was now in disgrace. The thought of spending the rest of his life watching over weaklings in mining camps made the blood surge through his veins, giving him a complete and powerful rush of anger.

Eldin took a low swing at Nagarr's legs; the dark elf parried it beautifully and with more power than his previous blocks. With his free hand, he struck Eldin in the face, drawing blood from his lip. He then took hold of his sword with both hands and swung it over his head toward the side of Eldin's chest. Eldin blocked it with a fast upswing that sent Nagarr's sword flying out of his hand and up onto the stacks of hay behind him.

After receiving a kick to the face, Eldin hit the ground with force, leaving Nagarr with a free moment to spin around and leap on the bales of hay to retrieve his sword. He reached for his weapon and glimpsed a few other prisoners closing in on his position. Frantically, he looked around him but failed to see any of his troops still standing.

Eldin took advantage of Nagarr's panic attack. He rose swiftly to his feet and swung his blade at his opponent. The tip of his sword cut through Nagarr's sleeve, the blood turning the left side of his uniform a brownish crimson. The dark elf let out a wounded cry and leaped from his bale of hay to fight on more solid ground.

Their swords met yet again and the two warriors' faces were now a few hairs apart. They spent a moment that seemed an eternity to them staring into each other's eyes. Each was trying to intimidate the other, when Eldin suddenly broke the staring contest with a smile. "You've lost," he spat at his dark opponent while catching his breath, "Look around you. You'll find you stand alone."

Captain Nagarr sneered and looked behind Eldin, then up into the air. He saw no one, not even a single Dracal. Fear swept over him. He could not die this way…not like this, not in his own camp, by a group of prisoners that should be too weak to run—let alone bring down a warrior as mighty as himself. He was Captain Nagarr, a trained fighter under the leadership of Commander Zelgot. He would not let such a thing happen. He would slay every last prisoner himself and tell tales for years to come of how he had single-handedly stopped the uprising.

"Today you lose, Nagarr. Not just you, but your dark elf buddies too." Eldin's words were full of confidence. There was no doubt in his mind; he would not fall before the dark elf captain. "The tide of this war turns today. Here and now."

"Never, human!" Nagarr snapped back in disgust. "Tomorrow will remain the same as today. The only exception is that your head will decorate my wall." With that, Nagarr pushed Eldin away from him to release their locked weapons. With renewed vigor, the dark elf warrior lunged toward Eldin. Each of his mighty blows was blocked as Eldin held his ground.

Their swords continued to clash in a feverish frenzy until Nagarr made a fatal error. He swung his sword with such fierceness that he lost control. He missed Eldin all together and hit a bundle of hay behind him. The bundle wobbled off its stack and fell to the ground, causing Nagarr to lose his balance and tumble with it.

Eldin swung his sword at the Captain and it tore into his precious, form-fitting uniform. The cut began at his chest and ended at his stomach. The medals of dedication flew from his chest and into the air as he fell to the ground.

Nagarr's sword fell out of his hand; his left hand clutched his stomach and chest in turn, as if to hold the blood in his body. "This is not the way it will end, human. You will all join me in death and I shall triumph over you in the afterlife." Captain Nagarr's breath was short and erratic.

Ayku came to stand near him and watched as his life escaped. As much as she hated Nagarr, a tear came to her eye. She actually felt pity for him. She found it sad that even in the end, his heart was full of hatred rather than forgiveness.

Nagarr turned his head and looked at her. A disgusted look appeared on his face and he tried in vain to spit the blood that was pouring out of his mouth at her. "My only regret is that you still live. I wanted the joy of being the one to extinguish your kind forever." His breaths were shorter and his body was now convulsing.

The look of disgust now shifted onto Ayku's face and she knelt down beside Captain Nagarr. She flipped off his visor and put her hands over his face. Her body began to pulse and glow in intensity. Never before did she remember producing any form of light that strong. Nagarr bathed in her fairie light. "Let me light your path and help guide your soul to the spirit world."

Captain Nagarr tried to get out one final insult when the last breath escaped his lips. Ayku's light faded as she turned to Eldin, "He will never again hurt my people. For this, I thank you."

Eldin gave Ayku a shocked look, seeing how grown-up she had become in a matter of minutes. "C'mon. There's no time to lose." They started for the door of Nagarr's quarters. He turned to see that Tye and Gusseus had at last joined them. "Where is everyone else?" he asked Tye.

"All dead. The remaining few took it upon themselves to head for the front gate," Gusseus responded.

Tye moved his head from side to side and up in the air, searching for his friend, "Where's Wyndle?"

"I'm here." The Winged Angel flew up so she was hovering beside Tye's face. Tears were streaming down her cheeks. "Everything happened so fast. There were too many to protect. I couldn't save them all," she cried as she leaned on Tye's shoulder.

"Wynd, you did everything you could do. You gave us all a fighting chance. You can't protect everyone. You've done more than your part in all of this; we all owe our lives to you." Tye had an understanding, sympathetic tone in his voice and Eldin again seemed surprised at the unexpected maturity that was blossoming within their group.

Wyndle suddenly leaped from Tye's shoulder and threw her hands in the air. She encased the small group in a protective force field just as fire engulfed the haystacks around them. The group looked up and saw a red Dracal flying away, preparing to come back for a second pass. Tye readied his bow and Gusseus picked up a throwing axe. Ayku's body shrank down to one-fifth its size as she flew above her friends.

Wyndle thought it necessary to briefly inform the group of the limitations of her spell. "I can't keep my force field up when you attack the Dracal. When the force field is up, weapons and spells can't come in or go out."

"Then keep it up until the Dracal is done shooting its flames. We'll have to hit it the moment after it spits and starts to fly away for another pass," Eldin ordered as he picked up a metal shield that had remained in the weapons pile.

The Dracal flew in fast and low over the group. Although Dracal possessed the ability to fly, they flew rather clumsily and could only rise about ten feet into the air. It opened its mouth just before it reached the group. Its underbelly seemed to recede within its body as it took a long, deep breath, then shot scorching flames from its mouth. The flames covered the domed force field, but because there was nothing to burn, they quickly went out as the Dracal finished its pass.

Ayku flew in front of the beast as it retreated before another pass, dancing directly in front of its face. The Dracal stopped in mid-air, flapping its huge leathery wings, and tried to swat her out of the air. Her tiny body started to pulse as she once again called on her powers of light. She grew to full size while glowing and she threw her hands out toward the Dracal's eyes, blinding it. Its hands had flown up in front of its face and it fell back in the air, flapping its wings rapidly to avoid falling to the ground.

Wyndle, taking full advantage of the Dracal's distraction, lowered her force field and closed her eyes to recover from her spell. The other members of the group wasted no time either. Tye shot an arrow into the Dracal's underbelly and Gusseus hurled his throwing axe at the creature's neck. The beast cried out in pain and fell toward the ground.

When the Dracal came within arm's reach, Eldin plunged his sword deep within it. The exhausted Dracal hit the ground hard and let out a whimper; then its eyes began to flicker.

Wyndle flew close to the Dracal's head and gave it a brief examination. "Yup. I'm almost sure of it," she said, as she looked it up and down. She stared into its eyes. "This is unthinkable. How could it have been done?" The Dracal's eyes flickered once more and then turned black. She was suddenly aware of screams in the distance, and she could see figures at the front gate shaking and convulsing as electricity danced all over their bodies from the blue Dracal's breath.

"We've *got* to help them!" Wyndle rose from the Dracal's body and hovered in the air, looking at the group for approval of her decision. But it was too late; even in her mind she knew it. If they had been closer, maybe they would have a fighting chance until Wyndle could erect a force field around them, but there was no hope of getting there in time.

"C'mon. We're next if we don't get out of here." Eldin gave Wyndle a sympathetic look and led the group to Nagarr's quarters. The heavy wooden door was closed. Eldin didn't bother to check to see if it was locked; that would use up their valuable time. He took the blunt end of his sword and smashed the door handle. The door swung open and they entered their destination.

****

Queen Valeria sat in the dark elves' quarters next to Aldara. The sudden cry of a Dracal just outside Nagarr's quarters told her that the battle couldn't be going as well as she thought. *Why weren't the prisoners dead by now? Surely, they had no weapons and must be too weak to fight. Why was the battle still going on?* She looked over at Aldara, who was sitting calmly at the other end of the bed.

"Stay here, child. I must see what is going on. It is obvious to me that Captain Nagarr has spent too much time giving orders in this camp, and that he has forgotten how to fight." The Queen stood up and tightly grasped her staff. She looked at the Globe of Imprisonment, which sat at the end of her staff, looked at Aldara, and then gave the room the once-over. The Queen's eyes fell on a spell book on the far end of the room. Her eyes tightened as she looked back at Aldara. "On second thought, come with me. I wouldn't want you to come to any harm."

Aldara looked over at her and sank into the bed. She had been listening to the battle through Valeria's ramblings and knew it wasn't going well for the Queen. Somehow, someway, the prisoners were winning. Now, if only she could get the Queen to leave her side for a fraction of a moment, she could make her escape. "Thank you for your concern, but I'll be fine here."

"I insist." The Queen reached out and grabbed Aldara's arm, lifting her out of the bed with ease. Aldara wasn't sure how she was being lifted; the Queen's grip wasn't tight and yet, there was so much force behind it. Aldara rose to her feet and they both made their way toward the door of the chamber when they heard a slam. Valeria looked over at the two spell casters, who were just coming out of their brief meditation. "You two stay there. I will handle this."

Queen Valeria and Aldara came out of the elves' quarters to see a group of prisoners charging the stairs. They were well-equipped and had a look of hard determination in their eyes. A human was leading the pack, and behind him were a dwarf, a fairie, a small Winged Angel, and a light elf.

Aldara's eyes widened in disbelief. "Tye?" she shouted to the group on the stairs. She looked at him to confirm that it really was her friend running toward her when the Winged Angel caught her eye.

"Aldara?!" Tye exclaimed in disbelief as he came closer to Aldara and the Queen. He looked at the Queen and a rush of fear came over him. *What was she doing here? What was Aldara doing here with her?*

The Queen looked at Tye and then over at Aldara; this was a reunion that would end in misfortune for them all. The Queen raised her staff, and the Globe of Imprisonment started to glow.

Aldara tried to grab the Queen's staff, but Valeria's grip was tight. She wouldn't let go and Aldara struggled with it as the globe discharged. A round, mysterious bubble shot out from the globe and hit the wall. It popped instantly on impact.

The Queen's eyes were full of hatred as she whipped her head around to face Aldara. She jerked her head in the air and Aldara's grip on the staff was released, while Aldara was knocked back a few feet against the stone wall. The Queen was raising her hand toward Aldara when she saw Wyndle. Valeria's eyes lit up like a small child who was just about to receive a present. All of the Queen's attention and focus was now off of Aldara, away from the group of prisoners, and on Wyndle alone.

Aldara, remembering what the Queen had said about the angels being the only ones who could stop her, suddenly reached out and grabbed Wyndle. A few feathers flew out of Aldara's hand, and then she brought her arm back and threw Wyndle as hard as she could into the dark elves' quarters. If the Queen was that afraid of the angels, this one may have the power to destroy her while making for a good distraction.

"Aldara, NO! Wyndle!" Tye was screaming at the top of his lungs, his voice cracking with fear. He started for the Queen.

The Queen paid him no attention and followed Wyndle into the room. She raised her staff and pointed the Globe of Imprisonment at Wyndle. Queen Valeria tightened her grip on the staff and another bubble squeezed out of its end and shot out at the Winged Angel with such force that it could not be avoided.

The bubble pressed itself against Wyndle's body and the force of it was overbearing. She struggled to resist it and tried to push it away when her hand was sucked inside. The bubble's pull worked its way up her arms, finally pulling her entire body inside it. Her screams of horror were suddenly muffled as the bubble hardened into a globe and fell toward the floor. The Queen quickly stepped forward, reached out her hand, and caught the globe in her palm.

Gusseus pulled Tye by his shirt. "No, lad!" he shouted. "There be nothin' you can do fer her now. Only way ta help her now is ta escape and come back fer her. We're no match fer tha Queen in our present state."

"The dwarf is right. Let's make our way to the top of the building as planned. We must get to those horses." Eldin and Gusseus grabbed Tye and pulled him closer to the next flight of stairs. Aldara followed nervously behind them.

The Queen turned and watched them run by the doorway. She looked back into the newly formed globe that contained Wyndle and smiled. She pointed at one of the spell casters. "Kill them," she ordered coldly.

The spell caster nodded and made his way to the door. He stopped briefly to look at the Queen's prize, then continued out of the room.

The group made its way to the top of Nagarr's living structure. They ran as quickly as they could out onto the circular balcony that encircled the whole building. There, they could smell the foul stench of death below them. Adrenaline coursed through their veins as they came to a sudden stop, confused at which direction to take.

"Left!" Eldin ordered. "This will take us to the back of the building where the horses are." Eldin looked over at Aldara. "I don't think yer comin' with us, honey." He raised his sword toward the half-breed.

The sound of leathery wings was heard to their right, and looking over, Aldara saw a yellow Dracal fly close to the structure. She also saw a dark spell caster approach the top of the stairs and silently raise his hands into the air while chanting quietly.

Aldara also threw her hands into the air, pointing them in Eldin's direction. Her fingers began to glow a greenish color. "Get down, human," she ordered him.

He raised his sword above his head and then turned quickly to look behind him. He saw that the Dracal was now hovering over the balcony's edge and had just taken a deep breath. Eldin dropped to the ground just as the creature opened its mouth and sent a stream of acid in his direction. It hit the stone wall and splashed on to the dark elf who was deeply involved in his spell casting. The elf let out a horrifying scream as his flesh was eaten away by the powerful acid. The elf's spell fizzled immediately as he grabbed his face in a vain attempt to stop the pain. He lost his balance and went tumbling down the stairwell.

The Dracal took in another deep breath just as Aldara's

spell was completed. Three green darts shot from her finger-tips and pierced the Dracal's eyes. She could hear its eyes sizzle as it covered its face. *A rather nice shot*, Aldara thought.

Eldin quickly rose to his feet and plunged his sword deep into the beast's chest. Another scream was heard, this time from the Dracal, as Eldin pulled his sword out. The creature's wings stopped flapping and he fell spiraling to his death in the flames of the haystacks.

"Let's move!" Gusseus's stout body waddled as he ran to the other side of the balcony.

"There!" Ayku looked over its edge, "the horses are still there!" Ayku backed up, raised her hand in the air and then looked at Aldara. "Why should we bring her? She betrayed us and now Wyndle is in the hands of the Queen."

"I had no choice! Queen Valeria would have killed you all to get her. I thought the angel would have the power to destroy the Queen. I thought I was doing the right thing. I've learned so much about the dark elves from my trip to Under Hollow. I can use that knowledge to help get Wyndle back." Aldara trembled as she defended herself. Had she come all this way only to be abandoned by her friends and left here to die?

"Shut up, traitor. We've got to get down there!" Eldin exclaimed. "It's now or never, fairie." Eldin put his sword in its sheath and gathered the group close together.

"What about Aldara?" Ayku asked as she waved her hand over the group.

Eldin changed his mind and roughly pulled Aldara into their small circle. "She comes with us." He looked into Aldara's eyes. "She was with the Queen. Maybe she can tell us something useful. If not, we kill her."

Ayku's hand was waving over the tightly circled group. Shimmering fairie dust showered all over them. It was a beautiful sight that few creatures had the privilege to behold. As the fairie dust covered their bodies, their feet slowly lifted off the ground, and they were soon levitating in the air.

The escaped prisoners jumped over the wall and glided down to their horses just as the Queen reached the top of the stairs. She walked slowly and calmly out onto the balcony. The remaining dark elf followed her and stood at her side. She turned to see the blue Dracal that was guarding the gate approach her position. She waved her hand in the air, signaling for the Dracal to stop. Obeying her command, as always, the Dracal flew down onto the structure and folded its wings, standing quietly while waiting for another command.

The Queen and her minions walked over to the side of the balcony and silently watched as the ex-prisoners rode off into the horizon, all the while maintaining a firm grip on her prize.

"Should we have the Dracal go after them? Riding on horses, they would be no match for it," the spell caster suggested as he watched his beloved Queen stand coldly with a chilling smile on her face.

Queen Valeria smiled at the dark elf and then held the globe up to her face. She watched Wyndle struggling to get out. Her small body was cut and bruised and her face was covered with tears. "No. I've got what I want. This trip has been a complete success." Her gaze rose from her globe to the group of renegades on their horses, galloping towards freedom. Her focus settled on Aldara and she smiled once more. "A complete success."

Chapter V

—◦◦◦—

Shades of Gray

Hot, watery beads of sweat slid slowly down the right side of Tye's neck. A droplet ran down and covered Ayku's head. She was still enjoying the feeling of being a few inches tall and was asleep on Tye's shoulder. Being close to him like this was such a treat for her. She hadn't been able to sleep peacefully in months, and though they weren't out of danger completely, she felt safe just knowing he was next to her. She missed being close to him and although his shyness compelled him to hide his feelings as best he could, he enjoyed her company just as much. She enjoyed using Tye's shoulder and neck as a bed and pillow, however, she did not enjoy her head being enclosed in a drop of his sweat.

"Wha—" She opened her eyes and shook her head violently, like an animal shaking the rain off its coat. She looked up at Tye, who had turned his head to see what all her fuss was about, and gave him a frown. "Eww. You know, sometimes you can just be so gross, Tyelander." She was now using her hands to brush the sweat from her face.

"Don't call me that." Tye knew she called him by his full name to annoy him. Although he knew it was said in fun, he didn't want the rest of their party to hear the name and get used to calling him that, especially Eldin. "I'm glad you had a chance to sleep."

"Yeah, after what we went through, I needed it. Now if only I could get a bath that wasn't in salt water." She brushed her soaking wet hair out of her face, "How long was I out?"

"We've been on these horses for hours. Not a single Dracal in sight," Tye responded, excited to report the good news.

"Yeah, nice and peaceful without the enemy in sight for miles around." Eldin's voice came from behind on Tye's left and Tye caught him flashing a look at Aldara. "Funny, that." He held his gaze on Aldara, wondering what response she would give him—*how would she react if he were to push her buttons? Was she friend or was she foe?* "I guess the enemy doesn't have to follow us with her here." Eldin craned his neck forward, trying to see inside Aldara's hood for a reaction. She gave none, keeping her head bent toward the ground and remaining steady on her horse.

"What are you trying to say? She's a spy or something?" Tye was annoyed by Eldin's accusations. In fact, he'd been annoyed with Eldin since he first met him.

Eldin caught the protective tone in the young elf's voice. "How naive. Grow up, junior. How you survived the labor camp is beyond me." Eldin shook his head. "Ask her to explain why she was at the labor camp with the Queen and how Valeria just let us ride away without a fight."

Tye tugged on his reins and pulled his horse slowly to a

stop. The others followed his lead. He turned back to the right and bent down to look under Aldara's floppy hood. "Aldara?"

The young half-breed raised her head when her horse came to a standstill. She took hold of her hood with both of her hands and gently pulled it back. She gave Tye a sympathetic look, then turned to Eldin. She eyed him up and down. Aldara had heard of the nomadic humans who roamed from province to province, never really having a land of their own. They were the last to enter Sylvanor and all of the land had already been divided up. They were the final straw for the dark elves, and in a way, the beginning of the war—a war that was almost over, with the Overlord winning. Most of the humans tried to prove their worth by banding together and forming knighted circles that roamed the land, helping village dwellers fight the Dracal when their towns were in trouble. These humans earned the respect of the people of Sylvanor. Eldin was one such person. A man of discipline, he was used to giving orders and having them carried out by his men. Now he was with children, risking his life to free young adolescents so they could help a Winged Angel reach her contact in Solaris Arbor. But now the angel was gone and Eldin had become unsure of his purpose. He wondered if he should leave to rejoin his old group or perhaps even find the few humans that chose not to fight against the Overlord's forces. Those humans had journeyed into the desert, never to be seen again.

Aldara had never seen a human before. Eldin was her first. Normally, she would engage him in conversation, asking him everything she could think of about his race. But he would not answer any of her questions. She was hated among this group. She even suspected that Tye, her childhood friend, now hated her as well. They used to play together when they were young, but each time Tye's parents saw him playing with her, they scolded him and finally forbade him to talk to her ever again. Life had never been easy for Aldara, a half-breed; her loyalty was always in question. No one had ever fully trusted her. Just when she thought she had made some friends and found herself reunited with her childhood playmate, they had been captured by Captain Nagarr's forces and enslaved. Aldara had narrowly escaped with Wyndle, but parted ways with her to pursue her own ideas on how to rescue Tye and her new-found friends. But here they all were now, free—and each and every one of them hated her.

"Your ego is too big, human. The Queen didn't care about any of you. She wanted the Winged Angel. If I hadn't given her over, Valeria would have killed us all." She held Eldin's gaze to prove to him that she could be just as strong as he was.

Ayku frowned and her eyes narrowed at Aldara. She leapt from Tye's shoulder and flew between Aldara and Eldin, growing to full size as she flew. Her wings of light fluttered as she hovered between them and she crossed her arms. "So before trying everything else, you sold one of us out?" Rarely did Ayku get this angry. Wyndle had quickly become a friend to her. "We owe our lives to her, and this is how she is repaid? By being taken to Under Hollow or maybe even killed?"

"I thought she had some power to stop the Queen. Looks like I was wrong, as are you, Ayku. You owe your lives to *me*. In order for us to escape, a sacrifice had to be made." Aldara's words sounded harsh and cold.

Ayku found herself clenching a fist and before she could stop herself, it landed on Aldara's jaw. Aldara fell from her horse and landed on the ground, engulfed in a dry, dusty cloud. "Why didn't you throw *yourself* at the Queen then?" Ayku asked her sarcastically.

"Ayku!" Tye jumped off his horse and ran over to stand between his friends. He was concerned about Ayku's temper, but he was also concerned for Aldara's well-being. Unsure of what to do, he stood looking from one of them to the other.

Aldara took her middle finger and raised it to the corner of her mouth. She wiped her lip and then looked at her finger. She was bleeding. She looked at Ayku and the thought of summoning the winds to send her spiraling away crossed her mind. The thought left as quickly as it came and she sat up. "Do you think I don't regret what I have done?!" Aldara's voice was loud and angry, and as she continued to speak, it was obvious she was fighting back tears. "You weren't there in Under Hollow or for the journey to the labor camp. She spoke of Wyndle like she feared her. I thought the angel had a power that could defeat the Queen. My decision was born of poor judgment and I'm sorry for your loss. But we *are* free. I have learned where the entrance to Under Hollow is and I have found out so much, we could go and get her back." Aldara stood up and dusted off her cape.

"Until the next time we get into trouble and you decide to turn on someone else." Eldin looked at her as if she were the enemy.

Tye looked over at the knight and raised his finger at him. "Shut up, Eldin! You aren't helping matters any." Tye didn't fully understand why Aldara had done what she did, but he knew in his heart that she wasn't working for the Queen and he felt that he should defend his friend over a stranger.

"Hold on there, laddie." Gusseus was trying to climb down from his horse. He lost his footing on the side of the saddle and tumbled to the ground. He rolled a few feet from the horse and struggled quickly to stand up, hoping no one would notice his vertically challenged *faux pas*. He ran over to Tye quickly while dusting off his buttocks. "I'm thinkin' everyone just needs ta be calmin' down. Just over tha hill there is tha border ta tha mixed province. Take tha horses there and get washed in tha river. It's about time we've all been havin' a bath." Gusseus lifted his arm slightly and briefly sniffed his armpit. A frown came over his face. "We don't want ta be offendin' anyone in Frentier. We'll be wantin' ta blend in and be as least conspicuous as possible." He walked over to stand by Aldara. "We'll be meetin' ya there. I'm wantin' a few words with this one." Gusseus and Aldara slowly started walking in the direction of the water.

Eldin grabbed the reins to Aldara's horse and started to gallop toward the hill. He turned and looked back at Gusseus, "Find out everything she knows so we can be done with her. I've brought her along just about as far as I want to," Eldin said, his voice lower than usual. His gaze turned to Aldara and he stiffened his brow, "Just don't turn your back on her."

"Aye, laddie. It's been my experience that things aren't always what they seem." Gusseus watched as Tye got back on his horse and the group rode up the hill toward the river. "C'mon, young one," he said to Aldara, "we'll take tha long way around. I'm wantin' ta hear yer tale."

****

Ayku stood on a rock on the side of the river, taking in

her surroundings. There were more trees near the river and the grass there was much more dense and vibrant. She closed her eyes and took a deep breath. A large grin appeared on her face as she became even more captivated by the nature around her. A soft cool mist was spraying the left side of her body and she looked over to see a fairly decent-sized waterfall, its water sparkling in the sunlight as it cascaded down some rocks and ended in a foamy pool before continuing downstream. A roaring sound was coming from the waterfall as Ayku again closed her eyes and enjoyed the sounds of life around her.

"In ya go!" Tye's hands were hard on her back and Ayku found herself falling off of the rock and into the water. Screaming as she plunged into the cool water, it had all happened too fast for her to figure out what was happening in time for her to escape Tye's mischief.

Ayku sank quickly and Tye could no longer see her move under the gentle current. He moved to the edge of the riverbank and looked into the water. "Ayku?" he called. Just then, with a splash, Ayku, now considerably smaller, flew up out of the water at his feet. The force of her movement showered his legs with the running water and she stopped to hover in front of his face. Tye looked at her in a daze as she opened her mouth and squirted water all over his nose. "You do that again, and I'll bop you!" Ayku shook her tiny fist at Tye, then burst into laughter. "You are such a jerk sometimes," she smiled.

A faint smile appeared on Eldin's lips as he remembered his youth. His adolescence had also been tough. His own realm destroyed by dragons, he had to flee to Sylvanor and start over, only to be fighting again to save his life. "Hey Ayku," he shouted. "Why do your clothes shrink when you change size?" His smile faded a bit when Tye turned around to face him, frowning.

"Don't be so rude, Eldin!" Tye grabbed at his shirt and pulled it over his head.

Ayku looked over at the knight. "It's part of a fairie's glamour." Ayku winked at Eldin, who smiled back, and then she turned her attention back to Tye. He had his shirt off now and she was looking at the muscle tone he was starting to develop. His body clearly reflected the months of hard labor it had endured.

Tye caught her looking at him and as usual, became embarrassed. "Ayku," he started. She looked at him and blinked. "Would you turn around?" He was now fully embarrassed and looked over at Eldin, only to find him stripping off his own clothes and laughing.

Ayku shrugged, smiled, and turned around. She grew back to her full size and flew up in the air and dove back down into the water.

Tye finished removing his clothes and dove in after her, followed by Eldin. The water was freezing and Tye came up screaming about how cold it was. He shivered a bit, then bobbed up and down in the water until he got used to it. Eldin had no complaints. *For once,* Tye thought.

"Now that you boys went through some embarrassment by removing your clothes, I should point out that what good is a bath if you're just going to get back in the same dirty, smelly clothes? You should have kept them on." Ayku giggled.

"Oh." Tye couldn't think of anything to say to her so he swung his arm out in the water and splashed Ayku as hard as he could. He swam over and without leaving the water, pulled his clothes in.

Ayku's giggling was now full-on laughter, "Gotcha back."

Tye soaked his clothes and was now wringing them out. "These rags are so old, they'll probably be ripped to shreds before I'm done washing them."

Eldin wasn't quite as embarrassed as Tye. He walked right out of the water and picked his clothes up off the ground. "Don't worry about it, junior. The first thing we're going to do when we hit that town is get some new clothes." He looked over at his horse, which had its reins tied around a tree. He noticed that his sword, strapped into the side of the harness, already had a few chips in it from their previous battle. "And some decent weapons." He walked back into the water at a steady pace, as if the water temperature were the same as that of the air.

Ayku looked beyond Eldin and leaned her head from side to side, trying to get a glimpse of Gusseus and Aldara. They were not in sight. A rush of questions came over her. *Was being alone with her safe? What if Aldara had a Globe of Communication and was now using it to give the Queen their location after knocking Gusseus unconscious? Was she even capable of such an act? Of course she was. If she could turn Wyndle in to the Queen, she could turn on anyone. Or could she?* Ayku looked over at Tye, who was squeezing the water out of his clothes. *Would she hand Tye over too if she were to find herself cornered again?* she pondered. Ayku knew that Tye and Aldara went back a long way, but Ayku had only known her for a few hours before they were captured in Frentier. All she knew about Aldara was that she had run to save herself then and then she had turned one of them in to save herself again. Sure, Tye knew her when they were children, but did he

really know her *now*? She couldn't keep her questions to herself
any longer. She had to let her doubts and fears out in the open.
"Tye?" she asked softly while wading through the water toward
him. "Can we trust her?"

Tye stopped washing his clothes and threw his wrung-out
shirt onto the grass next to the river. He looked at her sad face
and could tell by the tone of her voice that she was more than
curious; she was genuinely concerned and even a little frightened. "I've known Aldara for a long time, Ayk. She's done a lot
of things that I guess were wrong since I've known her. But
she's not a bad person." He saw Ayku shake her head and realized that he'd have a hard time making her see the girl that he
saw. "From all that I know about her, she did what she thought
had to be done."

Ayku let out a gasp of disbelief. *Could Tye really be that blind?*
she thought. She felt like asking him that question directly, but
thought it best to avoid an argument. Instead, she skimmed her
arm across the surface of the water and splashed him, hoping
he wasn't so blind as to not catch her hint of disgust.

Tye shook the water off of his face. "Oh, Ayk. Don't get
me wrong. I'm not making excuses for what she did. She was
wrong. *Really* wrong, but she knows that now. All I'm sayin' is
that we at least listen to her first. We need her to help us get
Wyndle back." He shrugged and continued, "I guess it would
just be easier if we wouldn't be fighting the whole time."

Ayku folded her arms. "Okay, Tyelander. I'll listen." Then
she shook her finger at him. "But it doesn't mean that I'll start
liking her. I'll be watching my back. And yours." She thought
it best not to wait for a response from her friend. She quickly
disappeared under the water and continued to wash up.

****

"But what were they doin' there?" Gusseus walked along-side Aldara with a puzzled look on his face. He shoved his hands in his pockets and kicked his feet as he walked along.

Aldara watched him do this and for the first time, she saw Gusseus in another light. She saw how genuine and true he was. He was a kid in an adult's body. Sure, he had grown up, but his heart had stayed young. Aldara secretly hoped she could be so lucky. Or was it too late for her? "I don't know. I never figured that out. They traveled to Under Hollow of their own free will and were on their way to a portal. I was yanked out of line and taken to the Queen at that point."

The stout dwarf raised an eyebrow. "Portal? What portal?" he asked, "Where were they goin'?"

Aldara sighed briefly and shook her head. "I don't know. My guess is that they were going to see the Overlord." She paused, trying to reach back in her memory. "I don't remember seeing him anywhere in the castle." She continued on toward the river. "From what I could tell, the castle looked more like it belonged to Valeria than to the Overlord. He must be some-where else."

Gusseus kept his stride beside her and was starting to envision all sorts of scenarios. "If the Overlord don't be on Sylvanor, it's gotta be fer a good reason. We gotta be findin' out where he is and why."

"I wish I knew," Aldara replied while looking forward. She closed her eyes for a moment and she sighed heavily. "I guess I didn't learn as much about Under Hollow as I thought."

"Nonsense!" Gusseus exclaimed. He turned and looked

up at her face, which was still steadily looking forward. "Any bit o' information helps at this point." His pace slowed and he scanned the ground for a walking stick. "Not even tha elders know much about what's goin' on. How tha dark elves can be keepin' so much a secret is amazin'. Aye, their brotherhood is astoundin'."

"Yes, they possess a harmony that the other races seem incapable of," she replied coldly.

Gusseus stopped upon finding his walking stick. He tapped the ground with it a few times and started up again. "And ya thinks ya remember tha way back ta tha Queen's castle, eh?" Hearing Aldara's admiration of the dark elves, he thought it best to briefly change the subject.

Aldara was looking around at the beauty of the landscape. She took in a deep breath. "Yes. I'm sure of it. I made very careful mental notes. They have some unique plants and things down there that I used for landmarks." She stopped and sat on a rock so she could be at eye level with Gusseus. "I know we can get Wyndle back. I remember the way. I will go on my own if I must; I owe that to her."

Gusseus looked deep in her eyes; he could see the regret. "Are ya sure ya don't want Eldin ta be goin' with ya?" he smiled.

"Eldin's reacting the way anyone would. I can't blame him." Aldara heard the knight's obnoxious voice booming from over the hill; she frowned at first, then smiled. "But if he's gonna be the only one coming with me, I'd rather go alone."

Gusseus laughed and grabbed his belly. His laughter caused him to bounce up and down and Aldara was reminded of a huge play ball she had when she was a child. She watched him laugh and realized how lucky Tye was to have been brought up by Gusseus. She was developing respect for him. He was, after all, the only one in the group who was talking to her, trying to find out what really happened before making any judgments about her.

The little dwarf's laughter died down and he composed himself once more. "So, how's Wyndle fittin' inta all this? Ya said tha Queen wants her, but why?"

"I don't know. She said the angels had the power to destroy her. She wants to learn the location of the angel's portal so she can kill them too." Aldara tightened her boots a little and dusted them off.

"Well, tha portal be safe in Solaris Arbor, everybody be knowin' that. But its exact location's been a mystery fer a long time. She canna get ta it, it be protected by tha Breathing Forest. Tha Queen canna touch it. She's tried before, and it was really tha only battle that Zelgot ever lost, methinks. And they didn't want ta be tryin' that again." Gusseus now had his walking stick in both hands and was seeing how far he could bend it without breaking it. "Wyndle was actin' very strange when she was givin' that Dracal tha once-over. She didn't get a chance ta share what she found." He shook his head as if trying to remember more clearly. "Aye, 'twas all very strange."

"The Dracal themselves are strange," she said as she continued to dust off her pants. "I was hoping to discover their origins when I was down in Under Hollow, but all I found out is that they are incredibly stupid creatures with no minds of their own whatsoever." She smiled, "But I guess it wouldn't take a trip all the way to Under Hollow to figure that one out."

Gusseus chuckled, then looked skyward, as if hoping that the answers he was seeking were spelled out in the clouds. "We need ta be findin' out who they be and why they'd be formin' an alliance with tha dark elves. Mebbe they be related ta tha dragons. Aye, maybe that's where tha Overlord be stayin', in the dragons' realm."

"Could be," Aldara said as she nodded in agreement. "I just wish I had more time down there to find out more about them. Talk about your best-kept secrets…" she trailed off.

"Aye." Gusseus raised his finger to his mouth and bounced it off of his lower lip. "Wyndle knew something. I'm sher o' it. She be actin' really strange when lookin' at a few o' their bodies."

Aldara looked toward the ground. "Had I known it was something the angel knew and not some power she had that the Queen wanted, maybe I would have thought twice about what I did." She closed her eyes briefly. "But then, maybe not. Stories of my escape will spread throughout Sylvanor and bring hope to those who have little left." She may not have learned where the portal led or just who the Dracal were, but a wave of self-importance came over her when she suddenly remembered the globe and the dark elves' spell book she had previously pilfered.

Gusseus put his hands on his hips and his voice sounded deeper. "Don'tcha go snowin' me, child. That's a lie as long as any bridge I've ever seen. Why do ya thinks yer more important than tha Queen?"

Clever little man, thought Aldara. He's not as foolish as she thought. There's a bigger brain behind his big heart than she realized. Perhaps she found out more on that trip than people realized. She grabbed hold of her bag and squeezed it in various places, making sure her collected objects were still inside.

"The Queen made a fatal error in letting me go this morning. I intend to take full advantage of that," she stated aloud.

Gusseus narrowed his eyes a bit. "Did she now?" The Queen had never made a mistake to date, much less a fatal one. He couldn't put his finger on why exactly the Queen would let them all just walk away. True, she may have got what she wanted, but why not kill them all anyway, just for sport. That was more her style.

Aldara sat up to her full height, as if to remind the dwarf of her size. "Look, old man, I don't have to prove my loyalty to you, the angel, or anyone else. I know where my loyalties lie and I will do whatever I can to obtain my goals."

A look of disappointment flushed Gusseus's face. "Even if that means sacrificin' an innocent life ta save yer own?"

Aldara crossed her arms and suddenly had a more pompous air about her. "If need be."

"Again, stop snowin' me, child. I know ya be regrettin' what ya done. Ya said so yerself. Why do ya put on these acts o' hot 'n' cold?" Gusseus found Aldara to be most intriguing. She seemed very mature, but at the same time, she seemed the most immature brat he had ever known. He was beginning to see why Tye's parents didn't want him playing with Aldara when they were younger.

"Perhaps that's because as much as you people distrust me, I distrust you all just as much." Aldara raised an eyebrow and continued to play 'Miss Grown-up.'

Gusseus continued to bend his stick, pleased to find it more flexible than he originally thought. "Yer heart may be in tha right place, Aldara, but yer in fer some hard lessons before ya be findin' it."

Aldara looked at the hill and listened to the sounds of the others playing in the water. "Aren't we all?" she replied.

Just then, Gusseus's stick snapped in half and he stumbled back a bit from the fright it gave him. "Oh, shuckinspoo! Now I be needin' ta find a new one." He let out a sigh, then offered his hand to Aldara. "Come on, then. We best be gettin' back ta tha others."

Aldara placed her hand in his and Gusseus helped lift her off the rock on which she was sitting. They started off toward the river and toward the laughter of their companions, now louder. Aldara didn't particularly care for the idea of going back into the fray of accusations, but she had to get it over with sooner or later. She squeezed Gusseus's hand a little tighter and then quickly let it go. He gave her a look as he discarded his broken walking stick. "Gusseus," started Aldara as she kept her head forward and her eyes on the group in the river, "Thank you."

He looked at her and smiled as they rejoined the others. It was perhaps the most confusing conversation he had had with anyone in his lifetime. Aldara was a heavily confused child, he thought. A child who had escaped the Queen's imprisonment and whose morals weren't totally sound. Although she would not admit it, she needed the support of her friends. If she was going to make it through these trying times, Gusseus had to help make the others understand…somehow.

"Hey," screamed Eldin from the river, "You've been gone so long I was beginning to think the witch turned you into a Pythian flower!"

Gusseus heard Aldara sigh. He wasn't sure if it was a sigh of defeat or disgust. "Come into tha water with us, Aldara. It be gettin' dark soon."

"Thank you Gusseus, but I'd rather not. I've got some thinking to do." Aldara looked around and saw some rocks jutting out at the top of the waterfall. "I'll be up there in my thoughts and meditations."

"Suit yerself." Gusseus walked away from her and started to remove his tattered clothes. As he was undressing, he looked over at Tye and Ayku splashing each other in the water. "Ya love things better be getting' out. Tha sun'll be goin' down and we need ta be settin' up camp."

Aldara looked over at Tye. She saw the way he was laughing with Ayku. If only he would look at *her* like that. If only things were different. If only Ayku was the one who was an outcast. Aldara let out a sigh, pulled her bag over her shoulder, and climbed the rocks on the side of the waterfall. It was an easy climb that took only a moment or two. From the top of the waterfall, she could see the entire area. She had many things to look at but her gaze fell immediately back down to her childhood friend and the fairie. *As soon as I pay my debt and rescue the angel, I'm out of here,* she thought as she watched Ayku fly out of the water and onto the riverbed. *If I make it that long,* she sighed. She slipped her bag from her shoulder and thought she'd eavesdrop a little while opening it.

"So if the Dracal can't enter Solaris Arbor through the Breathing Forest, why don't they just fly over it? Or why doesn't the Queen put them in a boat and sail around it?" Eldin had a few obvious, though valid, questions, but it was clear that he didn't stay in any one spot for long or he would have known that the answers to his questions were just as obvious.

Idiot, thought Aldara. As much as she wanted to sit upon

the rock, high above everything, and not be bothered, she could not keep silent. "The Breathing Forest won't let anyone through who isn't pure of heart and the Dracal can't fly high enough to escape the tree limbs." She saw that Eldin was a little embarrassed about his questions as he got out of the water. "And they can't enter by boat because of the barrier spell that surrounds all of Sylvanor. Have you never *been* there?" Aldara decided she was through with the conversation and reached into her bag.

"Thanks for the tip, honey," Eldin shouted up at her sarcastically.

Aldara ignored him and started to fumble around in her bag. Her hands came across the smooth, leathery feel of what she was searching for. She grabbed hold of it and pulled it out of her bag, making sure no one saw what she was doing.

The dark elf spell book sat heavy in her hands and it made Aldara's mouth water. The spells, the hidden knowledge of the dark elves, would soon be hers. She carefully opened it. It didn't take her long to see that the pages of the book, like its cover, were of the highest quality. The paper was smooth and refined and the ink was a nice contrast to it. Each page contained various types of runes, along with the written language of the dark elf.

Thanking the gods for her knowledge of the dark elf language, she began to read. She read very quickly at first, then realized that this was not a book to merely glance over, so she slowed her reading. She found deciphering it to be difficult, discovering at the same time that her knowledge of the language was not as vast as she thought it was. She knew it would all become clear to her; it would just take time.

Back down below the waterfall, the rest of the party was setting up camp. They bundled sticks near a group of rocks and dragged huge tree leaves over. Gusseus already had some rocks in his hands and was banging them across another larger rock in the hope of making some sparks for a fire. He soon gave up on the idea and looked for the two pieces of his walking stick, thinking he would have better luck rubbing them together.

Ayku set down a few more branches and then turned to look for Tye. She found him half dressed with his leg resting on a rock as he watched the sunset. As she looked more closely, she saw a tear slowly roll down his cheek and drop to the ground. She stopped what she was doing and walked over to stand beside him. "Tye?" she said in a soft voice while placing her hand on his shoulder.

"I'm worried, Ayk." Tye brushed his hand over his cheek and wiped the remaining tears away, hoping to get rid of them before Ayku could see them. "It's getting dark and Wyndle's out there. She's alone with none of her friends to help her. She's in the hands of Queen Valeria now. We've got to get to her soon." With that, he leaned to his side and rested his head on Ayku's shoulder.

"I know we do." She started to stroke his hair lovingly. Usually, he would smack her for it and run away in his playful manner, but this time all that was on his mind was his Winged Angel friend. "Tomorrow, we'll be in Frentier and we'll get what we're going to need to get her back."

"Yahoo!" Gusseus began to jump up and down as the fire started to roar. "Gather 'round everyone! Yer clothes'll be dryin' faster!" he suggested. He looked up at Aldara and saw she was focused on something that had her thoughts a million miles away, "and plus, I've got a story ta tell ya that may help yas understand our half-breed friend a wee bit more." The group started to gather around the fire, and realizing they had little sunlight left, Gusseus began to tell them what Aldara had told him earlier. There was already plenty of hatred and fighting going on in the realm of Sylvanor and they certainly didn't need any of that here, with each other.

Aldara heard Gusseus relay her story and she lifted her eyes from her pilfered spell book. She thought it best to remain where she was until Gusseus's tale was over, even though there was little light left to read by. Sitting on the rock, Aldara listened to the chatty dwarf spin the tale and hoped that in the morning she would find more acceptance and understanding from her friends.

Chapter VI

—◈—

Cat's Eye and the Killing Jar

Queen Valeria strode across her throne room chamber. She was dressed, once again, in her royal gown, which flowed around her feet, giving the impression that she was gliding on air. Her hands cautiously cupped the globe that imprisoned Wyndle. It was a clear, pale golden sphere and the Queen held it as if it was the most precious item in the realm. Perhaps it was.

The Queen's throne room was one of the largest rooms in the castle. It was three stories high, with huge, thick columns rising from the black-and-white tiled floor to support the heavy stone ceiling. Against the main wall sat her throne itself. It was on a raised platform and sat even higher than the seats alongside it. It was a wide throne of dark wood, with various runes carved into it. The arms of the throne were heavy and thick. The seat and back of the chair were lined with plush dark violet velvet. The smaller chairs on either side of the throne were similar to the Queen's, but their lining was a dark charcoal black. Those chairs were reserved for her royal guards, dark elves of the highest spell casting ability. They traveled with her whenever she journeyed in Sylvanor, except when she was on her own missions that were kept from the Overlord or Fenrik, like her journey to the labor camp. Although a total victory in Valeria's eyes, she could see that if Fenrik found out about its details, he would certainly spin it as a failure in his reports to the Overlord.

Above the throne was a window cut into the stone wall in the shape of a crescent moon. Dark blue stained glass filled the window and the eerie light of Under Hollow shone through, casting an unearthly glow throughout the room. The throne room was a room of power, and all the power belonged to Valeria, Queen of Under Hollow.

Queen Valeria approached her destination across the room. It was a metallic stand, made of the finest silver in Under Hollow. The stand had three legs that reflected the blue light of the moon window. The legs of the stand extended into the air, spread apart at the top and curled in, forming the perfect resting place for a globe. And indeed, that was its purpose. While traveling back from the labor camp, the Queen used her Globe of Communication to instruct her craftsmen in Under Hollow to make this special silver stand to support her Globe of Imprisonment. She reached the stand and carefully set the globe in its silver fingers. It was a snug fit. Once again, the craftsmen of Under Hollow had demonstrated their superiority in their crafting abilities. Valeria smiled at the thought that there was nothing a dark elf couldn't do, and nothing would be done with less than perfection. Truly, her race deserved not only Under Hollow, but also the entire realm of Sylvanor as its own.

"Minh-Soo," the Queen uttered as she raised her hand above the stand. The air above it seemed to warp and glow; soon, there was a ball of dim light hovering directly over the globe. The light was soft and did not cause the Queen's eyes any strain whatsoever.

Inside the globe, Wyndle was tossing and turning and trying to push on its smooth walls. The Queen watched her with fascination, like a child who had just caught a jar of fireflies for the first time.

Wyndle continued to struggle inside the globe. She had been imprisoned inside of it for well over a day now, but she was not giving up. She would fight for her freedom until the very end. A tiny stream of drying tears ran down her cheeks and a few feathers from her wings could be seen lying around the bottom of the globe. Although she was unsuccessful when she had previously tried to cast a spell to free herself from the globe, she raised her hands to try again. She put her hands in the air, palms out, and pushed them in so her palms were facing her. She continued performing this fanning motion several times, but stopped when she heard the Queen laugh.

"Your powers will not work in the globe, tiny one." The smile on Valeria's lips was that of a wolf who had just cornered its prey and was about to satisfy its appetite. "There is nothing you can do to escape your prison. Any attempt to do so will be in vain."

Wyndle acted as if she didn't hear the Queen at all. She continued to pound on the globe. Like a butterfly trying desperately to escape its killing jar, she flew to the top of her spherical prison and pushed up on it. When this accomplished nothing, she flew to the globe's side and pushed on it. Out of breath, she took a moment so sit on the bottom of the globe and look outside of it at her new surroundings. Remembering what she had learned from the labor camp, she reminded herself that you must know your surroundings if a successful escape was ever to be made.

A successful escape *was* made, at least for her friends, and Wyndle was thankful for that. As long as they were alive, there was hope. Regretting that she didn't have the opportunity to fill them in on what she knew about the enemy, her only hope now was that they could somehow piece it all together and find their way safely to Solaris Arbor.

Wyndle knew that her fate was sealed. Once a dweller from above was brought down to Under Hollow, they were never seen or heard from again. That is, until Aldara. She had to have been working for the Queen, Wyndle thought. As long as Aldara was with Wyndle's group of friends, they couldn't be safe. If only she could break free of her prison to warn them.

"In your new home, you will not find the need to breathe. Everything you have known and found necessary to sustain your life, you will no longer require. Air, food, sleep—these mortal traits no longer apply to you. You will not grow old. You will never die." The Queen narrowed her eyes and added, "and you will never be free." Valeria then tilted her head to its side. "Unless, of course…you help me."

Wyndle looked at Valeria in puzzlement. "What sort of help does the Queen of Under Hollow need from a Winged Angel?" she asked at last. Finally, after over a day of imprisonment and without a word as to why she was here, she was finally going to get some answers. She halted her vain attempts to find any weaknesses in the globe and sat quite still with her arms folded, awaiting the Queen's response.

Valeria took her time answering Wyndle's question. She looked her over from head to toe and then stared her in the eye. Wyndle's eyes were older than Aldara's and the Queen knew her motherly act wouldn't work with her. In fact, Valeria didn't quite know how to handle the angel at all. She had never interacted with one, nor had she even seen one in her life. All she knew about the species was that they kept the karmic balance of the realms, to make sure the elves' magic didn't get out of hand. Deciding on the direct approach, Queen Valeria stated her demand. "You will help me find the portal to your homeland so that I may seek an audience with your kind."

"Don't you mean, so that you can continue the genocide that you have started here, in Sylvanor?" Wyndle, though tiny in size, was no child. She knew the way of things and was not blind, like her people had recently been, to what was going on in the realm.

The Queen arched an eyebrow at Wyndle's defiance. "You *will* help me or you and your kind will die." Valeria kept her usual cool and calm composure.

"My people are not afraid of death. Your threats mean nothing to me," Wyndle dismissed Valeria, Queen of Under Hollow, with a wave of her tiny hand.

The anger rising in Valeria was turning her dark gray complexion to a deep red. She could no longer hide it from her prisoner. She roughly plucked the globe from its stand with the intent to smash it into oblivion. The force of the jerk caused Wyndle to bang her head on top of the globe then fall back down to its bottom. The Queen composed herself once again and carefully set the globe into its housing of silver. As quickly as she could, she reached back into her memory to when the angel was caught. A smile curled her lips and she wiped the globe once with her hand, as if to remind Wyndle who was in control. "Perhaps not, my tiny adversary. I imagine your friends here in Sylvanor feel quite differently about it. And once I've captured them, you will sit helplessly in this globe as they suffer before your eyes. You will watch them take their last breaths. The fairie, the human, the dwarf, and…" Valeria paused and continued to think back to the scene. She remembered Tye as the one who was most upset by her capture. The one the others had to drag away. "The light elf," she said, pausing briefly to watch Wyndle's reaction, "he will suffer like no other. When his death is upon him, he will welcome it. I *promise* you that." A look of satisfaction washed over the Queen's face.

"They slipped through your fingers once. They'll do it again." Wyndle delivered her words with conviction, but deep down she did not believe them. She knew that her young friends were no match for the Queen's forces. She could only hope that they were safely on the other side of the Breathing Forest, in Solaris Arbor, telling the elders their tale and hoping they would figure out what Wyndle already knew.

The Queen's eyes narrowed at Wyndle and she was about to rebut when she heard a familiar voice speak from the doorway. She turned her head and saw Fenrik hobble past the two royal guards stationed at the door. Fenrik had free access to go wherever he pleased in the castle, permission granted to him by the Overlord. He even had permission to enter the Queen's throne room without waiting for approval from her elite guard.

"Ah, good…you're back," Fenrik wheezed as he hobbled

toward the Queen, his cane for support in one hand and his Globe of Communication in the other. "The Overlord wishes to see you immediately."

Valeria looked at Fenrik's frail, old body and gave him a sympathetic smile before returning her eyes to Wyndle. "Later, Fenrik. I am much too busy right now." She leaned to her right to block Fenrik's line of vision, in part to show the disrespect she had for him, and also, to keep him from inspecting her find.

Fenrik briefly wrinkled his nose to adjust his spectacles, "I'm afraid the matter is urgent. He...*commands* that you contact him at once." Fenrik walked around the Queen and saw what she had imprisoned in the globe. His eyes widened, then quickly returned to normal to hide his enthusiasm from Valeria.

Queen Valeria continued to show her lack of respect by not looking at him while addressing him, and she stuck her arm out to him with her palm open. "Fine, then. Hand me your Globe of Communication, the one that you use to report my every move."

Fenrik placed the globe in his pocket and smiled at the Queen, "I'm sorry, Your Majesty, but the Overlord wants to see you *in person*." He tilted his head, still smiling, waiting for the Queen's response.

"I see." The Queen turned to look at Fenrik's smug face; the fact that he was untouchable and could get away with such insolence made her blood boil once again. She stood fully upright and turned her back to Wyndle's prison, "Prepare the portal at once."

"Your Highness," started a voice from outside the throne room. The Queen turned toward the doorway and saw

Commander Zelgot standing on the other side, behind her royal guards. Valeria waved her hand at the guards and they moved aside to let Zelgot enter. "Perhaps *I* should do that for you."

Fenrik's nose wrinkled as he looked at Commander Zelgot. He turned his head to the Queen and saw a smile appear on her face, a smile, he noticed, that appeared all too often when she was further from her husband and closer to Zelgot.

"Thank you, Commander. It is refreshing to see a dark elf of honor and integrity. One who need not prove his worth to me." Valeria shot a look at Fenrik and he bowed his head to avoid her gaze. "While I am gone, I will entrust Under Hollow to you, Zelgot."

"Under Hollow will remain as you leave it, Your Highness." Zelgot folded his arms behind his back and bowed to her in respect. He then motioned to the doorway, "If you'll follow me, I will escort you to the portal."

"Fenrik," the Queen turned to look at him, "Keep an eye on our prisoner and report any unusual activity to me at once. Is that clear?"

"Very much so, Your Majesty. You can count on me to report, in complete detail, anything I find strange." Fenrik walked closer to the Globe of Imprisonment.

Valeria shot him a look of hatred and she knew her visit to the Overlord would not be a pleasant one. "Somehow, I knew I could." She turned from Fenrik and followed Commander Zelgot out of the throne room, her royal guards trailing right behind her.

Fenrik reached up to his spectacles and moved them to the very edge of his nose to get a better look at Wyndle. He studied her silently for a few moments, then took his index finger and ran it back and forth on the globe. "I have such plans for you, my dear Winged Angel," he said with a cackle.

A look of horror appeared over Wyndle's face and she knew he wasn't referring to the Queen's plans at all. She saw how sinister Fenrik was and she was suddenly more terrified of him than she was of the Queen. Whatever it was that Fenrik had planned, it was sure to be more evil than she could ever imagine.

****

The town of Frentier was once a cheery, playful town. Tucked between the Dwarven and Gnomish provinces, its cobblestone streets and thatched wooden cottages were a welcome sight to any visitor. Children of all races used to be seen playing everywhere, and the scent of fresh baked pies always filled the air.

Everything had changed. The town was now under the control of the dark elves. Its streets were no longer washed and swept daily, but were now cracked and blood stained. Chunks of wood had been lopped off the buildings in sword fights and some of the buildings were charred, their thatched rooftops burned into nothingness. The children of the town were now in the streets carrying baskets of food and supplies for their dark elf masters. If a child dared rest before his designated break, he or she was sure to feel the snapping whip of the Dracal. The foul stench of the Dracal had replaced the sweet smell of baked goods and the lingering after smell of death was always present.

This is the town where Aldara had first met the rest of the group. Hours later, they had been captured in almost the same spot where she stood now. She was overcome with a mixed look of sadness and hatred, but it was hidden under her floppy hood. The crescent moon clasp on her cape was the emblem of the dark elf, allowing her to walk through the town unnoticed (as long as she kept her hood up and her arms folded, so as to not expose her pale skin). It was early morning and although it was a comfortable temperature, Aldara brought her folded hands just under her face and blew on them as if she were cold. She opened her hands a little and Ayku popped her head out of them and over Aldara's cape.

"I got a few looks from some Dracal and townsfolk, but so far everyone has, for the most part, ignored me," Aldara whispered as she continued to blow on her hands.

"I'll scout out the area and see what we're up against and what the safest streets are to use to get to the inn. They sell everything there, including weapons, if you know how to ask for them." Ayku squeezed out of Aldara's grasp. She was only as big as Aldara's finger and could, hopefully, move about the town unnoticed by flying above everyone's head. She had a lot of practice doing that and this time should be no different—at least that's what she kept telling herself. The tiny fairie started to fly away from Aldara but paused when she heard her name called out. Ayku turned around and flew in front of Aldara's face, hiding as best she could in the hood.

"Don't get swatted." Aldara smiled at Ayku and she could tell by Ayku's half smile that she wasn't all that amused by the joke. Aldara had to work on her sense of humor but she was making progress. For a moment, she had let her guard down and made a hearty attempt.

The tiny fairie darted high in the air and flew above

everyone along the cobblestone thoroughfare. Aldara watched her zig zag from street corner to street corner, occasionally looking into windows to see what was going on behind the closed doors of the once festive town.

Aldara kept her eye on Ayku as the fairie danced in the air about the town until she was no longer in sight. "If I remember correctly, that old woman's shop is near by. The dark elves should have left her alone because she has means of gathering food and supplies." Aldara was used to talking aloud to herself. Over the years, society's lack of acceptance had made her become her own best friend. She gave the Town Square the once-over, making careful mental notes of the Dracal on every corner. One of them stared at her, so she thought she had better not stay in the same spot too long. She began to walk down the street, tugging her hood over her face as she walked. If only she could cover her nose as well. Everything had a burnt cedar smell to it, which was making her nauseous.

She walked past the once-infamous Travelers Inn and flashed a glance at its doorway. There, she saw the innkeeper attempting to tempt a few dark elves inside for some ale. They wouldn't be paying, of course, but the best way to stay alive was to be as hospitable to the enemy as you possibly could. As long as you kept their stomachs full, clothed them warmly, and kept quiet during their meditation hours, you were allowed to live.

"Can I tempt ya, m'lady?" the innkeeper turned from the dark elves that were entering his establishment and spoke to Aldara. A bartender for most of his life, he was able to determine Aldara's gender through her body language and the way she walked and carried herself, even though her face and feminine features were hidden under her cape. "The finest ale in Frentier."

"No, thank you." Aldara noticed a strange look appear on the innkeeper's face as she spoke. *Too polite*, she thought, she was forgetting her role as a dark elf. She turned from him and continued down the street at a faster pace.

She walked another block when the foul stench of burnt cedar was replaced by a pleasant familiar scent. "Quin-Ti," Aldara said out loud as she remembered tasting the fruit for the first time in the Queen's carriage. She put her nose in the air and breathed in the rich aroma. Her mouth was already watering. It had been over a day since she had tasted any real food, and she was starving. She had to have at least a bite of the delicious fruit from Under Hollow.

The airborne scent was stronger from the left side of the street, so she followed it down the road. Turning the corner, she saw the small shop she was looking for and noticed a few Quin-Ti pies cooling on the windowsills. *Finally, something is going right. I found the shop and I'll get something decent to eat.* She might as well have said her thoughts out loud, so strongly were they echoing in her mind.

The thundering sound of a horse-drawn carriage was suddenly so loud, she found that it was almost on top of her. How could she have not heard it approach? Were her thoughts too involved in food so as to not be aware of a potentially dangerous situation? The horse's hooves were slamming down on the cobblestones and Aldara pulled her hood over her face to make sure she was properly concealed. She took a hurried step back as the carriage raced past her. Just after it whisked by, she had the courage to lift her head for a glimpse of who was inside.

It was by no means as elegant as the Queen's carriage. Large wooden wheels were shaking on its side and it looked as if they might fly off if it went any faster. This carriage had no roof. Aldara saw six robed figures in the transport, noticing that the one in the middle was wearing the robes of a light elf elder. Had one of the elders foolishly wandered out of Solaris Arbor and was now on his way to Under Hollow to be 'questioned' by the Queen? Or was he one of the elders Aldara was with in the Queen's castle? In any event, they were certainly in a hurry to be somewhere. Aldara would have loved to have had a horse handy to be able to follow them, but she was on a mission. She needed to get suitable clothes for her and for her companions, along with weapons and other supplies. Lifting her nose in the air again, she caught another whiff of the Quin-Ti pie. Food would have to come before any of the other things they needed.

Aldara stepped into the street, looking to her left and right to make sure another carriage wasn't coming along. She held a fast, steady stride across the street and approached the porch of the shop.

The shop was still in very good condition, surprisingly good, in fact. The wooden roof was intact and the shop's walls were free of battle damage (unlike many of the other buildings in town). She peered through its large dusty window and saw rows of food and various items such as backpacks, racks of clothing, and some gardening items. She had indeed remembered the correct place. Hopefully, this would help redeem her in the eyes of her friends.

Sitting on the windowsill was a furry animal. Feline in appearance and about as long as Aldara's arm from fingertip to elbow, the creature turned its head and looked at Aldara. It grinned at her almost stupidly and she thought she heard laughter from behind the window. She frowned at the animal as she placed her hand on the doorknob and opened the door. It opened with a loud creak. She craned her head inside before entering and saw no one. Aldara looked outside before entering, noticing a patrol of Dracal marching down the road. She quickly stepped inside the store and closed the door with a thud.

Inside, the store was so quiet that whenever Aldara took a step on the old creaky floor, she thought for certain that the Dracal patrol outside would hear her and discover there was a renegade in the town. She carefully made her way through the store to the front counter, stopping along the way to look at miscellaneous items. A box of flint and steel brought a smile to her face as she remembered Gusseus slamming rocks together to try to start a fire.

"Can I help you? Can I help you?" The words were followed by a giggle and Aldara whipped around in bewilderment. She saw no one in the store. She looked over at the window and saw the same cat-like creature she had seen before she entered. It was swinging its tail in time with the ticking of a clock that hung on the wall. It sat there staring at her, grinning from ear to ear.

"Just *what* are you grinning at?" Aldara asked. She found the cat amusing, yet annoying. Still, there was something strange about it that she couldn't quite put her finger on.

"I can help you. Can I help you?" the cat asked her while still wearing his grin, his tail still whipping in time with the passing seconds.

Aldara raised her eyebrow and folded her arms. She took a few steps closer to the feline. "Ah, so you *do* speak." She looked him over from head to swinging tail. His furry coat was a mixed brown and tan. His golden eyes held her gaze and his whiskers poked out from his smiling face. "Maybe you can help me. I am in need of supplies," she stated, rather than asking politely.

"I not helping you. Not my shop," the cat answered as it lifted its head and turned back to the window, as if to dismiss Aldara.

"I see you have made a friend." A tired, cracked voice came from the back of the store. Aldara, startled, turned around and raised her arms, preparing to defend herself. It was then that she saw the voice belonged to a stocky old human woman wearing a tattered blue dress. An apron was tied over it, covered with soiled handprints. She had most of her hair tied up on top of her head, with a few strands hanging down in front of her face.

"I did not mean to startle you." The old woman backed up and covered her eyes with her hands, adding, "please do not hurt me."

The cat, still looking out the window, began to snicker. Its tail flicked from side to side and although it seemed as if it was not paying much attention to the affairs in the room, it was, in fact, hanging on to every word spoken.

"It's okay. I'm not going to hurt you, old woman." Aldara retreated from her defensive posture and watched as the plump older human put her hands back to her sides and smiled. It was almost the same stupid grin that came from the cat, minus a few teeth here and there.

"I see Ali-Mimi likes you, My Lady." The old woman picked up a wicker basket full of clothes and walked behind the counter. She placed the wicker basket on the floor and took the clothes out of it, folding them neatly.

"He does, does he? Well, *Ali-Mimi* was just very rude to me." Aldara watched the old woman fold her clothes, then looked at the pies on the counter. The store was filled with the sweet aroma of the Quin-Ti desserts. Aldara turned from the tantalizing pies and gave the feline a look.

Ali-Mimi turned from the window and looked right back at Aldara with his usual grin. "Can I help you?" he began to snicker.

"Aww, he's just playing with you, My Lady. In fact, you're the first umm, well…the first person he has talked to in a long time besides me. He won't even talk to my husband." The old woman's voice was a little shaky as she tried not to suggest her cat didn't like the dark elf race.

"She different Mama Toothy. She ain't all bad." With that, Ali-Mimi leapt from his windowsill and over Aldara, swatting at her hood with his paw, knocking it down behind her. The cat landed on the other side of the counter, next to the Quin-Ti pies.

The old woman dropped the clothes she was holding and gasped. "What are you doing back here, child? It is awful risky these days." The old woman recognized Aldara from when she frequented the town before it fell to the armies of the Overlord.

"I am surprised you remember me." Aldara stepped away from the window, loosened her cape and pulled her hair from behind it, letting it flow down her shoulders. She looked at

Ali-Mimi and noticed him staring at her intently, never looking away—not even blinking.

"I never forget a face, child. Especially, umm, one as pretty as yours." The old woman stammered, but Aldara knew what she meant. Aldara was likely to be the only half-breed the woman had ever known. The elderly woman cut a piece of pie and handed it to her. "Times have changed, deary. What can I help you with? We must be quick, before my husband returns."

Aldara grabbed the piece of pie from her almost rudely. She ate it quickly, not caring about the crumbs falling down her chin and onto her cape. She understood the old woman's comment about her husband. It was obvious that, while *she* was sympathetic to Aldara, her husband would not be. For their shop to be in this good order, he must have offered his services to the Overlord. Aldara expected that more and more people of all races would choose that way of life over death or enslavement.

"Yes, how can we help you?" the cat giggled as it walked back and forth on the counter in front of Aldara, raising its tail in the air each time it walked in front of her.

"I need some clothes and some weapons. That is, if you still keep them down below." Aldara knew that the old woman and her husband kept their weapons in the basement. Everyone in town knew, except for the elder dwarf councilman assigned to watch over Frentier's affairs. For some reason, the well-known weapons had always remained a secret from him. "Not just for me, but for some friends of mine as well. We are in desperate need of your help and cannot make our journey without it."

The old woman stood behind the counter watching Aldara eat her food and beg for her help. A tear came to her eye as she remembered her own daughter asking for the same assistance. She had denied her daughter help, thinking it would be better for her if she stayed and helped keep the store in top shape for their new dark elf masters. But when Captain Nagarr's forces raided the town and claimed it for the Overlord, he took a fancy to her daughter. He forced her to go with him as his personal pleasure girl during his stay in town while his labor camp was being constructed. She was never seen or heard from again.

"Bring your friends quickly, child." The old woman brushed the tear from her eye and pointed at the ticking clock hanging on the wall, "My husband will be back shortly and if he catches you here, he would surely turn you in. I would not be able to help you at that point."

Aldara nodded her head in acknowledgement and headed for the doorway. "Thank you for this," she said gratefully, while tucking her hair back and pulling up her hood.

"Me go with you! Can I help you? I been waitin' so long for missing part." Ali-Mimi jumped into the air and landed on Aldara's shoulders. He grinned at her and settled in.

Missing part? Aldara asked herself. Clearly, this animal was magical in nature and was capable of joining itself with another magical being to form a bond of unity. "Is he your familiar?" Aldara asked aloud, looking from Ali-Mimi back to the old woman. "No, he couldn't be. You're human. You aren't a practicer of magic."

"I suspect he's yours now, child. He only hangs around here for warmth and for food. Every day he sits and looks out the window as if he was waitin' for someone. I guess now he's found who he's been a-waitin' for." The old woman smiled her toothless smile at Aldara and Ali-Mimi.

"Lucky me." Aldara smiled sarcastically back to the old woman and then addressed Ali-Mimi, "Just stay out of my way and let me handle everything. Got it?" She knew her time was running out as she walked swiftly toward the door. She opened it, looked back at the old woman, back at her laundry duty, and exited the store.

"You see. Lucky to have me. I help you. You see." Ali-Mimi held onto Aldara's shoulders as she crossed the street. He had been waiting for a long time for a companion. His species was never complete on its own and he was eager to bond with Aldara.

Aldara's stride turned into a semi-jog down the street. She reached the corner and when she turned it, she felt the dull thud of a wooden staff against her forehead. She whipped her head back and her hood flopped down around her shoulders. Ali-Mimi dug his claws into her cape to keep his balance. She lifted her head to see that she had run into a dark elf. He was standing on the corner and in her haste, she did not see him in time to slow down or to even move out of his way. His hood was down and his eyes were hidden behind his dark visor.

"Well, well, what do we have here," he said coldly as he focused his attention on Aldara's light complexion and the silverish gray streak of hair falling in front of her face. The sun's reflection on her nose ring made the dark elf wince even behind his visor; the reflection was a strong one. "And just where are we going in such a hurry?" There was a curl to his lip that Aldara found more menacing than his sarcastic tone of voice.

"I was just leaving." Aldara stood up to her full height to make her look as confident and sure as possible. "Now, stand aside," she ordered. Ali-Mimi's eyes narrowed and he hissed at the dark elf.

The dark elf chuckled for a fraction of a second, "I think not." He raised his staff above his head. It was a long wooden staff with a large pointed crystal clasped to its end. Hanging from ropes around the base of the clasp were three smaller crystals, one about half the size of the large crystal and the other two no longer than his thumb. The large crystal now glowed with a soft blue light as Ali-Mimi perched to strike. He arched his back and was about to leap onto the dark elf when a set of two large hands grabbed the dark elf on each side of his head, jerking it quickly to the side. A snap came from the neck and the hands threw the dark elf into the side of the wall. He hit the wall with a thud and slid down to the ground, his staff falling beside him with its crystal fading back to its original clear state.

"Eldin! What are you doing here? Are you mad? If anyone sees you, they'll kill you for sure." Aldara seemed more annoyed than grateful to see her rescuer. Ali-Mimi settled back down on her shoulder, quite relieved that he wouldn't have to jump on the attacker.

"Oh, you're welcome, witch. Think nothing of it." Eldin's voice reeked of sarcasm. He shook his head at her and then tilted his head, trying to figure out what sort of creature Ali-Mimi was.

"We could have handled him on our own. I didn't need your help, big man. Now get out of here before someone sees you!" Aldara pulled her hood up over her head and looked up and down the street.

"*We?*" asked Eldin. He looked at Aldara with her hood up, and then at the animal on her shoulder, and it finally clicked.

"Ahh, so the little witch has a familiar, does she? How cute. But if I remember correctly, you were supposed to be here with Ayku scouting out the area for supplies. You weren't supposed to be here finding yourself a pet." Eldin sounded like a father scolding his child.

"Will you shut up and help me get rid of this body?" Aldara was already bent over, grabbing the dark elf by his ankles. She looked around and saw some old wooden barrels behind Eldin. "There. Help me put his body into one of those barrels before someone comes along. These streets don't stay empty for long."

"We could use some extra help here, guys," Eldin said as he helped her drag the body over to the group of barrels.

Aldara was wondering who Eldin was talking to when she saw Tye rise from behind one of the barrels and Gusseus stepping out from behind another. Gusseus looked at Aldara and shrugged.

"All of you?" Aldara sighed. "Haven't any of you ever heard of sticking to a plan?" She helped Eldin stuff the dark elf's body into a barrel. "How did all three of you manage to make it this far without being spotted by anyone?"

Tye pointed his finger toward the sky. "We had an amazing tour guide." Aldara raised her head and saw Ayku hovering above the buildings, looking down at each street in turn, then flying down to join the group.

"There are a few Dracal escorting a human down the road. We had better get out of here fast," Ayku alerted the rest of the group. Ali-Mimi stuck out his paw to swat her but she jerked away quickly, avoiding his swing.

Aldara bent down and picked up the dark elf's staff. She

held it in both hands and a large smile appeared on her lips. She was a lover of material things and this magical staff would make a fine addition to her treasures. She would have plenty of time for testing it out later; she wanted to see what would happen if the crystal were allowed to glow further. But for now, they had to get off the street. "Follow me, I found an old acquaintance who is willing to help us." She darted off across the road, glancing back to make sure they were all following her and keeping up with her pace.

In no time at all, they reached the old shop. Aldara pushed open the door and she and her companions entered the store. They slammed the door shut behind them and Aldara leaned over and looked out the window.

"We back, Mama Toothy!" The group was taken back when Ali-Mimi spoke. Obviously, there was much more to him than they thought. *What other surprises did this little creature hold?* they wondered.

The old woman came out from the back of the store. " 'Tis good to see you again, child. I took the liberty of stuffing some backpacks for you and your friends on your journey." She raised her finger, silently counting each of them. A frown appeared on her face. "Oh dear. I'll have to pack another one. I'll do that while you and your friends try on some clothes." She looked everyone over, a human, a dwarf, an elf, and a fairie. " 'Tis a good thing Frentier is, or was, a mixed town. There are clothes down these two aisles. You'll find shirts, pants, and boots. Don't worry about finding something that fits perfectly. There isn't time for that. I put a mending kit in one of the backpacks so you can alter them later."

The group wasted no time and followed the old woman's

instructions without question. Ayku grew to her full size and whisked her way down the aisle. She immediately found a loose, light pink shirt and some pants that looked like they might be too tight on her, but could possibly be stretched.

The clothes were divided by race as well as by size, separated by orc, dwarf, elf, gnome, and human. There were also various types of armor that seemed to fit many different races.

Tye threw his outfit together. Dark green pants were the first thing he picked up, pairing them with a brown shirt and a forest green button-down vest. He looked at Ayku and saw her shaking her head at him. "I know, I know. So I'm predictable." It was typical for light elves to dress in the colors of the forest. Tye looked around and saw a pair of heavy brown gloves. "These will come in handy for bow shootin'! I'm tired of rippin' my fingers open on the bowstring."

"Aye, we don't have time fer fashion, laddie. Get in yer clothes as quickly as ya can." Gusseus was following Eldin's lead. They were both veterans; clothing didn't particularly matter to them. They threw on whatever came close to fitting and headed for the armor. Gusseus found a suit of studded leather armor and was pulling it over his body. He had a hard time buckling it. "Aye, I gotta be puttin' meself on a diet. Nothin' fits anymore," he said. This was followed by a large belch, intended to clear some room in his stomach and perhaps even lose a few pounds. Tye let out a giggle, as he knew that Gusseus was famous for his rude bodily noises.

Eldin was already in his leather armor. It had plates of steel in its shoulders and hung loosely on small hinges over the knees and elbows. He was trying on boots when he looked at Aldara. She sat near the door watching out the window, her staff in hand and Ali-Mimi still on her shoulder. "Hey, witch. Aren't you gonna change, or do you want to wear the clothes of the enemy this whole journey?"

Aldara turned to look at Eldin; she had known this would be coming. Why can't anyone ever just leave her alone and let her do her own thing? She let out a disgusted sigh. "It's because of these clothes that I was able to walk down these streets in broad daylight. Who knows what other town we'll come across or what circumstances will arise? Why ruin a good thing?" Aldara made a valid point and Eldin had no choice but to agree. He nodded to her and found a pair of boots that fit. They were a tough, thick leathery pair, plain and of no special design, unlike Tye's, which were tied up the front, or Gusseus's, which were folded over the top. Because Ayku could simply fly over any dangerous ground, she chose not to wear any foot attire.

The old woman finished packing the last backpack and threw one to each of them, excluding Aldara and Ayku. "I don't think the bag would shrink with ya, honey." The woman winked at Ayku and the fairie smiled back at her. She looked at Aldara. "And I see you've already got your own."

"Yes," Aldara replied. "Everything I need is in it," she answered.

The old woman hobbled to the back of the store and lifted a large board in the floor. "Down in the cellar is where we still have some of the old weapons we used to sell. We had to keep them hidden for legal reasons and now they're just sitting there collecting dust. Take whatchas want. Don't worry about cost. Since these dragon people took over the land, money means nothing. We work now just to stay alive. I'd rather have them go to those fighting for us than to those who would kill us."

Ali-Mimi jumped from Aldara's shoulder and onto the steps that led down into the cellar. "This way! Pointy things are this way!" He ran down the stairs and disappeared from view.

The old woman picked up a torch from behind the counter and lit it. She handed the torch to Eldin and turned to look out the window. She gasped and her face seemed to turn a ghostly white. "My husband!" She ran to close the front door. "Go down in the cellar and get your weapons! Shut the door behind you and do *not* make a sound until I come and tell you that it is all right to come out."

"But I don't—" Eldin started to question the old woman's words when he looked past her and outside the window. He could see an older, stout man being escorted across the street by two red Dracal. He threw a look at the old woman as if he and his friends had just been betrayed.

The old woman recognized the look. "I'm doing my best to help you, but he is doing everything he can to help the dark elves in the hope that they will return our daughter. Now go quickly! If he finds you here, he will surely turn you in. I beg of you, go now. I will try to send him away on some errand before he discovers you—if he does, we'll all be in trouble," the old woman ordered as she pointed to the cellar door.

Eldin didn't put up an argument. He took his torch and walked swiftly down the steps, shutting the cellar door behind him. Taking a deep breath, the old woman opened the front door to the shop and began to plead with her husband to go down to the river and return with some water so she could finish washing some robes for their dark elf masters.

Down in the cellar, Gusseus could hear their muffled

voices from above. "Find yer weapons quick, laddies," he whispered. "I don't think he's gonna be buyin' her story." Gusseus picked up a battle axe about the same time Eldin picked up a sword that was about twice the size of the dwarf. Tye picked up a sword and dropped it. The sword fell to the ground and the sound echoed throughout the cellar.

"Watch it, junior! Do you want them to know we're down here?" Eldin tilted his head and leaned his ear toward the stairs, hoping to be able to tell if they heard Tye's blunder.

"Sorry! It was too heavy!" Tye said in a whisper. He fumbled through the weapons again and found a small box that contained some throwing knives. "Now yer talkin'!" Tye slid the knives between his belt and his trousers; there were six in all and they were sure to come in handy. He searched a bit more and found a dagger in a sheath, which he also attached to his belt. He swung a quiver of arrows over his shoulder and was pulling on various bow strings trying to find the best one.

Eldin offered a small knife to Ayku, but she shook her head. "I get by without using them," she playfully ran her fingers through her hair. "This girl has her glamour to take care of her." She shrugged her shoulders. "Besides, weapons don't shrink and grow like my clothes do. My people find them to be a burden."

Gusseus was getting a little tired from all the excitement and sat down on one of the cellar steps. "Aye," he started with a sigh, "Now we just be waitin'. Waitin' and prayin' her husband don't be discoverin' us down here." With that, the group sat in silence, wondering what the next few moments would bring.

Chapter VII

———ↁↁↁ———

A Dark Affair

Queen Valeria strode down a long corridor. It was a narrow hallway that could fit no more than two people walking side by side. The only light available was a soft, mint-green glow oozing from small floating orbs of light placed every so often down the hallway. Escorting the Queen were two dark elves dressed in robes of the highest quality. They resembled the elves of her royal guard, but these spell casters were bodyguards to the Overlord. They were treated with the same respect and dignity that the Queen received. That fact greatly annoyed Valeria. She didn't like the fact that her respect had to be shared, nor did she like the idea of having them escort her to see her own husband.

The Queen was still dressed in her royal gown. She always wore it on visits to her husband. Not only did she like the way she looked in it, but it was also a reminder to him that she was not just a wife, but a woman of power, at his side. Valeria possessed several great accomplishments of her own since the

Overlord's siege of Sylvanor began, a spotless record of dicta-
torship that Fenrik somehow managed to tarnish every chance
he got. Valeria wasn't quite sure why she was here, but she
knew Fenrik had to have been behind it. If only he wasn't the
Overlord's personal friend and confidant; she would have had
the pleasure of killing him a long time ago.

She soon reached the huge two-story solid wooden doors
that led to the Overlord's throne room. The wood was glossed
and polished to a waxy shine that looked beautiful in the wash
of green light. The door handles were made of steel and they
were also kept polished. They looked brand new, due to the
fact that the Overlord seldom received visitors.

The royal bodyguards took their usual places on either
side of the door and stood motionless, facing forward. Valeria
looked at each of them and took a breath. She then closed
her eyes for just a moment and her hard exterior seemed to
melt away. Her composure became softer and a tender smile
appeared on her lips. Seduction was written all over her face
and she looked at the guards as if looking at them for the first
time. She placed her hands on the handles of both doors and
pushed them down. There was a loud click that echoed down
the hallway and the doors silently swung open. Queen Valeria
stood silhouetted in the doorway to the throne room in a sea
of green light, her royal gown draped around her slender body.

The throne room was a large chamber that had a cold look
to it. It was not a place of comfort, by any means; it was used
exclusively as a show of power. There was nothing of interest
in the room except for the throne, for when in the presence of
the Overlord, nothing was to distract you from his awesome
power. The wall behind the throne was curved and made up

entirely of several large windows that ran from floor to ceiling. The windows were tinted and let in the daylight in a very comfortable way. There was a royal guard placed in the shadows of each corner of the room, and although Valeria could not see them, she knew they were there from previous visits. The Overlord was an old elf and he was quite aware of his fading powers. Surrounding himself with bodyguards made him feel more at ease.

Valeria's eyes then focused on her husband. Seated on his throne of power and shrouded in his cloak, he remained motionless. Her gaze then dropped to the floor. She looked at the embedded Circle of Identification just a few feet in front of her. Each time she had visited the Overlord, she had gone through this ritual. No one was allowed to enter the chamber until they entered the Circle of Identification and stated who they were and their purpose for entering the chamber. Only after the circle verified their identity could they proceed. The Queen took a few steps forward into the center of the circle. The magical runes lit up faintly and soon, the ring of the circle glowed a brilliant green. Valeria bent down on one knee, bowing before the Overlord.

"I am Valeria, Queen of Under Hollow. I am here answering my summons." The Queen continued to look at the ground, never once looking up at the Overlord.

The rim of the circle now pulsed and the green light moved around it, trying to identify the Queen. After a few moments, it returned to its stable lighted form and then went dark.

The Overlord raised his right hand in the air and waved it. The royal guards emerged from the shadows one by one and exited the chamber. The door was shut behind them and the clicking sound of the lock was faintly heard from the other side of the door. "Rise, my Queen." The Overlord's voice was one of power and it echoed in his throne room.

Valeria slowly rose to her feet and approached him with a warm smile on her face. "My dear husband, it has been too long." She stopped a few paces before his throne.

The Overlord was still shrouded in mystery. The hood of his cloak covered much of his face. His pointed ears tented the hood upward on each side of his head. On each finger of his aged hands were rings holding the most precious stones of Sylvanor, Under Hollow, and a few that even Valeria did not recognize.

"You waver from my plan, my wife, and I want to know why." The Overlord's voice was cold and steady.

The Queen's eyebrows rose in surprise. "Everything is on schedule, Your Highness. Your plan is working beautifully. The only province left to fall is Solaris Arbor. After that happens, all of Sylvanor will be ours."

The Overlord sat quietly for a few moments and then continued, "What is this relationship you have developed with a young female half-breed?"

"I see that Fenrik, once again, is filling your head with false reports. Why is it that his word is taken over mine? You really should—" Valeria's words were cut off sharply by the Overlord.

"Answer the question, my Queen."

"Very well." Valeria folded her arms and a faint look of irritation came over her face. She hated to be talked down to this way and was not accustomed to it. "We all have great confidence in your plan, Your Majesty. But what if the council of light elves does not comply? This girl will bring us an alternative means of breaching the barrier of the Breathing Forest and entering Solaris Arbor."

The Overlord sat up slightly in his throne. "I will not have my plan jeopardized. We have come too far to falter now." He leaned forward and his grip tightened on the armrests of his throne. "Remember your place, my Queen."

Valeria placed her right hand on her chest and bowed slightly. "It is, of course, by Your Majesty's side." She was doing an excellent job hiding her rage, remembering that while she was here, pleasing the Overlord must always be at the front of her mind.

"You will cease this plan of yours at once. You will start by killing this half-breed. She is a danger to us. Should she discover the City of the Ancients, there is no telling what will happen. She could also summon the Winged Angels to return." After this announcement, the Overlord sat back in his seat of power.

"My forces have thoroughly searched the entire realm of Sylvanor. We have not come across the Lost City or the portal to the angels' domain. Are you sure they still exist?" The Queen was certain the Lost City was no more. But the angels' portal, it must still exist in Solaris Arbor. Her thoughts briefly shifted to her tiny prisoner. *Where had she come from? Had she come from the old portal in Solaris Arbor or does the realm have another door into her world? Why hasn't Fenrik told the Overlord that she had this one prisoner? Surely, he would have ordered her to kill it at once.*

"Of course I am not sure. But because of this uncertainty, I must figure it into our plans as if it does exist.

Nothing will stand in our way now and soon Sylvanor will be rid of every race that is not dark elven. At this very moment, the council is on its way back to Solaris Arbor to discuss my 'offer'. All we need them to do is believe that their province will be spared if they let us use their land as a base of operations. If we can convince them that it is my wish for both our races to rule the land, as in the past, they will allow us passage through the Breathing Forest. Once inside Solaris Arbor, victory will be ours." the Overlord's voice was full of confidence.

The Queen frowned slightly and debated whether she should continue adding her opinions to the conversation. She bowed her head, then lifted it quickly. "I do beg your pardon, my husband, but what are the chances that their council will be tricked so easily? Surely, they will come to realize that they are safe beyond the Breathing Forest." This was the first time Valeria had questioned the Overlord's plans. Up until now, everything that he presented had been flawless and made perfect sense to her, but now, with this final phase of the plan, she could not believe the enemy would be so foolish as to fall for his deception.

The Overlord chuckled and his body was gently bobbing with each laugh. "You underestimate me, my Queen. I have taken the proper steps to make sure their council sees things my way."

Queen Valeria's right eyebrow rose with interest. "What do you mean?"

"Let's just say that there are those who are smart enough to realize that we have won. They have come to know the importance of self-preservation." The Overlord's voice was strong and sharp and did not match that of his older body.

"I see," she said with a seductive smile. Valeria felt almost foolish for second-guessing her husband's plans. "I am sorry for my doubts, husband. I meant no disrespect."

The Overlord waved his hand as if to dismiss the Queen's mishap. "You have done well on your own with Sylvanor. Will you be ready for our final assault?"

Queen Valeria walked seductively toward her husband's throne. She glanced out of the huge windows behind it and looked down at the ground below them. She caught a glimpse of their forces below. She turned her gaze from the window when she approached him and stood at his side. She placed one hand on the headrest of the throne and slowly pulled his hood back with the other.

The Overlord turned to look at Valeria. His facial features were still hidden in the shadows of the room. His long white hair rested on the Queen's hand and his blue eyes were like ice in her heart. He was older than Fenrik and although just as wrinkled (if not more so), his body didn't seem quite as frail.

"I do miss your company, husband." Valeria massaged his shoulders and he sank in his throne. She often did this when she visited him. It seemed to be their only form of physical contact for the past few years.

"Soon, we will be together. The entire realm of Sylvanor will be ours to rule. Anything you desire, my Queen, will be yours for the taking." The Overlord's head drooped as Valeria continued to massage his neck.

Her hands extended from his neck out to his shoulders. After a few moments, they wrapped around his chest and she placed her head next to his and gave him a gentle kiss on his lips. "That day cannot come too soon, my love."

****

"What are you going on about, Kaytle? We have barrels of water out back, plenty for you to wash all the clothes that need laundering." The old woman's husband was a stocky fellow. He was well dressed and well groomed. Those who pledged their allegiance to the Overlord were easily spotted in any town. Their way of life had changed little and they did not live the lives of slaves, provided that they could be of use to the Overlord's plans.

The old woman bit her lip and waved her hand at her husband. "Did I say water?" she asked, followed by a chuckle, "I meant to say that we needed more soap to wash them more thoroughly."

Her husband's eyes narrowed, "You always were a terrible liar." He looked around the store and his eyes fell to the crumbs on the counter and the missing piece of Quin-Ti pie. He craned his neck in an attempt to see into the back of the shop. "Who's here?"

"No–no one," the old woman stuttered. "I had company earlier, a few dark elves, but they left. They said something about going to the Inn." The old woman struggled with her words and she knew they did not come out of her mouth sounding believable.

"Is there a problem, Morgan?" asked a dark elf that just stepped through the doorway, "Anything I can help you with?"

Morgan turned to his dark elf friend. "Nothing you can help me with, sir. Just having a disagreement with my wife."

"Ah. I see." The dark elf looked at the two Dracal standing on either side of the doorway, "You two go back to your posts. If you see anyone looking suspicious, even a dark elf, bring them into custody and report it to me at once." The Dracal looked at their master for a moment and then exited the shop. The dark elf removed his visor and turned back to Morgan.

"You are even questioning dark elves? What's goin' on, if I may ask." Asking such a question would be unthinkable to anyone else; however, Morgan had established a solid working relationship with his dark elf master over the past few months. They, on occasion, would even share ale together.

The dark elf removed his gloves while answering his friend's question, "There have been reports of a few members of the Circle of Thirteen, a traitorous faction of dark elves, sighted in this area. It is my job to find them."

"Traitorous dark elves? I can assure you that if I see anything suspicious I will report it to you at once, sir." Morgan always did his best to please his friend. He also liked to trick himself into believing that the dark elf was really his friend, rather than his master, to help hide his hatred and to hopefully develop a better relationship with the dark elf.

"You human males should learn to control your females. What's the disagreement about?" the dark elf asked, changing the subject.

Morgan looked at his wife, then took a breath and looked back at his friend, "We were just having a disagreement about how the shop has been kept lately."

The dark elf moved closer to the married couple. "You are as bad a liar as your wife. Lying to me will not help get your daughter back. You know this." At the end of his sentence, there was a large clanking sound that came from the back of the room. The dark elf's head spun towards the cellar. "Who is down there?"

Kaytle's eyes widened and she began to answer, again with a slight stutter, "No—no one. Just our pet, he plays down there often." The old woman smiled a toothless grin, pleased with her answer.

"You always let your pet play in the cellar and shut the door behind it?" the dark elf asked coldly. He looked at the old woman's face for a few moments, not saying a word, and then suddenly struck her across the face with the back of his hand. Kaytle let out a scream and fell to the floor, her husband standing by her side but afraid to help her.

Down below, Aldara frowned when she heard a scream from above followed by a thud. She moved toward the steps and started to climb them.

Gusseus, sitting on the steps, grabbed her ankle firmly as she started past him. "Where ya be goin' missy?" he whispered to her.

"I will not sit down here and cower while my friend gets a beating. She has been too nice to me and has helped us all out a great deal. I won't listen to her suffer."

"Aldara," interjected Tye in a soft whisper. "Sit down. All the help she's given us will be for nothing if we get caught."

"Tha lad be right. If they be catchin' us, they'll do more ta tha old woman than beat her. They'll kill her fer hidin' us." Gusseus, as usual, made sense. As much as Aldara hated the idea, she had to agree with him. She leaned forward on her new-found staff for support and listened to the conversation above with interest.

"If you are lying to me, old woman, I assure you that will not be the last time I strike you this evening," the dark elf's voice was full of anger, yet at the same time, pleasure. He seemed to enjoy hitting the woman, as most spell casters enjoy having a physical advantage when they can.

The dark elf hurried over to the cellar door. He bent over and grabbed hold of the handle. He pulled on the handle and the door barely budged. Embarrassed at his lack of strength, he threw Kaytle an evil glance, hating her even more for being physically stronger than he. Turning his attention back to the door, he grasped it once again. This time using both hands, he pulled the door open with all his might. The door swung open easily this time and almost knocked the dark elf off his feet. When he regained his balance, he peered down the stairway. As a member of the elven race, he was able to see into the darkness of the cellar easily.

The dark elf's eyes widened when he saw Aldara standing on the stairway. "I knew something like this was going on here. Just how long have you been harboring renegades, old woman?" His eyes never leaving Aldara, he continued, "I will make sure that you never see your daughter again and that you spend the rest of your golden days in the slave mines."

At that, Ali-Mimi let out a growl and jumped from Aldara's shoulders toward the dark elf. He extended his claws while in mid air, struck the elf's face with his paw, and raked the right side of his cheek. The dark elf managed to strike Ali-Mimi and send him spinning to the floor near Kaytle.

"On second thought, I will enjoy killing you now. All of you," he said coldly as the blood ran from his wound down his neck. He threw his hands up and the air around his fingertips began to glow a greenish color.

Aldara, still standing on the stairwell, pointed her staff at the dark elf and squeezed it tightly. As if it read her mind, its crystal tip instantly turned from its clear state to a bright blue and a beam of fluorescent blue light shot out of it, hitting the dark elf dead center. Swirls of blue light danced around his body and seemed to penetrate his chest and arms. His body was thrown against the counter and he let out a scream of agonizing pain. The light soon faded and he fell to the floor writhing in agony, his body jerking.

"Stop this at once!" Morgan shouted out. He stood between his wife and his dark elf master, unsure of whom to tend to.

Using what little strength he had left, the dark elf pointed his finger toward Aldara and it began to glow once again. He started to whisper the words necessary to perform his spell and once again Aldara pointed the staff at him. She could not get a clear shot at him and ordered Morgan to step away.

"Surrender yourself! If you kill him, all hope of retrieving my daughter dies. I have sacrificed too much to have you ruin it," Morgan stated, standing his ground.

The dark elf's finger was now a brilliant green. Kaytle let out a gasp and reached behind her counter. There she grabbed hold of her rolling pin, still covered with flour from her freshly baked Quin-Ti pies. She raised it above her head and took a few steps forward. She threw a quick glance at Morgan, too wrapped up in his conversation with Aldara to notice her, and brought the rolling pin down on the dark elf's head with a dull thud. His finger turned back to its dark gray color and fell to the floor, lifeless.

Morgan spun around to see his wife drop the rolling pin and take a few steps back. Her eyes rose to meet her husband's and she waited in silence for his response.

"What have you done, woman!" Morgan stepped closer to his wife and grabbed her by the arms. He started to shake her violently in a panic. "What are we to do now? We're all as good as dead!" he yelled, his voice cracking, his speech shaky.

Aldara emerged from the stairwell with her friends behind her. Upon seeing her, Ali-Mimi leaped onto her shoulder and looked down at the dark elf's body lying on the floor. Aldara raised her staff in the air and brought it down somewhat roughly between Morgan and Kaytle. "Take your hands off her or I'll be zapping you next." Aldara felt the rush of power and she enjoyed being in control of a situation for once.

"By the Gods!" Tye exclaimed as he looked at the dead body. He put his hand on the sheath that held his dagger and looked at Aldara's staff. "I wanna trade weapons!"

Morgan backed away from his wife and looked at the group, surprised at how many there were. He could do nothing but begin to weep softly and hold his head in his hands. "Everything is changed now. What are we going to do?"

Eldin walked over and kicked the elf's body to make sure he was really dead. He gave Aldara a smile, "Nice shooting, witch." Remembering all the hollering and the screams, he moved to the windows to look outside, wondering if anyone had heard them.

Gusseus scratched his head and twisted his beard. "Aye. Let's all be puttin' our heads together and do some thinkin' on this one," he suggested.

Aldara leaned on her staff and took a moment to think.

She pointed her finger upward, as if to pull an answer out of the air. "I heard him say something about looking for traitors."

Kaytle stepped forward. "That's right, he did! Dark elf traitors!" she said with excitement while looking at her husband, trying to jog his memory.

Aldara pointed to the dark elf's body, "There's your traitor."

"That's crazy! They'll never believe that! They will never take the word of a human over a dark elf. We're doomed for sure." Morgan's voice had no optimism in it whatsoever.

The old woman's face began to beam. "Perhaps," she started as she pulled a tiny silver key from her cleavage and walked behind the counter. She bent over, cleared several jars and boxes from a shelf, and picked up a small wooden box. She placed it on the counter and unlocked it. She dug into it and pulled out a small silver charm. "If he had this on his person. It belonged to our daughter. It was given to her by the elf who delivered her."

It was a tiny piece of jewelry shaped like the sun. Tye recognized it immediately. "A sun medallion! I haven't seen one of those since I left home!"

Aldara was quick to devise a plan. "Excellent! Now you've got some evidence. Put it in his pocket. Tell them you saw him kill another dark elf and that he put his body in a barrel down the street at the corner. When you questioned him, he tried to kill you and your wife and you fought back in self-defense. With any luck, they will believe they have found the traitor they were looking for and you will emerge a hero."

"What barrel? I know nothing of a dark elf in a—" started Morgan, thoroughly confused.

"Trust me, he's there," Aldara answered. She didn't have to

say she was the one who put him there; that much was obvious by her tone of voice.

Ayku looked at Aldara and she noticed that Aldara was a little too comfortable with the whole situation. "You sure are very quick to think and cover your tracks, Aldara."

Aldara looked at her with scorn, then turned her back on her and continued to converse with Morgan and Kaytle.

While the plan was forming, Eldin was looking out the window and up and down the street. It was dusk and the faint sound of cheering could be heard from the Inn down the road. His attention fell onto a little human boy, about nine years of age, walking down the street with a basket of fruit on his head and holding onto it to make sure it wouldn't fall. It was a common sight in the town, children used as slaves. He also noticed a female dark elf standing across the street. Eldin crouched down to hide himself further, not knowing if she was watching the shop or the little boy.

The boy looked over at the dark elf and picked up his pace. Not watching where he was going, he stumbled on a rock and the basket fell from his head and onto the ground. The boy, losing his balance, fell on top of his spilled items.

The dark elf looked to her left and then to her right, then ran across the street toward the boy. Eldin put his hand on the hilt of his sword. *If she harms that boy in any way...*, he thought.

She reached the boy and bent to help him up. Eldin could see her lips moving. She dusted the boy off while looking around and quickly helped him gather his fruit back into his basket. She handed the basket to the small boy and swatted him on the butt. The boy then continued his journey down the road.

A look of puzzlement came over Eldin's face and he lifted his head to make sure the boy was safely on his way, which, in fact, he was. He looked back at the female dark elf and was surprised to see her standing tall on her feet, looking straight at him. She held his gaze for a few moments, then turned her head and walked in the other direction.

Dozens of thoughts rushed through Eldin's mind. *Why did she help the boy?* She clearly saw Eldin, a human knight, and possibly his friends. *Why didn't she call her Dracal forces to capture them?* He seemed to jump a mile when Ayku walked up behind him and tapped him on the shoulder.

"Anything wrong?" she asked.

Eldin looked at her and shook his head while rising to his feet. He walked over to the rest of the group. "Stick to the plan, my friend," he said to Morgan. Eldin turned his head back to the window and looked blankly through it. "I have a hunch it'll work."

"Kaytle says we can leave through the back door. We can pile up the water barrels and get over the city walls. It's too risky to go back for the horses so we'll have to continue on foot," Aldara reported to Eldin.

"It sounds as if many of the dark elves are in the Inn getting drunk. But still, we had better hurry." Eldin led the group to the back of the shop, toward the back door.

Tye strode along behind them at his usual slow pace, Gusseus prodding him along. Tye glanced over at the shelf and his eyes lit up. He reached out his hand and grabbed a long wooden flute. He held it up to Kaytle and she nodded and winked at him in approval. He smiled back and tucked it in his belt.

Aldara stopped at the old woman and took her by the hands. "Thank you for everything, Kaytle. We will not forget what you and your husband have done for us. You have given us a fighting chance. We could not have continued our journey without your help." Aldara kissed her on the cheek. "I hope your daughter comes home soon."

Gusseus stood, watching Aldara from the back door. Again, she had managed to surprise him. He cleared his throat and tapped his foot, signaling that it was time to go.

"I'll draw their attention this way and feed them the story as you make your way away from here. Hopefully, they will believe it and you young ones will make it out of here safely." Morgan seemed to be a little more confident with his situation now and he watched the group exit the shop through its rear door.

"Here we go." Morgan drew in a deep breath, and kissed his wife.

"Good luck," replied Kaytle as she looked at her husband and at the back door, finally resting her eyes on the small wooden box of her daughter's belongings. She shut its lid and locked it tight. "To all of us," she added as she looked back at her husband, who was making his way out the front door and yelling to get a dark elf's attention.

****

Commander Zelgot stood outside the Queen's chambers alongside two of her elite guard. He began to straighten his uniform when he heard footsteps approaching from around the corner. He stood at attention with a smile when he saw Valeria, escorted by two more of her guards, turn the corner and make her way toward him.

"Your Royal Highness," Zelgot bowed, "Welcome back to Under Hollow. May I ask the well-being of the Overlord?"

Queen Valeria smiled slightly back at Zelgot. "It is agreeable to see you again as well, Commander. The Overlord sends his regards to you and to all dark elfkind on a job well done. He is anxious to complete the final phase of the war and foresees victory in a matter of weeks, if not days."

"Splendid news indeed. There is a matter of slight urgency, however, that we must discuss at once, Your Highness. It is…of a delicate nature." Zelgot looked around at the Queen's royal guards.

The Queen cocked her head and raised an eyebrow at Zelgot. "You guards are dismissed," she ordered, "Call upon the next shift and go get some rest."

Her royal guards bowed in unison and proceeded single-file down the hallway and around the corner to the stairwell. Zelgot placed his hand on the handle to the Queen's quarters and opened the door for her. He waved his hand in front of her. "After you."

Valeria entered, followed by Zelgot, who carefully closed the door behind him. As soon as the door was shut, he pulled the Queen close and kissed her passionately on the lips. After a few moments, Valeria broke the kiss and pushed Zelgot away gently, her hands resting on his chest.

"Not here in my quarters. It is too dangerous. If the Overlord found out, he would have both of our heads," Valeria's words were full of annoyance that she was under constant watch.

"Fear not, my sweet. Fenrik has been gone for hours. I

have sent my Captain of the Guard personally to watch him, as usual. We will know when he returns. Until then, the night is ours." Zelgot saw the smile of agreement on the Queen's face and kissed her again.

Valeria took him by the hand while kissing him, and led him to her bed where they both fell onto its red satin blanket. Queen Valeria wrapped her arms around Zelgot and ran her finger down his spine and continued further down the side of his leg.

"Before we go any further, my love, there is a matter of good news we must discuss," Zelgot said, breaking the kiss and moving slightly away from Valeria.

"Good news?" Valeria asked while leaning her head on her hand for support. "Go on."

Zelgot smiled at the beauty of his love. Seeing her, especially like this, took his breath away and made him long for the day, if it would ever come, when they could be together without fear. "It seems as if a member of the 'Circle of Thirteen' has been found and terminated in a city above ground."

The Queen frowned. She sat up straight and started removing her high black shiny boots. "That is what you call good news? All that means to me is that the reports are true. We do have traitors in Under Hollow and the fact that our own people would turn against us troubles me. It will be good news, Commander, when they are all rounded up and executed. I want your full personal attention on this matter," Valeria ordered, setting her boots alongside the bed, "You know Fenrik will be reporting this to the Overlord, and when he does, I want a handle on the situation."

"Of course, my Queen. I will give the matter my full

attention. I am sorry to say that he was killed before he could be questioned. Let's hope the reports have been exaggerated and that the circle has not grown beyond its founding thirteen members. However, I will find out who they are and put an end to it before it spreads any further, My Lady." Zelgot took hold of the Queen's hand and gently kissed it.

Valeria rose to her feet slowly and walked across the room to a finely crafted wooden cabinet. She opened its glass doors and reached for a bottle of water. She picked it up and shook her head, giving it a disgusted look. She set it back down and reached for a bottle of wine. She carefully poured herself a glass, then turned and held the bottle slightly in the air to offer some to Zelgot. The Commander nodded and she poured a second glass. She then put the cork back in the bottle and placed it on the shelf. She closed the cabinet doors almost lovingly, picked up the two glasses of wine, and walked very sensually back to the bed. She offered a glass to Zelgot.

"There is one more matter that is of higher importance that I want you to tend to first, and I am hoping you can resolve it before the Moon Festival begins," Valeria ordered as she slowly took a sip of her sweet beverage. She held up her glass and swirled the wine, releasing its bouquet.

"Higher importance than would-be traitors?" Zelgot also took a sip of his wine.

"The Winged Angel is not being cooperative. I must find other means to get her to tell me where the portal is to her realm. Torture will not work with her and I can't risk any harm coming to her." Valeria took another sip of the wine, her favorite. "She has a group of friends and there is one in particular of whom she seems very fond. I want your forces to find this boy and bring him before me. I think she'll begin to talk when she sees the pain and suffering I will bring to him."

Zelgot sat up fully on the Queen's bed. "That will prove to be a difficult task. Sylvanor is a big place. Finding him will not be easy."

Valeria sat down on the bed next to Zelgot and continued to swirl her wine. "I will provide you with his last known location and the direction he was heading as well as a sketch of him. Tomorrow morning, you will bring our finest artist to my quarters."

Zelgot tightened his brow. "I feel it is necessary to remind you, my Queen, that if he has traveled into Solaris Arbor, there will be no way for my forces to retrieve him."

"I am aware of that fact, Zelgot. Fortunately, the barrier of the Breathing Forest will no longer be of any concern to us in a short time. The final phase of the Overlord's plan has begun. Soon, this war will be over and a new era will begin. The dark elf race and this realm will be no match for any other." The Queen's words were filled with nothing but confidence and pride.

"What of your backup plan? What of the girl?" Zelgot asked curiously.

Queen Valeria smiled, "My plan remains intact. Either way, Solaris Arbor will never know what hit it. The first test of the girl will happen tomorrow. I am confident everything will go as I have foreseen."

"I am surprised the Overlord approved of your plan. I thought for sure he would order you to dismiss it." Zelgot took one last mouthful of wine. He savored the last bit for a few moments before swallowing what Valeria had often referred to as 'the nectar of the Gods.'

Valeria shrugged, "He ordered me to kill the girl, which will happen in due time. But as for the rest of my plan, well, what Fenrik doesn't know, my husband doesn't know."

The smile disappeared from Zelgot's face as his words took a more serious tone, "You are playing a dangerous game, Your Highness."

The Queen raised her right eyebrow, "*We* are playing the game, my sweet. Dangerous is too strong a word as long as we continue to be careful. She threw a glance at the doorway. Speaking of Fenrik…"

Zelgot cut into her question, "He has been gone for some time. He surely will be back soon."

Queen Valeria downed the last of her wine and placed the glasses on the floor. She lay down next to him. "Then we haven't much time to play our game, do we?" Without waiting for an answer, she leaned in and kissed him.

Chapter VIII

─═ↁↁↁ═─

Queen Takes Pawn

The fog was thick in the rolling hills of the Dwarven province, as it usually was in the early hours. It clung to the trees, hugged the rocks, and greatly reduced visibility. It seemed to absorb what little heat the sun produced at sunrise and chill to the bone any who dared venture out in it.

The band of renegades had been traveling all night on foot and were weary as they tried to find a place to rest without the fear of someone, or something, sneaking up on them. It was much too dangerous to rest while the fog was steadily creeping over their shoulders and they had no choice but to press on and challenge their endurance.

Tye kicked his legs playfully through the fog as they walked. The thick, misty air became so dense around his knees that it was impossible, even with his natural infravision, to see the ground. His hand came to rest on his flute and he fumbled with it while trying to remove it from its snug fit on his belt. With a jerk, it came free, flew out of his hand, and disappeared through the fog. "Shuckinspoo," he muttered, using a Dwarven slang word. He'd heard Gusseus use the word many times, but his stout little friend was always hesitant to translate it for him. It wasn't hard, however, for Tye to draw his own conclusions about what it meant. He stopped in his tracks and took a few steps back to where he dropped the flute. The others looked at him, shaking their heads slightly…all of them but Gusseus.

"Where's Guss?" Tye whipped his head from left to right and saw no sign of him. "I haven't heard him say anything for hours!" Tye began to panic. He bent down and moved his hands frantically about the fog. Just then, he heard a gasp followed by a thump. A fraction of a moment later, he felt a mass slam into his leg, causing him to jump back as he let out a yelp.

Through the fog, they saw a wooden flute being shaken violently, followed by the grumbling of an angered dwarf, "This fog be dangerous enough fer me without ya droppin' yer toys fer me ta trip over, boy! Bend over so I can be boxin' those big ol' ears o' yers!"

Tye quickly grabbed the flute out of Gusseus's hand, then began to chuckle. "I'm sorry, Guss. I didn't mean to drop it," he apologized through his laughter. He quickly composed himself as much as he could when he didn't hear a response. He could actually see Gusseus's point. The thicker fog, which came up to Tye's knees, encompassed half of Gusseus's body.

"I hope ya weren't plannin' on playin' that thing!" Gusseus grumbled.

Tye was wedging his flute back into place on his belt. "Of course not! Sound carries for miles in this fog. I just wanted to look at it." Tye was growing up. He was old enough to know when some things were appropriate and when others were not.

He was able to think and take care of himself, a fact he wished he could get his overbearing father figure to see.

"I sure hope we're going in the right direction," Eldin said as he looked around him. He could make out the trees immediately around him and every once in a while he could spot a branch breaching the density of the fog.

"Aye, we are, Eldin," Gusseus replied as he continued to move forward. "I know this land like tha back o' me hand. There should be a road comin' up ahead and then tha hills get bigger. Once we be reachin' tha higher ground, tha fog'll clear and we can be restin' our tootsies." Gusseus took the lead and the rest of the group began to follow him.

"Restin' our...?" Eldin began to ask Gusseus.

"Feet," interrupted Ayku. She was walking near Tye and noticed that her pace had started to drag. Not wanting to fall behind the group, Ayku jumped into the air and shrank in size. She flew next to Tye and landed on his shoulder.

Tye looked at her as she began to curl up on his shoulder, "Tired, eh, Ayk?"

"Mmm. Hmmm." Ayku looked up at Tye and smiled at him. She closed her eyes and rested her head on his neck. She had a right to be tired. They all did. They had been walking since dusk the day earlier and had traveled a significant distance from Frentier. It was a pace they must get used to, however, for Under Hollow was many days away.

Ali-Mimi was also resting. He was sitting on Aldara's right shoulder, his tail reaching around her back and curling around her other shoulder. Suddenly his eyes widened and Aldara could feel his sharp claws begin to sink into her flesh. He turned to her and began to whisper in her ear. "Speaky talk from up front."

Aldara stopped, threw back her hood, and made a conscious effort to listen. Her long, pointed elf ears moved slightly and she squinted, trying to hear what was ahead of them. Like Ali-Mimi, her eyes widened and she put her hand out in front of Eldin. He walked into it and flashed her an annoyed look.

"You tryin' to grope me, witch?" Teasing Aldara was second nature to Eldin now. He didn't like her and he saw that his teasing annoyed her. He had hoped that she might snap and reveal her 'true' self to everyone.

As predicted, Aldara gave him a glare of annoyance, "Will you shut up and listen," she nudged her head forward, "dark elves."

Eldin immediately put his hand on the hilt of his sword and Ayku quickly flew from Tye's shoulder and up into the air to get a better look at what was ahead of them.

Tye slid his bow from his left shoulder and reached over his right to grab an arrow out of his quiver. He loaded his bow and stood still. "I hear them too. It sounds like they are arguing."

Ayku soared high into the sky. She flew in front of the group and scanned the ground in search of the dark elves first detected by Aldara's familiar. At first, she saw nothing but gray mist in every direction. On the second pass, she slowed her scan to examine the area more thoroughly. She flew a little further and spotted a small glowing light just over a hill that the group would soon encounter. Ayku flew closer to the ground and saw that the light was coming from a small campfire that was strong enough to burn off the fog. Sitting in the glow of the warm firelight was a group of dark elves. They were all shrouded in their thick cloaks to help keep warm.

Next to the group was an old wooden carriage, lying on its side. One of its huge wooden wheels was smashed into several pieces all over the road. The carriage had no roof and the back of the carriage was split and barely hanging on to the frame. The horses that pulled the carriage were tied to a nearby tree.

Ayku turned her attention back to the group of elves. They were arguing among each other. There were few languages in the land of Sylvanor and almost everyone knew how to speak a little of each of them. But since Under Hollow remained much of a mystery to most generations of species, only those who made an effort to learn could understand the strange language of the dark elf. Ayku could only understand words that she had picked up from her previous captor, Captain Nagarr. She only heard a few of those words now and they translated into 'idiot' and 'fool'. They were clearly arguing, but about what, she could only guess. She surmised that the broken carriage wheel and the resulting accident must have been the issue.

Continuing her reconnaissance mission, she counted the number of dark elves so she could finish her report and deliver it to her friends. She counted five in all but noticed something different about one of them. Ayku let out a gasp as she saw that one of them wore the robes of an elder light elf. She cocked her head, puzzled. He was not bound and was merely sitting on the ground near the horses, not included in the argument. Ayku decided it was time to return to the group and give them all the information she had uncovered before they came looking for her.

She flew as fast as she could back to her friends who were already gaining ground on her position. She flew down to them. "Just over the hill here are four dark elves having an argument about a carriage wreck they had," she paused a moment, "at least that's what I *think* they are arguing about."

Eldin slowly drew his sword from its sheath. "Taking them shouldn't be too difficult as long as there are no Dracal around," he stated.

Aldara looked into the sky and began to scan it. Ali-Mimi arched his back and stuck his nose into the air. "Smell nuttin'," he said as he continued to sniff.

Aldara nodded at Ali-Mimi and looked over at Eldin. "Something is wrong here. Dark elves *never* travel without the Dracal," she had a worried tone in her voice.

Eldin smoothed over his moustache, "Do you think it could be a trap?"

Ayku flew over to Tye and floated in front of his face. "Could it be the fact that they have a light elf elder with them?" she asked.

"An elder?!" Tye exclaimed, "Why is an elder with them? They don't have the strength to wander this far out of Solaris Arbor. We've got to free him."

Gusseus walked toward the hill holding his battle axe tightly in his hand. "Aye laddie, but we mus' be careful. Even though there be no Dracal, 'tis still a dangerous happenin'."

Aldara shrugged her right shoulder violently, knocking Ali-Mimi off. He fell to the ground and disappeared into the fog. "Ali, you go distract them. If they have been there for a while, they may be hungry."

The fog began to swirl around Aldara's feet as Ali-Mimi circled around her legs. "No! I ain't made for the nibbles! You go! You more meat than me!" He leaped into the air in an attempt to jump onto Aldara's shoulder, but she leaned out of the way and he landed back down on the ground. "You mean when you don't get your way," his voice could be heard from under the fog.

"I'll go. I know where they are and I could easily sneak past them and give them a little light show." Ayku flew over to Gusseus and then to Eldin while offering her services. She hovered before them, waiting for approval.

"No way! It's too dangerous. I don't want you putting yourself in that kind of danger!" Tye was always very strong about his feelings for Ayku. He sometimes appeared overprotective of her. He looked over at Gusseus and put his head down. He saw that he was treating Ayku the way his father treats him. Like Gusseus, Tye had to learn that they each had to take chances if this mission was going to be a success. "Ayk, just be careful." As much as he hated the idea, he had to let her go. He had no real right to hold her back and he hoped Gusseus would get the hint and let Tye have a little more freedom.

Aldara folded her arms and looked at Ayku in disgust. She hated the way everyone liked her, especially Tye. However, at the same time, she had to admire her bravery. Maybe she would like her a little more if she didn't hold Tye's heart. Aldara looked over at her secret love and sighed to herself. The rage swelled within her and she adjusted her bag on her shoulder. Feeling the dark elf spell book as she grabbed her bag brought a smile to her face and her emotional low seemed to fall by the wayside of her new-found rush of power. Tye could feel her eyes watching him and he looked over to catch her gaze. "Let's go free your elder," she said to him.

The group headed toward the hill and Eldin kept his stride

in time with Aldara's. He looked at her and eyed her up and down. His looking soon turned into a stare when his eyes fell upon her bag. "I'll be watching you, witch. Try to remember whose side you are on this time."

Aldara kept walking forward, never looking at Eldin. She let his comment go for a few moments, and then she replied, still looking forward, "My patience for your comments is almost at an end, big man. Do not continue to provoke me or you will regret it."

"Save yer anger fer tha enemy and quit yer yappin', both o' ya!" Gusseus demanded as he started up the hill.

Ayku took to the sky and darted over the hill without another word. She flew across the dirt road where the carriage lay on its side and past the dark elves without any of them noticing. She positioned herself a short distance from them and hovered behind a tree, waiting for her friends to reach the top of the hill. She watched the dark elves continue to argue and flash glances of anger at the elder who was still sitting on the ground, propped up against a tree, his wooden staff lying nearby. She cleared her voice and prepared for her light show while waiting for her friends.

Tye was the first of the friends to reach the top; he already had his bowstring pulled back and was aiming at one of the dark elves. The rest of the group followed and crouched down in the fog to hide themselves.

"We won't have much time to get to the bottom of this hill before they hear us coming," Eldin started. He then looked over at Tye, who was adjusting his line of sight as best as he could through the fog, "How's yer aim, junior?"

"I used to be able to knock apples off of fences, but it's

been a while. I'm sure I could still shoot one off someone's head," Tye was confident in his words and kept his hands steady on his bow, never looking away from his target.

"Perhaps you could help him practice, Eldin. I'd be happy to go hunting for an apple to place on your head," Aldara said in a calm voice as if she meant every word of it.

Eldin curled his lips in a small smile at her and then raised his hand in the air, signaling Ayku that they were all ready and in position. "Cover us, junior. I hope your aim is as good as you say it is," he said to Tye.

Ali-Mimi looked at Aldara and walked over to Tye. "Me stay with you," he said to Tye, "Too much hurt gonna be down there." He looked over at Aldara and sat down while sticking his nose in the air, telling her with his body language that his decision was non-negotiable.

Ayku saw her friends reach the top of the hill and then disappear in the fog. She flew out from behind the tree, making sure not to expose herself enough to become an easy target for the dark elves' spells. She hovered there unnoticed until she heard a horrible imitation of a Noctil bird, which she knew had to have been the signal from Eldin. She took a deep breath and began to glow, soft and yellow at first, but rapidly becoming more brilliant. Soon, she lit up the area, and when she was at her brightest, she began to sing. Her voice was high and beautiful and it echoed through the trees and pierced its way through the fog.

The dark elves immediately ceased their bickering and turned their attention to the brilliantly lit fairie. They pulled their visors tight around their eyes and looked in wonder. The light elf elder grabbed his staff and used it to slowly push himself up to his feet. They began to talk among themselves but none could be heard over Ayku's high vocal range.

One of the dark elves raised his hands in the air and shot four green energy arrows from his fingertips at Ayku. She flew as quickly as she could behind a tree as two of the projectiles whizzed by her. The other two struck the tree in small explosions. Bark flew off of the tree as the energy bolts hit it, and sparks from the energy blast showered all around Ayku.

Looking past the small explosions, Ayku could see her friends running down the hill. She was just about to start singing again to drown out their advance when she realized it was too late. One of the dark elves turned, saw them, and alerted his comrades with a yell.

Tye pulled back as far as he could on his bow and released. The arrow flew from the top of the hill with lightning speed and struck one of the dark elves in the shoulder. He fell to the ground with a scream as he tried to pull it out.

The group was on them in an instant before they could cast any more spells. The three standing dark elves defended themselves with their staffs. Gusseus was the first to reach them, ready to strike with his battle axe. The dark elf was quicker than the aging dwarf and struck him in the side with his staff, causing Gusseus to tumble over. He rolled quickly a few times and recovered swiftly to his feet, only to find Aldara stepping in front of him.

"This one is mine, Guss. I don't like it when my friends are picked on." With that, she tugged at the moon clasp to release her cape, throwing it to the ground in a single motion. She raised her staff above her head, twirled it with both hands, and swung it at the dark elf. It was met with a block from the dark elf's staff and the two continued to duel.

Eldin swung his sword at another dark elf, who blocked it with his wooden staff. Eldin's sword stuck into the elf's weapon and he pulled to get it out. Not only did he pull the sword out of the staff but he also pulled the weapon out of the dark elf's hands. Both weapons flew to the ground. The dark elf immediately raised his hands and began to chant. Eldin took a few steps forward, formed a fist, and punched the dark elf square in the face. The blood rushed out of his nose and he was tossed back into a tree. He continued to chant and his fingertips began to glow. Eldin grabbed the elf's arms and turned the glowing fingers toward the dark elf while plunging his knee into the elf's stomach. The dark elf screamed as the energy flew from his fingertips into his own chest, which seared and burned; some of the energy struck Eldin's armor, propelling him backward onto the ground. The dark elf writhed in agony as his chest was set ablaze. He let out a final scream, then sank to the ground. Eldin, quick to get back on his feet, then saw Gusseus engaged in a new battle.

Eldin, judging that the two fighters were about evenly matched, stayed out of the brawl, but stood ready to help if need be. The dark elf swung his staff at Gusseus and the dwarf blocked it with his battle axe.

Meanwhile, the injured elf on the ground seemed, at least for the moment, to have been forgotten. He lay on the ground, arrow in his shoulder, chanting in whispers while watching Tye reload his bow. His fingers lit up and his energy arrows shot forth toward Tye.

Tye leaned to get out of the way as the energy bolts flew past him. One of them clipped his shoulder and sent a deep burning sensation through his arm. Tye fell to his side and looked down at the elf, who was already chanting to send more magical arrows his way. Acting quickly, he rose to his knees, continued loading his bow, and aimed at the dark elf.

Ayku, dimming her glow, gasped when she saw the wounded dark elf start his assault on Tye. She looked at the tree next to her and started to tug on the fruit it was bearing. She grew in size to give herself more strength and the red, rounded fruit snapped off its branch without restraint. She swung her arm back and hurled the fruit through the air at the dark elf, who was rising to his feet while casting his spell. It hit him square in the back of the head, exploding on impact, filling his hair with its red stickiness.

This small distraction was all that Tye needed to finish his aim. He released the arrow from his bow and it flew with breakneck speed toward its target, hitting him in the dead center of the chest. The dark elf fell to the ground with a yell, his arms grabbing at the arrow emerging from his body.

The elder could no longer just watch as his would be rescuers risked their lives. He stepped up to the dark elf Tye had shot and raised his wooden staff. He lowered it down on the dark elf's head, putting him out of his misery.

Gusseus looked over at the elder and then saw, out of the corner of his eye, his opponent's staff coming at him. He leaned to the side and rolled away, dodging the blow and recovering his footing at a speed only a dwarf could pull off. Most opponents of dwarves are larger than they are, forcing the dwarves to develop the skill of rolling as a primary means of defense. They are able to recover quickly and catch their opponent off guard, which Gusseus had indeed accomplished.

He rose quickly to his feet and swung his battle axe, striking the dark elf in the leg. It sunk in deep and the dark elf, losing his balance, fell to the ground. Gusseus raised his weapon and with a final swing, buried it into the elf's chest. He pulled it out, dropped it on the ground, and stood over his victim's body. His attention now turned toward Aldara, who was fighting their last adversary.

Aldara had been fighting her foe with success the whole time, blocking every thrust and attempting to strike every so often. She was toying with him, but now she was aware that all eyes were on her and it was time to end her game. She twirled her staff with both hands in the air and brought it down with force. It struck the dark elf in the side and he took a step back. He grabbed his staff with both hands and blocked another thrust from Aldara. While he blocked her attack he pushed her back with his staff, then swung it with one hand and slammed it into the side of her leg. She lost her balance and stumbled. Tightening her grip on her staff, she thrust it into his chest, forcing the air out of his lungs, causing him to gasp for air. She took that moment to rise to her feet and with another swing, she knocked the staff out of his hand.

He took a step back toward the light elf elder and quickly drew a dagger from the inside pocket of his cloak. He held it up to the elder's neck and Aldara lowered her staff, waiting for his demands.

"Drop your weapon or I will kill him, right here, right now, half-breed," the dark elf wheezed. He looked at her in disgust. Then he looked at her weapon, the magical staff of a dark elf. He knew she had to have killed to get it and he was going to do everything he could not to be her next victim.

Aldara laughed at him, "Kill him. Do you really think that you will live after you do so? You are in a no-win situation. You should spend the last few moments of your life asking the Moon Goddess to grant you a safe journey to the other side." Aldara knew she was taking a chance with the elder's life, but she was gambling that her enemy would surrender and plead for his life.

The dark elf looked around at the group and smiled to himself when he saw Eldin, a human knight of honor. "I will release the old man if you give me your word of honor as a knight that you will spare my life," he bargained with Eldin.

Eldin looked at him and watched him tighten his grip on the dagger. A small drop of blood surfaced on the elder's neck and slowly dripped onto the ground. Eldin realized that any sudden move, either by him or by the group, would surely end in the elder's death. Seeing no other way to save the old elf's life, Eldin replied, "You have my word of honor. I will cause you no harm. Release him and I will not harm you." Eldin looked at the others in the group and motioned with his hand, signaling everyone to lower their weapons.

Aldara hesitated as she looked at Eldin coldly, and then dropped her staff to the ground.

"Perhaps your race isn't as savage as it's rumored to be," the dark elf continued, again speaking directly to Eldin. Relying on the stories of a knight's honor meaning everything to him, the dark elf threw the elder forward, causing him to fall to the ground. Gusseus ran over to the old elf and helped him stand up. Bowing slightly to Eldin, the dark elf began to run away from the group.

Aldara watched him run for a few moments and then raised

her hands. "Mintok Salim Nufar," she spoke in the tongue of the dark elf. As she spoke the words of their enemy, small flames began to grow around her fingers.

Tye and Ali-Mimi reached the group with Ayku's help; she was already tending to Tye's wound with bandages and ointment the old woman had packed in his bag. "Aldara, what the…"

Tye could not finish his sentence before Aldara's spell was cast. The flames now danced around her hands in a ball of fire that was as big as a melon. She threw her arms out in the direction of the dark elf and the fireball hurled toward him. The fleeing elf, hearing his native tongue, turned back to see if help had arrived, only to see a ball of fire flying toward him. He tried to move out of its way but it was too late. The ball engulfed him in flames. He ran around in a small circle briefly before falling to the ground. His screams were short and then he fell silent. His body burned in the misty fog.

Eldin moved close to Aldara shaking his finger at her. "Damn you! I gave him my *word* that I would not hurt him and that he would go free. You damned witch!" His face was red and full of anger.

Aldara looked at him calmly. "And you were true to your word, knight. You did not hurt him and you did let him go." She turned to look at his burning body with no remorse. "Pity the fool didn't ask each of us to do the same."

"Aldara!" Tye exclaimed, "That fireball is a spell of the dark elves! How do you know how to cast it?" His question brought all eyes to Aldara and made Eldin tighten his grip on the hilt of his sword once again.

"When I was visiting your labor camp, I stole a spell book

from one of the dark elf spell casters. I've been studying it every chance I can," she started to explain. She looked around at her friends' doubting faces. "Look, I am using any means necessary to help free Wyndle, and perhaps all of Sylvanor, from the Overlord's forces. You should be thanking me instead of constantly doubting me," she said, clearly annoyed.

"Aye, we'll be discussin' this further after we've rested. Right now we gotta be settin' up camp." Gusseus looked at the carriage on the road and at the horses tied to a nearby tree. "We can use those horses ta travel up the hills away from tha road. There's no reason anyone should be travelin' that way and we should be safe there fer tha rest o' tha day and well past tha night. Tha short trip will be allowin' us ta be gettin' ta know our new friend better," Gusseus bowed to the light elf elder.

Eldin gave Aldara a final look and made his way over to the horses. He untied them and led all four over to the group by the reins.

Aldara walked over to Tye and Ayku. A look of concern washed over her face as she looked at Tye's shoulder. It was blackened and Ayku was rubbing a healing cream on it. It was a popular substance used to treat burns. It was extracted from a plant that was commonly seen throughout the forests of Sylvanor. "Are you alright, Tye?" she asked him, her voice genuine and full of concern.

"Yeah, I'll be fine. It stings a little, but it'll be okay." It hurt more than Tye was letting on, but if he wanted Gusseus to see him as the adult he wanted to be, he had to learn to hide his pain. He looked at Aldara and saw the sadness in her eyes. He wasn't sure if it was because of the distrust most of the group felt for her or because the feelings she had for him. He was aware of them, but being the young adolescent that he was, he tried his best to ignore them. "Thanks, Al." He saw the smile appear on her lips and was glad he could make her feel better.

Aldara opened her mouth to continue the conversation when she was rudely pushed aside by Eldin and his group of horses. "There are only four of 'em so some of us will have to double up," he looked at Aldara, "or one of us could walk."

Gusseus kicked some dirt through the fog at Eldin. "None o' us'll be doin' any such thing. Aldara can ride with me and Ayku will be ridin' with Tye." Gusseus addressed the elder, "What'd ya say yer name was?"

The elder looked at Gusseus, and using his wooden staff as a walking crutch, moved to one of the horses. "My name is Outoo," he said softly, "and I am…grateful for your help. Thank you."

Aldara struggled to help Gusseus onto his horse. When he was comfortably in position, she turned to Outoo and eyed the elder from head to toe. "Just how did you come to be in the company of the enemy?" she asked, thinking back to the group of elders she traveled with to Under Hollow. The baggy hoods draped over their faces made it impossible to distinguish any of them. *Was this simply a chance meeting? Or was the enemy escorting him back to Solaris Arbor?*

The old light elf turned to face the inquisitive half-breed and nodded. "I know of what you refer to, young one. I know of the meeting between some of the council members and the Overlord," he sighed. "I refused to have any part in it and in fact debated the issue for several weeks. But alas, I lost the argument and the meeting happened without my consent." Outoo began to stroke his horse as he had always done before mounting it. It was his way of getting acquainted with the animal, to let it know it just wasn't only a method of transportation but a friend as well. "As for me being here, that is a tale that will have to wait, I'm afraid. I am much too weary to tell it and answer the many questions that no doubt you will link to it."

Eldin stepped over between Outoo and Aldara and lowered his cupped hands to help Outoo onto the horse. "You don't have to explain yourself to her, old man. You are a legend everywhere in this realm. Why you are here is your business. Now on ya go." Eldin did not have any way whatsoever with words and had been told numerous times throughout his life that he'd do better if he kept silent. The elder placed his foot in Eldin's hands and Eldin raised him up onto the horse. Outoo straddled it and was now sitting upon it safely.

The vision and mind of a knight is totally one-sided and indeed, Aldara thought, *Eldin is a fool. Was he ignorant to the fact that even the most honorable of men were not beyond corruption?* She looked at him in disgust and let the matter drop for the moment. She mounted Gusseus's horse and sat behind him, placing her hands around his waist. He gave her a soft pat on the leg, letting her know that in spite of the fact that Outoo was an old war hero, she was right to question him. With that, he pulled the horse up with a swift jerk to the reins. The rest of the group followed, and they journeyed up the next hill and away from the road as quickly as possible.

****

Tye was the last to secure the reins of his horse to a tree. He gave them a tug to make sure they were tied tightly and gave his horse a pat on the head. He joined the others as they opened their packs and spread out their contents on the ground. Tye had a few large, thin pieces of cloth in his with some makeshift medical kits and some dried fruit. He looked at the others' belongings and they each had essentially the same assortment of food, but some also had clothing, mending kits, and blankets.

"There be enough in each pack ta be puttin' together three shelters. We be doublin' up tonight, laddies," Gusseus stated as he looked around for some sticks to prop up the pieces of cloth. Being from the hilly Dwarven province, finding sticks and stones was not a problem and he found what he needed almost immediately.

Tye was eager to help and he gathered some long, narrow dead branches. "You sure this place is out of the way enough, Guss?" he asked, while throwing his findings down at Gusseus's feet.

"Take a look around ya, laddie. There be a cliff ta tha east and we be at tha top o' a very high hill. There ain't be a town fer as far as tha eye can see. There ain't bein' no reason why anyone would come here." Gusseus pulled some heavy rope out of his pile of supplies and got to work with the help of Eldin and Ayku. The dwarf looked over at Outoo, who was sitting near a tree, rolling his staff in his hands and watching the group. "I'm lookin' forward ta be hearin' yer tale once we be set up," Gusseus said to him with a smile.

Aldara leaned up against a tree that was close to Outoo. She stood, arms folded, and watched him look over the group. She shrugged Ali-Mimi off of her shoulders and onto the ground, where he walked off on his own in search of something to eat. "I'm not willing to wait that long," she said coldly as she unfolded her arms and walked toward Outoo.

Outoo turned his head toward her when she approached him. He could tell by her body language that this wasn't going to be a pleasant conversation. "What is on your mind, child?" he asked her as he continued to roll his staff in his hands.

Aldara stood in front of him and crossed her arms again. Outoo was an old elf who had held a seat on the council of light elves for as long as anyone could remember. His name was known throughout all of Sylvanor and it struck Aldara as curious that he would be seen this far away from Solaris Arbor and under the arrest of dark elves. "I saw you late yesterday evening, in Frentier," she said in a tone that was accusatory.

Outoo continued to roll his walking staff and looked at Aldara. His face was smooth except for around his mouth and eyes, where a few deep wrinkles could be seen. He had an androgynous face that hid his age quite well. "My dear, you must be mistaken," he said, maintaining eye contact.

Aldara stepped forward with her right leg and sat it to rest against Outoo's walking stick, preventing him from rolling it. "No. I saw you and the dark elves and the wooden carriage you were in." As she spoke, she held his stare and lifted her eyebrow. "What I can't figure out is, you were heading north. When we found you, you were south of the city. How do you explain that?"

Ayku was helping Eldin put one of the shelters together while watching the conversation from afar. They were all listening but they kept on working. Twilight was upon them and they needed their rest soon if they were going to get an early start in the morning. She had just finished tying a piece of rope to a stick that Eldin had hammered into the ground when she gave him a nudge. He looked at her inquisitively and she cocked her head in the direction of Aldara and Outoo. He took the hint, stood up and walked over to make himself part of the conversation.

Outoo looked somewhat confused and then he began to laugh. "Oh yes," he began as he shook his head, "My captors departed the city the wrong way. My guess is they were in too much of a hurry to deliver me to the Queen that they weren't watching where they were going. They soon realized and turned the carriage around." Outoo was still chuckling at the embarrassing way the dark elves handled his capture.

Aldara's eyes narrowed. She didn't like him and she wasn't sure why. She secretly wondered if it was because he was a person of great fame and importance, or if he was a newcomer who was had been too easily accepted into their group. "But your carriage broke down far away from the city. You weren't even on the main road," Aldara continued her inquisition.

Outoo's face became more serious. Never in a few hundred years had he been treated with such disrespect. "As I told you, child, our driver was of poor direction. To simply put it, we were lost in the hills when we broke down. They didn't know where they were and I wasn't about to clue them in." Outoo pulled his walking stick from under Aldara's feet and set it beside him.

Aldara narrowed her eyes again, then rubbed her temples in an attempt to fend off an oncoming headache. "Why were you in Frentier? Why were your hands not bound if you were a prisoner?" she continued to question him.

"Okay, witch. That's enough," Eldin intercepted, "Have some respect for an old war hero. None of us would even be here if it wasn't for his courage and bravery during the last Great War." He looked at Outoo's aged body and then back at Aldara's pompous stance as she stood over him. "Let him rest."

Outoo waved his hand at Eldin. "I appreciate you coming to my defense, son, but it is not necessary. I have valid answers for her questions." He looked at Aldara and a tired look washed over his face. "But I fear they are not enough to appease her." He now spoke directly to Aldara, who was waiting to hear his responses. "I was in that town because I was a fool. I was trying to accomplish one more mission of glory before I depart this life. I, well…" He looked down at his hands, the hands of an old man that shook as he held them up at Aldara. "As for binding me up," he chuckled, "I guess they didn't find it necessary. Would you?"

Aldara could see his point. He would be no match for his dark elf captors and he certainly couldn't run away from them. She raised her hands to her head again and rubbed her temples harder. The pain was growing in intensity and she looked over to see how the shelters were coming along. They were all but finished, for which Aldara was thankful. All she wanted to do now was close her eyes and sleep off her headache, even though it meant ending her interrogation of their new-found ally. She lowered her head and took notice of the high quality boots Outoo was wearing. She had recognized them as stamina boots. They allowed their wearer to walk or run for long periods of time without getting winded. She closed her eyes and hoped her headache would go away faster.

Outoo looked at her curiously and waited for Aldara's pain to subside. "Now…I have some questions for you, my young half-breed."

Aldara looked at him and a smile curled her lips, "Oh?"

Outoo's face became very serious and he leaned forward. "You question my loyalty when that spell you cast, that fireball, was a dark spell. Your ability to cast such dark spells has me curiously cautious of you." He eyed her up and down and then continued, looking into her eyes. "I hope you won't succumb to the alluring power of the dark elves." He tightened his stare. "Just where do your loyalties lie? Have I been rescued only to be captured again?" he asked her.

"I was wondering the same thing, witch. Just how much of the dark arts do you know?" Eldin interjected.

"A spell is neither light nor dark. It depends on how you use it and what you use it for. I would expect you to know that, given your age." Aldara disliked old people. She didn't hold the respect for them that everyone else in their group seemed to. She looked at Eldin, ignored his question, and gave him a look that said to butt out of their conversation.

"Good answer, my dear. It seems you do have a decent head on your shoulders after all. How long you can keep it is another story," Outoo replied.

Aldara gave him a phony smile as a response. "We will have to continue this conversation at a later time." She grabbed her temples once more and walked away from Outoo and Eldin. She headed toward one of the shelters and stopped to look at Gusseus.

"Aye, tha tent on the end is fine, Aldara." Gusseus pointed to it. "I'll be sharin' my tent with Outoo tonight. I've always been wantin' ta meet him and would like ta exchange tales. Ya don't mind sharin' with Tye tonight, do ya?" he asked her as she walked toward her tent.

She turned to look at him and a brief smile overcame her pain, "No, of course not."

Gusseus smiled. "Aye, I thought not." He winked at her. There wasn't much that passed Gusseus's eyes. He knew the whole group pretty well for the short time they had been together and he quickly became their foundation.

Tye followed Aldara into their tent, asking questions about her well-being. When the two disappeared into their shelter, Gusseus suggested that the group not light a fire and instead turn in early. He received no argument and one by one, each member of the group slowly found their way into their respective tents for the first good night's sleep they'd had in days.

****

Aldara, the echoing female voice called out to her.

Aldara tossed and turned in her sleep and finally sat up, her eyes open but still sleeping. She looked forward but saw nothing. "Yes. I hear you."

Aldara, the voice repeated in her mind. *You are in a lush green field. Beautiful flowers surround you. Do you see them?* the familiar voice asked.

Aldara moved her head from side to side inside the tent. "Yes, I see them. They are beautiful," she commented. Aldara continued to move her head from side to side and then looked up at the imaginary sky. She threw her head back with a jerk when she looked skyward. There in the clouds was the faint glow of Queen Valeria's head. It was transparent and beautiful and hovered in the clouds like it truly belonged there.

Rise, my sweet little girl, the Queen commanded in her

motherly voice, *Rise and walk with me; I wish to spend some time with you.*

Aldara rose to her feet and exited the tent. She bumped into Tye's leg on her way out, startling him.

Tye opened his eyes and saw Aldara just as she left the tent. "Al—?"

Be careful! Watch out for the rocks! said the Queen from inside of Aldara's head. *I wouldn't want you to hurt your feet.*

"Yes. Don't hurt feet," Aldara muttered while in her trance.

Tye stuck his head out of the tent and watched Aldara walk closer to the edge of their campsite and to the edge of the cliff that they were camped upon. *Sleepwalking*, he thought as he exited his shelter, following her but keeping a few steps back, trying to figure out how to bring her out of it. He had heard stories since his youth about how dangerous it was to wake someone when they were sleepwalking. He wasn't sure if he believed them, but he wasn't about to test the stories on his friend.

Keep walking, my sweet child, the Queen commanded as Aldara walked closer to the edge. *You have the most beautiful wings, Aldara. With those wings, you could fly across the entire realm in a heartbeat. True freedom would be yours. Do you see them?*

Aldara looked blankly over one shoulder and then the other. She saw wings of an almost transparent material slowly flapping on her back. They were shining in the moonlight and were a sight to behold. They glowed many brilliant colors when the light hit them and were unlike any wings she had ever seen on any creature in her life. "Yes. I see them. They are beautiful," she commented as she reached the edge of the cliff. Below her was nothing but a steep, rocky hillside. Tye called out to her but she did not hear him. The only sound in Aldara's head was that of Queen Valeria and the gentle flapping of her cellophane-like wings.

You can fly, Aldara, the Queen's voice was growing with excitement. *Fly!* her voice echoed in Aldara's head, *Fly! Feel what it is like to be free. Fly!*

"Yes, freedom. I can fly. I *will* fly." Aldara's voice was full of so much confidence, it was like she had never believed anything so much in her life. Sure that her wings would support her and glide her around the realm, she slowly took a step off the rocky edge of the cliff. Tye quickly grabbed her by the waist and pulled her back, shaking her body violently while doing so.

The Queen's laughter began to echo through Aldara's head. The sound was almost overwhelming, and then, in an instant, it was gone. Aldara awoke in Tye's arms. She looked around quickly and then over her shoulder. She saw no wings. She then looked over the cliff and saw what a long way down it was. She then turned her attention to the sky. It was full of stars and stars alone. Valeria was no longer among them.

Tears began to stream down Aldara's face and she held onto Tye tightly, fully recognizing the fact that he had just saved her life. She laid her head against his chest and gently sobbed. "What's happening to me?" she asked through her tears. She looked up to his eyes but they offered her nothing but confusion. She returned her head to his chest and continued to sob. It was the first time that Tye had ever seen her like this and he stood holding her, rocking her gently from side to side. "By the Gods," she asked again, "What's happening to me?"

Chapter IX

———⟨◦◦◦⟩———

Ties That Bind

Tye inhaled a deep breath of the early morning air. It was crisp and fresh, the kind of breath that lets you know you're alive. He closed his eyes and enjoyed the calm peacefulness that was all around him. He wondered what it would be like to live in a world without war, a world where he could go walking outside without looking over his shoulder—a world that was actually worth living in. He took another deep breath and let out a sigh. He kicked his legs back and forth silently as they dangled over the edge of the cliff that looked down to a grassy valley that disappeared into the early morning mist.

He thought back to when he was younger. Back then, it was safe to play in the streets and in the woods, but life was always full of strange apprehension. He was told never to wander beyond the Breathing Forest. He was scolded time and time again by those who cared for him whenever he entertained the thought of exploring the rest of the realm. A look of disgust washed over his young, innocent face and for the first time, he realized that his race, the light elves, was wrong. They lived safely in Solaris Arbor, almost without a care. It was as if they had no desire to help the outside world. Sure, they wouldn't mind if strangers breached the forest and entered Solaris Arbor for solace, but they would never leave or journey out to save anyone. Would the war be different now if his people had stepped in? That was a question Tye could not shake out of his head.

He turned back to look at the makeshift tents that held his sleeping friends. He needed answers; when Outoo awakened he would get them. He let out another sigh as he looked at the tent where Gusseus and Outoo slept. Even Gusseus was reluctant to tell Tye what it was like beyond the Breathing Forest.

He looked at his bow, which was lying next to him, and frowned. He should have hit the dark elf in the chest with his first arrow. Archery was one of his favorite pastimes. He had enjoyed it for as long as he could remember. He was a champion among his friends and had now proven himself to be a worthy adversary in battle.

He quickly shook off his feelings about missing his target when he suddenly became aware that his absolute favorite pastime, the flute, was still wedged in his belt. He slid it out carefully and looked at it. It was a long wooden flute, about the length of his arm from fingertip to elbow. He raised it to his lips, but no breath escaped him. Remembering what Gusseus had said about not wanting to attract attention, he lowered it.

He looked past his feet at the valley below and saw nothing. Moving his hair away from his ears, he listened carefully, still nothing. It was as if they were all alone in the realm. Tye let out a heavy sigh. He wasn't even sure where in the realm he was.

His home had been taken from him. His freedom had been taken from him. He looked down at his flute. "They won't take away my dreams," he said aloud. He raised the flute back to his lips and quickly looked toward the tents of his sleeping friends, "They should be awake by now anyway."

The breath poured out of his lips and through his flute. It made a soft murmur at first, but the sound soon rose in pitch, though it remained soft. He moved his fingers up and down the flute, covering the various holes and getting a feel for the new instrument. His thoughts wandered to his friend, Aldara, and to the night before. How, for the first time ever, he had seen her cry. Even when she was younger and the other children picked on her for being a half-breed, she always stood tall, never letting it show how much she hurt. But this time was different. She wasn't being made fun of; she was being possessed. *How was Queen Valeria taking control of her? When would it happen next?* Before Tye realized, his warm-up had turned into a full-blown tune that sailed on the wind, flying from him to the bottom of the cliff, blanketing all of Sylvanor, it seemed.

Inside the tent, Aldara sat up while rubbing her eyes. The gentleness of Tye's song almost made her forget that her mind and body were no longer hers. She peered through the slit in front of the tent to see Tye sitting on the cliff's edge. She recognized the song he was playing. He used to play it for her when they were younger—whenever she was upset—and he was playing it for her now. She wiped a tiny teardrop from her cheek and exited the tent.

Outside, she stretched her arms as she thought of her relationship with Tye. When they were alone, they were comfortable. They had been friends since birth, but when there were other people around, they both became distant. It was something she had learned to live with. Tye was always immature when it came to his feelings, and he still had some growing up to do. She also thought about how she wished Ayku had never come into the picture. She could see that Tye's heart belonged to her, even if he couldn't, and it made her jealous. If only he could feel for her the way he feels for that fairie.

Aldara let out a sigh and walked up to Tye, basking in his song. When she reached him, she gently put her hand on his shoulder.

Tye let out a gasp and the flute fell to his side. "Oh, it's only you," he giggled, "I thought you were some dark elf who was a music critic." He stood up so he could talk to her face to face.

"I'm sorry I startled you, Tye," replied Aldara as she looked sadly into his eyes, "That was beautiful. Reminded me of when we were children."

Tye lowered his head as he tucked the flute back into his belt. He continued the conversation that way, pretending he couldn't fit it in snugly so he wouldn't have to look in her eyes. He always bowed his head this way when he felt sentimental. "Yeah, I thought you might need a reminder that you're with friends. Whatever that evil witch is doing to you, you can beat it. I'll help you; you know that." Securing his flute, he raised his head and looked at her, "What are you going to do, Al?"

She watched Tye fumble with his flute. His shyness was one of the many things that she liked about him. As quickly as he was growing up, he was trying so hard to hold onto his innocence. She wondered what it would have been like to have grown up surrounded by friends. Because she was on her own most of the time, she had been forced to grow up quickly.

Throwing her childhood away, Aldara had completely immersed herself in her studies, learning everything she could about both of her halves, light and dark. She had hoped to meet others of her kind one day so they could help continue her education and accept her as one of their own. She quickly discovered that there was no one else like her in the realm and there hadn't been for a very long time.

Her gaze met Tye's in a soft, caring exchange. Her midnight black hair fell into her face, her grayish streak covering her right eye. "I don't know," she said steadily. "I'm not sure there is anything I *can* do."

Tye looked at her for a moment and then pushed her hair aside. He then took his finger and pointed it at her chest. She looked down and he raised his finger, softly striking her chin. He smiled at her in an attempt to cheer her up.

Aldara's lips curled slightly but her expression quickly returned to its solemn state. "Tye, I have to go," she said, unsure of the words as they flowed from her lips.

Tye's eyes widened as he asked, "Go? But you can't!" Quckly, he tried to regain his composure. "I mean, if you are out there on your own, you won't have anyone to protect you! If I wasn't here last night, the Queen would have killed you for sure." He could see that Aldara was still frightened by the whole incident and that the prospect of being on her own was sure to drive that feeling deeper into her heart. "Where will you go?" he asked softly after a moment's pause.

"I don't know," she replied. She turned her head from Tye and looked out over the cliff, past the valley, and into the future. "Thank you for last night," she sighed, while continuing to hold her gaze on tomorrow. "The longer I am with you, the more danger you are all in. I had no control last night. She could have easily had me set fire to all of your tents. I care for you too much to allow that to ever happen."

Tye moved in closer to her. He looked to the horizon but he couldn't see what Aldara was seeing. "How can the Queen's hold over you be broken?" he asked her. "Are there any spells, light or dark, that could help you?"

"I don't know," she replied again. She squinted and her face turned from fear back to its usual hardened state. She squinted once more, as if she was trying to see what tomorrow looked like more clearly. She turned her head back to Tye. "Before I go, I will help free Wyndle. It is my fault she was caught and I promised to get her free. That I will do, and I'll be damned if Valeria is going to stop me." Her words were now full of strength and defiance.

"Al, none of us blame you for what happened to Wyndle. You reacted quickly in the situation and our response to judge you for it was probably even quicker," Tye surprised himself at how 'adult' he was starting to sound. "We probably do owe you our lives. They all know it. They just won't say it."

A smile found its way to Aldara's face, "Gusseus has. He has really done his best to help look out for me. He is a sweet little man. You are lucky to have him for a father."

Tye knew Aldara must think very highly of Gusseus. He knew that she rarely ever voiced her opinion, and she never spoke so highly of anyone but herself. "He's a great guy. A little pushy and overbearing at times, but I'm glad he's around," Tye said as he started to slip back into his adolescent 'too cool to care' attitude. He reached down, picked up his bow, and slung it over his shoulder. "So…what are you going to do in the meantime to keep control so the Queen doesn't come back?" he asked her as he adjusted his quiver of arrows next to his bow.

Aldara opened her mouth to reply when she heard a rustling from a bush near the tents. She quickly turned and raised her hands, poised to cast a spell if need be. The leaves moved once again and Ali-Mimi sprang out from behind them. He sprinted up to them, interrupting their conversation.

"Long look all night for food, Ally. Took long time but crawly lizards taste not bad." He grinned up at her. He looked at Tye and gave him the same silly grin. In one movement, he looked back at Aldara and jumped onto her shoulders, finding his usual spot to sit.

Aldara shook her head at Ali-Mimi, smiling but not really wanting to. She thought back to the village where they first met and remembered him saying he wanted to bond with her. She looked over at Tye, who was laughing at Mother Aldara and her Child. "I have an idea that may be able to help reinforce my position."

"Ya be playin' that flute again, boy, and I'll be boxin' yer ears good fer ya," Gusseus grumbled from outside his tent. He was standing with his arms folded. Judging by his stance, he had been there watching them for some time. He threw down the head of a small lizard that Ali-Mimi had left outside his tent and walked toward his young friends.

"Oh come on, Guss," Tye whined, "There's no one around for miles. No one heard anything!"

"Ya don't know that, laddie." Gusseus walked to the edge of the cliff and pointed his finger sharply over its edge. "There could be a whole fleet o' Dracal marchin' down there."

Tye looked at him with serious eyes. "I don't care," he said sternly, "I'm not afraid. I refuse to cower anymore. They aren't gonna kill me before they kill me."

Aldara looked at him and cocked her head to its side, leaning it on Ali-Mimi, confused by his words.

Gusseus stood still for a moment. Tye had talked back to him before, but never with such fire or passion in his eyes. The old dwarf knew this was not an argument he could win, nor did he want to. He saw that Tye was growing up quickly. As much as he wanted Tye to keep his heart young as long as possible, the winds of war would eventually take their toll and harden it. He nodded at Tye and gave him a smack on his behind, giving his approval to his adopted son without actually saying it. Tye smiled back at him as a silent thank you for not embarrassing him in front of Aldara.

"Now, we best be wakin' up tha others. We be havin' a long road ahead o' us and we best be movin'," Gusseus stated as he walked away from his kids. He considered anyone close to Tye part of his family and he made sure they knew it.

Aldara laughed for a moment as she watched him walk back to camp. "He is truly amazing," she acknowledged out loud. She felt his love and knew he had taken her into his heart. She was thankful for it and for the first time in her life, she was actually starting to feel comfortable. She looked at Tye and then back at the ground, realizing that, as comfortable as she felt, she would have to leave the group as soon as they freed Wyndle...provided she was still alive when they got there. She closed her eyes for a moment and hoped her control could hold out for that long. She knew she had to be the strongest she had ever been, but she questioned if even that was going to be enough.

"Come on, let's wake everyone up and get goin'." Tye looked at her and laughed as they started for the tents, "*You* can wake up Eldin."

Aldara walked toward her tent, passing the shelter that housed Eldin and Ayku. In one swoop and without stopping, she pulled on the cloth that covered the makeshift structure and threw it inward, collapsing the tent on the two sleeping inside. "Wake up," she said loudly. A look of complete satisfaction visited her face. There wasn't a more perfect way to start her day than to annoy the two members of the group who disliked her the most.

Ayku fluttered around inside the tent, but Eldin found his way out of it as quick as lightning. He cursed Aldara while placing his hand on the hilt of his sword to further display his anger.

"You bad! They nice people," Ali-Mimi complained to her while still resting on her shoulder. That was his comfort spot and Aldara was getting used to him using it as his traveling bed.

"It was an accident. I slipped," she replied as she reached her tent. She thrust her right shoulder in the air and sent Ali-Mimi sailing to the ground, where he landed on his feet. She kneeled and began to pull the sticks that supported her tented cloth out of the ground. The tents weren't very elaborate. They were held up by one stick on each corner and another, longer stick in the front center. Within minutes, she had the shelter completely collapsed and was folding the cloth to a size that would fit in with the rest of her gear.

Tye strolled over to the first tent, which housed Gusseus and Outoo. He opened the flap, made his way into the tent, and walked into something solid. It was a shock that sent him falling on his backside. He sat outside of the tent scratching his head. He looked up to see Outoo exiting the shelter. Outoo had an annoyed look on his face and made no effort to hide it from Tye.

"I…I'm sorry sir," Tye stuttered, "I didn't see you there." The young elf stood up clumsily and wiped the dust from his trousers. He smacked his legs quickly to remove as much dust as he could as quickly as he could. When he was done, he looked at Outoo, who was standing quietly in front of him, not saying a word.

"Perhaps you would have known I was there if you possessed some manners and knocked before you decided to barge in," Outoo finally said. His voice was cold. He studied Tye silently; seeing the young elf in front of him, his hair all moppy and his carefree attitude, sent him hurling back through time to when he was a lad. Back to the last Great War, when *he* had been on a quest to save Sylvanor from the dragon onslaught. Back then, he wasn't much different than Tye was now. He was young and inexperienced, and he was the cause of getting his friends into trouble more times than he could count.

Outoo's mind returned to the present and his eyes seemed a little warmer. "Forgive me, child. Perhaps I have spent so much time sitting in a chair making laws that I have forgotten what it is actually like to live with them." Outoo looked around at the rest of the group as they packed their shelters. "Or live at all," he finished sadly.

Tye suddenly became uncomfortable and fumbled with his belt, making sure his flute was secure. He also adjusted his bow and the quiver of arrows slung across his back. "That's okay. It was my fault." Tye tried to make Outoo feel better. "There is some water I carried up from the bottom of the hill earlier. It's over by the fire. You can wash up if you want to," he suggested.

Outoo stretched, making sure his walking stick was solid to the ground. "Save the water for drinking, Tye. When you are traveling across the realm you never know how long it will be before you come across any." Outoo looked around the campsite. "Or food, for that matter," he continued, not seeing any traces of wild game.

Tye followed Outoo's gaze, tracing the entire perimeter of the camp. "Yeah, I'm hungry too. I've only seen a few lizards here and there but they are way too fast to catch. I dive for 'em but I just end up with a face full of dirt." Tye shrugged.

Outoo laughed and again was swept away with his memories. He looked around the campsite once more. "It is too grassy here. Not a good weed to be found. Our camping site should have been chosen more carefully."

Tye's head cocked to the side in confusion, "What do we need weeds for, camouflage?"

Outoo laughed as he placed his hand on Tye's shoulder, "To lasso lizards. It is a skill I learned long ago. Perhaps if the opportunity arises, I will teach it to you." He took his hand from Tye and walked toward the small, flickering fire. "Come, let's drink before we start our journey. Gusseus filled me in on your quest to free Wyndle. You will need all the strength you can muster if you want to achieve success."

Tye walked by his side, matching Outoo's slow pace. He kept silent for a moment, pondering his thoughts, and then spoke. "Can I ask you something, sir?" Tye's voice was a little unsteady.

"By all means." Outoo looked over at him. "But only if you start calling me by my name. I am not different than any of you, just older. I've been called sir for more years than I want to remember."

They reached the fire. Outoo breathed in the deep, smoky flavor of the air and exhaled heavily with a moan. He enjoyed the smell of burning wood and smiled, thinking back to times when it was his responsibility to gather wood and to light the fires for the group. He bent down and picked up a crude bowl that Tye had made from the soft wood of one of the fallen Mushuar trees. "We are a lot alike, you and I. More so than you'll ever know, I'd imagine," Outoo said as he sipped the fresh stream water from the bowl.

Tye watched him drink while he got up the nerve to ask Outoo some questions about his private life. "What mission *are* you on? What would make you travel so far from Solaris Arbor by yourself? You had to have known you would be caught by the Dracal or by the dark elves." Tye was on a roll now, and without thinking, the questions poured from his mouth. "With a group, you can fight your way out of trouble. But one man," he paused, "One man can't accomplish much on his own."

Outoo slammed his walking stick into the soft ground. "You're so wrong, boy. Learn this here and now," Outoo paused as a faint mist appeared in his eyes. "One man can be responsible for changing things more than an army ever could."

Tye took a step back, shocked by Outoo's sudden change in mood. He watched as the wetness in Outoo's eyes came and went. "I'm sorry. I didn't mean to offend you," he apologized. Tye didn't know what else to say or how to recover from the situation. *Next time, Tye*, he told himself, *think before you speak.*

"None taken, my young friend," Outoo's voice became soft again as he regained his composure, "Just remember, you seldom get a second chance. When you do, you must seize the opportunity." He took a second sip of water and wiped his mouth with the back of his hand.

Tye was putting two and two together. He knew Outoo carried a great burden on his shoulders and he was anxious to find out what it was that made the elder seem to regret so much of his life. "Is that what you're doing now?" he asked, "Seizing an opportunity?"

Outoo chuckled at Tye's insight, "The mission I was on has all but changed now. It is too delicate to involve my new-found friends. What matters now is saving your friend, Wyndle. The Overlord must know what a catch he has, so time is of the essence." Outoo put the wooden bowl back down near the fire. "Perhaps she could shed some light on where these Dracal came from."

Tye thought of his special friend and could only imagine the horror and pain she was going through. "Why did the Queen want her so badly? When Wyndle was captured, she just let us go! From what I've heard about the Queen, I expected her to kill us, not let us just walk away and wander the realm freely. I wonder if…" Tye stopped as he looked past Outoo at Aldara. She was busy stuffing the cloth of her shelter into a pack. He thought back to the night before, when the Queen had control of her. If the Queen could see that there was a cliff nearby, she might be able to determine where they are. The color drained from his face as Tye realized they had never been set free. As long as Aldara was with them, so was the Queen. "We've got to leave this place right away," he said sternly to Outoo.

Outoo looked curiously at Tye's face, still drained of all color. "Patience, young one. As soon as everyone has packed up their tents, we will be on our way. I know the angel is your friend and the deadened forest of Glinfel is not far. We will be there soon." Outoo looked over his shoulder and watched as Aldara sat petting Ali-Mimi. He turned his attention back to Tye. "You are overly concerned about her. Why?"

Tye found that he was sweating. If he told the others about Aldara's possession, they would surely leave her behind. He could not let his friend wander Sylvanor alone, especially this close to Glinfel. She must remain part of the group. "No reason. I just always worry about her."

Again, Outoo put his hand on Tye's shoulder. "We all have our secrets, boy. However, if those secrets are so strong that they could hurt everyone you care about, are they really worth protecting?" Outoo sighed, remembering that he was given this lecture once, long ago. "By keeping your secret now to protect her, you may only end up hurting her or others in the long run."

Thinking back to the night before, Tye knew Outoo was right. If the Queen could make Aldara believe she had wings and could fly, she could surely make Tye, Ayku, or anyone else appear to be a Dracal that needed to be slain. He looked into Outoo's eyes and spoke softly, "It's the Queen. She was in Aldara's mind and could see through her eyes! I dunno how or why, but she can. Maybe it's because Aldara is half dark elf." Tye shook his head and then lowered it in shame, feeling guilty that he had just betrayed his childhood friend.

Outoo glanced back at Aldara and then back at Tye's

bowed head. He gently grabbed hold of the young elf's chin and raised his head, where he saw the pain in his eyes. "The Queen has possessed her, hasn't she?" he said gently.

"NO!" Tye snapped back. He whipped his head to the side to release Outoo's hold on it. "I never said that!"

With a sigh, Outoo slumped his shoulders. He knew the news he was about to give Tye would be hurtful, but it was necessary to deliver it. "You didn't have to. I've seen it before." This time, it was Outoo that bowed his head. "It can happen to the best of people."

"Is there any way to break her free of it?" Tye asked as he grabbed hold of Outoo's robes.

"Sadly, no," Outoo answered, "At least, there is no way that I am aware. The few I knew who were possessed died, either by their own hand or by someone else's, before any attempt could be made to free them of her wicked grasp. It was always the same." He sighed again. "I'm afraid your friend's fate is sealed."

Anger rose in Tye. He would not let himself believe Outoo's words. In a panic, he said in a voice that was much too loud, "We're not leaving her!" Suddenly aware of the increase in volume, he looked past Outoo and saw Aldara watching them. If she didn't know what they were discussing before, she did now.

Outoo put his arm around Tye, trying to reassure him that they were friends, not adversaries. "I have no intention of doing so. With her here, we can watch her. There is no telling what the Queen will have her do if she is on her own." Outoo looked over at Aldara to let her know that they were not talking in secret about her, and that she would be made aware of everything that was said. "Besides, Gusseus tells me she was in the

Queen's castle. We need her to find the way into Under Hollow and then guide us through the castle to free your friend." He looked back into Tye's eyes. "If anything, I will make it my duty to watch over her. But for now, I think you may be right, my young friend. We must leave this place at once."

Outoo started to walk away from the small crackling fire then stopped. He removed his hand from Tye's shoulder and closed his eyes. After a moment, he waved his hand through the air and then over the fire. The air churned and sent gusts of wind between them, following Outoo's gesture. The flames danced wildly and were quickly snuffed out. Outoo lowered his arm and headed for the tents.

Tye looked at him in amazement and with a little envy. "I never had the time or hung out with any light elves long enough for them to teach me the magic of the elements. I know very little," he confessed.

"You learn what you need as you go along in life, Tye," Outoo responded. "Right now, the skill of archery is what you need to depend on. Soon, you will learn the light magic of controlling the earth, air, fire, and water. That is a skill that takes time and patience." He paused and looked at Tye. He could see the look of hunger and striving for perfection in the young elf's eyes. Tye had the same personality traits he had, and he could already see the young elf getting angry that he wasn't already a master of the light arts. "Just remember, the dark elves are more in tune in the ways of magic. Our people have taken to nature and playful lives in the woods. Perhaps if we hadn't become too comfortable in our land of luxury, this war might have been different. Our pride is at fault here. After the last war, we were too proud. We insisted, with some coaxing from the Overlord, that the angels leave us alone to care for ourselves. We thought we were smart enough and capable enough to manage on our own. Obviously, we were wrong," Outoo shook his head as he thought back to the past.

"But when we free Wyndle, we can get them to come back and help us!" Tye became very excited at this thought. He was always quick to jump to the conclusion that the realm was on the verge of becoming free from the evil that grasped it.

Outoo frowned. "If they will listen, yes. Perhaps they could help us. Perhaps this war could have been prevented in the first place had we not been so ignorant." They reached Outoo's tent and found that Gusseus had just finished packing it up.

"I didna wanna disturb ya laddies so I packed our stuff up meself," Gusseus said in his usual jolly tone. "As soon as Ayku and Eldin be done packin' we can get a-movin'," he pointed to their friends, who were having a problem with their entangled tent.

"I really don't think it's as hard as you're making it out to be, Eldin," Ayku said in an annoyed tone. "Just grab those two corners and walk toward me." Ayku sounded like a mother teaching her child how to fold for the first time.

Eldin flung one of the corners up in the air and sent a backpack flying through the air, its contents spilling out on the ground as it landed. "It wouldn't have been so tangled if that witch didn't collapse it in on us," he snapped back angrily. He looked over at Aldara, who was drawing a circle in the grass with a stick. Inside the circle was nothing but her and Ali-Mimi. Curious, Eldin grabbed both corners of the cloth and walked quickly toward Ayku, handing it to her. "I'm going to see what she's up to," he said, setting out on his new mission.

"Oh leave her alone, Eldin," Ayku scolded him, "It's no wonder she knocked the tent in over you." Ayku continued to fold the cloth as she watched Eldin approach Aldara. "Next time, I'm sleeping with someone else," she said under her breath.

"Hey, witch," Eldin scoffed as he approached Aldara. "What are you up to?" he asked her rudely. He saw that she had laid out five rocks in the pattern of a pentagram and had just finished tracing an invisible circle with her stick around it. He watched as she sat down quietly in the center of the circle, legs crossed, with Ali-Mimi sitting in front of her and staring blankly at her.

She turned to him and let out a heavy sigh, letting him know just how much he was bothering her, and that right now she would not stand for it. "Go away, human. Do not cross into the circle or I'll turn you into a toad." Aldara's eyebrows were slanted inward and her eyes were narrowed as she tried as hard as she could to make herself appear threatening. It seemed to have worked.

"Yeah," Eldin lowered his voice and took a few steps back. "Right. Whatever." He wasn't sure if she had a spell to actually do it, but from what he had seen in the last battle, he wasn't about to tempt her. He walked backward, never taking his eyes from Aldara, and backed into Ayku.

"Ow!" she exclaimed as he trod on her foot, "Watch where you're goin', you oaf!" She pushed him off of her foot and slapped him in the back.

Eldin turned to face her and saw everyone had gathered together. "Sorry there, girly," he apologized in his usual Eldin way, "What's she doing anyway? We should stop her. She may be trying to cast a spell to kill us all."

Outoo glanced at Eldin and then turned his attention back to Aldara. "How did you ever live long enough to achieve your current age, human?" He realized how rude it must have sounded and raised his hand in apology. Outoo knew that humans were nothing more than roamers who knew virtually nothing in the ways of magic. "She is bonding with her little friend. He is to be her familiar," he explained as he put his hand down at his side. "There is no need for fear."

Aldara looked out of the corner of her eye and smiled. It took everything she had not to burst into laughter about the scared look on Eldin's face when she threatened to turn him into a tiny amphibious creature. That was the oldest line an elf could use on a human. Apparently, it still worked.

Ali-Mimi sat calmly in front of her, saying nothing. He watched and waited until the smile disappeared from her lips. Aldara's posture became stiff and her eyes rolled back in her head. She put her hands in front of her, palms together with fingers pointing to the sky. She closed her eyes and chanted to herself. The others tried to hear her words but they were spoken too softly for anyone to hear but her and Ali-Mimi.

The invisible circle that she had traced earlier began to illuminate a soft whitish blue that grew in intensity. The five stones that outlined the points of a star also started to glow. They soon became a brilliant fluorescent white and no longer resembled mere stones of the earth.

The two sat inside the glowing circle of light, not moving for a few moments. Then suddenly and silently, Ali-Mimi stood up on his hind legs like he was begging for a treat. He took a step closer to Aldara, his legs never faltering. His face was now only a lock of hair from hers. Aldara stopped chanting and opened her eyes. She was no longer aware of life outside her magic circle, unaware of the battle that raged on throughout the land or of her group of friends looking on with amazement as she merged her being with her strange and tiny friend. All that was everything to her at that moment was in the circle. She looked deep into Ali-Mimi's eyes. She looked through the windows to his soul, into the core of his being. He offered her the same look in return, his eyes widening as he did so.

They sat in silence for several moments. Eldin nudged Outoo while keeping an eye on Aldara. "They haven't moved in quite a while," he observed. "What are they doing now?"

Ayku sank her elbow into Eldin's stomach to shush him. Having glamour of her own and the power over light, Ayku was no stranger to magic; she knew that certain spells took time. She was enjoying the show Aldara was giving them and she was pleasantly surprised that she was letting them all watch. Perhaps this was Aldara's way of opening up and extending the hand of friendship. Maybe she wasn't just bonding with Ali-Mimi—maybe she was bonding with the rest of her friends as well.

The silence lasted a few moments more and then Aldara broke it. "Yes," she said to Ali-Mimi, never taking her eyes from his. "I can hear you." Ali-Mimi's voice was loud in her mind, but silent to the outside world. The first link had been established.

"Me hear you too. Loud and clear I do," Ali said aloud. The two now possessed the power to communicate at will via telepathy. Their thoughts were still their own but when they needed or wanted, they could now carry on full conversations without anyone else knowing.

They sat in silence a few moments more until suddenly Aldara gasped and sat back. Ali-Mimi followed her jolt with one of his own. Their eyes never leaving each other, they continued to stare. Aldara's eyes widened as she became completely immersed in Ali-Mimi's being. She saw the darkness of his pupils and the golden color of his eyes was brilliant as she stared into them. Her vision began to twist. She saw a fleshy oval appear and start to work its way into focus. The oval took on a form. It was a face—her face. She could now see herself, through what seemed to be a fish-eye lens, in full detail. The gray streak of hair hanging to the right side of her face and the nose ring capturing the fluorescent white light of the circle told her, without a doubt, that the bond was almost complete. She could now see what Ali-Mimi saw. She closed her eyes, her sight returning back to its own view, and prepared for the final phase of the joining.

Ali-Mimi sat and watched Aldara slowly reach for her right arm. She dug her nails into her arm and a small drop of blood appeared. Ali-Mimi let out a yelp and winced in pain. The two continued to stare into each other's eyes. Ali-Mimi slowly lowered his front paws to the ground and tilted his head up slightly to keep his gaze into her eyes. He took his paw and extended its claws, then scratched his left front leg. Aldara let out a brief cry of pain and a tear formed in her eye. It glowed in the light of their magic and slowly ran down her cheek. The tear worked its way to the edge of her chin and dropped off. It found its way to the top of Ali-Mimi's head. With that, the spell was complete. The two were now one.

Aldara blinked and Ali-Mimi licked his fresh wound. She

watched him as the stones dimmed and the lighted circle went dark. "The circle is broken, we have met, we will part, we will meet again," she spoke aloud as she stood up and retraced the circle.

Ali-Mimi hopped over to the water bowl and began to drink thirstily from it while Aldara scattered the stones of the circle. Her friends approached her. All of them were cautious except for Outoo.

"I am proud of you, young Aldara," he said to her. "It is clear that you have mastered the light arts, and at such an early age." He paused for a moment while she finished dispersing the stones, "And you are well on your way to increasing your knowledge of the dark arts as well, most impressive. You are accomplishing that which has not been done since the time of the ancients. I applaud you. Hopefully you will be able to master them soon and then you can…" Outoo quickly trailed off pretending that he accidentally stubbed his toe on a nearby rock jutting out of the ground. He looked at Tye, silently asking for help in changing the topic of conversation.

"Okay everyone, let's get our packs on and untie the horses. We've been in one spot too long." Tye had caught on to what Outoo was trying to do and he gave the elder a smile.

The group walked back to their belongings, secured their weapons to their belts, and slipped backpacks over their shoulders. Ayku walked over to Tye and checked his bandage. "This looks okay. The heat of that energy dart seared the wound. Aside from it stinging, you'll be fine," she smiled at him and gently patted him on the cheek.

Aldara grabbed Outoo as he started to walk away and pulled him in close. "I know Tye told you what happened to me last night." She looked at him with a very serious look on her face. "Is there any help for me?" She paused, then asked, "What do you intend to do?"

Outoo looked at her with sad eyes, then shot a glance at Ali-Mimi lapping up the rest of the water from the bowl. "Perhaps you have just helped yourself," he said to her. "You now share your mind with that creature. Your two souls are now one for life. The Queen may not be able to control you so easily now." He saw a gleam of hope appear on Aldara's face. "As for my intentions, the rest of the group need not know. You already scare the human. There's no telling what he'll do if he finds out the Queen owns part of you. I intend to watch you closely," he narrowed his eyes at her.

"Outoo," started Aldara, "If the time comes when I would become a threat to the group or our mission…" She looked at him, hoping she wouldn't have to finish the rest of the sentence.

Outoo nodded. "I will do as needed," he said reassuringly. He kept his face warm and sincerely hoped it would not come to that. He squeezed her shoulder gently. "Come on, let's get on our horses and resume our quest."

Aldara nodded her head in agreement. "Outoo," she started as he turned and looked at her. "Thank you." He smiled and walked away from her to rejoin his friends.

Ali-Mimi ran up to Aldara and began filling her head with telepathic conversation. His thoughts were almost overwhelming.

"That's all the water we've got. You're going to have to wait until we come across another stream. We've gotta go now." She then replied to him aloud as he looked at her in silence, again filling her head with chatter, "I said no. It's too risky for us to stay any longer."

Ali-Mimi put his back up and walked over to Aldara's horse. Aldara followed him and thanked Tye for untying her steed. "And will you please stop talking to me in my head? I've spent enough time talking to myself. Speak aloud unless we have a need for it otherwise. Okay?" she asked Ali-Mimi as she climbed on to her horse.

"Boy, you want everything your way. Okay, Ally, ok for now," he replied as he leaped from the ground to her shoulders.

Aldara secured her staff to the side of her saddle, and mounted her horse. She looked around at her friends and saw that they were all ready to go. Tye was riding with Ayku on his shoulder, as always. Gusseus and Outoo shared a horse and Eldin rode by himself. She gave them a nod and smacked the reins down on her horse while nudging it in its side. The others followed and they continued their journey toward the deadened forest of Glinfel. More confident than the night before, but more afraid than ever, Aldara cleared her mind of its chaos and focused on self-control. The days ahead would be the most trying of her life and she needed all the control she could muster. That, along with the help of her newly bonded familiar and her small group of friends, may allow her to break free of the sinister hold Queen Valeria had over her.

Chapter X

—◈◈◈—

Hidden Agendas

"Faster!" The words erupted from Ayku's lips as she frantically held on to Tye's collar. The tiny fairie couldn't take the chance of letting go and flying on her own. At the speed her friends were now galloping, she wasn't sure if she could keep up with them. Her blonde hair whipped across her face as they desperately tried to escape their dreaded Dracal pursuer.

The red Dracal swooped toward Tye's horse and extended its claws, but curiously enough, refrained from discharging its fiery breath. Its glowing eyes fixed on its target, the humanoid dragon acted as if the rest of the renegades weren't even there. Tye was its world now, and the Dracal would stop at nothing to get him.

"Hang on, Ayku!" Tye yelled to her. He reached to the side of his belt and pulled out one of his throwing knives. He held it steady in his right hand while holding the horse's reins in his left. With every muscle he had, he tightened his grip around the knife…he could do nothing but wait for the Dracal to strike.

Ayku, however, didn't have to wait quite that long. As the Dracal neared, she flipped her hair out of her face and threw her hand into the air. She instantly grew in size and her hand pulsated rapidly with a bright white light. She waved her hand at the Dracal as if she were smacking it across the face, and a brilliant beam of light struck its eyes.

The Dracal thrashed its head blindly from side to side and swung at Tye. Its claws dug into Tye's shirt at his shoulder and tore the fabric. Crimson streams of blood poured down Tye's arm as he thrust his knife into the creature's soft underbelly. The beast cried out in pain as it passed him, failing to grab the young elf; it felt strange, new burning sensations dance all over its body. It turned to its left just as Aldara pointed her staff at it, shooting beam after beam of electrical energy. Hitting it only once was enough to momentarily divert its attention from Tye. The energy bolts did little damage to the creature itself, as most of the energy was absorbed by the Dracal's thick, scaly armor.

Still not seeing clearly after Ayku's blast of light, the Dracal took a quick, yet deep, breath and exhaled a ball of fire from its gaping mouth. The fiery ball was expelled clumsily toward Aldara. She threw her body to one side to avoid the flaming breath and lost her balance on the horse. She fell to the ground with a hard thud, the momentum of the horse causing her to roll several times in the dirt.

Eldin drew his sword as he halted his horse and turned around. The others did the same, drawing weapons and readying themselves for battle. Outoo watched the beast spiral upward into the air with great curiosity. As the Dracal reached the top of its spiraling retreat, it looked down at Aldara, then focused its attention back on Tye. Suddenly, it began to dart out of the air, heading full force at Tye, its claws once again extended and its face devoid of any expression.

Gusseus waited for the right moment to strike. Just when the Dracal was a short distance from his son, he hurled his battle axe through the air. It quickly sped, end over end, toward the creature's soft underside. The creature arched its back in pain as the axe drove deep into its chest.

Eldin saw his opportunity and dug his heels into his horse's side. The horse sped to the Dracal's position and Eldin swung his long sword at the beast, striking it in the neck. The sharp blade penetrated the Dracal's armor and sank in deep. The Dracal flung its head to the side, causing Eldin to lose his grip on the weapon. The Dracal's leathery wings flapped wildly to keep itself in the air, but it soon began to lose its balance and it fell to the ground, its arms slowly moving, trying in vain to reach for Tye.

Outoo rode his horse up to the Dracal, silently watching it writhe in agony. Doing nothing to end its suffering, he watched as the Dracal's arms fell to its sides and the yellow glow disappeared from its eyes, the glow replaced with a black void. At last, the beast was dead. Outoo raised an eyebrow at the Dracal's lifeless body. He had never seen one die this close to him before. He had, however, seen full sized dragons die in the days of the Great War, and it was nothing like this. This Dracal had shown no sense of self-preservation or awareness. It seemed that all that it had lived and breathed for was the light elf. Lost in his curiosity, he turned to Tye, who was clutching his arm. "Are you all right, my young friend?" he asked.

"Yeah, I'm fine," Tye replied through clenched teeth, trying to hold back the pain. "I'll be okay once I bandage it up. It's just a scratch, really." He knew that the others, especially Gusseus, would not buy his story. A scratch it may be, but it had been made with razor sharp claws and needed attention immediately.

"I'm okay," Aldara said as Ayku helped her up off the ground. "Just a few bruises," she added as she dusted herself off. She looked over and saw Tye dismounting his horse with Eldin's help. "Go help Tye, he needs it more than I do," she said to Ayku.

Ayku nodded to Aldara and sprinted over to her best friend. His blood-soaked shirt was more than enough to tell her it was more than a mere scratch—his wound needed attention right away. She carefully slid Tye's backpack down his good arm and opened it up. "I'm sure that old woman said she had put some bandages and stuff in these bags," she thought out loud as she threw the contents of Tye's pack on the ground. Sure enough, she found them.

"Hold on there, honey," started Eldin, "If we're going to stop and rest and patch junior up, we'd better get off the road here. There's no telling who's gonna come by."

"No!" Tye winced through his pain. "I don't wanna slow the group down!" He clenched his teeth and grabbed hold of his arm. "Help me out with the bandages and let's keep going."

Ayku shot a look at Gusseus and when he nodded, she wrapped Tye's arm in the cloth bandages. "Times like this, I really wish Wyndle were here," she sighed as she looked into her wounded love's eyes. "Are you sure you don't need to rest before we start up again?"

"Aye," Gusseus replied as he nodded a thank you to Aldara for retrieving his battle axe. "Tha lad's right, I'm afraid. There never be just one Dracal. There's sher ta be more where he came from. We gotta be gettin' out o' here as quick as we can."

Outoo trotted his horse to the side of the road, stopping near the lifeless body of the Dracal warrior. Its shiny red scales were now covered with blood. His gaze fell upon the cold blackness of its once glowing eyes. He prodded the beast's carcass with his staff. "This was not the death of a dragon," he stated with conviction. "They have never died in this fashion before. I feel as if there's something more sinister going on here than any of us could imagine. We must rescue your angel friend before it is too late." He gave Aldara a sympathetic look and continued, "For us all."

Eldin raised his head and looked past the rolling hills. The windy dirt road on which they were traveling seemed to go on forever. He saw that Ayku had almost finished tending to Tye's wound. "Hey, witch," he called, his focus falling upon Aldara, who was climbing back onto her horse. "How much farther is Under Hollow?" The tone of his voice was one of annoyance. Eldin had no quarrels with showing Aldara his disrespect of her very existence.

Already used to his condescending attitude, she answered calmly and politely, as if Gusseus or Outoo had asked his question. "The entrance to Under Hollow is on the far side of the deadened forest of Glinfel. The forest itself is about a day away. We have traveled a considerable distance, human. No doubt all of this looks unfamiliar to you, a creature with your limited resources." Aldara loved to talk down to Eldin, and she loved it even more when she got the chance to embarrass him, especially in front of the whole group.

"Yes. From what I remember, Under Hollow is a total of about two sunrises away." Outoo stepped in and offered his knowledge of the land. "But we had best leave this road as quickly as possible." He raised his staff and pointed to the east. "Over these hills marks the beginning of the Crystal Fields, which are full of gemstones."

"Gems?" Eldin interrupted. The thought of making a little money during the adventure suddenly piqued his interest. "What kind of gems, old man?"

A sigh came from Outoo's lips, followed by a frown. "These gems are worthless to you, my young friend. They are strange crystals that grow from the ground. They seem to absorb the sun's light, storing some of it and reflecting the rest. It is almost blinding by day and still glows brightly after nightfall. The dark elves do not travel through the land because of it." A smile appeared on Outoo's lips. "They also believe that the land was blessed, or rather cursed, by the God of the Sun."

"Sounds like the perfect place to continue on," Tye said gratefully as he climbed back on his horse with Ayku's help. Tye smiled at her for tending his wound and trying to help him get back on his horse. After a brief struggle, he managed to throw his leg over his steed, ready to journey with the rest of the group. "I, for one, could do without any more surprise Dracal attacks for a while." He looked down at his arm, saw that his bandages were already soaked red with blood, and let out a gasp of pain. "I just hope I can hold together long enough to get into Under Hollow," he winced.

"Indeed, we should be safe there," Outoo said. "At least from the Dracal anyway." With that, Outoo nudged the side of his horse and it moved forward toward the Crystal Fields. "Once we are safely inside the field, we will rest so you can change the dressings on your wound. We will also take some time to gather our strength. Being this close to Glinfel, it will most likely be the last chance we will have to rest before we reach the Queen's castle in Under Hollow."

****

A stream of hot breath escaped Fenrik's lips as he slowly opened his eyes. Meditation was a favorite pastime of the dark elven race, at times enjoyed for itself, but often necessary to re-focus their minds and re-channel their magical energy. Without performing this ritual of deep thought and reflection, their powers would be rendered nonexistent. It was for that very reason, long ago, that the race of the elves split apart. The light elves chose to commune with nature and to celebrate life by living each moment to the fullest, rather than giving up half of their days immersed in meditation to control the elements and bend them for their own selfish needs.

The amount of time spent meditating varied, depending on the difficulty of the spell to be cast. Fenrik had been in this particular relaxed state for approximately ten hours, but now he was coming out of it. His eyelids flickered, and he was soon staring blankly at the ceiling as if paralyzed. Slowly, he returned to the world around him; he moved his fingers and his toes and carefully sat up in bed. He reached for his nightstand, slapping it harshly in search of his spectacles. Finding them, he placed them on the end of his nose, took a deep breath, and let it out with a groan. He was now ready to start the evening he had planned, the one for which he had yearned for so long. He leaned his body forward and to the side and grabbed hold of his staff. He leaned into it and used the heavy wooden stick to help him out of bed.

Once on his feet, he shuffled to a small table across the room. He rested the staff against one of its chairs and poured himself a cup of water from a fine silver pitcher. The water sparkled as it flowed into a matching cup.

Setting the pitcher back down on the table, he took the cup into both hands. He raised it to his lips and paused. A faint smile appeared on his lips as he watched his old reflection dance among the tiny waves inside. Time was visiting him like an old friend—not in a threatening way, but with a kind and gentle demeanor. It was reminding him how fortunate he was, not only to have lived a long life, but also to be surrounded with all the wealth and luxuries he could ever have wanted. His was the kind of life that all dark elves should lead.

A sour look overcame over his face and he stared into the cup with such hatred that had it been a man, it would have turned to stone from fright. With all his might, he threw the cup across the room. It struck the stone wall with a loud metallic crash and fell to the plush carpet with a deadened thud. The water ran down the wall in unison with a tear that fell from his eye and down his cheek.

He bowed his head and stood there, unmoving, for a few moments. If someone had walked into his room, it would have appeared that Fenrik had merely fallen asleep while standing up.

Suddenly, while keeping his head bowed, he lifted his arms in the air and slowly brought them down, tracing the outline of an invisible hourglass or a figure of a woman, in one fluid motion. A faint whispering issued from his lips and his arms, outstretched, came to a halt at his waist, with his palms facing upward. Once his arms were locked in their new position, a shining prismatic oval of light appeared and levitated above them. Rays of soft pastel colors shot forth from it, flooding his chambers with a soft and delicate hue.

Inside the oval, the soft, petite frame of a young woman appeared. Fenrik raised his head and stared into the vision of beauty he had just created. Her face was thin, hidden by locks of jet-black hair that curled around her cheeks. Her eyes were of deepest blue, nicely complimenting her dark gray skin. A hint of a smile appeared on his face. He closed his eyes and tilted his head back as if to feel her full red lips on his.

Suddenly, his eyes sprang open and his arms fell to his sides. The shining oval flickered and the woman's image wavered. "Enough." He spoke softly, yet sternly, as he waved his hand in the air to dispel the image. Now was not the time to become overwhelmed with emotion. He needed all of his concentration on the here and now if he was going to perform successfully.

Once again, he grabbed hold of the wooden staff and hobbled over to a large wardrobe. Unlike everything else in his chambers, the wardrobe was old and tattered. The corners were chipped and scratches covered its wooden surface. This particular piece of furniture was of great sentimental value, worth more to him than all the other treasures in his quarters.

He gently pulled open its rickety doors and examined the contents within, making sure that everything was exactly where he left it. He knew that nothing he kept in the Queen's castle was private and that the moment he left her castle, Valeria would be searching his room in vain attempts to find something to discredit him in the eyes of his best friend, the Overlord. Fenrik chuckled at the thought of her being so desperate. Did she really think him such a fool as to keep anything that might seem suspicious in her castle? He opened a small drawer within the wardrobe and let out a sigh. Perhaps he was slipping in his old age.

In the drawer was a tiny pin, placed with care on a small violet satin pillow. To anyone's eyes, including the Queen's, it would seem to be a mere pin resting on top of a pillow. But to Fenrik, it was so much more. It was a spell component, a vital ingredient necessary for him to complete a spell—a spell that would be perhaps the most important of his lifetime.

He set his staff against the wardrobe and carefully picked up the tiny pillow with both hands, holding it as if he were holding his own child. He walked to the center of his room and placed the pillow on the ground, making sure the pin was still on top and in its center. He then stood up and pointed his index finger at the floor. He chanted softly as he spun around once, tracing an invisible circle on the floorboards. The large circle encompassed him and his tiny spell component.

"I call on the elements of Sylvanor to serve me, to do my bidding without question and without hesitation. Let this circle be bound and know that I, Fenrik, am your master," he said aloud. The circle remained invisible, but he knew the forces he had just conjured were there. He could sense them.

Knowing that his spell was proceeding successfully, he carried on. He sat inside the circle and faced the pillow with his legs crossed. Focusing his attention on the pin, he began to utter the words of his incantation. The words were spoken just above a whisper. So quietly, in fact, that if anyone had been listening outside his door, they would have been unable to recognize the nature of the spell.

Fenrik sat motionless for at least an hour's time, chanting into the pin, when his wrinkled lips finally stopped moving. He watched as the pin began to glow, softly at first, then with such a brilliance, he was forced to momentarily close his eyes. When he opened them, he saw the pin appearing and disappearing, as if it were phasing in and out of space and time. He looked on with fascination until it came to a stop. It now sat before him just as it had when he first took it out of his wardrobe drawer…at least, that's how it would seem to any other creature.

He reached out and pinched the pin between his thumb and index finger, then opened his left palm. Chanting once again, he plucked his palm with the pin. A shot of light pulsed through the pin and a small dot of blood appeared on the surface of his skin. He pulled the pin out of his flesh and held it up to his face. Satisfied with the amount of blood on it, he carefully returned the pin to its pillow. He smiled as he stood up, and once again, he pointed his index finger at the floor, this time tracing the circle in reverse.

"I unbind this circle and set free the elements that have served me. Go until summoned again." With that, the spell was broken. Fenrik picked up the pillow with a smile. He retrieved his staff, then closed his eyes and sighed as he used it, once again, for support.

As he headed toward the door of his chambers, he looked

down at the pin, now shining a deep crimson. "Now for the blood of the other," he said to himself with a devious smile.

****

Wyndle's eyelids blinked open as she woke from her nap. Sleep was something that she didn't need to do, but there was nothing else for her to do in her timeless prison. At least when she was asleep, she could dream of happier times and happier places. It was the only escape from her dark reality. She had tried every possible means to break free from the Globe of Imprisonment, but to no avail. There was no way out. She was a prisoner of the Queen forever. "No!" she screamed as she leaped forward and struck her fist against the side of the globe. It struck the smooth, transparent wall with a thud, doing nothing more than, once again, bruising her hand. "I will *not* give up. Everything has its weakness. This globe is no different. I will not accept my situation, and I will not give in to the Queen's demands," she said aloud as she struck the wall again. "Valeria will die of old age before she gets anything out of me." Wyndle was quite aware that she was talking to herself. It was the only way she could maintain her sanity.

She grazed her hand over her fist and in an instant, healed her bruises. While rubbing her knuckles, her thoughts drifted once again to her friends. Hopefully, they were safely beyond the Breathing Forest by now, and in the care of the people of Solaris Arbor. If that were so, the forces the Queen had sent out to capture Tye would not be able to touch him. Even Commander Zelgot's clever Captain of the Guard would not be able to breach the living forest. What would the Queen do with her then? Would she sacrifice her to the Moon Goddess during the following night's eclipse? Or would she hand her over to the Overlord?

The latter thought made her tilt her head to the side. She had not seen the Overlord since she was brought down under the forest of Glinfel to Under Hollow. Surely, if he knew the Queen had captured a Winged Angel, he would have been the first to question her. Wyndle sneered as she thought about it. Maybe he *didn't* know she was here. Perhaps the Queen was saving her as a surprise, a gift on the night of their beloved Moon Festival.

If the Overlord wasn't in Under Hollow, where was he? Filling her mind with questions was her only escape when she was awake. If there was one good thing about being imprisoned, it was that it gave her time to reflect and try to solve the mysterious puzzle of the dark elves. It was obvious that the Overlord never fulfilled his promise to slay the great dragons. He must be in their realm, keeping some kind of alliance fueled. *But how was he persuading them to change their form? For that matter, why would the dragons even side with him? Many realms had fallen to them; the world was already theirs for the taking. Why seek an alliance now?*

She channeled all of her thoughts into energy, once again directing it to her fist. She struck the wall of her prison with all of her might, again without result.

"Such a fighting spirit for a creature of peace. Interesting." The words were spoken from the shadows.

Wyndle whipped her head around and saw a silhouetted figure emerge into the soft blue light in the air directly above the Globe of Imprisonment. She could tell it was Fenrik long before he entered the light, recognizing his small stature and his unique hobble. "Well, if it isn't the Overlord's lackey," she said as he approached the globe. He was aware of his reputation throughout the realm, but it was something that he no longer let bother him. She smiled as her next line of insults came to her. "Or are you catering to every whim of Valeria now as well?"

Fenrik grimaced and tapped softly on the small globe. "I can assure you, little one, that I am here of my own accord. I do have agendas of my own." He flashed her a wicked smile and reached into his pocket.

The smile disappeared from Wyndle's lips and she backed up. Fenrik was the only dark elf she feared. She found him far more dangerous than even Valeria. "You have an air of death all about you." She took a step forward as if to examine him. "You are playing with forces you do not or could not fully comprehend, necromancer. The dead should be left alone to rest in peace." A look of surprise came across Fenrik's face. "You may hide your dark art from everyone else, but to me it is obvious."

Fenrik dismissed her with a disgusted look. "I am not here to have my existence judged by a Winged Angel," he said coldly as he opened his right hand and exposed the shining silver pin resting atop the small pillow.

Wyndle backed up again, raised her arms in the air, and assumed a defensive position. "What is that?"

Fenrik did not bother to answer her. He dropped his staff to the floor, where it fell with an echoing thud. He then grabbed hold of the pillow with both hands and silently chanted. An intense bright light shot from the pin; in an instant, it was gone as quick as it had come. The old dark elf continued to chant and the pin disappeared and reappeared several times.

Wyndle's eyes widened and she threw her head from side to side, looking past Fenrik for anyone that could be in the room. Panic overtook her when she realized that even if anyone else was in the room, they surely would not come to her aid.

Fenrik held the pillow in his left hand and carefully pinched the pin with the fingers of his right hand. He moved toward the globe. The pin gently struck the globe with a metallic click, and once again, it phased in and out of space. The globe shimmered as if it were a pool of water struck by a raindrop, and then the pin pierced its surface.

"Do not be afraid, my tiny friend. I have no desire to hurt you," Fenrik stated as Wyndle hurled herself against the far side of the globe. It was a useless attempt to avoid the inevitable. She had nowhere to go. She was completely at the mercy of a necromancer, a person who harnessed his power through the life force of others.

The pin approached her and poked her gently in the arm. Wyndle let out a short scream as a trail of blood ran down her arm. The blood also covered the small spell component, mixing with Fenrik's blood that remained on it from just moments before. The pin once again burst with light for an instant and Fenrik carefully pulled it out of the globe. The sphere wavered as the tiny instrument was pulled through, then quickly returned to its solid state.

"Thank you, sweet angel," Fenrik said as he cautiously placed the pin back on top of the pillow. "That is all I need from you." He bent down and picked up his staff while holding his treasure as steady as possible.

Wyndle ran her hand down her arm and immediately healed her puncture wound. She held her hand on her newly healed arm and raised her eyes to meet those of her attacker. "What are you going do? What are you up to, necromancer?"

Fenrik snickered. That was his only reply. He need not explain himself to her. He silently held her stare without expression, then turned and hobbled back into the shadows of the room before disappearing through the doorway.

Wyndle watched him leave. She looked down at her arm and then back at the doorway. Whatever Fenrik was up to, she was sure it was nothing but evil. She sat in her spherical confinement, feeling more defeated than ever. Fearing that Sylvanor had finally and completely fallen to the dark elves, she began to weep, for there was nothing else for her to do.

****

The Crystal Fields were almost blinding and Aldara was on the verge of a splitting headache. Her half-breed heritage made her eyes more sensitive to light than those of her friends. She laughed to herself as she thought of all the things she had pilfered since her journey began—her bag, a spell book, an energy staff—and not once had she thought of taking a visor from one of her victims. *You've got to remember to be prepared for any situation*, she reminded herself.

Yes. Good to be ready all time. Bad man pound always, Ali-Mimi scolded her telepathically while his tail moved gracefully through the air and brushed elegantly against her face. "Pretty gems, they no hurt my eyes. You close yours and I steer big horsy thing for rest of day," he offered aloud.

Aldara waved Ali-Mimi's tail out of her face. Although it was nice and useful to have a friend linked to her, she frowned at the thought that her mind was no longer her own. Her shoulders slumped as she remembered that her mind was also shared with Queen Valeria's. How much time would pass before there wouldn't be any of it left for her? She let out a sigh and looked at Ali, who had repositioned himself on her right shoulder. She knew there was a way to block all thoughts from a spell user's familiar and that there was a way to communicate with it only when one desired, but having a familiar was still new to her. She knew it would take time to fully understand and control the joining spell she had cast. "That's okay, Ali. I can see enough to control my horse. I can't wait until nightfall though. The field should still be pretty bright; hopefully, a lot of the glare will be cut down and seeing will be more comfortable for me," she replied out loud to her familiar.

"Indeed," Outoo commented from in front of her without turning to look her in the eye. "The moon will soon rise, bringing a chill to the air but comfort to all of our eyes," his tired voice continued to speak, letting Aldara know that she wasn't alone in her discomfort.

"It sure would be nice to find a resting spot soon so we can stretch," Tye interjected. "My legs have fallen asleep and I'm thirsty."

"Aye," agreed Gusseus as he loosened his grip on the reins and swung his stubby legs up and down in the air. "Me bones be weary too, laddie." It was rare that the two would agree on matters of stamina but this journey had been hard on all of them. They were relieved to realize that the deadened forest of Glinfel was only about an hour's journey away and underneath it lay their final destination: The Queen's castle in Under Hollow.

Outoo's old face cracked a smile when he saw a familiar

sight, a large crystal formation that towered overhead. His thoughts traveled back in time again, to when he was a boy. He had rested here with his friends, hiding among the crystals to escape their foes, the dragons, during the last Great War. His mind snapped back to the present. "Just past that large formation is the Lake of Rainbows. We can set up camp there and rest. The lake has some minor healing properties. They won't completely heal your wounds, my young friend, but it will ease the pain of our eyes and minds that these crystals have caused."

"It's so beautiful," Ayku commented as they passed the largest of the crystal formations. The gigantic prism jutted out of the ground, bathing the entire group in a wide array of colors. "What a shame this place is so close to Glinfel. No one has a chance to appreciate it."

"Yes," Outoo agreed as he awkwardly dismounted. "In times long ago, this was a place of great celebration—one of Sylvanor's most sacred places. Lovers would travel here to wed, then return at a later time to give birth to their first child. It was considered of great fortune to celebrate those occasions here." Outoo finished dismounting and the rest of the group followed his lead.

A crashing sound was heard as the group turned around to see Aldara smashing some crystals with her staff. Shards of crystal flew everywhere. A few more whacks with her wooden weapon exposed an arm. It was, for the most part, intact. "Looks like people only come here now to die," she alerted the group.

"What are you talkin' about, witch?" Eldin asked rudely as he marched his horse beside her. His eyes widened as he knelt down at the body. "It's a dark elf," he said, loudly enough for the whole group to hear. He lifted the arm off the ground and examined it for a few moments before letting it drop lifelessly to the ground. "By the looks of it, it's only been here a day or so."

Tye tilted his head skyward, then lowered his gaze to the field of shining crystal. "The sun must make these crystals grow really quick for them to cover that body so fast," his keen eye observed.

"The question is," Aldara started as she leaned against her staff, "what is a dark elf doing dead in a field that they most fear? And so close to their home." It was a valid question that seemed to puzzle everyone…except Outoo.

"I believe I may know the answer," said Outoo mysteriously as he looked past the crystals and on to Glinfel.

Ayku's wings of light began to glow and flicker behind her; she took to the sky and rested her hand on top of the large crystal formation. She scanned the ground and whistled at what she saw. The whistle echoed throughout the field and caused several of the smaller crystals to shatter. "There are more of them. About two dozen or so scattered all around," she informed the group. "And hmm…strange, there's an old structure just by the lake over there." As soon as she finished speaking, she darted toward it. It wasn't a far fly, just minutes from the group's current location.

"What do you make of this, old timer?" Eldin rudely asked Outoo as they headed toward the ruins Ayku had found.

Outoo looked at Eldin and frowned. He hated being addressed as 'old timer', calling out the fact that he was indeed past his prime. It made him sound like he was no longer useful, that he had nothing further to contribute to the welfare of his people or the realm. "It would appear that two and two do not make four in the human race," he replied sharply. Satisfied with his rebuttal and Eldin's answering grumble, Outoo changed the subject to answer the knight's question. "It is clearly obvious that these bodies were put here after death. The dark elves have a strict code of not entering these parts, for fear of being struck down by the forces of light. Even Queen Valeria has been rumored to steer her carriage around them. Something, or someone, hid these bodies here so they would not be discovered."

"Aye," Gusseus twisted his matted, wiry beard. "While ya laddies ponder that one, I'll be makin' my way ta tha lake. I'll be fillin' up flasks ta quench tha beast o' a thirst that has us all by tha throat." With that said, Gusseus made his way to the lake and placed his backpack on the ground. He pulled out two flasks and filled them with the pure cool water, stealing a couple of swigs for himself before refilling them for the group.

The rest of the party reached the ruins just in time to answer the question of what Ayku had found. The dilapidated structure was composed of four stone objects in the ground that stuck out straight into the air, reaching the height of an average elf. They curved inward toward one another, as if to form an outline of an invisible circle. On the northernmost stone was a round indentation, where a sphere or a globe might have rested. The stones were covered with dust and coated with a thin layer of crystal.

Outoo nodded in remembrance of the object in question. "It is an old portal. Long ago, we used these to travel around the realm almost instantly. It was a quicker, much more efficient way of traveling, as many things were in those days. Alas, like so many other objects and ways of life, they were destroyed and forgotten, first by the war with the dragons and now by the perverted and twisted mind of the Overlord."

"We learned about these in school back in Solaris Arbor," Tye said with fascination as he knocked on one of the stones, smashing away the fine crystal skin it had grown.

"Aye. Tha short time ya were in it!" Gusseus scolded in a fatherly tone. He quickly stopped and paused to think about Tye's education. *Would he have learned more back in Solaris Arbor, studying under an elder, than being out in the realm seeing the harsh place the world had become?* Unsure of his answer, he shrugged the question off completely, as if he had never asked himself in the first place. "Here, laddie," he said to Tye while handing him a flask. "I brought ya up some o' that water from tha lake. It'll help heal yer wound and give ya yer strength back."

"Thanks, Guss!" Tye said gratefully as he took the flask and began to drink. He instantly felt a tingle in his arm and he stopped to remove his bandages with haste. His wound had scabbed over and was no longer bleeding. "Not bad," he mumbled. "Not as good a job as Wyndle could do. But at least I'm not gonna bleed to death now." He sent a smile to Ayku, who returned it with her usual grin. That grin could warm the heart of any man…or any boy.

Aldara studied the northernmost stone and traced the embedded circle with her finger. "How do they work, Outoo?" she asked with a smile as Ali-Mimi traced the circle with his paw, following Aldara's lead.

Finishing a sip of the cool lake water, he passed the flask to Aldara as he answered. "The traveler would place his Globe of Direction in the stone. The globe would flash images of the other teleport sites in the realm. When the traveler saw the image of the site he desired, he simply pressed the globe and he would be sent there in an instant."

Aldara handed the flask to Ayku, resting a hand on her bag while Outoo explained the use of the stones. She reached in and caressed the globe inside—the globe Valeria mistakenly thought was broken and of no use. "You mean a globe like—" Aldara's words were cut off when dark shadows were cast from above.

Two Dracal, one red and one blue, were closing in fast. They seemed to have come from nowhere and were already on top of the group. Their large, leathery wings were outstretched as they glided gracefully across the sky. The red Dracal was circling the group while the blue one opened its mouth and shot a bolt of lightning toward the party.

"Guss! Look out!" Tye sprang forward toward Gusseus and the two flew through the air before landing on the ground a few feet away. The lightning bolt had just missed the stout dwarf and instead struck a cluster of crystal formations. The force of the blast was hard and the crystals exploded on impact. The horses let out whinnies of fear and fled from the battlefield, far away to the horizon.

Eldin managed to grab hold of the blue Dracal's foot as it flew near, and he drew his sword with his free hand. He sank his blade into the beast's thick, scaly armor. The brave knight gave the Dracal's foot a quick jerk, which twisted and separated it from its body. The Dracal fell silently to the ground, without any cry of pain.

For the moment, the rest of the group ignored the circling

Dracal and concentrated their efforts on the fallen beast before it could spit another bolt of energy. Ayku flew in and shot a burst of light into its eyes, blinding it. Gusseus was quickly on the beast with his battle axe, hitting the Dracal squarely in the chest. Aldara released her hold on the globe and it dropped to the bottom of her bag. She grabbed her staff and pointed it at the beast. Its crystal tip glowed and a bolt of energy shot from it, landing on the head of their enemy. Even Outoo hit the Dracal with his staff as hard as his old body could. Before the Dracal could draw another breath and defend itself, its head flopped lifelessly to the side and darkness covered its eyes.

Tye was the only member of the group to keep back. He eyed the circling Dracal above and drew an arrow from his quiver. Before he could load his bow, however, the Dracal swooped down and grabbed hold of his shoulders. As quickly as it had descended, it rose back into the sky and toward Glinfel.

"Tye! No!" Gusseus shouted. He threw his battle axe at the Dracal but it was no use; it was already out of range.

Aldara pointed her staff at the Dracal and thought of what might happen if she missed and the energy struck Tye. Deciding that it was a chance she had to take, she squeezed her staff and a bolt of blue light shot forth. It struck the Dracal in the back. The beast wavered but held on to the light elf. Aldara squeezed her staff again but this time the Dracal was out of range. The burst of energy flew forward, then sank to the ground, hitting some of the crystals and exploding them on impact. The sound was deafening as crystal shards flew everywhere.

Ayku shrank her body to a mere one-eighth of its size and

took to the air. "I may not be able to take down the Dracal myself, but I am not going to let Tye be taken by himself. I'll follow them and I'll bring him back to you, Gusseus." The round dwarf nodded to her in agreement, realizing there was no time for further words. "I promise you that." With that, Ayku darted after the Dracal, knowing full well that it was much faster than she, but hoping with all of her might she could fly fast enough to stay on its trail.

Soon, the two flying creatures, one friend and one foe, were out of sight. Aldara walked over to Gusseus and placed her hand reassuringly on his shoulder. "I believe the fairie." She tried to believe her own words, but they wavered as they left her lips.

Gusseus sighed and his shoulders slumped under Aldara's touch. "I can only pray ta tha Gods above that yer right, Aldara. If that Dracal reaches Under Hollow I'm a-fearin' rescuin' both him and Wyndle will be impossible."

"Then come on," Eldin commanded. "Let's start after them." He looked around for their horses but they were nowhere to be seen. He let out a disappointed sigh and shook his head. "All right, we'll go on foot then." After his second command to the group, he started walking toward the deadened forest of Glinfel, the forest in which lay the entrance to Under Hollow. "What about you, old man," he turned to look at Outoo, "can you manage?"

"Worry not for me, human. Worry for your future and the future of the realm," Outoo said dryly as he glanced down at his stamina boots, grateful that they provided him with the energy he needed to keep up with with his young companions. "If we don't get those two back before the Dracal reaches the

Queen, all will be lost. There are too few of us as it is. Our situation may seem grave but we must prevail." He followed Eldin's lead, as did the rest of the group. Gusseus looked up at him, silently thanking him for his words of encouragement. They may not have been much, but it was all the comfort anyone could offer at the moment.

Following behind was Aldara. A tear ran from her eye and Ali-Mimi gently licked it off of her cheek. She was once again filled with guilt. Although it was perhaps the right thing to do at the time, she was responsible for the capture of Wyndle, and because of that, she now felt responsible for the abduction of her best friend. *He can't die, Ali,* she said telepathically to her familiar. *We've got to save him before the Queen gets him. If he goes down to Under Hollow, she will surely kill him without hesitation.* Ali-Mimi let out a soft purr of remorse, settled on her shoulders, and lovingly licked the second tear that leaked from her eyes.

The group pressed on into the sun that was just beginning to set, on to the deadened forest of Glinfel, on into a future that seemed more bleak and uncertain than ever.

Chapter XI

———⟨ဏ⟩———

The Circle of Thirteen

The image of the Overlord's shrouded face twisted and wavered before coming into focus. His large ears caused his hood to tent up on each side and his dark gray chin was jutting out of the shadows his hood made over his face. "Is everything in order for our offering to the Moon Goddess, my Queen?" his voice projected from her Globe of Communication.

"Everything is ready, my love. The festival tomorrow evening will be so grand that it will surely please the Goddess," Valeria smiled into the image of her husband. "I am confident we will receive her blessing for our final assault on Sylvanor." Her black hair framed her face perfectly and the Overlord was reminded of when he first fell in love with her, many years before.

"I regret I can not join you for the festivities in Glinfel," he said solemnly. "There is much work to be completed here. I expect the group of elders I sent back to Solaris Arbor to contact me with an acceptance to my offer any day now. The taking of their land should commence by the end of the week and I want to be ready."

Valeria held the globe tightly in her right hand and walked to the oblong window on the side of the tower wall. From there, she looked down at the courtyard of the castle and out into the forest of Under Hollow. The beauty of the electric blue light shining from the protective domes above as it bathed the foliage of the forest took the Queen's breath away every time she looked at it. It was more beautiful than anything above ground had to offer, but nevertheless, the Queen wanted the domains above. She turned her attention back to the globe with a slightly sunken face. "My sweet, you are our Overlord, our leader, would you not offend the Moon Goddess if you were not here to praise her tomorrow evening?"

"Fear not, Valeria," the Overlord replied in his usual powerful voice. "I will be conducting my own rituals to the Goddess from here. She will acknowledge my thanks; in that I have no doubt."

Valeria knew that when something was wrong, the Overlord's voice took on a tone of overconfidence to mask his true concern. She wrestled with the idea of asking what was bothering him, but she did not want to seem disrespectful. Still, he was her husband and she should be allowed to ask questions about his well-being without sounding like she was questioning his judgment. "My dear husband, you seem troubled. Is there anything wrong? Anything that I can assist you with?" she found the courage to ask him.

The Overlord raised his hands, palms pressed against each other, just under his chin. His fingertips tapped softly against each other. "Thank you for your show of concern, my wife.

There is in fact a slight problem; however, I'm afraid it is something that you cannot aid in. Actually, the main reason for this communication was to summon Fenrik to assist me."

"Fenrik?" the Queen asked with a bitter taste in her mouth. Again, Fenrik was on the mind of the Overlord. His regular reports to his master were bad enough, but what really turned the Queen's stomach was how the old elf had managed to work his way so deeply into the Overlord's master plan. She despised the fact that anyone but she could be so close to her husband and so important to him. She should have to share the glory and power with no one on Sylvanor and yet here she was sharing it—and with a lackey, of all things. "Surely I could assist you just as efficiently as he could, if not more so," she offered.

The Overlord knew of the Queen's intense jealousy toward his old friend. It had always been there and he had grown tired of it long ago. He sat back in his throne and ceased tapping his fingertips. His hands were still poised just below his face and he rested his chin on the tips of his fingers. He sat in silence for a moment, gathering his thoughts. Admitting there was a problem, no matter how slight, was always hard for him to do. But Valeria, the love of his life, shouldn't be kept in the dark about all things. She deserved to know. "It is the Dragon Heart. It seems to be losing some of its power. I need Fenrik here to make some minor adjustments to it." He sighed but continued quickly, once he saw Valeria's lips open to respond. "It is," he interrupted her before she could even begin to speak, "his creation. He knows more about it than anyone. You will see that he comes immediately." His voice took on a sternness that told her it was the end of the discussion.

The Queen bowed her head, letting him know she

understood perfectly. "I will see that he comes to you without delay, Your Majesty." She was fully conscious of when she should address him as her lover and when she should refer to him as her leader. She managed to conjure up a smile and gazed into the globe with a seductive, yet saddened, look upon her face. "I do so miss you, husband."

"And I you, my love." He paused as he took a moment to fall into her eyes and immerse himself in the world of her love. "Soon, the realm will be ours and we will be together again. We will fortify it and make it strong together. With our combined powers, we will then bring down the barrier that surrounds Sylvanor and conquer the lands that fell so long ago to the dragons." He smiled and leaned in closer to his globe. "There will be no one to stand in our way, no one to stop us."

Again, Valeria offered a slight bow in agreement. "I will send Fenrik to you, my sweet," she said in conclusion. She was about to deactivate the Globe of Communication when the Overlord raised a long, bony finger.

"There is one more matter that must be addressed." He saw Valeria's eyebrow rise and knew she would not find what he had to say very palatable. "You will order Zelgot to free all light elf prisoners."

"What?" Valeria snapped, forgetting to whom she was talking for a moment. But that moment was all it took to have the Overlord come down hard on her for her tone.

"The subject is not open for debate. It is necessary for my plans to unfold." The look of puzzlement and disappointment on his Queen's face told him he should offer her a reason for his actions. "As a good faith gesture, I told the elders that all light elves were to be released immediately." He smiled at his own cunning. "We can't very well coexist in this realm when we are holding half of them in labor camps." He noticed that Valeria's look remained a stern one. "It matters not, my Queen. They will return to Solaris Arbor with the traitorous elders I have sent back. They will see I am sincere. Once that happens, they will grant us passage through the Breathing Forest and we will kill them all just the same."

"Yes, My Lord," Valeria agreed as she forced a smile to her lips. It was completely phony, but believable. "May the Goddess of the Moon hold you in her care and protect you until you are safe in my arms." With that, she released her tight grip on the globe and watched the image of the Overlord inside of it fade as the globe turned black. She lowered her arm and took another moment to gaze upon the beauty of her land. She shook her head and turned from the window, tossing the globe carelessly onto a plush, velvet-covered bench near the wall.

"Is something wrong, my Queen?" A familiar voice asked warmly from the doorway of the chamber.

Queen Valeria turned to see Commander Zelgot in the company of two of her elite guards. Her eyes swept over his broad shoulders and square jaw, his young, strong arms and legs. He truly had the body and mind of a natural leader. His efficient use of time and resources had helped organize their Dracal army and take the realm quickly. Their attack was like a hurricane sweeping over the land, taking each province in turn swiftly and without pause. That is, until they got to Solaris Arbor and the barrier of the Breathing Forest. The Overlord's plan for taking the final province was taking too long. Would this delay make her beloved dark race appear to be losing its edge? Valeria had to continue with her own plans for taking the realm. Seeing Zelgot like this in her doorway reassured her of her decision. The strength he was emanating should be continuously displayed to the realm.

"My Lady?" Zelgot asked again while cocking his head slightly to one side. He knew something must be wrong. He could see it in her eyes as she looked him up and down.

"Guards," she spoke at last, "leave us." As her elite guards turned from the doorway, she abruptly stopped them. "Fetch Fenrik for me as quickly as possible." The guards nodded to her and turned back toward the door. "Thank you, my dark brethren." As they left the room, she looked over at Zelgot and then turned toward the window. Within a few steps, she was again looking down at the beauty of Under Hollow.

Zelgot entered the room and closed the wooden door behind him. He walked over to stand by Queen Valeria, put his arm around her shoulder and joined her in observing the land of the dark elves. "Under Hollow truly is a magical place," he said to her in a voice just above a whisper. "No other land in the realm can compare to the beauty of our homeland," he continued.

Valeria turned her head from the window to look at Zelgot. She rolled her shoulder to remove his arm and walked away from him. "But how long will it remain ours?" she asked him, a disgusted tone in her voice.

"Valeria?" Zelgot's raised eyebrow showed her that he was unaware of what she was talking about. It was not like the Queen to worry. She had always been a woman of calm and control, but now there was a look of concern in her eyes. "I don't understand."

"The Overlord has decided to stay on Caliron and not join

us for the Moon Festival," she announced as she waved her hand through the air in disgust. "I fear the Moon Goddess will take offense and not grant us her blessing on our eve of glory." She folded her arms and looked at him, not caring for a response, for she knew what it would be.

Zelgot had never been a religious man. He was one of the few dark elves who relied on his own inner strength, rather than asking it of a being that would never answer him back. He was almost alone in his disbelief in the gods. He possessed no magical ability for which to be thankful. What he had was his own cunning and a tactical mind that had been his since birth, not a gift given by some goddess. He knew this was a rather touchy subject with the Queen and he always tried to choose his words carefully, but whenever he delved into a religious conversation, no matter how hard he tried, he always came across as offensive. "I'm sure everything will be fine, My Lady. Your plan is foolproof, your people resourceful, the Dracal effective. We cannot lose."

"My plan is an alternative. One I am not even supposed to be thinking of carrying out. That, however, is not the issue." She paused. "My husband, the Overlord of all dark elves, is not here. He says he will perform a ritual from Caliron but I fear that isn't good enough. He should be *here*." She paused again, looking thoughtfully at the floor. "Perhaps if he were here more, we would have taken Solaris Arbor already."

Zelgot placed his hands behind his back and paced away from her, thinking about how he could possibly ease the mind of his Queen. Finally, he turned to her. "The Overlord has his hands full with the dragons. His confidence is in you to lead our people to victory. I do wish you would show the same confidence in our people that the Overlord shows my love. Place more faith in your subjects and not all of it in your Moon Goddess."

The Queen's eyes widened. She arched her eyebrow while raising her finger. "I told you never to speak heresy in this castle again, Zelgot," she replied coldly.

Zelgot extended his arms out to his sides and bowed slightly. "I apologize, my sweet. I meant no disrespect by it." He raised his head to see Valeria still looking at him with eyes of anger. He knew she was upset at the Overlord and that he had to be careful not to upset her further. The Overlord was a person she could not touch, but everyone else, including himself, was fair game. "What I meant was," he started, "perhaps the Overlord thought he would leave the offerings and celebrations in the hands of someone whose faith was more solid. Perhaps if he leaves it up to you and your unwavering devotion, we would surely receive the blessing we are asking for." Zelgot's face warmed and the faint hint of a smile appeared on it.

Valeria now raised both eyebrows in unison at the thought of what Zelgot was saying. Maybe his words did have merit. "I hope what you say is true, Zelgot. For us all." She walked to a small table in the room that held a few glasses and a small bottle of wine. She poured the wine into two crystal glasses. Keeping one for herself, she offered the other to her lover, who received it gratefully. "Now, how is the hunt for my light elf going?" she asked him as she raised the glass to her lips and took a sip of the sweet spirit made from Under Hollow's rare Obrae fruits.

"I should be hearing from my Captain of the Guard soon,"

he replied as he swirled the wine in his glass. "Rest assured, my sweet, that the light elf will be in the castle dungeon by the end of the Moon Festival. My captain has yet to fail me."

"Excellent. Then we will finally learn the location of the angels' portal. Once Solaris Arbor has fallen, the angels' realm will be next." She took another sip of wine, savoring its taste in her mouth before swallowing. "I have a personal score to settle with them."

"You…umm." Zelgot gulped his wine, neither savoring it nor appreciating it as the Queen had. "Heard of the Overlord's orders to free all of the light elves from the labor camps?"

"Yes." Valeria finished her wine and set her glass down on the table. Again, she walked to the oblong window and looked down just as a fleet of Dracal marched by. "The Overlord believes that releasing the light elves would show them he is interested in peace among the elven races." She turned from the window. "I believe it will be seen as a sign of weakness. It is a decision that I do not agree with but can do nothing about."

"Agreed," nodded Zelgot. "I have carried out his orders since the first day of this operation without questioning them. He has led us so close to victory, clearly showing the rest of the realm who the superior race is. We must bear in mind that he too has a vision and a master plan for all things to end in our favor." He moved closer to her. "This final phase of his plan does, however, paint a portrait, temporary though it may be, of weakness." A more serious look found its way to his face. "Give your enemy a glimmer of hope, and they will build upon it." He looked at Valeria as she continued to silently look downward. "Are you certain he would not even consider your plan?"

Laughter burst from the Queen's lips and Zelgot was taken aback. She turned to him with a sarcastic smile on her face. "He wanted to hear nothing of it. He had his plan and it was *his* plan. He takes pride in all of this as being his." Her laughter subsided. "Should it fail, he will thank me for having this alternative and then he will finally see me as an equal."

"Ah, I see the two of you are conducting business as closely as usual." Fenrik's voice interrupted. Valeria and Zelgot took a step back from one another when he entered the room. His usual tone of sarcasm was unmistakable and he followed it up with a twisted smile that told Valeria that he would be taking note of what he had seen, possibly to use against her in the near future.

Valeria's lips curled briefly before responding. "Ah, there you are, old man." She took a few more steps away from Zelgot and toward the wine table. "I summoned you a while ago. You must think of a way to motivate those old bones of yours, for I do not like to be kept waiting," the Queen ordered as she reached the table and poured herself another glass of wine.

Fenrik despised the Queen's habit of talking down to him like this, but he did not give her the satisfaction of letting it show. Instead, he smiled at her sarcastically and bowed. "Yes, my Queen. As usual, I will place your requests at the top of my list."

"See that you do," she commanded as she took a large sip of wine. "The Overlord wants to see you right away." Her gaze moved down his old body. "You'd best start walking down to the portal now, if you wish to get there before the Moon Festival," she snickered.

"Did he say why my visit was so urgent?" he asked her on

the way to the door, not expecting an answer from her. To his surprise, he received one.

"It's the Dragon Heart. It is weakened," she said in a stern, professional voice to him. "He needs you to perform some minor adjustments on it." She placed her empty wineglass down on the table and crossed her arms. "I hope your magic isn't getting as weak as your body, Fenrik. If the Dragon Heart fails us, so does your usefulness."

Fenrik was now officially tired of this cat-and-mouse game with the Queen. How dare she comment on his abilities? If it were not for him, the Dragon Heart would not exist and she would not be in the position of power that she held. Perhaps that was another reason why she hated him so. She had *him* to thank for where she was, but whatever the reason, he was now tired of it. He looked Queen Valeria square in the eye, "I can assure you, my magic is as strong as ever." He threw a glance over to Commander Zelgot and then back at the Queen before exiting the room. "I can also assure you that there will be some changes when I get back. I promise you, my Queen." With that, he hobbled out of the room to begin his journey to the portal that would take him to the Overlord.

Zelgot took a few steps toward the Queen and stopped when she held up her hand. "He has made his little threats before, Your Highness," he tried to ease her mind.

"Yes, he has." Her arms still folded, she looked at the door and then back at the Commander. "He is, nevertheless, a danger to both of us. We must be more careful. With his strong ties to my husband, there is no telling what damage he could do. It is best that we not give him any more gossip to feed to the Overlord."

"Agreed," Commander Zelgot answered as he placed a hand on the hilt of his sword to adjust it on his belt. He walked slowly past her and longed to kiss her but he knew that such affairs of the heart would have to wait. "I will check on the progress of my captain as well as the preparations that are being made in Glinfel for the Moon Festival," he told her as he reached the door.

"Zelgot." She stopped him. She stood motionless for a moment, then tapped her hand upon her heart, silently confessing her love for him. "Thank you."

The Commander smiled and he bowed honorably to his Queen and lover. "My pleasure, Your Majesty." He raised his head and flashed her a smile before he disappeared from the doorway to tend to his duties. He would make sure Valeria would have her prize, a young light elf, delivered to her by the Moon Festival.

****

Gusseus twisted his wiry beard, trying to make sense out of what he was looking at. A few hundred feet before him lay the bodies of two dark elves and one Dracal. Lying next to the lifeless bodies was his adopted son, Tye, his head resting in the lap of his best friend and love, Ayku. She was stroking his hair lovingly, with a caring but sad look on her face. Gusseus breathed a sigh of relief as he saw some movement from Tye's legs. "Aye, tha laddie's alive!" he said happily, though still full of worry.

His hand strengthened on the hilt of his battle axe when his eyes moved to the cloaked figure standing over his wounded son. He could peer just enough inside the hood to see that the figure was wearing a dark sun visor. Was it possible for Ayku and Tye to kill all but one of the abductors? He shook his head at his ridiculous thought. Even at full strength, his two friends could not take on such a force. Whatever the case was, there was only one enemy to face now. Gusseus looked out from the side of the large crystal formation that kept him and his friends, who surrounded the dark elf's position, hidden. A nod from each of them was the signal that they were all in place and ready to strike.

Eldin watched from behind his tall, thick crystal as the dark elf placed its hand under its cloak, digging into one of its pockets. The figure brought its hand out from under the cloak, now holding a small vial. Eldin quickly drew his sword and stepped out from behind his crystal barricade. "If you want to live, I would seriously think of dropping that if I were you," he said in a loud, powerful voice.

The cloaked figure turned to him and dropped the vial onto the soft dirt. "I was wondering when you were going to show yourself," a female voice answered from under the hood. "You and your friends have positioned yourselves around me quite well." She glanced around at each of them. "I'm impressed. Quite a good thing I have no intention of running, for I would have nowhere to go."

"Then it looks as if your intention is to stay and die, missy." Eldin took a few steps toward her with his blade in the air.

"Eldin, Stop!" exclaimed Ayku as she raised her head from Tye and focused on her friend, the knight. "She is here to help us. She's the one that killed the Dracal and the other two dark elves," she continued as she nodded her head toward each of the dead bodies.

It was then that the others came out of hiding. Gusseus stepped out with his battle axe still on his belt, confident that Eldin had the situation under control, while Aldara held her staff pointed at the dark elf just in case she had a trick up her sleeve and was too quick for the human. Outoo, being a little more cautious, stood his ground and continued to watch from afar.

The mysterious dark elf was aware of the others approaching but she kept her focus on Eldin. "You have traveled a long way. Frankly, I'm surprised you managed to get this far without being captured." She saw the human's look of confusion as she raised her hands and pulled her hood back.

Eldin's eyes opened wide and he lowered his sword upon recognizing the female dark elf. Her jet-black hair was short and cut around her large elf ears in a bob style. Her bangs hung just past her eyebrows and brushed her visor. She was the most beautiful woman Eldin had ever laid his eyes on. But she was the enemy. Or was she? "You are the dark elf I saw back in Frentier. The one that helped the boy." He lowered his sword further. "The one that told no one we were in the shop after seeing me."

"And you," she replied warmly, "my handsome human, were the one that helped me considerably with your lie about my dark brethren being a traitor." Her words were spoken with a strong, solid voice that was, at the same time, soft and full of gratitude.

The mysterious woman bent down and picked up her small vial. She handed it to Ayku. "This is a healing potion made by one of our finest healers. It will heal your friend's wounds and bring him to consciousness again," she said as Ayku took the tiny vial, opened it, and breathed in an obnoxious aroma. She pulled her face from the vial and gave the female stranger a worried look.

The dark elf smiled. "It is meant to heal, not to entertain the tongue."

Ayku raised Tye's head, parted his lips, and carefully poured the liquid into his mouth. She gently massaged his throat with her delicate fingers to help the liquid work its way down and throughout his body.

"Ayku!" yelled Aldara as she took a few steps closer, still pointing her staff at the dark elf. "What are you doing? We don't know what kind of potion that is! For all we know, it could be poison!" She looked at the stranger with a cold look in her eyes. "We have no reason to trust her."

The dark elf now addressed Aldara. "You are correct, half-breed. You are clever to be cautious, but I assure you, my only intention here is to help."

Aldara's eyes narrowed and she thrust her staff toward the dark elf as if reminding her who was in control and that lying would not be tolerated. "Just who *are* you?" she asked, never taking her eyes off of her prisoner.

"Her name is Ilayna." Outoo finally spoke as he approached the group. He nodded a hello to her and her eyes widened with surprise as she nodded back. "She is a friend." He could tell by her expression that she was not at all happy with Outoo for revealing her name to a group of travelers she didn't know. "It is all right, my dark friend. These are my companions. They were kind enough to allow me to join them in their quest and I was happy to join and help Sylvanor one last time before my body gives way to old age."

Ilayna placed her hands on her hips. "A new quest? What about the last one? Have you succeeded in seeing it to completion?" Her voice was now raised and full of worry, keeping Aldara from becoming comfortable enough to lower her staff.

A sad look came over Outoo's face and he nodded, a nod of agreement and of shame. "Yes. All of the elders' throats have been slit. None of them made it back to Solaris Arbor." When he raised his head, all of his new-found friends were looking at him in a state of shock.

Tye groaned as he regained consciousness. Ayku caressed his cheek and looked up at Outoo with a puzzled look on her face. "Outoo? What are you talking about? You killed your own kind? The council of Solaris Arbor is no more?"

"Traitor!" Eldin yelled as he stepped into Outoo's space, raising his sword. "I knew we shouldn't have brought you along with us! You had us all fooled pretty good, old man."

Outoo looked at his friends and waved his hand at Eldin. "Put down your weapon, my human friend, and allow me to explain." Were all humans as quick to judge as Eldin? Outoo looked at the sour faces on all of his companions and realized that they all had a right to judge him. He had kept them in the dark about his mission and now was the time to enlighten them. They had, after all, proven themselves trustworthy. The old elf took in a deep breath and began to tell the tale of his mission. "The Overlord called for a meeting with the high council of Solaris Arbor. It was to be a meeting of peace talks. Most of the elders gathered outside of the Breathing Forest and were brought to the Queen's castle in Under Hollow. From there, we were taken to a portal and transported to another realm where the Overlord had taken up residence. During the meeting, the Overlord discussed his version of peace, how both races would once again share the land, purified from the outsiders that settled here long ago." Outoo took another deep breath while shaking his head. "The elders were, of course, not foolish enough to believe his story. They did know, however, that the Overlord would one day find a way through the forest to conquer their land. It was not until he offered them positions of power that they began to listen seriously to his terms."

"In short," Ilayna interrupted, realizing that the border of the Crystal Fields and the deadened forest of Glinfel was not the best place to sit and have a lengthy discussion. "The elders sold out the rest of their race in order to save their own lives and hold on to some power. They were to be given positions of authority, keeping watch over labor camps." As she continued, her voice became louder and sharper. She was genuinely sickened by the story she was telling and she wanted to convey her feelings as best as she could among the group. "They were to go back to Solaris Arbor and convince the rest of their people that the Overlord wanted to sign a treaty with them, sharing the land as both elven races had in the past. The Overlord even went so far as to release all of the light elves that were held prisoner as a gesture of good will. Once they allowed the Overload passage through the Breathing Forest, it would have all been over."

"During the journey back to Solaris Arbor," Outoo brought the tale of his mission to its conclusion, "we stopped in the town of Frentier. It was then, while all of us elders were allowed to use the resting facilities, that I slit the throats of my comrades. I did it so their plan could not be carried out. I was caught trying to escape out the window." He paused to let out a small chuckle. "Acting like I was in my youth, old fool that I am. And it was on my journey to most likely be executed that your group found me and rescued me."

"I don't believe it." Tye said as Ayku helped him to his feet. He was dizzy but was gathering his wits about him. He looked over at his shoulder and saw that his wounds were completely healed. He looked around and saw his Dracal captor, dead, and then Ilayna, who smiled briefly at him; it was a warm smile, trying to let the young, disoriented elf know that she was a friend. "The light elves would never do such a thing!" he snapped at Ilayna.

Aldara lowered her staff and offered a look of sympathy. "It's true, Tye. I was there, remember? I was there for the journey from its beginning to just before its last step at the portal. The light elves went to Under Hollow of their own accord. It was then that the Queen pulled me out of line. It's true, I do not know what happened after that, but we have no reason to believe Outoo is lying. Why would he?"

"It pained me to kill the others, my young friend." Outoo said as he placed his hand upon Tye's newly healed shoulder. "Those people were my friends for many years. But you must understand, had I not done so, our home would now be in the hands of the dark elves, to shape it as they saw fit." He was taken aback when Tye jerked his shoulder away to release Outoo's loose grip on him. "It is time that you faced some harsh realities of our people, my young friend. They are not as innocent as you would like to believe. I have spent these months trying to convince them to help the outsiders, but they turned down all of my proposals, turning their backs on the humans, the orcs, the fairies…on everyone in the realm. They sat back and did nothing but hide behind the Breathing Forest while many innocents died at the hands of the Overlord." Outoo's shoulders slumped. "We are a proud race and we have no reason to be."

Tye's eyes filled with tears as he heard the words flow from Outoo's lips. Words that he did not want to hear, words that were so painful they tore at his heart. As much as he hated hearing Outoo's ill words of his people, he knew them to be true. Overwhelmed with emotion, he walked away from the group and sat on a smaller crystal formation with his back to them, pondering the ugly truth of his people.

Ilayna took a step forward and cleared her throat to draw everyone's attention to her and away from Tye. "That brings me to my question. Why are you all so far from Solaris Arbor and so close to Glinfel? Being this close to Under Hollow, you are all asking for nothing but death," she said in a matter-of-fact tone.

Gusseus moved over to Tye and was rubbing his back to help comfort him. He was overcome by a great sense of guilt for not telling his adopted son the truths about his people. If he had, none of this news would have been such a shock to him. He heard Ilayna's question and everyone fell silent. Were they not answering her for fear of what she might do with the news? Gusseus looked at her for a moment, then turned his attention back to where it belonged, on his son. "Aye, I'm sorry, laddie. It was wrong o' me not tellin' ya o' tha faults o' yer people, and fer goin' out o' tha way keepin' it from ya. I shoulda let ya make yer own judgments," he said.

"Yes, you should have, Guss." Tye managed to reply through his tears.

Eldin looked around at the group and then at Ilayna. He remembered when she helped the young boy who fell. He remembered staring into her eyes as she stared into his before turning away. He was taken with her. Dark elf or not, he knew in the pit of his stomach that she was true to her words. "We came here to get our friend back that the Queen took from us," he said at last.

"Eldin!" yelled Aldara, "Don't offer her information about who we are or what we're doing! We don't even know if we can trust her! By the Gods, we don't even know how she knows Outoo! She wasn't there in the carriage." She shook her head. "We don't even know if we can trust *him* anymore." She threw a vicious look Outoo's way before continuing her rant with Eldin. "It's so funny that you still can't trust me, but as soon as you see a woman that triggers your fancy, you're spewing all kinds of information to her!" she snapped.

"Listen, witch." The tone in his voice was that of anger. "She had the opportunity to turn us in when we were in the shop in Frentier, but she didn't. Unlike some people I could mention." His voice dripped with bitterness.

Ilayna raised her hand at Eldin to cut him off. She wanted this conversation to end quickly as it was not a safe place for debates. "I believe I can answer your question and perhaps put some of your fears to rest, half-breed," she said coolly to Aldara. "I know of the friend of which the human speaks. In fact, that is why I am here. Although I have not seen your friend, it is forbidden for anyone to speak with her, except for the Queen. I can tell you that she is alive and refusing to answer the Queen's questions. It is because of her that the Queen sent me out here to capture the young elf. The Queen believes that by torturing him, she will gain the information she needs from your friend."

Aldara leaned against her staff and the smug look remained on her face. "If that's true, then why did you let him go?" she asked while pointing to Tye.

Ilayna sighed and looked over at Outoo. "There is no harm in telling you, because the Queen will find out on her own soon enough." She cautiously looked around the area before continuing. "I befriended Outoo many months ago, when I formed a group known as the Circle of Thirteen. Believe it or not, there are those among us who do not share the Overlord's beliefs and know in our hearts that the genocide he has committed must be stopped. We have been working with Outoo, among others, to help slow down the overtaking of the realm. At first, our numbers were too small to be very effective, but we have grown in size and we will soon be able to make a considerable difference. I had no intention of turning the light elf over to the Queen. She wanted him badly and that was a good enough reason for me not to deliver him." A slight hum and a throbbing glow came from underneath her cloak, cutting her words off. She made no motion toward it it. "That is my Globe of Communication. They are most likely looking for a report on how my hunt is going. I must go back to Under Hollow and give the report that I have failed." She placed her fingers to her mouth and gave a whistle. A few small crystals smashed upon hearing the sound and they saw a horse in the distance galloping toward them. "If you choose to press on to Under Hollow to free your friend, I cannot help you. I cannot compromise my position. My people need me if we are ever going to break free of the Overlord's hold on us."

Tye stood up and turned around, his eyes red from tears, but he now forced them back to put all of his efforts on the here and now. "But we'll need all the help we can get if we're going to free Wyndle. You *have* to help us," he said to her in a harsh voice.

The horse halted next to Ilayna and she mounted it. "I have done all that I can, young light elf. I have freed you and your friend from certain death," she sighed as she grabbed hold of her horse's reins. "I can tell you, however, that the Moon Festival is tonight. The entrance to Under Hollow will be crawling with dark elves in the hope of gaining a blessing from the Moon Goddess. It is a costumed affair, so if you seek entrance to the land of the dark elves, tonight will be your only opportunity. I wish you luck." She nudged her horse and it trotted away.

"Wait!" yelled Ayku. The fairie darted toward the horse. She hovered in the air until Ilayna had brought her ride to a stop. "I want to go with you into Under Hollow and the Queen's castle. We have no map of the castle and my friends are going to need a guide to find where they are holding Wyndle." In an instant, Ayku shrank to a fraction of her size. "You can keep me in your pocket. No one will know," she pleaded to Ilayna.

"Ayku, no!" Tye interjected. "It's too risky! I won't let you do it. If you're discovered, they'll kill you!" He looked at Ilayna and begged her with his eyes to confirm what he was saying.

She understood Tye's look of desperation. "It is true. If you are spotted, they will kill you without ever asking you a single question," Ilayna told Ayku coldly.

"It's a risk I'm willing to take," Ayku replied bravely. She turned around and looked at Gusseus, who was generally considered the group's leader. They trusted him the most and respected his opinion on all things. This was good, for he gave it often. "Guss?"

Gusseus let out a heavy sigh and reached up to pat Tye on the back. "Aye, I'm afraid she be right, laddie. We'll be needin' a way o' gettin' out. We canna roam tha halls o' tha Queen's castle not knowin' where we be goin'. As much as I hate ta say it, we gotta be lettin' her go."

"Thank you," Ayku said gratefully. She flew in front of Tye and hovered in front of his face, hoping that he would give her his blessing. "Tye?"

He looked at her as if he were looking upon her for the last time. "I…I'm just afraid I'm gonna lose you," he confessed, as his youthful eyes teared up again.

She gently kissed him on the cheek with her tiny lips. "You won't. I love you too much to let the gods separate me from you," she confessed for the first time. She was surprised Tye didn't blush.

"We must hurry, then. It is too dangerous to stay here any longer," Ilayna said to Ayku as she opened a pocket on her cloak. "I will do what I can to watch over her, but I can promise nothing," she told the others. "Keep heading southeast. On foot, you should reach the entrance to Under Hollow by evening. The forest should be clear of dark elf activity, for it will be concentrated at the mouth of the entrance preparing for the celebration."

The group nodded in unison and Ayku flew into the pocket of their new-found ally. She waved at her friends and blew a kiss to Tye as Ilayna kicked her horse to gallop toward Under Hollow. Within moments, the horse was nothing more than a dot on the horizon, covered in the misty fog that blanketed Glinfel.

Eldin put his sword back in its sheath and removed Tye's bow and arrow from his shoulders. "Looks like this crazy rescue might actually work, if the fairie can manage to stay alive long enough to help us find the angel," he said as he handed Tye his belongings.

Tye grabbed them rudely out of Eldin's hands and strapped them around his shoulders. "She'll be fine," he spat at him.

"Easy, junior." Eldin put his hands up in a mocking defensive position. "I'm sure she'll be okay. She's in good company." His sentence trailed off as he looked back at the horizon to where Ilayna had ridden off.

Aldara looked at him in disgust. How could Eldin, the most non-trustworthy of people, fall for a dark elf? Were all human males that weak when it came to objects of beauty? She scoffed at his weakness and found him more pathetic than she ever had. "Unbelievable," she said to him. Then she walked over to Tye and lightly pushed on his back. "C'mon. Let's go get our friends back."

Chapter XII

——◦◦◦◦——

Festival of the Moon

The heavy charcoal smear started at Valeria's eyebrow, curved around her cheek, and ended below her lips. She tilted her head slightly to the side to admire her artistry in the looking glass. Pleased with what she saw, she smiled and continued to stare at her reflection. Tonight was the night she had been waiting for. She had always had a deep belief in and respect for the Moon Goddess, and now was her chance to demonstrate it to the Goddess herself.

Suddenly, the image of a young dark elf appeared behind her in the mirror; the elf was accompanied by two of her royal guards. It was Malsang, one of Under Hollow's finest clerics, a healer who skills were matched by few. Valeria had always secretly been jealous of the cleric's way of life; they had a stronger connection with the Moon Goddess—something Valeria ached to possess. But the calling of a healer had never come to her. Nevertheless, she was blessed with a strong magical ability all of her own. She had an especially strong respect for Malsang, as young as he was with such power at his command. Respect that would shatter in an instant if she was ever to discover that he was a member of the traitorous Circle of Thirteen.

"The face paint you requested, Your Highness," Malsang said. His voice was soft and caring, truly a healer at heart.

At first, the Queen did not turn to face him. Instead, she examined his reflection in the looking glass before answering. She watched as the torchlight flickered and danced upon his bronze armor, causing his body to shimmer in the light of the flame. His dark gray skin and piercing blue eyes were a deep contrast to his body armor, and that alone let anyone who gazed upon him know that he would also be a formidable opponent in battle. She was still impressed at how he could balance his healing talents and his warrior skills. "Thank you, Malsang," she replied at last. "Place it here on my dresser, please."

The young cleric approached the Queen, followed closely by her royal guards. He placed the tray of face paint where she had indicated. "These are made from the finest berries and plant life in Under Hollow. They will make you look even more radiant for the Moon Goddess, and their medicinal properties include excellent moisturizing properties for your skin," he offered with a smile.

She turned to look him in the eye. "Thank you again, my young cleric. You must share a drink with me this evening during the festival."

Malsang was taken aback, but tried not to let it show. The Queen certainly respected her people, but it was rare that she offered herself socially to them. It seemed to happen more often with the members of the cleric guild than any other. "It would be an honor to drink to the Goddess with you, Your Highness." With that, he bowed. Remaining in the care of her guards, he exited the room.

The Queen looked down at her tray of makeup and dipped her finger into a dark violet paste. She raised the finger and applied the thick, gooey substance to her lips, evenly covering them. It was a most agreeable shade, perfectly complimenting her skin tone.

She dipped her middle finger into another dish of paste. This one was silver, and it glittered in the torchlight. She applied it carefully to her eyelids, making them look like they were covered with hundreds of tiny diamonds. No sooner did she finish applying the glittery substance to her other eyelid than her Globe of Communication began to hum and throb with a soft yellow light. She frowned as she looked at it and quickly wiped her fingers on a damp cloth.

Quickly tossing the cloth on the table, she reached for the globe and squeezed it in her hand. Within moments, Commander Zelgot's image appeared. She smiled at the image of her secret love.

"Forgive my intrusion, Your Highness, but my captain has returned from the surface and I thought you would like to hear her report in person," his muffled voice issued from the globe.

"Excellent. I will meet you in my throne room," she replied.

"As expected." He smiled at her. "I am already there."

The Queen returned his smile. "You know me too well, Zelgot." She released her grip on the globe and stood up. Her royal gown clung to the top of her shapely frame, then flowed freely about her. She placed the globe in her inside pocket and turned from her dressing table. Eagerly awaiting the report from Zelgot's captain, she strode out of her chamber and down the hall to her throne room.

Commander Zelgot was waiting, as promised, at the bottom of the raised dais that bore the throne. He bowed as she entered, remaining lowered as she made her way across the room. Her royal guards took their places behind her seat of power as she sat upon it.

"You may rise, Commander." She disliked being this formal with Zelgot, but it had to be done in the presence of others so as to not give away their true level of intimacy.

Zelgot resumed his normal stance and gazed upon the Queen. Seeing her made up this way took his breath away. "May I say, Your Highness, you look radiant."

Valeria slowly blinked to draw more attention to her glitter-covered eyelids, then thanked him with a smile. "As do you," she commented, gazing at his formal dress uniform.

He was about to thank her when a movement at the doorway caught his eye. He turned to see his captain standing outside the room, waiting to be announced. He motioned toward the door. "May I present my sister and Captain of the Guard, Ilayna."

Ilayna took a deep breath and ran her finger along the top of the pocket in her cloak, making sure that Ayku was deep inside and well-hidden from anyone. She let out her breath and entered the room, bowing immediately to the Queen upon reaching her throne.

"Rise, my child," the Queen instructed Zelgot's sister. Valeria gave her a warm smile as she rose. "It has been too long since our last meeting, Ilayna. How goes the hunt for my young light elf?"

Ilayna took another breath and swallowed. She had plenty of time to think of a reason why she did not have Tye in her custody, but she was still nervous about delivering the news. Would the Queen and her brother buy her story? And would her made-up story avert any suspicion that she was a member of the Circle of Thirteen? "I regret to report that the light elf eluded my grasp, Your Highness," she said as she bowed her head in shame.

The Queen's face tightened as she listened to Ilayna. "How did this happen?" she asked coldly.

Ilayna began to tremble underneath her cloak. If any of that showed, she hoped it would be attributed to the fear of disclosing her defeat, rather than the fear of lying directly to the Queen of Under Hollow. "I came across him and his companions just outside the city of Frentier."

"In which direction were they headed?" interrupted the Queen as she sat forward in her throne. She was gripping its armrests very tightly.

As Ilayna watched the Queen's expression, she immediately realized she should have picked a different location. "They were headed north toward Solaris Arbor. They were not riding the horses they had when they escaped the labor camp." She hoped her lie about the horses would explain why they hadn't covered much ground in the days since they broke free of the labor camp. "At first, they were no match for my forces. Most of the escapees were killed in battle, and the rest retreated."

The Queen raised an eyebrow and looked over to Commander Zelgot. A look of complete dissatisfaction covered her face and she turned her attention back to Ilayna. "You did not go after them?"

Ilayna now unconsciously opened and closed her hands as if to air out the sweat gathering in her palms. "That was where the Circle of Thirteen came in," she answered. She was aware of a report that a member of the Circle had been found and killed in Frentier. "Although it was reported that one of the members was killed in a shop in that town, there were more members on the outskirts. Their attack on us was sheer surprise and the light elf slipped away during the battle."

Queen Valeria's look of disappointment turned into disgust, but she kept her composure as the details of Ilayna's failure unfolded before her. "And what of this Circle of Thirteen?"

Ilayna forced a smile as she continued spinning her web of lies. "It was a tough battle, but in the end, the members of the Circle were vanquished. Only one of their soldiers survived the battle." She looked at the floor. "Sadly, he died during the journey back to Under Hollow."

Commander Zelgot had remained silent during his sister's report to the Queen but now he felt he should step in and play up his sister's victory. "Then the mission was not a total failure," he said to the Queen. Her reply to this declaration was nothing more than an emotionless stare. "The traitors have been swept away. The Overlord will be pleased to hear that you have handled the situation, Your Majesty."

The Queen let out a sigh and sat back in her plush, oversized throne. "This was a failure we could not afford. When the Moon Festival is over, you will continue the hunt for the young light elf." She raised her finger in the air. "And you will not return to Under Hollow without him. Understood?"

Ilayna once again hung her head in shame. She knew she

would not have gotten off so easily if this had not been the first failure in her career. Fortunately for her, her years of service to her brother and the Queen had been flawless. "It is understood, Your Majesty." She raised her head to look upon her Queen. "I will return with the light elf. I promise you."

"See that you do, for that is the only way for you to return. Dismissed." She waved her hand in the air, shot a brief glance at Zelgot, then watched as her subject left the throne room.

"Thank you." Zelgot acknowledged the leniency the Queen had shown to Ilayna.

The Queen looked at him, feeling drained from the news. "Were she not your sister, Zelgot, she would now be living in a labor camp near the swamps, watching the lesser species dig through rock."

Outside the throne room, Ilayna felt a twitching in her pocket. She tapped it lightly, letting Ayku know that now was not the time to come out. The royal guards followed her to a stairwell and watched her descend before returning to their posts. Upon reaching the bottom of the stairwell, Ilayna found a dark corridor and walked briskly down it until she came upon a wooden door. It was unlocked and she opened it swiftly. It was nothing more than a closet that housed cleaning supplies. She looked up and down the hallway, making sure no one was watching her, and entered.

Shutting the door behind her, Ilayna held her pocket open and Ayku poked her head out, making sure the coast was clear before she darted out into the air. She took in several deep breaths of the moist, fresh air and shook her head from side to side. "Ah, much better," she said as she wiped the beads of sweat from her brow. "That was close. Wasn't mentioning the

Circle of Thirteen a bit risky?" While speaking, Ayku summoned her powers of light and dimly lit the closet.

Ilayna shrugged saying, "It was the only out I could think of. As far as being risky…well, if your friends do make it inside the castle, the Queen will know I was lying anyway. I will soon be forced to leave Under Hollow before she learns the truth, for I will surely be put to death. Fortunately, the Circle now has more than its share of members, so it can continue without me."

Ayku could certainly sympathize with Ilayna's banishment. She recalled her conversations with Wyndle and how she had been banished for interfering with the mortals of the realm. How she longed to have more conversations with her friend! She was somewhere in the castle and Ayku had to find her. "Ilayna, where is Wyndle being held?" she asked, biting her lip out of habit.

The young female dark elf folded her arms and shrugged. "Where we just were. In the Queen's throne room. In the far end, opposite the throne, is a long curtain that was put up after your friend was captured. My guess is that Wyndle is trapped behind it. She is almost impossible to get to, I'm afraid. When the Queen is not in her throne room, she gives strict orders to her guards to kill, without question or hesitation, anyone entering the room."

Ayku looked at the ground in thought and then back at Ilayna. "And the room is only guarded by two dark elf guards, right? No Dracal?" she asked. She had trouble believing that the guard on Wyndle was so light.

"That is correct," Ilayna replied. "The Queen likes to limit the Dracal to the courtyard and to their own housing in Under

Hollow. She believes that only dark elves should see the beauty and wonder of the castle. From time to time, some races from up above behold its wonders, but it is always the last thing they ever see…with the exception of your friend, the half-breed."

"On the subject of the Dracal, who or what are they? No one above knows and we need to know and understand what we're up against," Ayku asked. If anyone would know, she thought it would be a dark elf, especially Commander Zelgot's Captain of the Guard.

Ilayna bowed her head, shaking it from side to side, "I don't know exactly." She raised her head to see Ayku's clear disbelief. "But I will tell you what I *do* know. They come from another place, we assume from the realm of the dragons. They enter our realm through a portal—a portal through which only the Queen, Fenrik, and Zelgot occasionally pass through. They visit the Overlord, who, by the way, has not been seen since he and his troops entered the portal. Once in a while, a few dark elves are called upon to assist him. They never return either." Her voice had an annoyed tone in it. Of all the secrets she knew of her people, this one was limited only to those of the highest power in Under Hollow. She had asked her brother several times to clue her in on where they came from, but he always dismissed her. She shook her head before continuing. "Our guess is that they were summoned to help fight against the dragons."

Ayku had a quizzical look, followed by a frown. "But you said only a few dark elves were called upon every once in a while. The Overlord would need a lot more than that if he were going to fight dragons. Just one dragon is enough to level a whole town; a handful of dark elves would be no match for it."

Ilayna nodded in agreement. "Yes, we have thought of that, and that's what doesn't make sense. We have also heard talk, here and there, of something called a 'Dragon Heart'. Given the Overlord's lack of troops, we can only assume that the Dragon Heart was some sort of gift and the Overlord is working with the dragons to take over Sylvanor." She shook her head. "Why? I dunno." Ilayna saw Ayku's mouth open to ask another question, but stopped her before she could get a word out. "Time is precious, Ayku. I will be wanted up above for the eclipse and the Moon Festival. You must find your friend and help the others reach her. I'm afraid that from this point on, I can be little or no help to you."

Ayku nodded. "We are all grateful for your help. It is comforting to know that there are some dark elves who don't share the twisted minds of the Overlord and Valeria." Resuming her tiny size, Ayku sailed down to the crack underneath the door. She began to squeeze through it. It was a tight fit, but she managed to pass underneath it. "Good luck to you up there," Ayku said to her friend.

"And to you, fairie," Ilayna replied as she watched Ayku finish squeezing through the crack and undoubtedly make her way back to the throne room. "Looks like all of us will need it," she commented to herself before opening the door and stepping back out in the hallway.

****

The deadened branches of the forest of Glinfel towered overhead. They looked like skeletal fingers reaching out, hoping to grab hold of those who didn't belong. A shiver caused the hair on the back of Tye's neck to stand on end. "You can *feel* the evil of this place," he commented as he watched the light mist hug the trees as it chilled the bones of the intruders.

"Aye," agreed Gusseus. "It be quite clear we are na' welcomed here." They had been traveling for hours through the deadened forest without seeing a single dark elf or Dracal. For that matter, they hadn't seen any small animals either. He found it strange not to see any elves this close to Under Hollow. The Moon Festival must be bigger than he had previously imagined. They must all be there; otherwise they surely would have encountered someone.

"Look over there, Guss!" Tye interrupted Gusseus's pondering. "There's another one!" Immediately, Tye quickened his pace to examine the newly discovered object. It was a bright blue energy dome that rose out of the ground. Its light was brilliant, giving off an electric blue aura. Tye picked up a stone the size of his fist and hurled it at the dome. A sizzling sound was heard as the stone ricocheted off the energy field and hit him in the leg. With a small yelp, he began to rub his knee.

Eldin burst into laughter at Tye's foolishness. "What makes you think that one is gonna be different than the other fifteen we saw so far, junior?" he asked him through his laughter. "You know, we would have made more ground if you didn't have to stop at each one of those," he remarked snidely.

"You never know if one of them is going to have a weakness or be broken or something," Tye snapped back as he finished rubbing his knee and adjusted his vest. "If we found a broken one, it could be another way into Under Hollow for us."

Aldara stepped up to the dome of light and narrowed her eyes as she looked upon it. "I told you before, even if one were broken, land is a long way down. These domes sit on the ceiling of Under Hollow; only light and water pass through them. Also, Ayku isn't here to use her powers to ease our descent," she informed Tye in her usual know-it-all tone.

"Silence, all of you," Outoo commanded as he raised his hand in the air. "Listen."

The group strained their ears, and in the distance they could hear the faint sound of a drum. It was a constant, steady beat that grew louder as more drums joined in. Soon, the distant air was brought to life by the tribal beats of the dark elves.

"The festival has begun," Outoo announced.

"Look up there!" Tye pointed to the sky.

His companions followed his gaze and watched in awe as the moon turned from its bone white color to a dark crimson. The clouds seemed to separate as the drumming continued, leaving the Moon unmasked and open to watch without disturbance.

"The eclipse is starting," Outoo commented as he adjusted his magical boots. "We must make haste if we are going to seize this opportunity." With that, the group picked up its pace and pressed on, with caution, to the beat of the drums and the entrance to Under Hollow.

****

Queen Valeria's carriage emerged from the cave-like entrance to Under Hollow. It glided gracefully through the immediate circle of festivities before its fiery horses slowed to a complete stop.

Immediately, a small group of dark elves gathered around her carriage; when Commander Zelgot raised a finger into the air, one of them stepped toward the magical transport and cautiously opened its door. The Queen stepped majestically from her carriage and, with the aid of one of her smiling dark elf subjects, planted her feet firmly on the soil of the deadened forest. Her sleek, black royal gown shimmered in the light of the massive bonfire that danced in the middle of the circle, and her eyelids sparkled like the stars themselves. She looked upwards at the eclipsing moon, closed her eyes, and offered a brief, silent prayer to the Moon Goddess.

"You look like a goddess yourself tonight, Your Highness," Zelgot complimented her as he approached. He had to all but scream his words to be heard over the powerful cadence of the drums.

The Queen opened her eyes and mouthed a silent 'Thank you.' She looked around the festival and marveled at how grand her people had made it. The bonfire was massive; it sat in the exact center of the clearing, so as to not catch any of the dead trees on fire. Her fellow dark elves were either wearing costumes or had their faces painted like the Queen's in honor of the Moon Goddess. Barrels of ale were everywhere, as were groups of drunken dark elves dancing near them. Valeria took a deep breath and smiled as the smell of cooking flesh filled her lungs. Here and there, animals were turning on spits while chefs basted them in thick, gooey sauces.

"A glass of wine, Your Highness," a costumed figure offered her. Long, colorful feathers hung from his bronze armor and a huge painted mask covered his face. Its eyes were bulging and golden in color, the exaggerated mouth was painted bright red with its cheeks covered in stars and moons. He saw the Queen's grateful but quizzical look as she took the glass of wine from him. He thought of raising his mask, but remembered the festival was to be anonymous. Everyone's face must be kept either painted or covered, so that all dark elves would be seen as one in the eyes of the Moon Goddess.

"Malsang," she said with a smile. "It is hard to tell who is who underneath all these outrageous costumes. Be it not for the familiarity of your voice, I would not have known it was you." She took a sip of wine and continued to eye his disguise. "I commend you on your costume. It is obvious you have taken great time and care in creating it. The Moon Goddess will be most pleased."

"It pales in comparison to your beauty, my Queen," he returned the compliment.

"And what is it that you are wishing of the Moon Goddess, may I ask?" Valeria asked him.

Malsang thought for a moment, then responded, "The same as we all wish, Your Highness. Swift and total victory over Sylvanor." He saw the Queen smile and nod in approval of his response. Before he could say more, he was whisked away in the flurry of his dancing comrades.

The twanging of mandolins combined with the sound of various wind instruments. Underneath the light sound of the wind instruments, the dark, heavy beat of the drums could still be heard. From the thumping of the drums, a chant was born. It picked up in tempo and soon, hundreds of dark elves were dancing around the blazing bonfire.

Queen Valeria looked at her glass of wine. She saw the small bubbles rising slowly to its surface and looked through the glass at the dance that was going on. She smiled and raised the glass to her lips, emptying it in one gulp. She carelessly tossed the glass behind her and turned to Zelgot. "This is a celebration to be enjoyed to its fullest," she said to him with a smile. "More wine!" she shouted as she joined hands with a few dark elf children and danced with them in a small circle.

Tye and his friends looked on as they settled beside a near-by energy dome. Protected by its brilliant light, they were virtually safe there because of the dark elves' poor light vision. "Looks like a pretty good party," Tye commented. He looked over at a figure covered in various animal skins with a small feather-covered mask who was tuning some of the wind instruments away from the center of the celebration. He smiled at Eldin, "I wonder if anyone can join in?"

Eldin smiled back but grabbed hold of Tye's arm. "Hold on there, junior. We can't risk splitting up and getting lost now. We've gotta stick together until we get inside Under Hollow," he insisted.

"Wait a moment." Aldara leaned in close to the two, at which point she felt a little silly; there was, after all, no need for her to lower her voice because none of them could possibly be heard over the loud music and cheering. "If we are all going to get costumes, we're going to need a good distraction. We'll have to divert most of their attention to one area. I suggest livening up the band. That just might do the trick," she said with a wink to Tye.

"What a great idea, Aldara!" he replied playfully. "This music is flat anyway. I'll show 'em how real music is played!" He grabbed his flute, then paused. He looked over at Gusseus, his beloved adopted father, silently asking for his permission to follow through with Aldara's plan.

Gusseus stared at him, a worried look on his face, while

twisting his beard. His son was growing up; it was time he started treating him more like a man. As much as it pained him to do so, he nodded his head in agreement. "Aye. Play yer heart out, laddie. Play so tha dead'll rise and want ta join in tha dancin'!"

"Thanks, Guss," Tye said gratefully as he reached out and messed up the dwarf's coal black hair. He looked over at his would-be victim and saw how light the skins were that he was wearing. Shooting him with an arrow was out of the question. He would risk spilling too much blood over the costume. He looked over at Eldin. "I think I may need your help on this one, muscleman." He had a small, sarcastic tone in his voice that Eldin didn't catch.

"Let's go, junior," Eldin replied with a smile. The two immediately began to make their way over to the dark elf musician, hiding behind thorn bushes that provided little camouflage.

"They are going to need some help with this," Aldara said to Gusseus. "Let's see how the dark elves like their own magic used against them," she continued as she tapped her dark spell book through her bag. As the two approached the position of the dark elf, Aldara threw her hands in the air and recited a newly-learned dark elf incantation. Gusseus and Outoo looked on as she summoned the power of the earth.

While setting down a flute, the costumed dark elf looked down at his feet in horror as thick mud rose above his boots and worked its way up to just past his ankles. Roots sprang from the ground and fastened themselves around his legs. He tried with all his might to step out of them, but he was held fast, rooted to the ground. He looked up and saw Eldin bearing down on him. His screams were drowned out by the music and he tried in panic to grab hold of the earth that held him glued to the spot. Alarmed that his efforts were having no effect, he quickly threw his hands in the air, but it was too late. Eldin grabbed hold of his neck and jerked it to the side. The body fell quietly to the ground.

Aldara smiled at her own power. How much she had learned from her studies with the spell book. Her smile widened as she continued to marvel at just how powerful she had become. With a snap of her finger, the roots released their grip on the corpse's feet and sank slowly back into the mud.

"Good trick!" Ali-Mimi said aloud. "You do fancy stuff," he complemented her.

"Indeed, you do seem to be a prodigy with the arts, young one," Outoo nodded.

"Hide his body underneath the thorn bushes and cover it with mud," Tye told Eldin as he stripped the animal skins and facemask off of his victim. "I've got to get in there before the song ends and they take a break." He hurriedly put the skins on top of his clothes and slid the mask over his face. He looked down at his hands and suddenly realized that his light skin was a dead giveaway. He reached down into the mud and rubbed it all over his hands and wrists, covering them completely. When he was finished, he stood up and looked at Eldin as he was dragging the body away. "How do I look?" he asked.

Eldin paused and looked at Tye, letting out a brief spat of laughter. "Like a complete idiot," he answered.

Tye shrugged and lifted the flute out of its holder from underneath his skins. "Well, here goes nothing," he said as he made his way around the edge of the dancing circle and to the rest of the musicians.

He stepped onto the makeshift stage and tapped his foot to the beat, getting a feel for the song. *It's obvious they spend a lot more time learning spells then they do practicing music*, he thought to himself. *This is way too flat and boring.* After a few more notes, he raised the flute to his lips. At first he joined in with the others, following along while keeping in time perfectly. He noticed a few of the elves start to break away from their dancing and return to their barrels of ale. Deciding to attract more of the crowd's attention, his fingers moved rapidly up and down his flute. His notes were a combination of both low and high pitches and he forced the rest of the group to increase their tempo.

The rest of the small orchestra shot looks of surprise and bewilderment at him. Some were of disgust—he had ruined their planned song—but they sped up to match his playing. Tye lifted his head from the flute to see most of the elves gathering around and wildly dancing to the new beat. The arms of the drummers were now being thrown wildly through the air as they pounded their heavy drums fast and rhythmically.

From across the way, he noticed that the Queen had stopped dancing with the children and had focused her attention on him and him alone. She raised her finger without taking her eyes away from him, signaling for Zelgot to approach her.

"Is there a problem, Your Highness?" he asked as he stood by her side, his arms folded behind his back.

"That flutist," she pointed at Tye, "he plays like no other I have ever heard."

Zelgot followed her finger and he examined Tye. Keeping his eyes on the hidden light elf he leaned his head toward the Queen. "Shall I bring him before you, My Lady?" he asked her curiously.

Tye could feel the beads of sweat slide down his cheeks from underneath his mask. Suddenly the drums had ceased their beating and the rest of the instruments were winding down. Focusing back on the music, he helped bring the song to a close; he alone played the final few notes.

Instead of cheering, however, the elves stopped dancing. A profound silence fell over the festival. Tye stood nervously on the wooden stage with the Queen of Under Hollow and her second in command staring directly at him. The silence seemed to last forever and the sweat was now pouring under his mask as his legs began to tremble.

"No," replied the Queen. "Make him play it again," she said with a smile as she rose her glass to the masqueraded light elf.

Zelgot raised his finger in the air. "Again!" he shouted. His command was followed by cheers from all the dark elves, and the music began to rise into a deafening roar of beats, chants, and fast-paced flute playing. "And more wood for the fire!" he commanded.

"Woohoo!" yelled Gusseus as he slapped his knee. "That's me laddie," he said with pride.

"He is quite good. A fine son you have there, little friend," Outoo said affectionately. "But alas, we have no time to enjoy his song. We must get costumes for ourselves, and quickly." He looked up at the sky to see that the eclipse was now almost total.

"We may have a problem there," Aldara interjected. "Eldin is too big to pass as a dark elf and Gusseus is too small. They'll be spotted in an instant."

Eldin stroked his moustache. "The witch is right," he rudely agreed. He looked over at Gusseus. "But maybe...how much do you weigh, dwarf?" he asked Gusseus.

"Quite a few stones," Gusseus replied as he ran his hand over his plump belly. He then let out a large belch that surely would have echoed through the deadened forest and probably all the way back to Solaris Arbor if the music hadn't drowned it out. "Aye. Maybe a few less now," he touched his nose, then pointed to Eldin.

"I think I could manage to balance you on my shoulders," Eldin said mysteriously as he looked out at the group of fancily dressed elves beginning to gather some dead wood for the fire.

"What are you planning, human?" Aldara asked him with a worried sound in her voice.

"Just follow me, witch. I've got an idea," he replied as he led them closer to the group of dark elves.

The music continued to wail through the air and Queen Valeria stumbled drunkenly to sit upon a secondary throne that was constructed for her for the celebration. She placed her hand to her forehead and rubbed it in a circular pattern.

"Are you all right, Your Highness?" Zelgot asked her as he placed his hand on her shoulder and rubbed her back gently.

The Queen shook her head briefly, removed her hand from her forehead, and shook her finger in the air. "Your sister." She turned to Zelgot; his image was blurred from the wine. "She said most of the light elf's friends were killed in the effort to capture him." She paused and looked briefly at the Moon before turning her look back to Zelgot. "If Aldara was one of them, my plan is ruined. I must see where she is. If she had died, I would have felt my link to her sever."

"Your Highness, do you think that is wise, given your present state?" Zelgot asked her with care. "Could it not wait until tomorrow morning?"

The Queen sat back in her chair and clasped her hands together. "No. There is no telling where she is now. I do not want to miss my opportunity." With that, she forced a blank stare forward, blocking out all sound and acivity around her. She reached deep within her soul and then out across the realm. Her eyes widened as she began to see through the eyes of the young half-breed.

Aldara's eyes snapped open and she dropped the mask she was about to put on. She grabbed hold of Outoo's arm. "She's linked again. She is trying to find out where I am," she said in a panic. "I shouldn't have come here. She's sure to know where we are."

Outoo patted her on the back and tried to comfort her as Eldin and Gusseus looked over in confusion. "Fight her. Use all of your concentration and control to block her out as much as possible. Place your head to the ground so she sees nothing through your eyes," he told her, remembering when the Queen had possessed a friend of his long ago.

"She is here," the Queen said aloud to Zelgot as she reached out and grabbed his arm while keeping her gaze forward, her mind still in Aldara's.

Zelgot's eyes widened as he looked at her in disbelief. "Here, in Glinfel? At the celebration?" He looked around and saw nothing out of the ordinary. "Are you sure?" he asked her again.

"Yes. I am sure. She is near and—" The Queen's words were cut off as her vision twisted. She now saw Aldara's face looking back at her instead of seeing through her eyes. The image was distorted; it looked as if the Queen were looking at her through spectacles that were not made for her eyes. "I'm a cat," she said aloud to Zelgot.

Ali-Mimi lay on the ground looking up at Aldara. He stared at her with his cat eyes opened wide. He could feel the Queen's link to Aldara, and since he was also linked to her, the Queen had a hold on both of them. "Bad lady see through me too," he chuckled. "She not know what she sees," he said as he began to move his head from side to side, making Aldara's image waver.

"A cat?" Zelgot asked her as he raised his eyebrow. "I really don't think you are in any condition to continue this, Your Highness," he cautiously offered. "You have consumed too much drink, I fear."

Queen Valeria unclasped her hands and shook her head, ending the spell. She then looked at Zelgot. "I suppose you are right. My visions are clearly getting distorted with the drink. Fetch me some Lin-To juice to counter the effects of the wine."

"As you wish," he replied as he left her side in search of the fruit juice that contained the properties to relieve her drunkenness.

Tye continued to play along with the group as he looked out into the crowd, hoping to catch a glimpse of his friends. He had not seen them since he began playing and he was beginning to wonder if they had been captured. He dismissed that thought, thinking that if they had been caught, they would have immediately been placed before the Queen. As his fingers ran feverishly up and down his flute, he was beginning to run short on breath. He almost burst into laughter when he looked out and saw a large figure two dark elves tall. It was covered in a few sparkling cloaks and walking clumsily through the crowded dancing area near the bonfire. *Dark elves on stilts? I thought they were too clumsy for that. I hope they fall into the fire and burn themselves*, he thought to himself.

It was then that all fingers pointed upward and everyone raised their heads to see that the eclipse was now total. Everyone gasped at the beauty of the moon, now a deep, full red in color.

Various spell casters shot fireballs into the air while others shot their magical green energy arrows into the sky. Queen Valeria stood up from her throne and threw her hands together before lifting them to the sky. "Now is the time to offer our prayers!" she yelled before getting down on one knee and bowing her head in silence.

The dark elves were in a flurry, looking for places to meditate and pray. The musicians stopped playing and left the stage quickly to join in the offerings and the praying.

"Burn the books and literature of our enemies that speak of ill will against us and the Moon Goddess." Zelgot shouted into the crowd. "Let this be our first offering to her." Books were thrown on the fire as soon as Zelgot gave the order. Countless volumes of aged literature were destroyed, sacrificed to the Moon Goddess.

The thought of the dark elves completely wiping out all traces of every other race was making Tye's eyes swell with tears. They were more evil then he ever imagined, and it took all his might to keep himself from running up to Valeria and sticking his small throwing knife into her heart. He shook off the temptation when the stilted dark elves walked near him.

He was about to stick his foot out to trip them when the figure opened its top hood just a crack. Tye strained to look through the cloth and recognized Gusseus's bearded face immediately. His father gave him a wink as Eldin opened his hood. "Get yer butt movin', laddie. We best be gettin' out o' here before tha festival ends," Gusseus ordered Tye.

Not hearing every word, Tye looked to his left at the cave entrance to Under Hollow. There, he saw two costumed figures. One gestured to him right before they both knelt down to pray. While the remaining dark elves prepared to worship their Goddess after the last of the books were thrown onto the fire, Tye walked briskly to the cavern's mouth. Eldin and Gusseus walked clumsily behind him, swaying as they, too, reached their destination.

"Let us proceed with haste," Outoo suggested as he stood from his prayer stance.

Looking around before disappearing into the cavern, Tye saw that the dark elves were immersed in meditation and prayer. It was now or never. Giving one more look at Glinfel, he took a deep breath, wondering if their plan would work and if he would ever see the natural light of Sylvanor again. With that thought, he disappeared into the cavern with the others.

Aldara was the last to enter. She paused to look up at the total eclipse of the Moon and whispered a heartfelt thank you to the Moon Goddess. Perhaps, out of all the prayers being sent up to the heavens, Aldara's would be the one answered. She, too, gave the festival one final look and disappeared into the descending cavern that led to the dark elves' home territory of Under Hollow.

Chapter XIII

⟞⟋⟋⟋⟍⟝

The Masked Invasion

The once-thundering roar of the festival's drums was now only a faint rumbling from above. If it weren't for the echoing effect of Under Hollow's cavern entrance, Gusseus and his companions would not be able to hear the drums at all. They had traveled quite far down the vast tunnel and were nearing its end. The air was becoming thick, hot, and stale, sticking to their skin like moist cobwebs. Eerie mint-green energy balls, magically fused into the hard, stone cavern walls, dimly lit their descent into the land of the dark elves.

Gusseus held out his pudgy index finger and trailed it along the wall as they traveled. It was warm and wet to the touch. Occasionally, his finger would run into a patch of moss, which his finger would slice through with ease. His growling stomach was loud enough for the rest of the group to hear; he removed his finger from the wall and rubbed his belly in a circular motion as if that would calm it down and keep it quiet.

Tye prodded the dwarf's belly and found his hand slapped

away. Tye smiled but didn't say a word. Instead, he turned his attention to the wash of blue light that was ahead of them. It was getting bigger now, reaching into the cavern, telling him that they would soon be walking on the soil of Under Hollow. He smiled to himself at the ridiculous position in which the gods had placed him. He was not a trained warrior, he wasn't very disciplined, and yet here he was underneath Sylvanor—a place to which no light elf had journeyed and returned from alive since before the War of the Dragons. He realized how lucky he was, and trained or not, he was going to not only walk among the dark elves, but also enter the castle of their Queen to rescue his friend. He let out a sigh when he thought of his friends. He now had two of them in Valeria's castle. Were they all right? Had Ayku found Wyndle? Maybe she had and they had quietly slipped away…maybe he and his friends wouldn't even have to enter the castle. He sneered at his own thought. *That would be too easy*, he told himself.

Aldara, alarmed by the rumbling of her stout friend's stomach, turned around and offered him a look of sympathy. He was the only member of their group to receive such looks, other than Tye, her secret love. Gusseus had found a warm place in her heart. He was the only one willing to listen to her and extend the hand of friendship. The journey from the labor camp would have been much more difficult had it not been for her new small friend. "Your stomach will soon be satisfied, Gusseus. Once we're out of this tunnel and in the forest, several food options will be available to us. Trees that bear the most delicious fruit are plentiful," she reassured him. She was also reassuring herself.

Eldin licked his lips at the mention of food. It had been a

few days since he had eaten anything substantial and he, like the rest of the group, was starving. He tried to keep up his rough warrior-like exterior, but it was nearly impossible given his mode of dress. His armor was still well hidden by the large cloak he wore. At first, he was happy just to take Gusseus down from his shoulders, but he now wanted to get rid of his disguise altogether. If it weren't for the fact that he would need it again to enter the castle, he would have thrown it on the ground the moment he stepped into the tunnel and out of Valeria's sight. He caught Aldara glancing at him and smiling when she saw him holding up both sides of his cloak like a girl would her dress when walking through a muddy puddle. "You must feel at home here, witch. Knowing the area so well and all," he said sarcastically to her. He still didn't trust her and he was sure he would never like her.

Aldara responded without a care. She wasn't bothered at all by a wandering nomad who didn't care for her. "You should appreciate my experience, human," she said to him coldly, "For it may yet save your life." She took a few more steps before opening her mouth again. "Maybe we'll stop off at Ilayna's house on the way to the castle. You like her so much, you might want to stay there. You know, start a family and have little half-breed Eldins running around." She was pleased with her comeback, as childish as it may have been. Nevertheless, she was happy just knowing it would get a rise out of him.

"Enough, witch!" Eldin scolded her, "or I'll cut your tongue out." He saw the other members of the group, as well as Aldara, look at him in shock for his harsh response to the words said about Ilayna and himself. Dark elf she may be, but he saw something in her that he never saw in Aldara, or in any other dark elf he had come across—compassion. Ilayna was genuine and true. He saw the way she helped the young boy when he dropped his basket, and how she could have turned them in but didn't. He didn't know exactly why he was so drawn to her, he just knew that he was.

"Mmmmm," Ali-Mimi said aloud from on top of Aldara's shoulders. "Smellin' da pie fruit makes water run out of mouth!" He stood up and placed his nose in the air. His claws sank into Aldara's skin, causing her to wince as he stretched. He seemed hypnotized by the scent of the food and he sprang from her shoulders onto the ground. He leaped happily in front of the group and around the corner of the end of the tunnel.

Aldara caught the sweet scent of Quin-Ti and like Ali-Mimi, her mouth immediately began to water. *Don't wander off too far*, she said to him telepathically. Her hunger pangs were also great and she exercised all the control she had not to run ahead and join her familiar. She turned back to Outoo, who had kept silent during their descent, and wondered when he would have given up if it hadn't been for his magical boots. As much as she disliked the elders and old people in general, she had developed a deep respect for Outoo. He had spent his youth saving the realm and now, in his twilight years, he was doing the same, his dedication never wavering.

Outoo caught her look but didn't acknowledge it. He seemed to never miss anything that happened around him. That was one benefit of growing old, and he secretly marveled at the thought of how he had become so wise. He glanced over at Tye and saw how he was looking at everything, the cave walls and ceiling, not missing a trick. Outoo felt like he was look-ing at a mirror through time whenever he looked at his young elven friend. How he envied Tye; he was at the beginning of the adventure of life while Outoo was nearing the end of it. He could only hope that Tye would not have to grow old in a realm of death and chaos, as he had.

After an hour's worth of silently trekking through the cavern, Outoo finally spoke. "At last. We seem to be leveling off," he said gratefully as the dark blue light that illuminated Under Hollow began to wash his feet. "We will be safer once we are out of this tunnel and in the forest of Under Hollow."

A few more steps and the group reached their destination. As they turned the corner, they paused and gasped as they took in the wonderous sight of Under Hollow. It was a land like no other. Huge plants were everywhere; the flowers alone were the size of the Queen's carriage. Rubbery trees towered high into the sky, their leaves bending down—leaves that were large enough to be used to line a bed for two. The air was cooler than it had been in the cavern, but it was still just as moist. A roaring stream of water flowed in front of them, and its gentle misty spray was welcomed on their faces. It moistened their feathery costumes and caused their face paint to run and blend together.

They crossed a wide wooden bridge as they enjoyed the cool mist and made their way to the other side of the stream. Outoo closed his eyes for a moment, then opened them with worry. He looked around at the plant life covered in dark blue light and saw it appear to become lighter. The change in brightness was so small that it could only be seen with elven eyes. He looked skyward at Under Hollow's ceiling. It was covered with the blue energy domes they had seen from above. The domes were much darker now, but they were slowly returning to their normal state. "The eclipse will soon be over. We haven't much time," he stressed.

"Agreed." Aldara took lead of the group. "Follow me; there is a grove of Quin-Ti trees over here. We can eat their fruits as we walk."

She led the group from the main road into the forest. The leaves of the Quin-Ti trees were smaller than those of the Cocil trees but they still could easily be used as table covers. The fruits grew on a slim branch that rested on the tough, leathery leaves. Six fruits grew on each side of the branch. It was a fruit truly meant to be *enjoyed*. They tasted delicious, and the way they were presented on their own leaf made them a friendly and attractive meal.

Aldara plucked a fruit from its branch and sank her teeth into it. Its soft texture exploded in her mouth and its juices covered her tongue, making her close her eyes and smile with delight. She opened them moments later, when she was finished with her fruit, to see the other members of her group devouring them fiercely. "Slow down." She remembered the words of Queen Valeria when she first tasted them in her carriage. "You will get sick if you eat too many or too fast." Her eyes were resting on Tye as if to prove her point, but it was too late. In the time it had taken her to eat one, Tye already had 4 cores sitting at his feet. He licked his lips and then sucked each of his fingers in turn.

"That was the best fruit I've ever had!" He put his last core in his pocket. "I wonder if they will grow above ground," he thought aloud.

"I would advise all of you to put some fruit in your bags," Outoo stated as he placed some smaller Quin-Ti in the pockets of his cloak. "Assuming we make it out of here, it is a long way back to Solaris Arbor. Who knows when we will find another food source."

"Aye. Smart thinkin', laddie," agreed Gusseus. He began to stuff his bag carefully with the fruit and paused as he was finishing. His eyes looked upward and off into the distance. "Now *that* be a sight ta see."

The rest of the group looked at him curiously, then followed his line of sight past the forest and up a long, winding road to the top of a hill. There sat their final destination, the Queen's castle. It was huge and ominous, truly a vision of power and wickedness.

"Ah, it doesn't seem that far away," Eldin said as he stroked his moustache.

Outoo looked at him and nodded a thank you at Eldin, acknowledging his experience as an accomplished traveler, but he knew Aldara would be more of an expert on this terrain. He looked over to her and saw Eldin's face sour as he asked for her assistance. "Do you think we can reach the castle before the festival ends and the dark elves return?"

"Distances in Under Hollow can be quite deceiving, human," she said snottily to Eldin. She then turned to Outoo to answer his question. "However, I do believe we can make it if we hurry."

Tye felt the tension between Aldara and Eldin. Neither of them liked to be corrected, especially by the other. "Let's go, then!" he said as he trod off, happy in the thought that Wyndle was now closer than ever.

"Be careful, Tye," Aldara warned. "Dracal are placed all over the forest. We can't wander too far off the main road or we'll attract them. And since they never see anything but dark elves down here we'll get their attention immediately." She walked past him, snapping her fingers to summon Ali-Mimi to his usual position on her shoulders. She could have asked him via telepathy, but she was feeling a rush of power and knowledge about the land. Giving a command with a snap was a demonstration to the rest of the group, especially Eldin, that she had no fear and was in control.

Aldara led them through the forest, keeping parallel with the main road but also keeping out of sight from it. She stuck her hand out and silently signaled the group to stop. She pointed ahead of them and down the slope to a small village. It was composed of several stone buildings with one about twice as large as the others.

Eldin slapped her arm and pointed down and to the left. She followed his finger and her gaze rested on a green Dracal. It was slowly walking away from the village. Quickly, the group dropped to the ground and underneath the safety of the huge flowery plants that blanketed the forest floor. They sat and listened to the beast breathe…heard its footsteps stop…then start up again, this time getting louder. Aldara tightened the grip on her staff when Outoo stayed her hand. She looked at him curiously and watched as he pulled a Quin-Ti out of his pocket. He squeezed the fruit and it burst in his hand. He then ran the juice and flesh of the fruit over his robes and silently instructed the others to do so.

Following his lead, the group covered their festive costumes with the sweet scent of Quin-Ti. Aldara winked at Outoo, finally understanding what he was doing, then turned her thoughts to Ali-Mimi. *We are masking our scent with the fruits,* she silently informed her familiar. *I'm going to need you to jump out of these plants and pass his line of vision down to the village. Hopefully, the smell of the Quin-Ti will mask us and he'll think the noise he heard was just you.*

Ali-Mimi scrunched his tiny nose and continued their telepathic conversation, *No go for Ali. Ali stay here safe with friends.* He remained on her shoulders.

Aldara narrowed her eyes in anger, then widened them as the Dracal's footsteps drew nearer. *You'll be fine, Ali. Under Hollow is full of little critters. He won't bother you, I promise.* If only she could believe the words she was saying to him. Luckily, they had been bonded long enough to gain practice at hiding some of their thoughts from each other. Aldara hoped that her doubts about his safety were among the thoughts she could hide. Without giving Ali-Mimi a chance to respond, she flung him off her shoulder and he landed on some stray leaves on the ground with a crash.

A groan was heard from the Dracal and Ali-Mimi leapt up into the open. He jumped and scurried about, making as much noise as he could muster. The emerald green Dracal followed him with its glowing yellow eyes, watching him scamper out of sight and down into the village. It whipped its head back to its previous position and lifted its head slightly in the air. Its nostrils flared and it stood there for a moment with its tail wagging lazily behind it. Smelling nothing but the common fruit of Under Hollow, the beast turned around and headed back to its original path.

The group let out a faint sigh but patiently waited, without moving, for the Dracal to disappear from sight. They looked around for other nearby visitors but saw none.

Ali, Aldara asked, silently using her mind link to him, *Is it clear down there?* A few moments passed by without a response.

All safe here, boss lady, Ali-Mimi finally replied, annoyance in his voice.

"Let's go," she said to the group as she stood up and once again took the lead.

Aldara led the group down the slope and into the deserted village. There were several stone buildings; peeking in the windows told them they were living quarters. While the group checked out the houses, Aldara's curiosity brought her to the largest of the stone structures. It wasn't square like the other buildings, rather, it was rectangular. Its windows were in the shape of crescent moons. She pressed her face to the window, but it was too dark to see inside.

Fed up with straining her eyes, she looked out into the forest. Seeing and hearing nothing, she took the end of her staff and tapped it repeatedly on a small window. It remained intact. She applied more force and the window gave way with a large crash as shards of glass flew inside the building.

She peered inside and saw a few long tables in the center of the room. The rest of the building was full with row after row of books. Again, her mouth began to water—not out of hunger for food, but hunger for knowledge. A whole library lay at her feet. She speculated about the contents of the books. Could she steal some more spell books for herself? Would there be a map of Under Hollow somewhere inside? Her head flew frantically from side to side as they considered these questions. Realizing that she didn't just need a closer look, but that she needed to get in there, she left the window and began searching for the door.

She quickly followed the stone wall around the building. She knew she had to be quick. No doubt her friends heard the crashing window and they were on their way to investigate. Finally, she came to a large wooden door. It had been carved with beautiful decorations, then waxed and polished to a perfect shine. Aldara recognized the dark elf word for meditation written on the door and smiled. Where there are dark elves meditating, there are spell books. She tried the handle but it was locked. Frantically, she tried it several more times, even punching it with her fist. Not about to give up, she took in a breath of the moist air and pointed her staff at the door handle.

"Are you crazy, witch?" asked Eldin as he smacked her arm to change the position of the staff. "If you shoot that thing here, you'll have every Dracal in the area breathing down our necks."

She swung her staff back at him and again pointed it toward the door. "I've got to get in there. There are new spells and perhaps some maps, maybe even some plans the dark elves have to use against us," she started to squeeze the staff when she felt a tugging on her cloak. She looked down and saw Gusseus shaking his head.

"What good'll new spells get ya if ya ain't 'round ta learn 'em?" he asked her.

She gave Gusseus a thoughtful look, then turned to the others. Outoo gave her a nod, silently telling her that what Gusseus was saying made perfect sense. She released the strong grip on her staff and stood it upright to use it as a walking stick once again.

"Look," Tye exclaimed as he pointed to a nearby energy

dome in the sky, "you can see half of the moon now!" He looked around at the increasing bluish moonlight that was illuminating Under Hollow with a ghostly hue. The plants around them seemed to glow with a strange phosphorescence. The veins of the leafy plants throbbed and danced with a soft white light and the colors of the flowers began to subtly glow. Tye's mouth dropped as he took in the new view. This was a truly wondrous land and it saddened him to think that only the dark elves were given the chance to appreciate it.

Outoo approached Aldara and placed his hand on her shoulder. "As much as I too would like to go inside and learn something new of the dark elves, we do not have the time." He pointed his walking stick toward the castle. "We must get to the Queen's castle as quickly as we can and before she returns, or any hope of saving the angel and Ayku will be lost," he told her solemnly, his voice taking on a fatherly tone.

Aldara let out a heavy sigh. "You're right," she told him. She looked down at Gusseus and saw him twisting his beard nervously. "You both are." She looked back at the door that separated her from the wealth of knowledge. She stood there for a moment while the group resumed their quest. She felt a gentle push on her leg from Gusseus and knew that she had taken enough time away from their quest.

Ali-Mimi jumped back on her shoulders and shook his head at her, saying nothing. She playfully swatted his nose, then joined the rest of the group as the traveled to the Queen's castle.

****

Ayku sat quietly on the edge of a stone that jutted out from the castle wall near the ceiling. She had been sitting there patiently for hours, watching the guards change, and even glimpsing Valeria herself as she left the throne room to journey above ground. Now she sat listening to the dark elf guards engage in chatter in a language she did not speak. The castle had become deadly quiet once the Queen had left and Ayku wondered just how many dark elves went with her to celebrate the eclipse of the Moon.

She looked up and down both corridors from her convenient corner seat and saw nothing; not one dark elf was in sight. If she were to sneak into the throne room without being spotted, now would be the time. All she had to do was get past two guards. Given her current tiny size and the rate at which they were involved in their current discussion, getting inside didn't seem to pose the monstrous problem she originally thought it was going to be.

She was about to leap behind the guards to the crack of the door, but she stopped herself before doing so. If they were to spot her, even for an instant, everything would be ruined. She had to be more careful. She looked around and realized that her options were limited. Her glamour would also be of little use, because dark elves had a natural immunity to sleep or charm spells. All she needed was a small distraction. She thought back to the day she was liberated from the labor camp along with her friends and how, for a split second, her charm spell had worked on Nagarr. He shook loose of it rather quickly, but if a sleep spell had the same effect it was worth a try. All she needed was a swift distraction—she would be gone before they recovered.

With a smile, she snapped her tiny finger as all the pieces of her plan fell into place. She arched herself on the edge of the stone and silently attacked her victim with a wave of her delicate hand.

Her fairie dust fell gently and unseen upon one of the dark elves. As it rained down on him, his speech slowed and he wavered from side to side. He stumbled back against the wall and his companion rushed to assist him. Ayku immediately seized the opportunity. She darted from the stone, behind the unaffected elf who was struggling to keep his friend from falling.

The spell was over as quickly as it began, and the sleepy dark elf gained his composure once more. He shrugged the episode off as being a victim to heat and reached for a glass of water on a nearby table.

While he poured his water, Ayku squeezed her small body under the door. She momentarily got stuck halfway through, but with a stronger push, she succeeded. She breathed a heavy sigh upon entering the throne room and immediately looked it over. It had remained lit and comfortable so it would always be ready to receive the Queen. Disgusted by the sight of Valeria's twisted seat of power, she paid the throne no attention. Her eyes fell quickly on the curtain Ilayna had told her about and she cautiously flew toward it.

She put her ear to the ground at the curtain's edge and listened for any voices coming through from the other side. A few moments went by and she heard nothing. Curiously, she lifted the heavy curtain and peered into the segregated section of the throne room. It was a dark room illuminated only by a small blue ball of light that hovered in the air. Below the light source was a silver stand that housed a small transparent globe. This section of the room had no other furniture or décor; Ayku gave the room one more glance to make sure there was nothing lurking about in the shadows. Satisfied that she was alone, she flew up to the globe and peered inside.

Inside the globe was her friend Wyndle. She was lying down with her eyes closed, most likely trying to dream away her situation. Her blue dress was rumpled underneath her feathery wings. Ayku knocked on the globe with her tiny knuckles to get the angel's attention. There was no reaction, so she decided to use a more risky tactic, calling out her name in a whisper.

After a few quiet calls of her name, Wyndle opened her eyes and saw her friend hovering outside the globe. She saw Ayku, hands clasped together and, as always, biting her lip. Thinking she was still dreaming, she shook her head, but the image of her friend remained. Wyndle's eyes widened and she sprang up. "Ayku!" she said aloud and full of excitement.

Ayku put her finger to her lips and motioned for her friend to be quiet. "Yes!" Ayku whispered, "Are you all right?" she asked her, as she looked her over.

"Yes, I'm fine for the most part," Wyndle answered as she pushed her bangs out of her face. She looked around the room in search of the others. A frantic look appeared on her face when she realized Ayku was the only one in the room. "Tye! Where is Tye? Is he okay? The Queen sent people out to capture him. Have you seen him? Is he okay?"

Ayku waved away Wyndle's barrage of questions. "Calm down. Tye's okay. He's on his way here with the others to rescue you."

Wyndle pressed her face to the side of the globe. "Everyone is coming? It's much too dangerous. Go back and tell them to call it off!" she pleaded.

Ayku shook her head. "It's too late for that. And everyone

thinks it's worth the risk. They also think that you know something about the Dracal that may help us." Ayku pressed her cheek against the side of the globe as well, trying to be as much comfort to Wyndle as she could.

"Yes." Wyndle shook her head. "I think I'm on to something, or rather, I was…before I was captured by the Queen." She paused to catch her breath. "I believe my people have the power to stop the Dracal."

"Stop the Dracal?" Ayku asked, her voice rising a little above her previously whispered tone. "How? I didn't think there would be anything that could stop them."

"I'm not sure. There's just something odd about them. When I read their auras it's like they don't have any. They shouldn't be here." Wyndle saw the confused look on Ayku's face and knew Ayku needed more answers than she could provide. "What I *am* sure of is that the Queen fears my people. She's stopping at nothing to find the location of the portal to my world." She raised her finger so that Ayku wouldn't interrupt her. "Sure, she knows its somewhere in Solaris Arbor, that's pretty much common knowledge, but she doesn't know where. Her goal is to find it and destroy it so that the portal can never be opened again."

Ayku opened her arms. "Even if she did find out where the portal is, it's in Solaris Arbor, beyond the Breathing Forest. She knows her troops cannot penetrate the forest. It's safe there from her or any of the Overlord's forces. She must know that."

Wyndle shook her head from side to side. "No. I heard her speak of a plan to take down the forest. She doesn't seem to be worried about it at all. We've got to reach Solaris Arbor before the Queen does, or all will be lost. She will start to gather her forces after the Moon Festival."

Ayku's body grew in size, and in an instant, she was standing on the ground. "Then there is no time to waste. You are coming with me now." She grabbed hold of the globe and tried with all of her might to take it out of the silver stand. Using all the strength she had, she pulled on the globe. Her hands soon slipped and she fell backward. The globe remained snug in its holder.

"That won't help, Ayku. The Queen used a spell to fuse it to the stand. I fear that only a dark elf can dispel the magic that keeps me a prisoner," Wyndle said as her shoulders slumped. Had her friends come all this way, put themselves in such peril, only to be able to do nothing to save her?

Ayku ran her fingers through her hair and bit her lip as she thought about the new twist of events at hand. Suddenly her face lit up. "Maybe Aldara can help! She does know some of the dark elves' magic. She has one of their spell books!" she exclaimed excitedly.

"Aldara is here? She came with you all to free me?" Wyndle asked, stunned by the fairie's news.

"Yeah, who would have thought, but she has been a big help to us along the way. She made a vow to get you back. She claims she feels horrible about what she did to you and wants to make things right," Ayku shrugged. "I didn't believe her at first, but I think there is sincerity in her words."

"Perhaps," Wyndle replied. She was very capable of forgiving and she had hoped that Aldara was not beyond redemption. She smiled at the thought that the girl who was the cause of her imprisonment was now the only one who could save her, and that she was putting her own life at risk journeying to Under Hollow to do so. Aldara was quite capable of surprising everyone.

Ayku shrank back to her tiny size. "I've got to go now, Wyndle. I've got to find an alternate route out of here before our friends come. They are counting on me to do my part." She watched a sad look crawl across Wyndle's face. "We will free you. I promise." With that, she flew underneath the curtain and made her way to the throne room door.

"Be careful," Wyndle said softly as she pressed her hand on the globe. "All of you."

****

The brush was thick, making the task of maneuvering through Under Hollow's forests a difficult one. Aldara was beginning to tire and she stopped to catch her breath. She leaned her neck back and rolled it over to her shoulder to release some of the tension. While doing so, she felt a drop of rain land on her cheek, mix with her face paint, and roll down her face. "We cannot rest long," she informed the group, who had also stopped to catch its breath. "It is beginning to rain. If we are caught in it, it will destroy our costumes and face paint and we'll never get into the castle."

Tye had leaned over and placed his hands on his knees and was breathing heavily. He looked up and saw that the castle was not far off. "We're almost there. If the rain can hold out for a few more minutes, we'll make it."

Eldin wasn't as tired as the rest of the bunch and he began to wander from the group. "We can use the big leaves to protect us from the rain," he offered from the distance.

"Yes," Aldara agreed. "They would do nicely." She hated to

admit that Eldin had a good idea, but she was more upset that it was a simple one and that she should have thought of it first.

"Outoo!" Eldin's voice was again heard from the distance, projecting louder than anyone's comfort level. "You gotta come here and see this!"

The elder sighed and tightly grabbed hold of his walking stick. "Remind me to give our friend lessons in proper stealth techniques," he commented as he started off in Eldin's direction.

The rest of the group followed him to the knight's position. Aldara's jaw dropped immediately upon seeing Eldin's find.

"This is just like the one we saw in the Crystal Fields, isn't it?" he asked Outoo as he began to clear the small stone pillars free of the plants and vines that had grown around them.

"Indeed it is," Outoo agreed as he struck some plants with his walking stick. "A teleportation circle. And by the looks of it, it hasn't been used in a long time. Just like the others in Sylvanor." He raised his hand and rubbed his chin.

"You're wrong, elder," Aldara corrected him. "I'd say this has been used recently and fairly often." She had found the headstone and discovered it to be free of debris and plant life. The circular indentation on the stone was well taken care of. She looked down on the ground and saw muddy footprints on the shiny green leaves that covered the area. "Yup. It looks like someone has one of those travel globes. Or should I say... someone else."

"What do you mean, witch?" Eldin asked her as he picked a Quin-Ti from a nearby tree, devouring it before he was even finished asking his question.

"The Queen gave me a globe of this exact size when I was

with her. She believed it to be broken. She referred to it as a Globe of Direction and said she hoped it would help her find the Lost City of the Ancients." Aldara tapped on her bag, making sure it was still inside. "I found out that it works after all." A confused look came to her. "Oddly enough, it lit right up for me when I held it. But when she tried to activate it, it remained black. I still don't know why."

"Shhh! Listen!" Tye interrupted as he leaned his head into the air and put his hand up to one of his huge elf ears. "The dark elves are starting to come back. I can hear them singing. Sounds like its coming from the tunnel." He followed his alert with a chuckle. "They must all be drunk to be singin' and yellin' like that."

"Yes." Outoo also had his hand to his ear. "I can also hear them. We must make haste and get inside the castle at once." As soon as his words left his lips, he started toward the castle. "I would recommend that the dwarf get back on your shoulders, human, and that we resume the disguises we had above ground. I believe this will be our final need for them."

****

The castle courtyard was beautiful and exactly the way that Aldara had remembered. Its fountain shot water high into the air, and the sound it made as it crashed down into a foamy pool drowned out all sound near it. She held onto her bag tightly, making sure not to lose her globe. If the guards at the entrance discovered who they were, they would have to leave in a hurry and the globe would be their only hope…if it even worked at all with the teleportation device.

Eldin was fatigued from the long journey, walking

rather clumsily with Gusseus's weight on his shoulders. Aldara held his arms and treated him as if he were drunk and needing assistance.

Outoo looked around the courtyard through his large, painted animal skin mask. He marveled at how well-built the structure was and how well it had been kept. He let out a sigh and thought back to the days of the Dragon War, when he was once a friend to the Overlord. If he could build such beautiful things down here in Under Hollow, he could have been instrumental in helping to rebuild the entire realm…but greed had gotten the better of him and he chose to rule the realm on his own.

They approached the gates that led to the inner chamber of the castle. It was guarded by a dark elf dressed in full armor, along with four Dracal. The nostrils of the Dracal flared as the group approached but they could smell nothing but Quin-Ti. After they dismissed the fruity smell, they stood still and without emotion, their glowing yellow eyes staring off into nothingness as they waited for their next command.

The dark elf stepped in front of the Dracal and ordered the group to stop their advancement. "You are the first ones back from the festival. We didn't expect you back this soon," he said suspiciously.

Outoo was about to reply when he saw Aldara step forward. He had a good understanding of the dark elf language, having spent much time with his dark elf friends during the Great Dragon War, but he stood his ground and let Aldara handle the situation. If she failed too miserably in her conversation, he would step in and remedy the situation.

Aldara began their cover story. "My friends are drunk and

feeling hugely tree sick. There are more down road. They're a lot more drunk than we big books are here." She continued as she pointed down the road toward the cavern.

The gatekeeper's face hardened as he listened to her ridiculous responses. "Tell him to get down off of his shoulders. Such antics are not proper and will not be tolerated in the Queen's castle," he ordered harshly at Aldara.

Aldara began to sweat under her mask. "He would giggle to be my lord but umm." She hoped her stuttering would be a show of her drunkenness, rather than a lack of knowledge of their language.

"He can't, My Lord," Outoo interjected in the dark elf's native language as he held on to Eldin's arm, pretending to be supporting him. "His leg was broken up ground. We'd like to get inside quickly and have him prepped for when the clerics get back." He smiled inside and was just about to wonder if the guard would buy their story when she saw him raise his finger in the air.

The metal gates lifted with a loud screeching sound, loud enough to even drown out the fountain in the courtyard. The sound was worse than nails on slate and Aldara winced upon hearing it again. They soon came to a halt and the group took a step forward, but the gatekeeper held up his hand, stopping them again.

"Show me the leg. I studied for a time as a cleric before joining Commander Zelgot's military. I may be able to help you," the gatekeeper offered. His offer was a genuine one but it was said with a suspicious tone.

Underneath his cloak, Gusseus was sweating profusely. The heat of the garment combined with Eldin's unstable walk made his stomach churn. He took one hand off of Eldin's head and placed it on his own stomach. He silently wished he had taken Aldara's advice to heart and eaten his Quin-Ti more slowly. The sweet fruit was now churning in his stomach. He looked through his floppy hood to see the gatekeeper with his outstretched hand, telling him to expose his broken leg. Realizing that doing so would reveal that he was, in fact, not a dark elf, he began to think of an excuse why he couldn't show it. Panic overtook him when he also realized that he didn't speak a word of the dark elf language; he let out a belch to buy a little more time and also to make his stomach feel better. He soon realized that a lie was no longer needed. His belch had started as a low, obnoxious noise, but it soon became much more. The bile rose from his stomach along with the fruit of the juicy Quin-Ti he had eaten earlier. Gusseus leaned forward slightly and his vomit spewed forth from under his cloak and onto the gatekeeper's well-kept armor.

The gatekeeper shouted in disgust. "You fool! Look what you've done!" he shouted at Gusseus. "I can not let the Queen see me this way! How dare you..."

Gusseus waved an apology, then followed through with another belch that caused the gatekeeper to back off.

"Fix your own leg, you drunken idiot. And get out of my sight before I break your other one," he grumbled as he began to wipe off his armor.

"We are truly sorry about my friend's episode," Outoo said in the dark elven language, holding back his own laughter. "I will personally see it to that he apologizes to you in person to-morrow. I will also see to it that he compensates you for your armor." The elder would not hide his smile and if it were not for the mask he was wearing, surely the gatekeeper would have smacked his smirk clean off his face.

Aldara giggled under her mask, not even trying to hide it from the guard. It became louder as she passed him and entered the castle's great hall. Once inside, the group turned and watched as the iron gates were lowered. Feeling the ground shake subtly as the heavy bars struck the ground, they looked at each other in unison. The laughter had gone from under their masks and they stood in silence, each aware that there was no turning back. From this point forward, any mistake would certainly end in all of their deaths. They had reached their destination and now the most difficult of their tasks to date was upon them, to liberate Wyndle from her prison in Queen Valeria's castle and to escape the haunting beauty of Under Hollow itself. In the next few hours, the small band of friends would taste either the sweetness of victory that could help save the realm from the clutches of the Queen or the bitterness of defeat that could only result in their deaths and the fall of Sylvanor.

Chapter XIV

—❦❦❦—

A Secret Revealed

Gusseus pulled the door to the small chamber shut behind him. It closed with an echoing thud. Realizing that he might have closed it too quickly, he whirled around and took a quick count to make sure all of his friends were safely inside. Accounting for each one, he took a deep breath and sat his tired body down on a wooden chair.

"I don't think anyone saw us come down this last corridor. We should be safe in here for a bit," Aldara stated as she, too, took a moment to compose herself.

"They don't have to see us go anywhere!" Eldin exclaimed while sniffing his large cloak. He frowned and shook his head. "If the dark elves have any sense of smell at all, they'll find us any where we go. That fruit juice of yours is all over us, witch." Keeping his eye on Aldara, he ripped the cloak from his body and threw it to the floor.

Aldara frowned at him. She was reaching her boiling point with Eldin. "What are you doing, human?" she asked him in a raised voice. "You and Gusseus will stand out in a heartbeat if you aren't under that cloak. Put it back on and let's get going," she commanded.

Eldin took a step closer to her and shoved his finger in her face. "Listen, witch, you aren't in charge here. Give me an order again and I'll make sure you stay here!" He held her gaze for a moment then looked around the room at the rest of the group. He saw all of their eyes on him and made his best effort to regain his composure.

Aldara tightened her grip on her staff. She prepared herself for a heated debate with Eldin, then she, too, noticed all of the group's stares. Quickly calming down, she waved him off with her hand as if to dismiss him. "Have it your way, human. Go on your own. Better to have the dark elves kill you instead of me anyway."

Tye cautiously approached his friend and placed his hand on her shoulder. He knew that when Aldara reached this level of intolerance anything could happen. "Al," he started in his soft, boyish voice, "Eldin does have a point. The Quin-Ti camouflage was great outside but the scent is too strong in here. We're turning heads just walking by rooms that have elves in them. We really would be better off out of these clothes and keeping to the shadows." He looked into her eyes and saw no resistance from her. When Tye showed these signs of maturity, it made her even more powerless to his charm. "Besides, we still have the mud paint and masks. It'll fool people from a distance anyway."

Aldara looked into his face and could not hold back a smile. Tye looked ridiculous with his masked face, but he did make sense. She despised admitting she was wrong, especially in front of everyone, but she nodded in agreement.

She followed her nod with a glance around the room. It was a good-size room with small tables scattered about it and a bar in the far right corner. In the center of the room was a large oblong table with a game board etched in its center. Squares in a stepping pattern with a row of circles on either side made up the game board, and a crescent moon was present at the top. Aldara walked over to the table for a closer look and picked up one of the playing pieces scattered around the board. They were miniature figures about the size of her index finger, carved out of various materials—wood, stone, and precious gems. Some of them were standing upright in the circles and others were tipped on their sides in the squares. The largest of the pieces, representing the Moon Goddess, was placed in the center of the crescent moon. She saw a beautiful piece carved out of a transparent crystal, and as much as Aldara wanted to pick it up, she refrained from touching it.

Outoo took a few steps forward and now stood at her side, giggling slightly. "It's okay, my young friend," he started to explain to her. "It is merely a game, nothing more. Everything is quite safe to touch."

Aldara picked up a playing piece and twisted her hand back and forth, examining it thoroughly. It was carved in the likeness of a small girl with wings on her back at full spread. She marveled at its beauty and how uncanny the resemblance was to their friend Wyndle. She raised an eyebrow and rested her eyes on Outoo. "What is it?" she asked him dryly.

"Cre' Lu," he answered, rubbing his chin as he looked over the board. A smile passed across his lips as he remembered playing it in his youth with his dark elf friends. "It translates from dark elven to 'Ranks of the Gods'. The object is to pick an element and use its power to rise above mortal men to live among the stars, in the realm of the Moon Goddess." He picked up the figurine of the Moon Goddess, glanced at it, and placed it back in the crescent moon. "It's actually quite entertaining."

With a look of disgust on his face, Eldin stepped between the two. "Look, I hate to break up your play time but we're here to save the angel and I'd like to do it before all of those dark elves get back," his tone was commanding and snappish.

"We've gotta take time to study the dark elves whenever we can. We know so little about them and the way they live now. This is a great opportunity to learn about them," she scoffed. She carefully placed the figurine back inside the square from which she took it. She crossed her arms and looked at Eldin with a smug look on her face. "You've got to know your enemy inside and out before you can defeat him."

Eldin's mouth fell open and he rolled his eyes. "Oh, that's right," he taunted her, "I forgot, you know everything. You know, I dunno why the Queen spends all of her time looking for those Globes of Information when all she has to do is sit down and talk to you." He waved his hand at her. "If you want to learn how the dark elves pass their days, do it on your *own* time. We're going to free the angel," Eldin finished, gesturing to the rest of their party.

"Fine. Then that's *exactly* what I'm going to do," she snapped back as she leaned in closer to him.

An all too familiar puzzled look appeared on Eldin's face. "What do you mean, witch?" he began. "If you think that—"

His words were cut off as Aldara saw no reason to be polite

enough to allow him to finish his ramblings. "I'm through with you, human. I have no time for your gibberish. Go save the angel and I will do what I came here to do." The tone in her voice was sharp and decisive. It also rose in volume, but she did not care. Aldara had made a decision, not only about her mission, but also about dealing with Eldin as well.

As she started toward the door past Eldin, the knight grabbed hold of her arm. "What do you mean, what *you* came here to do? We're all here to free that angel and I'm not letting go of your arm so you can go off on one of your secret missions. We're staying together!" he ordered. "Once we free Wyndle and get out of Under Hollow, you can do what you want, but for now you're listening to *my* orders and *my* plans."

Ali-Mimi sat at Aldara's feet, growling at Eldin. Although he was linked to Aldara's emotions, his ill feelings toward the knight were his own.

Aldara began to laugh at the thought of Eldin's self-proclaimed leadership of the group. The words of her rebuttal were cut short before they even left her lips when a bright light filled the room. All eyes turned to the source of the illumination. It came from the crack underneath the door, through which Ayku was now squeezing.

"Ayku!" Tye exclaimed, "Did you find Wyndle?! How did you find *us*? Are you all right?" His questions seemed endless.

"I could hear you from down the hall," she answered, with a look of annoyance to Aldara and Eldin. "And yes, I found Wyndle. She's being held in the Queen's throne room. The guard on her is light, but I suspect it'll get heavier once everyone gets back."

"Then we must hurry," Outoo said as he straightened up.

"Wait." Aldara spoke again, turning her attention from Eldin to someone who would listen to reason. "Outoo, we have a great opportunity to learn here. One that perhaps we may never get again." She paused just long enough to draw a breath. "When I was here with the elders and the Queen discovered me, she was showing off her Globe of History. Before I could learn anything from it, she pulled my hand away. If I can make my way back to that room, there's a good chance we'll know what happened when the Overlord left Sylvanor. We'll find out what's going on with them and the dragons."

"Aye." Gusseus found sense in what Aldara was proposing. "Mebbe we can bring tha dragons ta our side o' this fight." He gave Eldin a glance and saw that he was trying to follow the logic of what Aldara was saying. "At tha very least, mebbe we can shut down tha portal tha Dracal be comin' through."

Eldin twisted his moustache. "I dunno about that Globe of Whatever, but shutting down the portal is worth a try." He turned to Aldara and lifted his hand in the air as he spoke. "But I'm not letting her go alone. I'm going with her." His focus now turned to her eyes. "Just to keep an eye on you."

Aldara scoffed at Eldin. "Just what is it that you think I'll do, Eldin? Do you really think that I made this journey just to turn all of you over to the Queen or to get caught myself? How stupid are—"

Gusseus hurriedly stepped between the two to avoid yet another argument. He reached up and rested his hand on both of their bellies. "Aye, I can see I best be goin' with yas. Someone has ta keep yas apart so yas won't be killin' each other."

"It's settled then," Tye said with relief. "Ayku, Outoo, and I will go free Wyndle, while you guys find that Globe and close the portal." He put his arm around his fairie friend and nodded at Outoo, signaling to him that he was ready to go.

The elder of the group acknowledged Tye's eagerness but raised his hand, signaling them to pause. "I do remember that the portal was located underneath the large dome room to the east. Do you remember the way?" he asked Aldara.

Her eyes darted back and forth as she remembered getting lost very quickly in the maze of hallways that led to the portal. She marveled at how Outoo, an aged elf, could remember such details. "I'm sure I can manage."

"You don't even know the way?" Eldin interjected in disbelief.

"Time is of the essence, my friend." Outoo's voice had become impatient.

"Outoo is correct," started Ayku, "the domed room is to the east of here. Just go left out of this room and follow the corridor. Keep bearing right when you can and you'll get there. We need Aldara to come with us, though. The Queen has placed Wyndle in a small spherical prison. We need Aldara's help to free her."

A smile of remembrance crossed Outoo's lips. "Valeria is still using her Globe of Imprisonment. I possess the knowledge needed to free the Winged Angel. Show us the way, Ayku," he directed, gesturing to himself and Tye.

"Finally! It be takin' an act o' tha gods fer this group ta be reachin' any kind o' decision! Let's go, and keep yer traps shut until we be reachin' that room!" With that, Gusseus placed his hands on the lower portions of Aldara and Eldin's backs and pushed them toward the door.

****

"Now that was a grand festival," Zelgot declared, swelling with pride, "Surely the Moon Goddess will be most pleased!"

The Queen looked at her secret lover with a cautious smile. Her passion for him knew no bounds, especially after consuming so much of the best wine Under Hollow had to offer. If only she still felt this burning passion for the Overlord, she would feel more like an equal instead of one of his underlings. She knew at times that the Overlord still loved her and deeply cared for her well-being, but she couldn't help but wonder how much of that love was diminished by Fenrik's tattletale reporting.

It was times like these, the most precious of occasions, when Valeria's guilt filled her heart. *What if the Moon Goddess disapproves of my secret affair with Zelgot?* she thought. *Would she punish me somehow, or would she know that her most faithful servant is never-ending in her faith? Either way, I must seek forgiveness.*

The trees began to spin; the dizziness quickly brought Queen Valeria out of her thoughts. She glanced around to make sure her subjects were out of listening range before settling her focus once again on Commander Zelgot. "Where—Where is Malsang?" she asked in a defeated tone, placing her hand on her forehead.

"He has already returned to Under Hollow to prepare some celebration remedy potions for our dark elf brethren who may have consumed a bit too much wine, Your Highness." Zelgot could tell from her flushed gray skin that perhaps the Queen would be Malsang's first customer. "Some more Lin-To juice,

My Lady? It will help counter the, um, nausea you may be experiencing," he offered.

The Queen's face went sour. "I have had more than my share of that damned juice. I think I may have been better off without it." She looked down at the half-empty glass on the arm of her makeshift throne and flicked it onto the ground. "I need the medicine of my most powerful healer."

"Then you shall have it, my Queen."

Valeria's thoughts returned to the forgiveness she felt compelled to ask of the Moon Goddess. Were these thoughts of shame or fear? Was she afraid of the Goddess disapproving and cursing her with a loss on the battlefield, or was she just consumed with shame over the way she had been acting behind the Overlord's back?

"The Globe of History," she said aloud.

"I'm sorry?" Zelgot replied, confused.

"In my prayer to the Moon Goddess, I will use the Globe of History to remind her of all of the achievements and sacrifices that I have made over the years in her name. She will see that my relationship with the Overlord was a necessary step to bring her glory back to all of Sylvanor," she smiled as she finished speaking, a look of total satisfaction on her face.

"I do not believe anyone has worked harder in her name than you, my Queen. I am sure the Moon Goddess is aware of this, but perhaps a gentle reminder will not hurt." The words were forced from Zelgot's mouth. The Queen knew of his disbelief in the gods and even though he tried his hardest to sound sincere, she narrowed her eyes at him in annoyance.

"Yes," she answered, after a brief and thoughtful pause. "That is what I shall do. Fetch me my carriage at once. I must pray to her while we still have her attention."

"Your carriage has already been prepped for you, my Queen. It awaits your departure."

Zelgot's proactive nature was one of the traits the Queen loved most about him. It helped advance the dark elf cause and bring honor and glory to their race. Surely, it had been a catalyst for their love. "And Zelgot, use your Globe of Communication with Malsang. Have him meet me in the history room with one of his potions."

Commander Zelgot flashed a smile, as he always did when Valeria showed a hint of vulnerability. "As you wish, my love."

****

The dark elf fell to the ground with a thud as Eldin withdrew his dagger from its back. After quickly wiping the blood off his blade, he attached the dagger back on his belt.

"Good work, laddie," praised Gusseus.

"These elves sure do die easily when you sneak up behind them," Eldin responded with a smile that he flashed Aldara's way.

"Fortunately, we half-breeds have an extra eye in the back of our heads that alerts us when there is danger…and it squirts a highly toxic venom at the attacker." Her tone was serious, but she chuckled inside at Eldin's gullibility when the look on his face told her he just might have believed her.

Ali-Mimi did not contain his laughter. "Human not so smart!" he chuckled.

Gusseus walked ahead of the group as Eldin dragged the body of the dark elf behind a pillar on the side of the corridor. As Gusseus peered around the corner, he gave a sigh of relief and waved his hand to his friends behind him, signaling that the hallway was clear.

The group turned the corner and cautiously walked down the hall until they came to a large circular junction. They now had multiple directions to choose from. Each of them was dark, with the familiar green glow seeping from half spheres that lined the walls; they all looked identical.

Gusseus gave Aldara's cloak a tug and she turned and looked down at his stout fatherly face. "Do ya 'member tha way, lass?" he asked her.

Aldara looked around, raised her finger to her lips, and cocked her head. "This is very familiar, but I cannot remember which way we were led."

"Perhaps I can assist you," a voice said, as a figure stepped out of the shadows. Upon this, Eldin raised his sword, Gusseus tightened his grip on his battle axe, and Aldara raised her staff.

He was a thin dark elf, dressed in high boots, dark violet pants, and a billowing white linen shirt. Aldara quickly recognized the emblem on the clasp of his cape as that of a healer.

"I don't think so!" Eldin took a step closer to the dark elf.

The dark elf raised his hand at Eldin. "Steady, knight, for I am a friend." In a friendly gesture, Malsang took hold of his hood and gently lowered it behind his head.

"And I'm the Overlord," Eldin retorted. "We don't have time for—"

Eldin's words were cut off by the dark elf. "Correct. Time is what you are quickly running out of. The Queen is now on her way back to the castle. If the Winged Angel is what you seek, I am afraid you are headed the wrong way."

Aldara stepped up and blocked Eldin's sword with her

staff. "Can you tell us the way into the room with the domed ceiling? The room that contains the Globe of History?" she asked the handsome dark elf.

A look of surprise washed over the dark elf's face as he wondered how this group of strangers not only knew that a Globe of History was nearby, but also were able to describe the room that held it. He decided not to pursue this line of questioning, instead answering Aldara directly. "If you follow the corridor, veer right at the end, then follow that to its end, you will find the history room that contains the globe you seek."

Eldin looked down at Gusseus. "How do we know we can trust him? What if he is leading us into a trap?" His eyes were now back on the dark elf. "Who are you? What's your name?"

"Surely, you don't expect me to utter my name in the echoing halls of the castle?" replied Malsang. "My comrade has told me all about your group. I am impressed you made it this far. And no, I will not utter her name to you either. Believe me or not, the choice is yours, but I cannot risk any more time talking to you, nor can you afford the luxury of interrogating me any further." With that, the dark elf pulled his hood up over his head to conceal his face once more. Without waiting for permission, he turned and walked away.

Eldin took another step closer to the dark elf, but Gusseus reached up and put his hand on Eldin's belly, signaling him to let the dark elf go. He pointed to Aldara, who wasted no time on making her way down the hall toward her treasure, the globe. Gusseus broke out in a swift jog to follow her, and Eldin, who let his gaze linger a moment longer on the image of the dark elf disappearing into shadow, brought up the rear with a swift walk.

They soon reached their destination, finding it to be unguarded. *Curious,* Eldin thought as he looked around to survey his surroundings. After making sure they were alone in the hall, he reached for the door handle. The doors were wooden and extremely wide and thick. They stretched from the floor to the ceiling, and their intricate carvings were polished to a shine that indicated they were cared for daily. The door handle would not budge. "Locked," Eldin said in frustration, and he struck it with the hilt of his sword.

"Stand back, human," began Aldara, "these doors are sealed with magic. Your violent temperament will not open them."

Eldin backed away from the door. "I suppose you know how to open them, eh, witch?"

"Indeed I do," replied Aldara in a snobbish tone as she brushed her cloak aside to access her shoulder bag.

While Aldara was fumbling for her spell book, Gusseus placed his hand on the door and traced a few of the carvings with his finger. They were very elaborate, displaying a curious story of dark elves battling dragons—with the dark elves appearing triumphant in the battle. He shook his head and smiled at the fact that history is written by the winners, rather than the losers. It is theirs to embellish and exaggerate. He saw a faint light out of the corner of his eye, and he backed away from the door, turning toward Aldara in time to see her casting her spell.

"Furloish Min Toye," she spoke as she twisted her right wrist.

The door handle flashed a brilliant white. It lasted only a fraction of a second, yet it still caused them all to shield their eyes. When the light of the hall returned to normal, Eldin reached for the door handle and turned it. The door opened slowly and silently. Eldin and Gusseus entered the room with Aldara, stuffing the spell book back into her shoulder bag, right behind them.

It was a grand room. There was a flight of stairs on the far side of the room leading up to the floors above and a large, shining silver door across the way that was closed. Sitting in the corner of the room was a large blackened globe on a stand.

Eldin glanced at the globe and immediately went for the large silver door. "Is this the way to the portal?" he asked Aldara in a gruff tone. He didn't bother to wait for a response before he grabbed hold of the handle.

A shot of electricity shot through his body and knocked him back. "This one is locked as well. See if you can unlock it, witch." When he received no immediate reply, he turned and saw Aldara already approaching the Globe of History.

Aldara placed her hand upon the globe and took a deep breath. She closed her eyes and the globe began to hum. A small point of light appeared in its center and grew until the globe, along with the entire room, was encompassed by its light.

****

Tye removed his mask and pulled on the bowstring with his fingers pinching the end of an arrow, increasing the bow's tension and readying for a fight as he peered around the corner of the hall to see two elite dark elves standing guard to Queen Valeria's throne room. He looked back at Outoo, who took a large seed out of his pocket, cupped it in his hand, and began to whisper words of magic into his palm. After a few moments, Outoo closed his fist around the seed and gave a nod to the young elf. Ayku caught the nod as well and followed it up with one of her own to Tye. With that, she flew her tiny body around the corner and in front of the dark elves.

The dark elves jumped in surprise and panic as Ayku clenched her fists and slammed her eyes shut. Bright yellow light burst from her body and flooded the area in an instant. The dark elves, not wearing their visors, threw their arms up in front of their eyes and uttered phrases in the dark elf language.

Just then, Tye's arrow struck one of the elves in the neck and he fell to the floor. His screams were muffled as he choked on the blood that poured from his wound.

At the same time Tye's arrow struck, Outoo threw the seed in front of the remaining guard. The seed let out a boom as it hit the floor, and it immediately began to grow into a thick wooden tree, its roots cutting through the stone floor with ease and quickly taking hold. The branches and vines of the tree wrapped around the dark elf's legs. A fireball erupted from the guard's hands as he hurled it blindly at the wall, where it seared the stone and quickly dissipated.

The guard managed to let out a horrifying scream before the branches and vines grabbed hold of his arms and slid across his face and mouth, silencing him. The elf was now suspended, motionless and silent, off the ground in the body of the tree.

"By the Gods!" exclaimed Tye. "Do you want me to finish him off?" he asked as he drew a dagger from his belt.

Outoo took in a quick breath, "No, my young friend. There has been enough killing today. This spell will hold him long enough for our needs. Come." He gestured toward the door. "We haven't a moment to lose."

Outoo pushed open the door to the throne room. It was a large circular room with a decorated throne of gold, silver, and precious gems sitting on a raised dais. On the sides of the room were a few tables with pitchers of water and some comfortable chairs lined with thick velvet.

Ayku's eyes widened when she saw the closed curtain behind the Queen's throne. "There!" she exclaimed. "Wyndle is being held in an orb behind that curtain." Throwing caution to the wind, she flew under the curtain. A few moments later, she was dragging the curtain open as she grew to her normal size to make the task easier.

The Winged Angel jumped with excitement, hitting her head on the top of her spherical prison. She watched as her friends Tye and Ayku approached her and wondered who the elder light elf was that accompanied them.

"Wyndle!" Tye was bursting with excitement. "It is so good to see you! Are you all right?"

"Yes. Please hurry. The festival is over and everyone will be back very soon." Wyndle's voice was serious, but she had a look of happiness upon seeing her friends.

"Prepare yourself, my tiny friend, as you will soon be free," stated Outoo as he placed his hand on the tiny globe.

Outoo lowered his hands and began speaking the ancient words of elven magic. His words rose in tone as his voice became more commanding. The silver stand holding the globe began to crack at its feet. The cracks traveled up its legs to the base of the stand. Metal shards splintered off, and with a mighty creak, the silver turned to dust and the globe dropped to the floor. Before it hit, however, the globe popped like a bubble and Wyndle flew up in the air, stretching her wings and legs as she did so.

"Thank you!" She bowed to Outoo, adding, "I am in your debt." Wyndle wasted no time flying to Tye and throwing her arms around his neck and kissing his cheek, all the while giving a wink to Ayku.

"I'm so glad you are okay, Wynd," Tye said in a somber tone. "I am so sorry this happened to you."

"We can catch up later; we must meet up with the others and get out of here," ordered Outoo.

Wyndle's expression turned serious as she spoke to Outoo. "We have to get to Solaris Arbor immediately. From there, I can use the portal and go back home. My people *must* be made to listen."

"But you were banned from your realm, Wynd. There is no telling what would happen to you if you went back." cautioned Tye.

"They will listen to me. My people have the power to end this war. It's the Dracal, Tye. They aren't alive. The balance of things has been disrupted. This is why the Queen wanted me so badly."

From out of the window and down below, the voices of the dark elves could be heard entering the castle. In a flash of light, Ayku shrank in size to match Wyndle's height. "Follow me. The group isn't far. Stick to the shadows and do not make a sound. With any luck, we will make it to the history room without incident. This part of the castle is empty. For now."

The group followed Ayku out of the room and down the

hallway, hastening to meet up with their friends and escape the castle of the dark elf Queen.

****

Aldara's hair whipped wildly around her head as images began to appear inside the Globe of History. She opened her eyes and her hair instantly stopped moving, flopping down around her head, her gray streak taking its place in front of her face. As if filled with water, the images in the globe shimmered and distorted underneath her touch as her fingertips gently glided back and forth on its surface.

Ali-Mimi's eyes widened as if he were in a trance.

"Show me the secret of the Dracal. Where did they come from?" commanded Aldara.

The images twisted once again inside of the globe and settled upon the dark elves in Under Hollow. Legions of spellcasters and soldiers of the dark elf empire could be seen entering a portal gate in large groups with the Overlord, Queen Valeria, and Fenrik leading the way.

In a flash of light, the image inside the globe changed; it now showed a barren charred land with a pink sky. The dark elves, led by Fenrik, were chanting around a large jewel while strange humanoid creatures stood nearby, shackled in bindings of pure energy. Their shapes were twisting as if they had no bones and were trying to escape the bindings, but to no avail.

A large red dragon was chained to the ground next to them. Its giant mouth was also bound as it lay helpless.

Aldara's arm was coursing with energy and beginning to burn. "I can't keep this up much longer!" she shouted to Gusseus and Eldin.

At that moment, Ayku flew into the room with the rest of the gang following. Everyone's attention was immediately focused on the Globe of History—except for Tye's.

"Aldara! What are you—" his words were cut off by a raise of Gusseus's hand.

"She canna' hear ya, laddie. Let her be."

From inside the Globe of History, a group of spellcasters could be seen waving their arms and chanting, and with a clap of Fenrik's hands, light shot out of the large jewel and into the dragon's eyes. The gem appeared to be sucking the very life out of the giant beast. In a few moments, the dragon's body went limp on the ground. It was dead.

Outoo's and Wyndle's eyes met before she flew in closer to get a better look. Her face was filled with sorrow, followed by horror and disbelief.

Inside the globe, the vision of the jewel pulsated with a yellow swirling light. The humanoid creatures were now desperately trying to escape when the light shot out of the jewel, hitting each member of the captured group at the same time. They stopped fighting their bindings and stood there, motionless, the energy filling their eyes and transforming their bodies. Their smooth, tan skin was turning red and thick scales began to form. Giant wings grew out of their backs and horns sprang out from their heads. There they stood, their eyes glowing an eerie yellow. A few dozen Dracal had just been born, and whatever creature previously stood in their place had ceased to exist.

The jewel was now contracting and expanding. It was beating like a heart with the life force of both the dragons and the humanoid creatures captured inside.

"How *dare* you," Queen Valeria said coldly as she flung her hands in the air and hurled a ball of green energy at Aldara.

Gusseus pulled Aldara's hand from the globe and pushed her to the ground. He took the full impact of the energy ball, and he screamed as his body sparked with electrical energy. It sent him spinning against a concrete pillar and he fell to the ground with a thud, shaking uncontrollably as he foamed at the mouth. He looked at Tye for one last, brief moment…and then his eyes rolled back in his head. He was dead.

"No!" Tye let out a scream. He quickly drew an arrow from his quiver, loaded his bow, and released it at the Queen.

With a wave of her hand, she deflected the arrow as if it were suddenly caught up in a tornado. She turned to Tye and again threw her arms up in the air. Another green energy ball flew out of her hands toward him. Wyndle popped up from behind Tye's shoulder and quickly enveloped him in her protective force field.

The Queen looked at Wyndle with shock. "How could you possibly…" she looked over and saw Outoo. The elder light elf she once knew in her youth. They were friends long ago—during the last Great War—but now, she felt nothing but rage when she looked at him. That rage quickly found its way to the surface as she screamed, "None of you shall leave here alive!"

As if on cue, her guards burst through the doorway and began hurling fireballs and energy darts toward Tye and his friends. Wyndle did her best, throwing up force field after force field, while other members of their party ducked behind pillars for cover.

Ali-Mimi was at Aldara's side, licking her face and hissing

at the Queen's minions. Aldara slowly stood up and recovered from her severed connection with the Globe of History. She grabbed her staff just as an energy dart sank into her left arm, searing her flesh and causing her to cry out in agony. Ali-Mimi doubled over in pain and cried out in response to Aldara's wound. Regaining her balance, Aldara pointed her staff at the Globe of History and squeezed it with all the strength she had left in her. A stream of energy shot out of her staff and hit the globe with tremendous force. The globe exploded so violently, every window in the room shattered and the outer wall next to the globe burst, throwing fragments out into the forest of Under Hollow.

Outoo saw that large chunks of a few pillars were also taken out by the blast and reacting quickly, he uttered a few words of magic, pointed his hands to the ceiling, and quickly lowered them to the floor. The pillars shook and began to crumble and the ceiling came crashing down into the space between them and the Queen's forces.

"Quick, out into the forest!" ordered Eldin.

As the group quickly sprinted past the rubble, Tye stopped and ran over to Gusseus's body. He bent down and cradled him briefly in his arms as tears streamed down his face.

"Tye," started Aldara, "there is nothing we can do for him. He's gone. We must mourn him later."

Tye shot her a look of hatred.

"I loved Gusseus too, we all did. He gave his life for me. We cannot let his sacrifice be in vain. We need to go now." She grabbed Tye's arm. He looked up at her, saw her charred wound, and stood up. He could see movement behind the rubble and knew it was only a matter of minutes before the Queen and her spell casters would blast through.

"She will pay for what she's done." He began to reach for an arrow from his shoulder pack.

"Not today, Tye. You cannot win now. Her day will come, but only if we leave now."

Tye saw the look of reason and the compassion in Aldara's face, and with a defeated nod, he gently pushed her toward the hole in the wall and out into the forest.

Ali-Mimi gave one last hiss in the Queen's direction and followed Aldara into the woods, constantly looking back to make sure his bonded partner remained safe.

The Queen's guards were shattering the rubble in chunks, but it was still some time before they could see the other side of the room.

"Hurry, you fools!" she commanded as she looked down at her bloodied arm and legs. Bits of the ceiling had hit her on the way down as she attempted to get out of their path. She winced at the pain.

Commander Zelgot came to the doorway and immediately ran to the Queen's side. "Your Highness, what happened? Are you—"

"Where *were* you?" she said angrily through clenched teeth. She then grabbed him by the clasp of his cape. "Kill them. Kill them all," she ordered coldly.

Commander Zelgot spun on his heel to his guardsmen. "Grab the nearest platoon of Dracal and hunt them down. Block off the entrance into and out of Under Hollow. They must not leave our domain," he commanded. He then turned back to the Queen. "I will lead the hunt myself, my Queen."

"See that you do," she replied, grabbing hold of her arm,

"and summon Malsang to heal these wounds."

****

Running through the forest as quickly as they could, they passed by the small village they had encountered on their journey to the castle. The group was panting hard and tiring quickly. Even Outoo, who was wearing the magical boots that allowed him to travel as if he were in his prime, was beginning to have trouble keeping up with the group.

They stopped for a moment to catch their breath and formulate a plan. The sound of chaos that erupted from the castle told them they had only seconds to rest.

"Where to now?" asked Eldin. "Surely, they will have that cave that leads above ground blocked off. There's no way we'll be able to get out of here."

"The cave is no longer an option, but there are alternate ways of travel throughout the realm," Outoo offered, as he looked Aldara's way. "Just up that hill lies the portal we discovered earlier."

Aldara gasped, "That's right! If we can make it there, we can use my Globe of Direction to get out of here!"

Suddenly, a boulder smashed near them, covering them all with dust and small debris. Wyndle quickly threw up a force field around her friends as the Dracal made a pass over them. Their breaths of fire and lighting ricocheted off the force field and into the forest, setting small fires on the ground and in the trees.

"We're pinned down. We can't move out of the angel's protection. There are too many of them," yelled Eldin.

Arrows also bounced off of Wyndle's force field as

Commander Zelgot's archers caught up to the fight. As the Dracal swooped in for another pass, they were hit by energy darts coming from the trees nearby. Most of the darts were absorbed by their armor, but some pierced a few of their soft yellow underbellies. Those Dracal lost control and fell to the ground.

A large group of dark elves now came into the clearing and attacked the fallen Dracal as a few spell casters hurled fireballs at those flying above. The Dracal fought back, spitting lightning and fire at anything that moved on the ground. The smell of burning elven flesh was everywhere.

Ilayna ran to over to Eldin. "Go. We will cause the best diversion we can, but we will not last long against the Queen's forces. Get the Winged Angel to safety and yourself as well."

"Let's move!" yelled Tye as Wyndle lowered her force field. Tye put his arm around Aldara and helped her move as quickly as possible up the hill. Ayku was flinging bursts of light into the sky in hopes of blinding the Dracal, while Wyndle was doing her best to provide her protection when needed.

"I hope we meet again, human." Ilayna said to Eldin as she quickly kissed him on the lips. "Now go, your friends need you." She turned from him, drew her sword, and joined the fight.

Ilayna's comrades were being massacred. Few were left on the battlefield when Commander Zelgot arrived on his steed. He dismounted, drew his sword, and sliced into the stomach of one of the traitorous dark elves, all in one swing.

From across the field, Ilayna watched her brother murder one of her dearest friends. She knew there was nothing she could do for him and that she must hide before she was discovered. She reached in her pocket and searched for a small vital of shimmering powder. She drew it out of her pocket. She looked up to see her brother, Commander Zelgot, looking her square in the eye. He looked at her in disbelief, and she mouthed the words 'I'm sorry' to him just before she threw the vial to the ground in front of her. It exploded on impact and her immediate area was covered in smoke. When it cleared, she was gone.

At the edge of the portal's circle at the top of the hill, Outoo did a quick count to make sure everyone was accounted for. Everyone except…Gusseus. He briefly reflected that they would no longer be able to benefit from the wisdom and guidance of Tye's father figure.

The remaining Dracal were closing in fast. Rocks and tree limbs exploded all around them and Wyndle threw up one force field after another. "I can't keep this up forever! We have to go now!" she pleaded with the group.

The Dracal would stop at nothing until Wyndle and her friends were vanquished. *Lifeless*, she thought. Without missing a beat, she took to the air above her friends and darted after a yellow Dracal who was spitting streams of acid to the ground, hoping to disintegrate those that helped save Wyndle's life.

The yellow Dracal caught sight of Wyndle and sent a toxic stream her way. She flipped in the air and turned sharply, narrowly missing the jet stream. She continued her path, sailed between the Dracal's legs, and came to a stop just behind him. He turned toward her and his face was now just a breath away from her. She quickly reached out with her hand and touched its warm scaly body. The glowing light in the Dracal's eyes began to flutter. The beast opened its mouth for another strike, but nothing came out. Its eyes flickered faster and then suddenly went dark. The Dracal went limp and quickly fell to the ground, dead.

Aldara grabbed the Globe of Direction from her shoulder bag and placed it in the indentation of the portal's control stone pedestal. The globe lit up and the landscape displayed in the portal's circle changed—slowly at first, then more rapidly. First, a forest appeared, then a swamp, then a desert, each rotating in turn. "Which one do I choose?" she asked Outoo, just as a bolt of lightning narrowly missed the globe, charring the stone pedestal.

"Anywhere! Just activate it now, witch!" shouted Eldin. They were now surrounded by a ring of fire with Zelgot and his troops quickly advancing up the hill.

Aldara pressed her palm to the globe and the image of a dark, foggy swamp appeared. She grabbed the globe out of the pedestal and the group ran into the center of the portal. Wyndle, trying to make sense of what had just happened between her and the Dracal, darted toward the portal just in time to join her friends the instant they vanished and the portal went dark.

Zelgot approached the top of the hill, finding no one to capture or kill for the Queen. His report would not be pleasant. He spat on the ground and growled at the thought of his own sister; his Captain of the Guard had helped his enemies escape. His own flesh and blood was a member of the Circle of Thirteen. Zelgot took in a deep breath and let out a heavy sigh. He turned from the portal and walked down the hill toward his steed to begin the short journey back to the Queen's castle.

Chapter XV

—⟡⟡⟡—

The Isle of Lost Souls

A brilliant flash of light disturbed the deathly calm of the misty, darkened swamp. One by one, figures appeared, seemingly from out of nowhere. In a loud swooshing sound, the materializations finished. There, in the center of a gate portal, stood the weary band of unlikely heroes.

Aldara was the last to appear and she did so with a cry of pain. She collapsed to the ground clutching her arm, as the pain was overwhelming. She choked on her tears between her cries. It was the most intense pain she had ever felt. Ali-Mimi lay by her side, also groaning and screaming through an odd catlike cry, feeling her pain.

Wyndle wasted no time rushing to Aldara's side with the rest of the group in tow. She could see Aldara's wounds through the tattered remnants of her cloak. Her arm was ripped open and covered with burns so deep there was very little blood. The heat from the energy dart had been so great that it had cauterized the wound. Wyndle tried to remove a piece of cloak that was stuck to her seared, blistered skin, and once again Aldara screamed out in pain.

"Your wound is very serious, but fear not, I shall heal it for you." With that, Wyndle laid her hands upon Aldara's arm. She could see the look of gratitude through the pain in the young half-breed's eyes.

Wyndle's hands glowed with a faint, soft white light. Aldara winced and cried out as the angel gently moved her hands up and down Aldara's arm. Before her very eyes, Aldara watched as the burns slowly disappeared. Her gaping wound closed in on itself and her skin returned to its smooth, light gray color.

The tears were leaving Aldara's eyes but their streams remained on her cheeks. "Thank you," she said sheepishly to Wyndle, bowing her head in shame. "I wasn't deserving."

Wyndle used her tiny finger to gently lift Aldara's head. "Everyone deserves a second chance, my new friend. I forgive you and know in my heart that you were doing what you believed was right at the time. There are no more words necessary on the subject."

Ali-Mimi's screams ended simultaneously with Aldara's. He sat up next to her and began purring, rubbing his face along her arm. "Me feel you fine," he said aloud in his broken speak. She acknowledged his comment using their telepathic bond and stroked his head a few times before standing up.

"How come you couldn't do that to Gusseus?!" Tye's words were harsh and spoken out of hurt. He had never spoken to Wyndle like this before and she knew his words came from his broken heart.

"He died too quickly for me to reach him and heal him in time," she said softly.

"YOU DIDN'T EVEN TRY!" his response was screamed at the top of his lungs. "You could have brought him back!"

"Tyelander!" Ayku began to scold him before Wyndle gently cut her off.

"Tye, you know it is forbidden for me to bring anyone or anything back from the dead." Wyndle's words were stern but still gentle.

"Just like how leaving your people to live on Sylvanor is forbidden? You've broken the rules before," he snapped back.

"Yes, and I paid the price of exile for it." Wyndle's words were not as gentle this time. "Even if I wanted to I couldn't have brought him back. We do not possess that kind of power. Not only is it forbidden, we simply cannot do it."

"Then what good are you?" he spat out as he shook his head, not fully believing her.

Tye walked away from Wyndle and Ayku followed him. In a flash, she grew to her full fairie size and slapped her friend across the face. Their eyes met and Tye hung his head in shame. He knew he was wrong to yell at Wyndle and he also knew, deep in his heart, that if there had been a way to save Gusseus, she would have done so. He walked back to Wyndle and apologized. She reached out to him and ran her tiny hand through his floppy blonde hair, signaling that things were okay between the two of them.

"Now that everyone has made up," began Eldin, "where are we?" He looked around. The shroud of nighttime still covered the land and there was a faint, misty fog in the air, which was slightly thicker toward the ground. He stepped out of the portal's circle to further examine the area. All of the trees had lost their leaves and their bare branches reached out in the moonlight like eerie bony fingers. As a gentle breeze passed through and parted the mist, he could see that the whole area was littered with tombstones, some new, some old and broken.

"We seem to have teleported to the Isle of Lost Souls," answered Outoo. "The ancestral burial grounds of Sylvanor."

"Creepy," said Tye as the slight chill in the air caused him to rub his arms. He moved out to get a closer look, as did the rest of the group.

Outoo continued, "This Isle was once shared, like most of the land, between all the races before the last Great War. Now it is only used by the dark elves. They bring their dead here as well as the dead of their enemies. They have a strange connection to this island that I have never quite figured out."

"Ow!" exclaimed Aldara suddenly as she tripped forward, making her friends laugh. "I could swear something just tried to grab my foot."

"It's your imagination, witch," chuckled Eldin. "Don't half-breeds ever trip?" he asked sarcastically with a smile. He started to walk away from the tombstones when a skeletal hand reached up from the misty fog and grabbed his leg. "What the?" he exclaimed as he jumped free of the hand and drew his sword.

The sound of earth moving and of stone grinding against stone was heard as dozens of skeletal and rotting hands began to reach up from the ground, their animated bodies now wiggling out of the dirt.

Eldin swung his sword at the skeleton that was unearthing itself at his feet. The impact shattered the bone and cracked its skull in half. The brittle bone fragments fell to the ground, no longer a threat. Aldara raised her staff and tightened her grip. Blasts of energy shot forth and struck another skeleton square in the rib cage. It, too, shattered and turned to dust. Tye wiggled his leg free and took a few steps back. Rising out of a nearby grave was a rotting corpse that still had a considerable amount of meat on it, although bone could be seen jutting out of the dripping flesh, along with its exposed, worm-riddled organs.

He drew an arrow from his quiver and shot toward the corpse. The arrow struck the zombie's chest, yet the creature did not waver. Instead, it continued walking lifelessly toward him.

Remembering what happened with the Dracal, Wyndle flew toward the zombie and touched its diseased, rotten skin. Though she expected it to fall to the ground, nothing happened. Her eyes widened. *How could this be?* she asked herself. In a panic, she yelled out to her friends, "Don't let them touch you. They are diseased, and if you get infected, I am not sure I will be able to heal you!"

Outoo threw a large seed down in front of the zombie and it instantly rooted to the ground. A tree sprang forth from the seed and its branches encased the zombie, neutralizing him. Satisfied with this result, he looked over at Aldara and watched her hands wave in front of her as she uttered the magical words of the dark elf. A fireball appeared in front of her hands and she hurled it at another zombie, engulfing it in flames. The stench of the burning, rotting flesh was unbearable as it continued to advance on her. Ali-Mimi shrieked in fear and jumped up on Aldara's shoulder.

Ayku looked over to a nearby mound and saw the silhouette of a short humanoid figure whose pointed ears were bent down. She illuminated the area with her command over light and the mist burned away. On the mound stood Fenrik, leaning on his cane, concentrating and watching the spectacle before him. The blast of light broke his concentration and the skeletons that were climbing out of their graves, as well as those engaged in battle, broke apart and fell to the ground. The zombies also fell as if they were marionettes whose strings had just been cut.

"You," Wyndle said coldly as she took up a defensive posture.

Everyone else had assumed the same protective stance, wondering about the identity of the dark elf. Everyone except Outoo; his posture remained unchanged as his eyes narrowed, trying to make sense of what was transpiring around them.

"What have you done, necromancer?" started Wyndle. "How is it that you can be raising the dead?"

Fenrik's aged lips curled in a smile that caused his old face to wrinkle even further. "Your blood is a very precious gift," he answered, followed by soft, wicked laughter.

A look of shock washed over Outoo's face. A Winged Angel on Sylvanor is a rare occurrence. Its blood in the hands of a dark elf necromancer was unheard of, and the thought of it chilled Outoo to the bone.

"My blood was no gift. You stole it from me while I was in that prison." Wyndle snapped back as she started toward him.

Fenrik flicked his wrists in the air and a dozen miniature orbs appeared. They hovered around him. They were dark green and purple in color and smelled of disease and decaying flesh. "That is close enough, angel. While I thank you for your blood, I must insist that you and your friends leave this place immediately. Consider me sparing your lives as my official thank you." His voice was solemn. "Everyone except Outoo." He gazed at Outoo through the spectacles on the end of his nose.

Everyone's eyes turned toward the elder. *How does this dark elf know Outoo and why was he sparing all of their lives?* They all thought the same thing and hoped an answer would come as Outoo spoke.

"Go, my friends. Take a boat on the east docks and cross the water to the shores of the Gnomish province. Wait for me there; I will join you shortly." Outoo's words were not what the group was expecting.

"No way, old man," Eldin protested, "we're not leaving you here alone with this dark elf!"

"You cannot win here, knight. This is not your fight. Go now, for our mission…Wyndle is our priority," he ordered Eldin, never taking his eyes off of Fenrik.

Eldin thought about it for a split second and chose not to put up a fight. Whatever was going on between Outoo and Fenrik, he did not know, nor did he really care. He had put a lot on the line to rescue Wyndle from Under Hollow; they all had. He was not about to put all of their hard work in jeopardy for a squabble between two old elves. "C'mon everyone." He waved to the group to follow him to the boats. He kept his eyes on the orbs that were hovering around Fenrik, knowing they could strike at any moment.

The group of friends followed Eldin to the dock nearby and boarded a small wooden rowboat. Wyndle stood her ground, hesitant to leave. She flew over to Outoo and leaned in close to his ear. "He took my blood. There is no telling what powers he now possesses or what he will do," she said, her voice just above a whisper.

Outoo leaned closer to her, keeping his eyes on Fenrik. "I agree, the situation is alarming, but your mission is of higher priority. You must go before he changes his mind and wants more from you than your blood. Go now." His response was also in a low tone.

Wyndle backed up and continued to hover near Outoo's head. She looked over at Fenrik and then back at Outoo. "May the gods protect you," she said to him, while she flew over to her friends.

Eldin and Tye picked up the oars and began rowing the boat away from the Isle of Lost Souls and toward the shores of the Gnomish province. Once they were out of sight, Fenrik lowered his hands and his hovering diseased orbs vanished.

Outoo took a few steps closer to him. "Now, my old friend, tell me what you are up to."

****

Queen Valeria stood in her throne room clutching her Globe of Communication. Although the wounds from the previous battle had been healed by her most trusted cleric, Malsang, the rage inside of her had not left. Her castle had been invaded. Her precious Globe of History had been de-stroyed. *How shall I pray to the Moon Goddess now?* She thought with a heavily angered sigh. But the most painful loss was that of the Winged Angel. The only thing in the realm that could put an end to The Overlord's master plan is now on its way to Solaris Arbor and the portal to her realm.

The Overlord…how am I going to explain all of this to him? Would he even let me live after such a huge failure? Her mind raced in preparation for her conversation with him. If ever she needed her skill of deception, now would be the time.

She squeezed the orb and it began to glow. "I wish to communicate with the Overlord on Caliron." The globe responded to her command and glowed brighter. "I wish to see him," she added. Just then, the air above the globe in her hand wavered as if it had become a window to a different realm—which, indeed, it had. The Overlord came into focus; his cloak covered his head as usual, with his large elf ears causing each side of it to tent.

"Your Highness, forgive my intrusion, but I have some disturbing news to report from Under Hollow." Her tone took on a serious and professional tone. The Queen slid into a submissive role, one she despised, but required, for this conversation. "There has been an insurrection."

The Overlord leaned closer to his globe, making his image larger for the Queen. "The Circle of Thirteen," he stated, without at all sounding surprised. "I was wondering when they would reach their moment of attack. I thought for sure they would hold off until our big push into Solaris Arbor." He tapped his fingertips together and sneered. "This could have all been prepared for, had it not been for your failure to retrieve the Globe of Future-Foretold or to find the Lost City of the Ancients."

Normally, Valeria would have defended her actions, but she knew that now was not the time and let his remarks go. "They had with them," she paused cautiously and lowered her head slightly, "a Winged Angel, My Lord." While keeping her head bowed in submissiveness, she lifted her gaze and cringed inside, knowing what would follow.

The Overlord growled under his breath, stood up, and backed away from the globe. He then erupted in anger. "How could you have let this happen? Where is the angel now?" He whipped his hood back to emphasize his anger. His face was cracked with age and his icy blue eyes were as cold as steel. His lips were thin and his upper lip quivered uncontrollably with anger. Once a man of exceptional beauty and charisma, he was ashamed of how his looks had eroded with time. He preferred to hide his face in his hooded cloak when around his subjects, and the Queen knew that his removal of his hood now was a sign that he was extremely angry with her and with the fact that his plans were unraveling.

Valeria cocked her head to one side for a moment. The Overlord seemed to have had no prior knowledge of the Winged Angel. With all of the gossip and reports of the tiniest setback Fenrik took pride in reporting to the Overlord, how could he not have told him that she had captured one and that it had escaped? This news would surely put an end to her reign in Under Hollow, and perhaps to her life.

She swallowed nervously before she answered her husband. "She is, regrettably, on her way to Solaris Arbor with the traitors. I have my best trackers after them, but they possess a Globe of Direction, which makes tracking them very difficult."

"And it makes their travel to Solaris Arbor that much faster, should they come across a portal." His tone was full of hatred now. The Queen wasn't sure if it was for her or for the situation.

"But what of your brilliant plan of the elders returning to Solaris Arbor and putting an end to the Breathing Forest to allow us passage into—" she started, but she was quickly cut off.

"The Elders are all dead!" he snapped at her, his voice loud. He could see the look of shock and panic over the Queen's face as at last, she fully understood the gravity of the situation. "We were betrayed by our old friend, Outoo. He murdered them on their way back to Solaris Arbor. Once that portal to the angel's domain is opened, they will surely put an end to our plans." He had lowered his voice, but he still spat out his words in disgust.

Valeria breathed in and her thoughts wandered to the previous battle, where she saw Outoo in her very castle. She knew it had to have been him that released the Winged Angel from her Globe of Imprisonment. Anger rose in her again as she recalled the image of Aldara destroying her Globe of History.

A wave of calm came over the Queen as she thought more on Aldara, and then a wicked smile came to her lips. The young half-breed was also on her way back to Solaris Arbor and the Queen's attempt to control her several nights ago when she slept had been a success. Valeria silently commended herself for placing that spell on Aldara when they first met.

"My Lord," she said at last, "there is still a way for us to be victorious." She saw the image of the Overlord's face look at her curiously through the globe as he waited for her to continue. "The half-breed," she began, "she was being held for execution after the Moon Festival. I thought it would be a fitting sacrifice to the Moon Goddess." Her lies now flowed with more confidence. "In order to learn more about her before she was destroyed, I placed the 'Kiss De' Lon' on her." The Queen referred to the kiss she had given Aldara when they first met. Her hope was that the Overlord would welcome this news instead of condemning her for not executing Aldara when ordered to do so many moons ago. "She was freed by the Circle of Thirteen and now accompanies the Winged Angel to the Breathing Forest."

The Overlord's sour look vanished and a hint of a smile appeared on his lips. "And I take it you have tested this spell?" he asked her, lifting an eyebrow.

"With complete success," she flaunted.

The Overlord smiled as he pulled his hood back up over his head. "You may have just redeemed yourself, my Queen." His voice was much calmer now; he seemed pleased that he was now presented with a path to victory.

The Queen regained her regal composure and her majestic air returned. "We must act quickly if we are to reach the borders of Solaris Arbor in time. I will need all of the Dracal on hand for this final assault."

"Although Fenrik's repairs to the weakening Dragon Heart have been successful, creating more Dracal is just getting underway. I will send you the few battalions that I do have, immediately."

"That should more than suffice, My Lord," she thanked him. "I will lead this battle personally to make sure we are successful."

"See that you do," he replied coldly, "failure is not an option and will not be tolerated," he threatened her. "The Dracal will be through the portal in moments. Good fortune to you. I look forward to your report." With that, the air above her Globe of Communication returned to normal and her globe went dark.

A knock sounded on the chamber door, causing Valeria to whirl around toward it. "Enter," she commanded.

The door swung open and Commander Zelgot entered the throne room. He approached her and bowed. "The hunt is ongoing for the angel and her friends; however, I am confident we will find them." His voice was stern and confident, but he knew that after the previous altercation, conversations with the Queen would now have to be handled very delicately.

"Never mind the hunt. Recall your troops," she ordered him. Zelgot's raised eyebrows and quizzical look let her know that this was not the response that he was expecting. "Prepare your men for battle. We leave at once for Solaris Arbor."

Thoroughly confused, Zelgot replied, "But my Queen, what about the Breathing Forest? Such an attack would be a futile effort."

She smiled at her lover. "My plans have been set in motion. Soon, that damned forest will be no concern of ours and in two more cycles, when the moon sets, Solaris Arbor will fall."

Commander Zelgot put his fist to his chest in acknowledgment. He started for the door when the Queen stopped him. He turned back to look at her.

"Zelgot. Your traitorous sister, she will die. After this battle, that will be your number one priority. Do you understand?" her words were cold and the tone in her voice was final.

"Understood, my Queen." Zelgot's answer was just as cold. He bowed to her and exited the throne room.

****

Tye assisted Eldin in pulling the heavy rowboat onto the shores of the Gnomish province. It didn't take long to cross the water and everyone was glad for the chance to rest, however brief it may have been. When Eldin let go of the boat, Tye's end came crashing down onto the shore and he made it look as if he had been the one to throw it down in victory. He looked up, and sure enough, Ayku was watching him. He flashed her a brief smile, then focused on the island and their friend who they had left behind.

Aldara caught the interaction between Tye and Ayku. Looking for something to distract her from her jealousy, she turned from the shore and back to the Isle of Lost Souls, which she could barely make out in the moonlight through the mist. "Outoo shouldn't be that far behind us. I wonder what is going on over there," she pondered aloud.

Eldin joined her as she stared at the island. "Who knows if that elder is even still alive." He turned to the group and shook his head. "That dark elf was really creepy. Who knows, he could be changing his mind right now and sending those corpses after us again."

Yes, dead people are going for a swim to kill all of us on the shore. Aldara thought. She thought of saying it out loud, but she got his point. "The human has a point, sort of. We cannot stay here for too long."

Tye nodded in agreement and then looked over at Wyndle. He approached her with his boyish smile and a sad look in his eye. "Wynd, you've got to go ahead of us. You have to fly to Solaris Arbor as fast as you can and talk to your people. We are only slowing you down." He knew he was approaching a sore subject. "They will take you back, right? To hear what you've learned?"

Wyndle saw the caring in his eyes and slowly shrugged.

"I was banished for interacting with all of you. Banishment is not something my people take lightly. Going back means I will surely lose my wings. But it is the only way to stop the Queen."

Tye knew she was right and that there was no use arguing with her about the sacrifice she was about to make for the entire realm. "Thank...thank you, Wyndle. From all of us."

"Be careful," she said to Tye. She looked around at the entire group of friends that had recently saved her life and finished, "Everyone." She started away from the group, toward Solaris Arbor, when she paused and looked back at her friends for a moment. She then darted away into the night, toward her destiny.

Tye's shoulders slumped. "It feels like I'll never see her again. First Guss and now Wyndle. We've gotta kill the Queen and end all of this." His expression turned to pure sadness as he thought of the murder of his father figure. He bowed his head to the ground in remembrance.

Aldara leaned on her staff and spoke to Tye directly, "We will. She'll pay for everything she has done to Gusseus and everyone else in the realm. This, I promise you."

****

Outoo eyed his old companion up and down. They had both aged so much since the time when they were the heroes, saving the realm from the dragons and the Demon Lord Voltanis. "I cannot believe after all this time you continue to serve the Queen and bring destruction to Sylvanor."

Fenrik looked at Outoo with disgust. "Let it be known, brother, that I have never served the Queen!" he thumped his cane on the ground for emphasis. "I served the Overlord as it fit my needs to do so, but from this point forward, my servitude ends."

Outoo raised his staff, ready for a fight. "You haven't won yet. I cannot let you off of this island to continue to destroy the realm, to turn its inhabitants into that," he pointed at the rotting corpses scattered about the ground, no longer animated.

Adjusting his spectacles on his nose, Fenrik ignored Outoo's defensive posture. "Why do you care so much about those who inhabit this realm? You held the same prejudice we all shared against those that were not of elven kind."

"But that prejudice never led to genocide!" his grip on his staff tightened. "You chose the wrong path, my old friend. You cannot have Sylvanor."

Fenrik began to walk slowly, in a non-threatening way, off of the small mound he was standing on and toward Outoo. It was then he began his confession. "You misunderstand my intentions. I have no desire to rule this realm; let the Queen and the Overlord have it. I have put up with her for one reason only: to get me to this point." He could tell by the confused look on Outoo's face that he still wasn't getting it. It still wasn't clicking. "The time is at hand and soon I will be reunited with Lavora."

Outoo's eyes widened; he now understood Fenrik's motivation. "You cannot bring her back. Your beloved, my sister, is gone forever." Trying to talk sense into his old friend, he continued, "even if you could bring her back, what would she be? One of these undead puppets? She deserves more dignity than that. And I will not allow you to desecrate all that she was." Outoo took a large seed out of his pocket, uttered a quick magical phrase into his hand and threw it at Fenrik. It exploded at his feet and as he expected, it grew instantly. Its branches encased Fenrik in a leafy wooden prison.

Fenrik's old hand grabbed hold of one of the branches and he murmured in his native dark elven language. The leaves on the tree turned yellow, then brown, and fell off of the tree. A creaking sound came from its branches as the wood split around him. With a swipe of his cane, the dead wood gave way easily and Fenrik stepped out of the broken cage.

"I wish you no harm, Outoo." As he spoke, small orbs appeared around him, the same rotting orbs he had conjured earlier for defense. "But I will not allow you to stop me. Go save your world and leave me to my affairs." He stepped closer to the gate portal with his putrefying orbs circling around him.

Outoo closed his eyes tight and slumped his shoulders. It looked as if he was about to admit defeat when he suddenly raised his staff in the air and called on the elements. He moved his staff in a circular motion and a wind tunnel began to form above his head. Quick to react, Fenrik threw out his hand, directing his diseased orbs, which flew to the old light elf and circled around him.

"Cease your call to the elements," Fenrik ordered his old friend, "or die."

Accepting that he could not finish his spell before the floating orbs would be absorbed into his skin, rotting him from the inside, Outoo lowered his staff and the wind subsided. His fate was now in the hands of his once best friend, the husband to his fallen sister.

"I do wish things would have turned out differently between you and me," Fenrik's voice was somber. "We made quite a team all those years ago." He made his way to the edge of the gate portal and inserted his Globe of Direction into the socket of its pedestal. "But now I must leave you, my friend, for I have one more task to complete. Goodbye, Outoo." The globe activated and the image of Under Hollow appeared in the portal's center. Fenrik pushed on the globe, then pulled it out of the stone and in an instant, he was gone. The orbs he'd left behind quickly dissipated.

A curious tear fell from Outoo's eye and he let out a heavy sigh. He was old now, a fact he knew but never really thought about. Seeing his old friend-turned-enemy and discussing his sister for the first time in hundreds of years left him yearning for the past... a time when she was alive, he and Fenrik were friends, and the Queen was nothing more than a catty, spoiled brat that always needed to get her way.

"Goodbye," he said to the empty space inside the portal's circle before turning away and walking toward the dock. There were still a few rickety wooden rowboats tied up and floating on the water. He untied the one that looked the most intact and pushed it into the water before climbing in, barely keeping his balance.

He sat down to look across the water, faintly making out his friends in the distance. "Wetil Lok Soo," he said aloud. The water around him stirred and Outoo gestured forward with his arm. The current of the water picked up and accelerated his boat until it was moving at an incredible speed.

He quickly reached the shores of the Gnomish province and snapped his fingers. The boat returned to its normal pace and glided softly onto the weedy beach. Tye walked over, grabbed Outoo by the arm, and helped him out of the boat.

"What happened over there?" Tye asked as Outoo gave

him a nod of thanks while they made their way toward the warmth of their small fire.

Sadly, Outoo responded, "The end of an old friendship and nothing more." He didn't expect anyone to understand him, nor did he feel like explaining what had transpired on the island.

Eldin finished up the last of the fruit they had gathered, except for one that he tossed to Outoo. "We better be on our way before he comes back." He tossed the core of the fruit to the ground and kicked it off into the nearby shrubbery. "The sooner we get to Solaris Arbor, the sooner we can have a real meal."

Outoo took a bite of the fruit. It was hard and not fully ripe, but he ate it all the same. "There is nothing to fear. Fenrik will not be returning. We will be safe here for the night. Rest easy, my friends, for tomorrow begins our journey home."

Chapter XVI

—◦◦◦—

An Unwelcomed Homecoming

The wind picked up quickly; soon, the air was swirling in a giant funnel cloud. Although the wind was moving at high speed, the landscape below was unaffected. A ball of white light pushed out of the storm, ejecting Wyndle. She flew a small distance from the storm and turned to look back toward it. In an instant, the light was sucked back into the cloud and the storm was over. The portal was closed and she was now home, in the land of the Winged Angels.

Since her departure from her friends, her journey here had been swift and uneventful. She journeyed through the Gnomish province and through the safety of the Breathing Forest before entering Solaris Arbor. Then, for the first time since she had been banished from her realm, she opened the portal that returned her home.

She looked around her homeland as she slowly descended

to the ground. It hadn't changed at all in the many years since she had last been here. The land was lush and the grass was greener than any she had seen elsewhere. There were many babbling streams that littered the landscape and they criss-crossed each other often. The healing waters flowed gently through them as if they were veins of a larger entity.

The sound of the trickling water and the stillness of the air made Wyndle take in a long, deep breath and close her eyes. This was a moment of peace that she had not felt in a long time. It was as if nothing here could hurt her.

How wrong she was, for she had come back. She had been banished from this land quite some time ago for interfering with those who dwelled in the land of Sylvanor. Her people are the karmic keepers of life. Their job is to make sure balance is kept among all of the realms. Interference is forbidden, except when required to restore the alignment of a realm, but only if that realm may have been misaligned by unnatural means.

'Unnatural means' was a term that was hard to understand by anyone who wasn't an angel. In worlds where magic was commonplace and war seemed to come as often as the seasons, their definition of 'karmic balance' remained a mystery to many. In some realms, such as Sylvanor, the purpose of the Winged Angels and the ignorance of their function was enough to cause a violent confrontation. A confrontation that had ended with the banishment of the angels to their homeland.

The decree of separation from the angels by the leaders of Sylvanor was something to which Wyndle had never paid attention. She could never understand why her people obeyed the ruling and left the realms to their own devices.

She still believed it was the duty of her people to protect all of the realms, regardless of emotional decisions by those living in them.

Wyndle had secretly traveled to Sylvanor during the last Great War and helped those whose situations were dire. She considered the Demon Lord Voltanis, who crossed over from the borders of its hell and into Sylvanor to ravage the land for his own means, to be the very definition of 'unnatural means'. Her people did not agree; they cared very little about what went on in a realm they had been forced to leave. Such a mandate was unprecedented and considered a high insult. When they discovered that Wyndle had broken this cardinal rule, they banished her to the world she seemed to love more dearly. The price she would pay if she ever returned home would be the ultimate punishment—the removal of her wings.

Wingless Angels were the social pariahs of her world. It was forbidden even to speak to them, and all other interaction with them was kept to a strict minimum. This law was very easy for the angels to follow, as a Wingless Angel was an extremely rare sight to behold. Wyndle couldn't recall ever seeing one in her lifetime, and she feared that coming home now would mean that she would see one every time she looked at her reflection, whether in a looking glass or in the healing waters of the streams that she loved so much.

The thought of losing her wings interrupted her moment of serenity and she slowly opened her eyes, surprised to see a pair of eyes staring back at her. She gasped and jumped back, taking to the air.

She was now looking at what she had never seen before. A Wingless Angel was staring at her from the spot where she'd just ascended. He was dressed in black pants and wore nothing on his sculpted chest but suspender-like straps that crossed his fit body. In this realm, the color white symbolized purity and was worn by everyone; wearing black was considered part of the shame, for a Winged Angel would never wear a color of darkness. His face was handsome and his black hair flopped down into his face, covering his green eyes. He bore the mark of shame that had been seared into his forehead at the time of his sentencing.

Wyndle looked shocked. "You...you're a—" she began as she slowly descended back to the ground, her look of shock now replaced by one of curiosity.

"A Wingless Angel," replied the fallen stranger. He carefully looked around to see if anyone was watching their exchange. "It is forbidden for you to talk to me."

Wyndle joined him, also looking around the grassy field. "My name is Wyndle," she offered.

"It is also forbidden for you to come back, Wyndle," he said, as if he knew who she was. "You were the object of talk here for quite some time. And, I must add, you were very inspirational to me, as well."

Wyndle knew it was forbidden to talk to him, but she also knew that by coming back, she would soon be one of them, so what would it matter? What else could they do to her? "I am sorry that my inspiration has caused you so much pain," she replied. She leaned forward and over to his side, looking to see if there were any remnants of his wings left.

Her new friend turned around to give her a better view of what she was hoping to see. Two large scars blemished his back and could easily be seen under the crossing of his black straps.

Judging by the look of them, it seemed that the de-winging process was not a painless one. He turned back around to see Wyndle lower her head. "My name is Yerel," he greeted her.

She raised her head and bit her lip. Not only had she returned home, but she was now socializing with a fallen angel. She was sure she had now broken every rule imaginable.

"Tell me, Wyndle. What brings you back home? What could you possibly want here that would bring my fate upon you?" he asked her. He could not hide the tone in his voice that belied his thought of *How could anyone be so stupid?*

"There is much happening in the realm of Sylvanor," she answered, catching the tone in his voice. "I came back not for myself, but to help those in the realm. There are many unnatural things happening there. I must tell my father and the other Winged Angels on the committee of what is transpiring, in the hope that they will intervene. It is Sylvanor's only chance of survival. The dark elves have these beings that aren't alive! It seems as if—"

"Do you really think your father is going to care?" he asked her sternly. "Do you think any of them will care what happens on Sylvanor?" His words were full of disgust.

Wyndle's eyes widened, "Yes! It is his duty, the duty of all our people."

Yerel laughed, "Sylvanor's leaders turned their noses up at him, at all of us." He saw her look of disappointment. "Much has changed since you left, Wyndle. The committee has gotten lazy and uncaring. It seems the only thing they care about is this place," he extended his hand to the field.

"I'm here now," she shook her head. "I am going to see my father. There isn't much time."

Yerel sighed, for he knew she had come back in vain. Her pleas would not be heard and her wings would be stripped away. With a slump of his shoulders, he admitted, "Sadly, I cannot take you to him as the way requires flight. But the committee's judgment platform is to the east." He leaned toward her. "For your sake, do not speak of our meeting, much less our conversation."

Wyndle nodded her head in acknowledgement. "Thank you, Yerel. It is comforting to know that I will at least have one friend here after my wings are removed."

Wyndle took to the sky toward the floating platform of the committee. She spread her wings and was determined to enjoy this flight as much as possible, for she knew it would be her last.

****

It wasn't until Wyndle was floating inside the Circle of Judgment with two winged escorts on either side of her that she finally realized the hypocrisy of her people. The Winged Angels kept the balance of all things without judging, yet she hovers here before the committee, waiting to be judged herself.

The platform itself was a large circular disc made of crystal; it floated high in the sky. The sunlight shone through it, causing breathtaking prisms of light to arc across the sky and down onto the fields before showering everything in a soft array of multiple colors.

On the other side of the disc was an area large enough to fit a few dozen committee members. Winged Angels filled the area to capacity and most of them were considerably older than Wyndle. They made all the decisions of her race, the realms connected to her homeland, and apparently, her fate.

Wyndle looked around the room sadly and her survey ended on the two angels by her side. *When were guards necessary?* she thought. She bowed her head and marveled at just how much her people had changed.

There was a rustling among the committee when the Proconsul, her father, finally reached the platform and took his place in front of them. Her father had always been a proud man, and Wyndle was about to find out how that pride had turned to arrogance and entitlement.

He was an old angel whose hair had gone gray, but his youthful physique remained intact. He held a ceremonial scepter in his hand, which pulsed with a glittering light, signaling that the judgment ceremony had officially begun.

"My daughter, Wyndle," his voice was intimidating as it boomed over the entire platform. "You have been deemed 'disharmonious' by this committee and banished to live out your years in the realm of Sylvanor. Why have you violated one of our most sacred laws and returned?"

Wyndle was taken aback. She had forgotten just how cold her father could be. Neither a greeting nor a look of empathy was on his face. It broke her heart, and the fact that his coldness still could affect her so much broke it even further. "My dear father," she said at last, "I wish you, the committee, and all of the Winged Angels no disrespect." She watched as all eyes were on her. All had blank, careless stares except for one, whose look of empathy caught her eye. She lost her train of thought for a moment, then focused on her father once again. "But there is a disturbance in the karmic balance in the realm of Sylvanor."

The empathetic angel raised his eyebrows with interest and looked at Wyndle's father, wondering if his reaction would be the same as it had been since the humiliation brought on by Sylvanor's rulers. He hoped that hearing this news from his own daughter would pique his interest once again, reigniting the purpose and the passion of the angels.

"Sylvanor released us from overseeing their welfare many years ago. Their problems are no longer our concern and haven't been for quite some time." Her father's reaction was, sadly, just as the empathetic angel had predicted.

"But the dark elven race has crossed over into another realm and is somehow harnessing the life force of dragons to create mindless armies of a new race of beings not capable of living on its own!" Wyndle spoke in a tone of anger she rarely used.

The empathetic Winged Angel shot a glance to an angel hovering beside him and their eyes locked in a moment of concern. "This is most alarming!" he protested. "Such a claim must be investigated!"

Wyndle held her hand up in front of her, her palm facing the committee. "Link with me and you will see what was shown to me in their Globe of History," she offered.

Wyndle's father ignored his daughter's request and snapped at what seemed to be her only ally on the committee. "You speak out of turn, Teluli. Remember your place on the committee," his arrogance coated his words. "It would also suit you well to remember that you are fortunate to be in this realm at all," he concluded, turning his attention back to Wyndle.

She hardly recognized her father. He was more of a tyrant now than Proconsul. Power had gone to his head, making him unreasonable. "It's true! And it is the duty of our people to set things right!" she demanded.

"You dare lecture me on the ways of our people? You, my own daughter, after breaking several of our laws yourself?" He paused to sigh. "Violating your punishment and returning here brings upon you the sentence of the removal of your wings."

"I accept my punishment, but you must listen to me," she continued to plead. Losing her wings, although devastating to an angel, was something she had expected on her return.

"Proconsul, we must see reason and listen to what she has to say. For too long, we have ignored the realm that has taken her away from us. We can no longer be ignorant of Sylvanor. If what she says is true, and the dark elves have crossed realms to create these soulless beings, then the problem could be spreading and it is only a matter of time before—" Teluli's voice of reason was cut down by the tyrannical words of Wyndle's father.

"Enough!" he shouted. "There is nothing left to discuss here. Wyndle, you will be taken away to have your sentence carried out. Your poisonous nature cannot be allowed to infect the angels in this realm." For the first time, he looked at her with a hint of sadness in his eyes. "Your actions, my daughter, are highly regrettable. I am sorry."

The Proconsul raised his scepter, and with a glittering shower of light, declared the judgment over. Most of the Winged Angels on the committee flew away, leaving a handful behind who crowded around Teluli and began whispering.

Wyndle's escorts gently took her by her arms. They did not enjoy the task they were about to perform. Removing an angel's wings was the highest form of dishonor among her kind;

most thought it a fate worse than death. They guided her away from the platform and all three disappeared to the land below, where she would meet her fate.

As the Proconsul took flight, the group of the lingering committee members caught his eye. "This session is adjourned, my brothers and sisters," he said sternly.

"No," answered Teluli, "we believe it is not."

Chapter XVII

—⟨ɷɷ⟩—

An Early Autumn

The clouds covered the sky, but here and there, beams of sunlight shone through and illuminated trees, bushes, lakes, and various other objects in the land of the Gnomish province. It was a beautiful sight to behold, and it almost made Tye forget about the ravages of war and the destruction it can bring.

Occasionally, he would snap back to reality when the heavens spotlighted the scorched terrain. Tye let out a heavy sigh. *Was Solaris Arbor the only safe place left in the land?* he thought. There had to be safe pockets for people elsewhere throughout the realm. They couldn't all be in Solaris Arbor.

Tye let out another sigh and shuffled his feet as he walked with his friends. They had been walking since dawn, and although they had rested well the night before, the journey was taking its toll. The changing landscape also played a role in his fatigue. The burnt trees, dead grass, and black dirt was much more common now than it had been when they left the shore that morning. There is nothing sadder for a light elf than to see nature dying like this on such a grand scale, and presumably for quite some time. Many seasons ago, tears would have come to Tye's eyes at this sight of such destruction, but sadly, he was becoming numb to its commonality.

Nearing the end of the semi-ripened fruit he had recently picked from a seemingly untouched grove, he placed its core on the ground. He covered it with dirt, and just above a whisper, uttered a short magical phrase. When he finished his incantation, the small mound of dirt covering the core began to quiver and a small tree bloomed from its center and grew to his height. Leaves popped out of its branches and small pods formed that would eventually turn into fruit.

He smiled at his handiwork. Tye didn't know much magic. At an early age, he was taught the basics to keep Solaris Arbor, and the realm, growing and full of life. Seeing this tiny tree now growing in the center of an ashen landscape gave him hope that perhaps one day, the land could be restored.

"Why don'tcha just leave a trail of breadcrumbs for the dark elves to follow, junior," Eldin asked, ruining the moment. He was a very practical man, always planning his next move, but he realized that sometimes his practicality appeared a little harsh. Seeing Tye's expression of hope fade, Eldin reconsidered. "I suppose one tree wouldn't hurt," he backtracked. "I mean, you never know who may happen along and need something to eat. Good thinking, kid." He waited, only for a moment, for the smile to return to Tye's face before turning his focus on the land ahead.

Eldin's thoughts were still on the young elf, however. Just yesterday, Tye had lost the only father he had ever known. On top of everything else, he was now an orphan. Eldin knew that the right thing for him to do, as a knight of honor, would be to take Tye under his wing and continue his education in the art of combat. Tye's further studies in magic and anything else that involved a book were best left up to Outoo. Eldin looked over at the old elf, their eyes locked, and they exchanged a brief smile.

"We are certainly taking the long way. It will take us days to reach Solaris Arbor. I just hope Wyndle will make it there okay," Aldara spoke out loud to Ali-Mimi, but it was loud enough for the others to hear.

"We are lucky to be out of Under Hollow at all," Ayku retorted. She felt bad for her friends and how tired they must be. For most of this journey, she sat quietly on Tye's shoulder, nestled in a wrinkle in his clothes and holding on to his quiver's strap.

Ayku didn't care much for Aldara. Her dislike did not run as deep as Eldin's, but she knew Aldara had strong feelings for Tye. She also knew that, given the chance, she would quickly act on them. "Complaining about our current situation won't help us any," the fairie concluded.

"The way is not too much further," Outoo interjected before an argument broke out. "Just up ahead, near those buildings, is our way home. You will be able to thank Aldara for getting us home so quickly."

Everyone displayed clear looks of surprise, especially Aldara, who obviously had no idea what Outoo was talking about. Outoo's meaning became clearer once they could make out a few stone buildings that were coming into focus. They were as burnt as the landscape. Their thatched rooftops were gone and the windows had been blown out. Some of them were damaged so badly, no one could figure out how they were still standing.

Upon reaching them, they could see that the buildings were arranged in a half circle around a gate portal. There were a few bodies on the ground. Some were burnt beyond recognition, victims of the Dracal, while others were shot with arrows or had been slain with a warrior's sword. It was clear to everyone that a battle had taken place here not too long ago, and its victims had gathered at the portal in a desperate attempt to escape.

"These gnomes didn't stand a chance," Eldin said as he bowed his head with respect.

"None of us do if the Winged Angel doesn't reach her kind," Aldara said in her own practical tone, but unlike Eldin, she offered no apology for it. "If they had a Globe of Direction, it was taken," she informed the group as she scanned the bodies for anything useful.

Ayku shot Aldara a sour look. "Should we bury them?" she asked Outoo.

"There isn't time to pay our respects to them, unfortunately." He pounded his staff on the ground in a mixed display of anger and sorrow. "But we can honor them by continuing their fight for the freedom of Sylvanor." he proclaimed.

Outoo motioned for everyone to enter the portal's center and nodded to Aldara. She caught on and pulled the globe from her bag. She placed it carefully in the indentation on the portal's chipped and battered pedestal.

"Patience and timing is what is needed now," Outoo said to her. "Wait until you can see the Breathing Forest around us before you press the globe."

Images of Sylvanor materialized around them, they rotated through a grassy land, the deadened forest of Glinfel, the Isle of Lost Souls—all of which were common places of travel—but when an image of the portal in Under Hollow and an image of the barren desert came into view, Outoo was startled.

How could this globe point back to the gate portal in Under Hollow? No ordinary globe used by the residents of Sylvanor has that ability. Only a few globes do and you must be dark elven to use them, he thought. What he thought was even more peculiar was the portal in the barren desert. In all of his travels, he had never seen a desert portal and frankly, he didn't even know of its existence.

A tranquil forest appeared around them and Aldara quickly recognized it as the Breathing Forest. "Got it," she said with confidence. She pressed the globe into the stone and then quickly plucked it out while taking a hurried step back inside the circle. In an instant, she and her friends vanished.

****

The fire that erupted from the horselike beasts that pulled the Queen's carriage was roaring as it left a steady trail of flame and smoke behind. The carriage was flying just above the ground at its usual high speed. Valeria's transport was the quickest method of transport available for those who did not possess a Globe of Direction. The Queen, of course, did possess such a globe, but she enjoyed the regal display her carriage put on.

She was now far from the deadened forest of Glinfel and her beloved Under Hollow. In a single night, she managed to travel out of the southern lands, through the old Dwarven province and was now passing through the marshlands that opened up to the beautiful wide open plains of Sylvanor.

The plains were grassy and still beautiful, because they were close to the light elves' Breathing Forest. Not many battles had taken place here and Queen Valeria was glad that some parts of the realm remained relatively intact for her people.

The Queen enjoyed the view from inside the carriage. She looked on what she believed to be *her* domain through the dark, parchment-thin lenses of her obsidian visor. She was dressed in her usual traveling attire for the journey to the land above. Her black leather fatigues fit snugly on her body, as did her dark boots and gloves. Leaning by her side was not the weapon that held her Globe of Imprisonment, but another staff—this one of pure silver with a long, pointed crystal at its end. It was similar to the staff Aldara had acquired from one of her dark elf victims, but the Queen's was much more powerful.

She raised her hand in the air and her carriage immediately slowed to a crawl. The trail of flame and smoke expelled by her carriage disappeared and the fire that once engulfed the hooves of the magical beasts pulling it were now gently licking the grass beneath it. The carriage came to a complete stop and lowered to the ground.

Queen Valeria opened the door, adjusted her visor, and stepped out of the carriage onto the ground of Sylvanor's plains. She surveyed the area and drew in a deep breath. The air was sweet and a gentle breeze seemed to almost constantly wash across the fields. It flowed all around the Queen. She took it all in. She was grateful to be out of her carriage to stretch her legs. When she opened her eyes, she looked off into the distance. Valeria could now faintly make out the outlines of tall, thick trees. *The Breathing Forest*, she thought as a smile curled her lips.

Raising her hands in the air, Valeria began to cast her magnification spell. She threw her hands up in the air and moved them in a clockwise fashion, her hands occasionally overlapping. In a few moments, the air in front of her twisted and the distant forest came into view. Its dense, leafy trees swayed in the wind and several light elves were milling about the area.

"Enjoy it while you can," she said aloud.

With a wave of her hand, the air returned to normal. The forest now appeared exactly where it was, off in the distance. Reaching into her carriage, she pulled out the small Globe of Communication and gave it a squeeze. "I wish to speak to Commander Zelgot, master of the dark elf army," she spoke her command to the globe.

The globe turned from its dark amber color to a brighter yellow. It vibrated ever so slightly in her hand.

"Greetings, my Queen," a familiar voice came from her globe. "How goes your trip to the Breathing Forest?" Zelgot asked her pleasantly.

"The night was long, my..." she paused, not sure of who could be listening on the other end, "Zelgot." Every time she felt the need to hide her relationship with Zelgot, she had a sickening feeling in her stomach. She was the Queen of Under Hollow and soon, the Queen of the entire realm; she should not have to hide anything. However, she was fully aware of what would happen to her should the Overlord discover her affair.

"My forces have left Glinfel and have circled around the Crystal Fields," he reported to her. "We are now in the

Dwarven province."

"Excellent," she smiled, "I have reached my destination and will await you and your army of Dracal here on the edge of the plains."

"Very good, my Queen," came Zelgot's voice from the globe. "We will meet you at the rendezvous coordinates at dawn. I trust that will be acceptable."

The Queen raised her globe to her lips. "Completely," she said to her secret love. "By this time tomorrow, Solaris Arbor will be ours."

Valeria gently squeezed her Globe of Communication and it went dark. She tossed it into her carriage without a care and threw her head back in the wind. She let out a gentle moan as she rolled her head on her shoulders. When she stopped, she looked upon the forest in the distance and flashed it a wicked smile.

****

In a whooshing sound and a flash of light, Outoo had returned home with his friends. The gate portal they had just materialized into was much different than those they had used before. This one was in perfect condition. The short walls that surrounded the portal's circle were intact and emerald green gems decorated its activation pillar.

The light elves who were going about their daily activities stopped what they were doing and assumed a defensive posture, not knowing who or what was coming through the portal. Some of the younger light elves made a dash for the forest and their home of Solaris Arbor beyond it. It wasn't until Outoo raised his hand in a friendly gesture that they cautiously went back to what they were doing, although a few elves continued to watch the group's every move.

The portal was located just on the edge of the Breathing Forest in the Great Plains. Tall grass was blowing in the gentle wind and the landscape seemed to stretch on forever. The setting sun made the endless sky burst with color. As pleasant a sight as it was, what brought even more comfort to them was the Breathing Forest itself. The forest was a dense, magical area that surrounded all of Solaris Arbor. Only the pure of heart were able to pass through its trees and into the haven beyond.

"I can't believe I'm finally home!" Tye exclaimed.

The forest was a welcome sight to everyone except Aldara. She looked upon it, remembering all the times she was teased within its borders. To her, Solaris Arbor wasn't a joyous, happy land. It was one of misery and sorrow. *I suppose it's better than Under Hollow, though it's not as pretty*, she thought.

She shook off her memories of the past in an attempt to compose herself. Much time had passed since she was last here. She had discovered the secret of the dark elves. She had learned the origin of the Dracal and had helped bring back a Winged Angel that would help them win the war. Surely, the light elves would not see her as a mere half-breed, but as a hero: *Aldara, Savior of Sylvanor*. She smiled, liking the sound of it.

"Maybe you should get comfortable out here, witch," Eldin jabbed her. "I doubt the forest will let you through." Eldin was the first to enter the forest and everyone else followed. Aldara rolled her eyes at him and shook off his remark. She was done fighting stupid.

As they made their way into the forest, they could not help but notice its calm, peaceful beauty. Small animals scurried on the ground and up into the trees. Birds whistled in song high up on its canopy, and the sunlight shone through its bright green leaves, striking the ground and lighting up the glittery, golden dust of its precious metals.

Ayku leapt from Tye's shoulder and twirled in the air. "Oh, how I have missed this place!" she giggled with delight.

Tye joined her in a laugh and she flew around his head. Laughter soon came over everyone except Aldara. But the deeper she delved into the forest, the happier she felt. Her sad memories of the place seemed to have faded away. She may get teased on the other side, but at least she would be safe from the evil hands of the Queen and her minions. The harder she tried to fight her smile, the harder it became and soon she, too, let out a burst of laughter. Outoo looked at her with a warm smile.

Their laughter came to a sudden halt as the branches of the trees began to move in their direction. The roots of the trees lifted slightly out of the ground and surrounded them as well.

None of the group was alarmed, for this was what happened whenever anything entered the Breathing Forest. This was the time where their hearts would be judged. If their intentions were pure and peaceful, they were allowed to pass. If their hearts were of ill intent, they would never make it out of the forest alive. It was for this reason alone that the Queen and her forces were unable to take Solaris Arbor. Every attempt ended with the forest taking her troops. Even the Dracal didn't stand a chance against the forces of nature itself.

Suspended on the thick vines that hung from the trees was a beautiful, sultry woman who was gradually lowered to the ground. She had smooth, cocoa-colored skin and bright green eyes, and she was dressed in a small outfit that seemed to cover only what needed covering. Her deep emerald hair was blowing in the wind, matching the flow of her arms, which swayed from side to side as she came closer to the ground.

She eyed each of them in turn and and her arms continued their gentle swaying as she walked around the group. "My name is Jade," she said at last. "Welcome to my forest." She did not wait for, nor did she expect, an answer from any of them. Jade was the embodiment of the forest and she was just as legendary. She had the respect of everyone in the realm, save those in Under Hollow. She had been Sylvanor's mother, in a sense, nurturing the realm and protecting all those who ran to her from danger.

Jade approached Outoo, whom she recognized immediately, and gave him a smile. She placed her hand on his chest and closed her eyes. "Your heart is pure and your intentions lawful. You may pass into the land of Solaris Arbor," she said after a moment.

Outoo gave her a nod and a thankful smile. Jade caught his eye and then moved on to the others. She placed her hand on the chests of Eldin, and then Tye, and their outcomes were the same.

Ayku grew in size in a burst of light that caused Jade's eyes to widen. She closed them slowly and then reopened them, placing her hand on Ayku's heart. "Welcome, member of the fairie folk. You may enter into the land beyond."

Aldara stood, watching Jade's judgment of her companions, nervously tapping her foot. This was not her first time in or out of the forest, but this judgment made her feel uneasy every time. After a lifetime of being judged by everyone, she was more than over it.

Jade approached Aldara with the same warming smile she offered to everyone. Aldara stood still and she stopped tapping her foot. With their eyes locked, Jade placed her hand on Aldara's chest and closed her eyes. A bead of sweat rolled from underneath the gray streak in her hair and down her cheek before finding its way to her neck.

Jade opened her eyes and looked at Aldara, studying her face. Jade's mouth opened just a crack, and then she closed it and shut her eyes once more. After a moment, the trees rustled. Eldin put his hand to his moustache and stroked it as he raised an eyebrow. *I knew she wouldn't make it through. Finally, everyone in the group can see what I knew all along,* he thought.

The branches of the trees came closer to Aldara and she nervously looked around. Just then, the roots sank back into the ground and the branches lifted around them. They were now free of their earthly confines.

"Your heart is pure and your intentions are lawful. You, too, may pass into Solaris Arbor, my ancient one," she said softly to Aldara.

Ancient? thought Aldara. She wasn't exactly sure what Jade meant, thinking her ancient comment was better suited for Outoo. "Thank you," Aldara said at last, in a voice just above a whisper.

"As is customary," Jade addressed the group as a whole, "you will be my guests this evening in the forest." She stood before them with her arms still swaying in front of her. Her body seemed to almost float in the air. "You will awaken soon after the morning sun with your spirit renewed."

Eldin took a step forward and opened his mouth to protest

but Outoo stopped him by placing his hand on his shoulder. They all knew time was of the essence, but Outoo also knew better than to refuse the offer of hospitality from Jade, as it would have been looked on as a high insult.

"Your offer is most kind, Lady Jade," Outoo replied.

Jade raised her arms in the air and thick patches of green moss and long blades of soft grass sprang out of the ground and appeared at their feet. The bedding that Jade had just provided was softer than anything they had slept on during their time in captivity and on the run.

Tye was the first to fall onto his makeshift bed. He let out a comfortable sigh and was asleep in no time at all. The others sank more slowly into their beds and were grateful at the comfort Jade had provided.

Aldara lay down in her bed after Tye and settled in. She looked over at him and marveled at how trusting he must be, to allow himself to fall asleep so easily. As she removed her shoulder bag, she pulled from it a small knife and subtly slid it beneath her pillow before resting her head. She was not so trusting.

When they all were settled in, a pair of thick vines once again lowered, this time behind Jade. Rather than carrying her back into the air, they lowered a large collection of thatched leaves for her to sleep in so she could join the wanderers in their sleep.

She seemed to float into her hammock and she waved her hand in the air. "Sleep well, my weary travelers."

****

The sun peeked over the horizon. The darkened sky already glowed faintly with deep reds and oranges. A new day was beginning in Sylvanor, a day that would forever change its destiny.

Aldara, a voice said softly in her head. Aldara stirred but remained asleep.

Aldara, the voice repeated this time more sternly. *You and your friends are in danger. The woman of the forest is not what she claims to be. You are all in grave danger.*

Aldara's eyes popped open, but she was still sleeping. She could hear the Queen's words echoing in her mind. She was falling victim, for the third time, to the Queen's 'Kiss De' Lon' spell. Its influence is so powerful, the thought of fighting it never occurs to those who are spellbound. *Danger. I must warn the others!* She accepted.

Ali-Mimi tossed in his sleep. To him this was a dream that Aldara was having. Being mentally linked with someone was confusing enough, especially when the being with whom you are linked is dreaming, let alone being controlled, through their subconscious.

No! There is no time! If you warn the others it will only give her the chance to kill you all, the Queen's voice continued to deceive her. *You must strike at her first. If you kill her, all will be well. Sylvanor will finally be free. That is what you want, isn't it? You would be a hero. Everyone would love you.*

Yes. Of course it is. A hero. Yes, I would be a hero, Aldara's thoughts made her sound like a zombie, as she became a mindless puppet of the Queen.

Do it. NOW! ordered the Queen.

Aldara reached under her pillow and grabbed hold of her small knife. She sat up in her bed and looked around. Everyone was still sleeping. Eldin snored loudly, Ayku gently purred, and Ali-Mimi's foot twitched back and forth. Jade was also fast asleep. As everyone had been found to be pure of heart, neither she nor the forest was believed to be in any danger.

Silently, as if pulled by unseen ghosts, Aldara rose to her feet and walked toward Jade. She stood in front of her sleeping body, watching her chest rise and fall in a peaceful rhythm. Jade had been so nice to them. She is known through the land as a gentle peacekeeper. She protected Aldara on more than one occasion in her lifetime; *how could she be bad?* Aldara raised her small knife and stood there motionless. Something deep within her was trying to fight the Queen's possession.

DO IT. The Queen's words were powerful and irresistible.

Without pausing another second, Aldara plunged the knife into Jade's heart. Jade's eyes opened immediately and a blood-curdling scream shot out from her lips and echoed throughout the forest and, it seemed, the entire land.

The Queen's wicked laughter now filled Aldara's head and the screams of Jade's pain snapped her out of the Queen's spell. She blinked and looked at the bloody knife in her hand. Ali-Mimi jumped out of his slumber and added a cry that also chilled her bones.

Jade's scream continued, waking all those around her. Aldara's companions stared in disbelief at what she had done and what was sure to follow.

Jade looked into the sky and her scream suddenly stopped. Her eyes focused upward as she drew her last breath. She now lay in her hammock, dead.

"What in all the planes of Hell have you done, witch?!" Eldin screamed at her.

Aldara opened her mouth to explain when a rustling was heard all around them. As the sun continued to rise, it illuminated the forest, revealing that the trees had begun to shed their leaves. They turned brown on their limbs before they fell and glided to the ground. It was like autumn had suddenly come, but this was not autumn. The forest was dying. The moss on the ground had turned a dark brown and the berries in the bushes had all shriveled up and begun to decay.

"It," Aldara stuttered, "it wasn't me!" She whirled around at Tye and Outoo. "It was the Queen! She came to me again. I couldn't stop it! I just couldn't stop her." Aldara sobbed uncontrollably at what she had done.

Outoo sighed and dropped his head. This was the beginning of the end. No longer did Solaris Arbor have its protection. The Queen's forces could enter, which they would, and they would overtake the land at any time she chose. All they could do now is warn those living beyond the forest to prepare for a battle that would take many lives.

"I *knew* you were working for the Queen!" accused Eldin. "You'll pay for what you've done here, traitor." Eldin picked up his sword and quickly drew it from its sheath. He took a step toward her, intent on ending her life.

"Stop!" Outoo slammed his staff into the ground, causing a shock wave that almost knocked Eldin off balance. "Our young friend was under Valeria's control. She was powerless to resist the charm. Although her actions have caused the death of the forest, she is not to blame," his voice was loud and stern. "You will not touch her or you will answer to me." This was a side of Outoo none of them had seen before and it was intimidating, even to Eldin.

"You knew about this…possession?" Eldin asked Outoo. Without waiting for an answer, he looked at Tye, who put his arm around Aldara to comfort her. "You both did?"

Outoo kept his gaze on Eldin. "Yes, we did."

"And you kept it from us?!" Eldin erupted in a rage. "Do you have any idea what you have done?" He gestured all around him. "The forest is DEAD. Our last hope to make a stand is gone. All of our hard work, gone. Our lives, the lives of the children over there in Solaris Arbor, gone." He pointed to the light elf domain on the other side of the forest.

"It is done, Eldin. We must enter Solaris Arbor and send the children away to safety before the dark elf forces arrive. There is no telling how much time we have." Outoo declared.

"And just where are they going to go?" Eldin asked sarcastically. "All of the lands have fallen."

Outoo paused, as he was about to reveal a secret of the light elves to a human. "Long ago, my people carved out large catacombs underneath Solaris Arbor," he began. "It was our version of Under Hollow, albeit on a much smaller scale. We can hide my brethren there. We can use our magic to cover them with nature. They will be safe for a while."

"A *while*?" Eldin answered. "Just how long is a while?"

Ayku walked over to Eldin and grabbed his hand, pulling him away from the conversation and away from Aldara. He lowered his sword and packed up his belongings. The others did the same. Ayku looked over at Aldara and shook her head in disgust. She had no words for her, not anymore. With a flash of light, she shrank in size and led Eldin and Outoo toward the land of the light elves.

Tye and Aldara lingered behind for a few moments before joining the others. Aldara composed herself as best as she could. Tye flung his quiver of arrows over his shoulder and took her hand.

"Eldin is right, Tye," she started, "I am to blame for this. I should have left that night she possessed me on the way to Under Hollow. If I had the courage to do so, none of this would have happened."

"You would have died on your own out there and we never would have made it to the Queen's castle to save Wyndle. We needed you," he said softly to her.

Aldara burst out in anger, "Look around you, Tyelander! We made it to the castle and freed Wyndle from a situation that *I* put her in! And where is she now? Is she here? No. She went back home to help us—to a place where she was banished. They've ripped off her wings, Tye. *That's* why she's not here! And poor Gusseus! He gave his life to save *mine*. Everything is my fault!"

Ali-Mimi circled her leg in a vain attempt to comfort her. He was too scared to interject himself into the conversation but eventually he looked up at Aldara and spoke, "Must help elves. Bad Queen coming. She will kill everyone, me think."

Aldara looked down at him. "You're right, Ali." Ali-Mimi jumped up to his usual spot on her shoulder. "I will help as many folk as I can and then I am leaving. It is not safe for me to be around anyone," she said to Tye.

"Al, you can't just leave…"

"I have to. What if next time she orders me to kill you or one of the others?" she shook her head. "My mind is made up. I will help clear out the children and I will stand with you and fight. Should I be lucky enough to survive, I will banish myself and leave in exile." Aldara didn't wait for a response. She picked up her things and started for the other end of the

Breathing Forest, Tye following close behind.

****

Solaris Arbor was as beautiful as Tye had remembered. It hadn't changed at all since he was last home. It was one of the largest provinces in the realm and one of the most remarkable. He looked upon the town of Terrenal. It was an ancient town built by the light elves, standing adjacent to the Breathing Forest, welcoming all those who enter Solaris Arbor.

Terrenal had no protective walls and battlements, for it had no use for them. White stucco buildings and cottages lined the edge of the town. Neatly placed cobblestones connected the buildings and led to a large town square, where an enormous fountain bubbled fresh, sparkling water high into the air that fell in soft splashes, collecting in a frothy pool at its base.

The tallest structure of the town was a large temple devoted to the God of the Sun. It was a two-story building that had a large spire stretching high into the sky. At the top of the spire was a large sunrise-viewing platform with a large bell attached to it that was used in conjunction with services to the Sun God. On the face of the building hung a large golden sun with its rays stretched out across the entire front of the building and wrapping around its side. Ordinarily, the temple was a place of peace, but now, with the death of the forest, it was in a flurry of panic.

Outoo and Eldin were already hard at work, spreading the word of the impending assault. Outoo stood on a large platform used for town events and raised his hand to quiet the fountain.

"My brothers and sisters, we do not have much time. You

must gather only those belongings which you can carry, make your way north, and enter the network of catacombs below Solaris Arbor as quickly as you can," he instructed. "You will be safe there, for the enemy has no knowledge of them. I will use our Globes of Communication to spread the news throughout the province. Those who are willing and able must stand to fight. We need to slow the Queen's attack while our citizens make their way to safety. We had best call upon the clouds to gather as quickly as we can. We will need their assistance in battle."

The crying children and the look of fear in everyone's eyes saddened Tye. He shook off his despair with a dedication to his new mission at hand; he must gather all of the archers and spell casters that he can.

"Tye?" a familiar voice came out to him from the crowd, "Tyelander, it *is* you!" A young elf came running up to Tye, hugged him tight and kissed him. It was Tye's best friend, Jencen, a friend he had known since birth. Excitement came over them and for a split second, the despair of the town seemed to disappear.

Jencen was a handsome young elf who, like Tye, was an accomplished archer. They had grown up together, attended the same schools, and had gone through more than their share of troubles. As much as they loved each other, they could not see eye-to-eye on a whole slew of issues. It caused them to quarrel often; in fact, they had an argument the night before Tye left Solaris Arbor for the town of Frentier all those months ago. It had been too long since Jencen had seen his friend and he had thought the worst. He spent every day hoping he would hear some news of Tye, but none ever came. He journeyed out into the realm on quite a few occasions to look for his friend, but each time, it had become more dangerous until finally, he was resigned to the belief that Tye must have been killed. If only he had gone with him to Frentier, perhaps things would have been different, but here Tye was, in his embrace, and he was ecstatic.

"I thought I lost you," Jencen said to him. "We all did."

"Boy, do I have stories to tell you!" Tye exclaimed. "I've been to Under Hollow and everything!" he couldn't help but brag.

"*You*, in Under Hollow?" his friend responded in disbelief. "This I have to hear!"

"I'll tell you all about it after we win this battle." Tye said, remembering his task at hand. "Help me gather up the others. We have to start fortifying the area." The two young elves took off and scurried about the town, organizing a defense team.

Outoo was inside the Temple of the God of the Sun. It was a grand spectacle. Its walls were adorned with precious metals and gems found only in Solaris Arbor. Its altar was made of pure gold and sparkled with the sunlight from a nearby window. He looked around at all of the faithful who crowded the room, hoping the Sun God would provide a miracle. *If ever there was a time to pray*, thought Outoo.

He had finished communicating with the watchmen throughout Solaris Arbor and placed the temple's Globe of Communication back on its stand. Making his way to the stairs that would take him to the top of the spire for a better look at the land, he was grateful, once again, for his stamina boots, for he surely would not be able to make it up even a couple of stairs without them.

Stepping onto the sunrise viewing platform, Outoo looked to the horizon. The sight was breathtaking. In the distance, he saw the majestic snow-capped mountains of Solaris Arbor and the purple water that filled the great lakes nestled in their valleys. He looked upon his homeland sadly, for he knew it could quite possibly be for the last time. He turned his attention to the dead, barren trees that had been full of life just a few hours ago. Never in his many years had he seen anything quite like the death of the Breathing Forest. A tear fell from his eye and he said a silent prayer to the light elves' Sun God.

He looked into the forest and leaned forward as if to get a better look. He set his staff against the stone wall and raised his hands. He began to twirl them, and the air in front of him twisted as he created his own magnification spell. He zoomed in on the horizon and gasped at what he saw: The forces of darkness were on the move, heading in his direction. *They couldn't be more than a couple of hours away*, he thought. With his focus on the Queen's carriage being pulled by her nightmarish creatures and Commander Zelgot on his steed, leading his army, he waved his hand away, ending the spell. He grabbed the rope to the temple's morning service bell and began to ring it wildly. They would soon be out of time and caught up in a battle that was sure to end in the loss of their homeland and perhaps their lives as well.

Chapter XVIII

—⟨❦⟩—

Solaris Arbor's Twilight

W hat was left of the Breathing Forest was now burning. The recently destroyed trees now produced billowing clouds of black smoke instead of delicious fruits and beautiful flowers. The flames were just starting to lick the grassy lands of Solaris Arbor when the Dracal burst from out of the lifeless forest and into the land of the light elves.

The Dracal were Zelgot's first line of attack. Their breath was powerful and they were more expendable then his dark elf brothers. The entire Dracal race was represented, the red, blue, green, and yellow, and they were all pouring into Solaris Arbor. It was a rare sight to see the Dracal this highly concentrated. They were deadly enough on their own, but together, with their attacks coordinated, they could not be stopped.

Arrows began to fly from the archers on nearby rooftops. They flew through the air with the usual light elf precision, striking many of the Dracal. However, the Dracal's thick, scaly armor provided more than an adequate defense and the arrows ricocheted off their bodies. A few archers were lucky enough to hit the Dracal's soft underbellies, but it would take more than a few arrows to bring down the beasts.

The archers on top of the closest building to the forest's edge were the first to feel the sheer power of Zelgot's creatures. A yellow Dracal swooped in and shot his acid breath at the building's column support structure. The stone immediately began to disintegrate where it was struck.

As the archers shot their arrows at their attackers, a green Dracal flew in overhead, opened its mouth, and let out a large, toxic cloud of gas upon them. Many of the archers fell to the ground instantly, choking on its fumes. Those who did not succumb to the poisonous gas were soon consumed by the fiery breath of the red Dracal that was closely in tow.

A blue Dracal was the last to swoop in. In a loud clap of thunder, a powerful lighting bolt flashed from its mouth and struck the columns that were still being eaten away by the acid from the yellow Dracal. The lightning hit with a thunderous boom and sparked on impact, lighting up the surrounding area. The columns gave way and the building crumbled to the ground, killing everyone inside and on top of the structure.

The light elf spell casters now joined the fray. Using their command of the elements, they channeled lightning of their own from the clouds above and shot it at the beasts. Funnel clouds appeared, whipping the Dracal out of the sky and onto the ground.

After Tye and Jencen had started the defenses, they took it upon themselves to assist the remaining residents of Terrenal to their horses so they could escape the battle. They knew there were too many of the Queen's forces at their doorstep and that this was a battle that could not be won, but they had to buy time to make sure as many of them as possible were out of immediate harm's way.

Tye helped a small child up onto a horse behind his father. As the small elfling placed his hands around his father's waist, a large Dracal came from the sky, landing directly in front of them. Its large red wings were impressive. It stood there, expressionless and ready to carry out its orders.

Tye quickly reached into his pocket and searched for anything he could use as a weapon, because he knew his small knives would have little or no effect on the creature. He pulled out the rotting core of the Quin-Ti fruit he had saved from Under Hollow. With a quick shrug of his shoulders and a magical phrase, he threw the fruit at the Dracal's feet. In an instant, a strong Quin-Ti tree grew out of it, encasing the Dracal in a cage of its thick branches.

Jencen hurried to Tye's side. He knew he had to act quickly before the Dracal used its breath of fire to escape. He clapped his hands together very forcefully and yelled into the sky, "Lerr Min Tah!" The lightning he summoned from the gathering storm clouds repeatedly struck the Dracal inside its prison. The creature thrashed around wildly as it was electrocuted. Its tail and arms were smashing the branches of the Quin-Ti tree, but by the time it had freed itself, it fell to the ground, dead.

"They do grow above ground," Tye referred to his Quin-Ti fruit core with a smile.

Jencen smiled back at Tye and slapped the rear of the horse. It took off, carrying its passengers out of the town and to the safety of the catacombs.

The battle was in full swing when Commander Zelgot

emerged from the forest on his mighty steed. With him came his army of swordsman and spell casters. "Kill anyone that would resist you," he ordered.

The dark elves rushed to join the chaos of the fight. The spell casters were conjuring up their energy darts and fireballs. The swordsmen soon found themselves locked in melee with anyone that was nearby. Unfortunately for some, their closest adversary was Eldin.

Eldin was a master with a blade and he towered above the shorter dark elves. None of them could match his strength. One by one, he cut down any who would dare challenge him. He couldn't help but wonder, as he looked at the battle around him, how this fight would be going if only they had been given time to call for help beforehand. He knew that Solaris Arbor would soon fall and he would either be dead or taken prisoner. Like the others, he knew he had to do his part by buying as much time as possible. He looked across the battlefield and his eyes focused on one opponent, Zelgot. If he could kill Zelgot, the loss of morale would slow the dark elves down for sure. With that thought in mind, he began slicing his way through the battlefield, doing his best to avoid anything that could be spat his way from the Dracal gliding through the air above.

****

Queen Valeria lagged behind the rest of her forces, save for a few of her elite guard. Her carriage was parked in the Great Plains just outside of the Breathing Forest. It would not navigate well through the density of the trees, which were now more like matchsticks engulfed in flames. She left her elite guard behind to watch over her precious transport and wandered the forest alone to join her forces, confident that she could handle anything that came her way.

Her eyes widened and she raised her staff in a defensive posture when she came across Jade. She was still lying in her hammock, her chest covered in blood. Valeria cautiously approached her body. She eyed the corpse up and down and focused on Jade's wound. *No breath,* she thought as she focused on her chest. She raised her head to the forest around her. Everything was dead and much of it was burning. The Breathing Forest was now lifeless. That which had stopped her before was no longer an obstacle.

With a smile on her lips, she took a step back from Jade's body and pointed her staff at it. She squeezed her staff and the magical words spoken in her native tongue flowed from her lips in a calm, seductive tone.

A blast of energy shot from the staff's crystal and struck Jade's lifeless body. Her corpse lifted off the ground and throbbed with pulsating light from head to toe. The area was engulfed in sparkling electricity as the corpse exploded in a thunderous boom, sending fragments of itself throughout the forest.

****

Aldara had just finished hitting her dark elf opponent in the head with her staff, knocking him unconscious, when she whirled around and struck another one with a bolt of energy from her weapon. *There has to be more I can do,* she thought. She looked around and her eyes settled on the Temple of the God of the Sun. She looked up at the platform on its spire. *Come on Ali,* she communicated telepathically to her familiar. *We're going to get a better view.* Ali-Mimi gave her a nod as he leapt off of the face he had just mauled to join Aldara.

Ayku was buzzing around the battlefield, shooting powerful beams of bright light into the eyes of the dark elves and the Dracal, blinding anyone she could. She caught Aldara's glance at the temple's spire and flew over to join her. "I'll provide cover for you," she offered. "Just keep us out of your line of fire." With a dismissive look from Aldara, she took off, filling the area with intense white light.

Outoo gathered arrows and supplies for the light forces, keeping a careful eye on the battle while doing so. At times, he envied the dark elves' magic. They were able to conjure fire and energy out of nothing, whereas the light elves had to have a source nearby to draw from.

A group of dark elf spell casters caught Outoo's eye when they gathered to focus their efforts on one of the last caravans to leave the town. He wondered how he could possibly stop them when the flames of the Breathing Forest gave him the answer he needed. He threw his hands up and called upon the fire to do his bidding. His hands reached out to the blaze, then he quickly pulled them in and twirled his hands. The fire poured in from the forest and engulfed the light elf's targets. With a sigh, Outoo turned his attention away from his screaming adversaries and back to the task of gathering arrows.

****

Queen Valeria stepped out of the forest and into the land of Solaris Arbor. This was the day she had been looking forward to for quite some time. She took a moment to give thanks, not only to the Moon Goddess, but also to herself. It was her plan that made it possible for her to walk into Solaris Arbor and claim victory. She gave herself full credit for finally winning the war.

Spotting Zelgot nearby, she made her way over to him. An occasional arrow flew her way, but most had not yet noticed her arrival onto the battlefield.

"How goes the battle, Commander?" she asked Zelgot. Looking around the town made her question more rhetorical than anything else. Her forces clearly had the upper hand.

"The fight should be over soon, Your Majesty," he answered her. "but I am growing tired of coordinating our efforts from afar." He looked at her and said in a nonchalant way, "I was thinking of joining in. I could use some sport."

"You have done well, my love," she smiled at him. "Go and have your fun."

Eldin was making his way across the battlefield toward Zelgot when he noticed the Queen. His eyebrows rose as he found a new objective. The thought of lopping off her head renewed his energy and determination.

His line of sight was overcome by a flash of light. It streaked across his path with a scream and ended in the town's fountain. It was Ayku. She grew to full size on impact and Eldin could see she was cut and bleeding. In a heartbeat, she was surrounded by couple of dark elves with their greedy hands pawing at her.

Eldin looked back at the Queen in disgust and ran to the aid of his friend. He made short work of the dark elves as he came up from behind, taking them by surprise. Ayku sat up on the fountain's edge. "You all right?" he asked her.

Ayku shook her head and stood up slowly with a groan.

"I'll live," she responded, "for a little while anyway." The battle around her reminded her of when her own land was attacked by Nagarr. The fight wasn't quite as spectacular; the fairie folk were a peaceful people. They had no real means of defending themselves and Nagarr had slaughtered them into near-extinction.

The fairie folk had been respected throughout the land. To gaze upon them, let alone hold a conversation with one, was considered a great honor. From afar, they could be seen lighting up the night in small dances of light. Like fireflies or stars that had come from the heavens, wishes were often made on them. But now, their numbers had dwindled from many thousands to a couple of hundred, at best.

In the span of a few hours, Terrenal was transformed from a beautiful city to a crumbling vision of the realm's apocalypse. "Eldin," Ayku said with tears in her eyes, "this is the end, isn't it?"

He took her hand and helped her out of the fountain. "I believe it will be, soon," he answered with a helpless sigh.

The fiery spectacle from above caught not only their attention, but also the attention of the Queen. Aldara had reached the top of the temple's spire and was blasting the Dracal with fireballs.

The Queen looked up just in time to see a blue Dracal engulfed in flames spiraling out of control to the ground, releasing its electric breath on the way down and making for quite a spectacular death.

"Aldara," the Queen said aloud. Her eyes narrowed as she quickly walked into battle. "She ends now."

She easily repelled anyone who tried to approach her with

blasts from her staff or with a wave of her hand, either of which sent them sailing away; she was determined to reach her target.

Tye and Jencen took notice of the Queen approaching the Temple of the God of the Sun and sprinted to intercept her. They were closing in fast when the Queen reached the temple. It had still maintained its beauty even through its surface was now covered in scorch marks.

The Queen let out an angry growl when she looked upon the golden sun that adorned it. She did not hesitate; she aimed her staff directly at it and squeezed. The image of the sun exploded, sending gold, cement, and stucco debris flying through the air. The two young light elves were buried in the rubble.

Valeria looked at the two light elves covered in the broken pieces of their God's shrine and laughed as she entered the temple. She didn't know what to expect inside. She was ready for a fight, but the temple had been abandoned. All of the windows had been shattered and the altar had been cracked. She made her way to the stairs, intent on reaching the top and killing Aldara.

Tye and Jencen slowly dug themselves out of the rubble. "Are you okay?" Tye asked his friend.

Jencen winced in pain. His arm was cut and bleeding and his face was covered in scratches. He sat on the rubble. "I'll be fine, you?"

Tye tried to stand, then fell down with a scream of pain. "My leg," he said through clenched teeth, "I think it's broken."

A shadow came over them and they looked up to see Commander Zelgot, the most feared dark elf in all of Valeria's forces. "Well, such hearty young elves. You will both make excellent slaves to the Queen," he said with a smile.

Valeria reached the top of the spire and she took no time walking out onto the platform. Ali-Mimi saw her out of the corner of his eye. *Trouble behind!* he screamed in Aldara's thoughts.

Aldara turned to see Ali-Mimi jump toward the Queen and scratch her across the face. It was a deep cut and the pain caused her to wince. Her staff fell to the ground and she looked at Ali-Mimi, who had just landed next to Aldara, with nothing but hatred in her eyes.

With a loud scream the Queen pointed her hands at Ali-Mimi and electric green energy darts flew from her fingertips and struck him. He spun across the platform with such force that when his body reached the support wall, it shattered the wooden frame to pieces as his body went tumbling toward the ground.

Aldara let out a scream of sadness, but even more so, of pain. With the death of her familiar, the link was now broken. It affected her thoughts and her emotions, and the physical pain was unbearable. She collapsed to the floor in agony.

Still full of anger, Valeria looked at her staff and then focused on Aldara. She didn't need it. She didn't require any magic to end Aldara's life. She saw her young adversary doubled over in pain, and just as Aldara looked at her, she felt the Queen's rage.

"You," the Queen began, as she kicked Aldara in her side, knocking her away, "stupid," she continued as she kicked Aldara closer to the edge of the spire, "insignificant," she kicked Aldara again, this time bringing her to the spire's edge, "girl," the Queen ended her insult with a final kick that sent Aldara flying over the spire's edge toward the ground. The Queen let out a satisfied laugh as she aggressively wiped the blood from her cheek with the back of her hand. Aldara had been useful to her in the past, but her usefulness was over. Death was her punishment for destroying the Queen's Globe of History and Valeria was more than happy to carry out her sentence. The Queen closed her eyes and took in a deep breath.

From the ground below, Ayku and Eldin watched the clash outside of the spire. They had witnessed their friend Ali-Mimi fall to his death just moments before and they now watched Aldara falling victim to the same fate.

With a gasp, Ayku flung her arms in Aldara's direction and the young half-breed was covered in shimmering pixie dust, just in time to slow her fall. Aldara hit the ground with a fairie's gentle touch.

Ayku and Eldin ran to assist her when a loud rumble stopped them in their tracks. They looked skyward and saw the clouds begin to twist and turn as the wind picked up. From a stone obelisk, a beam of light shot forth into the storm brewing above.

The Queen grabbed her staff and let out a gasp as the light hit the clouds. Lightning seeped out of the storm's center and wrapped around the clouds, clinging to them like a spider's web. With a clap of thunder, the portal opened and dozens of Winged Angels poured through. They filled the sky and wasted no time heading down to the battle below.

No, the Queen thought, *I will not be cheated now*. She eyed the obelisk across the town and made her way to the stairs of the spire and began her descent.

Teluli was leading the Winged Angels in battle. They

flew past the temple and were on the Dracal within seconds. Following closely behind Teluli was Wyndle—her feathery wings outstretched and flapping—delivering her to the fight.

As Wyndle had discovered days before, all it took was a touch from an angel to release a Dracal from the unnatural dark magic that maintained it. Wyndle didn't really quite understand how it was done, but the Globe of History told her all she needed to know, that the Dracal were monsters created from the life force of another. The Overlord and his Queen had broken the rules of nature and now it was time for the Winged Angels to restore the balance.

The aerial combat was astounding to watch from below. The touch of the Winged Angels sent the Dracal spiraling from the air down to the ground, dead. It didn't take long for the Dracal to figure out what was happening. Their new enemies were the Winged Angels, to whom they showed no mercy. The angels proved to be difficult targets, but the Dracal had their share of small victories, either by engulfing them in poison or by setting their light, feathery wings ablaze.

Commander Zelgot took his eyes from his new prisoners for just a moment, watching his forces begin to crumble before his eyes. Tye seized the opportunity and reached for a small knife in his belt. He leaned forward and jabbed it into Zelgot's calf. He twisted it with all his might and Zelgot let out an intense scream.

Zelgot backed away from Tye and drew his sword. "You'll pay for that with your life," he said coldly. He swung his sword just as Wyndle cast her protective force field around Tye and his lifelong friend. Zelgot's sword hit the protective sphere with so much force that it knocked him off balance.

After regaining his stance, Zelgot let out a growl and pulled the knife from his wound, throwing it carelessly to the ground. There was nothing he could do to his prey as long as the Winged Angel had her force field surrounding them. "We will meet again, young light elf. I promise you," he said to Tye. "And next time, there will be no angel to help you." He turned and limped his way across the battlefield.

Feathers were gently falling to the ground as the Winged Angels were slowly picked off by the dark elves and their deadly magic. The Winged Angels could only erect their protective fields around themselves when they actually saw the incoming danger, so many of them felt the dark elves' revenge from behind.

Teluli flew to Eldin and hovered in front of his face, quickly informing him of the angels' progress. "My angels have done what they can. It is up to you and your companions to do what you will with your adversaries. We have now witnessed the true defiling of the dragon race. I will travel back to our land and summon more angels to Sylvanor. Your world will be cleansed of this abomination." With a final look around the battered town, Teluli took off for the portal.

The Queen's quick stride seemed to go unnoticed as she moved across the battlefield unchallenged. A look of concern washed across her face as she saw her beloved, limping his way toward his steed. Even when injured, he was still able to successfully fight off any light elf foolish enough to think they had the upper hand in attacking the wounded dark knight.

She reached the obelisk just in time to see the last Dracal fall from the sky. The glow in its eyes sputtered and then went dark as it hit the ground. Valeria pointed her staff at the obelisk and unleashed all of its power. The blast from her weapon shattered the angel's portal on impact.

Teluli looked up and watched the portal to his home world collapse in on itself. His body was jerked violently as the Queen suddenly grabbed him. She held him tight in her fist. "Your portal is closed forever and there are too few of you left here on Sylvanor to oppose me," she smiled, "and now there is one less." She clenched her fist as hard as she could. Valeria's black leather gloves muffled Teluli's screams and cracking bones. A moment later, she opened her fist and shook his broken body to the ground.

Queen Valeria walked over to Zelgot, who was being helped onto his steed by one of the few remaining dark elves. She gave him a look of concern.

"Not to worry, my Queen," he said as he finished mounting his horse. "I can handle the remaining swine on horseback."

The Queen looked around at the smoldering town. Its streets were crimson with blood. Bodies of the Dracal littered Terrenal, along with the corpses of light elves and their dark elf brethren. The sight of white feathers sticking to the blood-soaked cobblestones made her think of what could have been had she had not seen the obelisk, the controlling stone to the Winged Angel's portal.

An arrow struck the last dark elf that was standing near the Queen. It plunged into his head and he was dead before his body hit the ground.

The Queen waved her hands in the air and a giant wall of fire appeared between her and her foes. "Come on," she said to Zelgot, "we are returning to Under Hollow."

"What? Retreat?" asked Zelgot in an insubordinate tone.

It was a word he seldom heard, and it was something he had never personally done.

"Let them have their victory," she told him with a smile, "for it is only temporary. The angels are now gone forever and the Breathing Forest is destroyed. Solaris Arbor is now ours; surely even the most foolish of light elves can see that. We will return with more Dracal from the realm of Caliron and then we'll make our victory official by taking its flag for my castle wall."

Zelgot offered his hand to the Queen and when she took it, he pulled her up onto his steed. She gave a quick glance around at the land to which she would be returning, a broken land that she believed belonged to her. *From this point on*, she decreed silently in her head, *I will now be known as Valeria, Queen of Sylvanor.* With a kick of her heels, their horse went speeding off out of Solaris Arbor and toward her carriage.

****

The remaining fires had been put out but foul-smelling smoke still filled the air of Terrenal. Most of the city had been destroyed, but the battle had been won. The brave men and women who chose to stand and fight did so bravely. Although many of them had lost their lives, most of the townsfolk escaped.

"The sacrifices made today were not in vain," Outoo said, finding it unbelievable that his own heart was still beating.

"Yeah!" said Tye excitedly. "We won! Did you see the way the Queen and her lackey took off out of here?" Wyndle had just finished healing his leg and Tye could now stand up, pain free.

"We won nothing, junior," Eldin replied solemnly. "The portal is closed. The rest of the Winged Angels can't come through and help us get rid of the army the Overlord has tucked away in that other realm," he sighed. "This land has fallen. It belongs to the Queen now. She'll be back. You can count on it."

"Speaking of the portal," Tye looked at Wyndle. "I can't believe they let you come back. Wasn't going back home the worst thing you could have ever done?" he asked her.

"Yes. When you are banished, it is forbidden to return home," she lowered her head in sorrow. "When I returned home, I received my sentence of having my wings removed and had it had not been for Teluli, it would have been carried out."

"I am sorry you lost him, Wynd." Tye said to her. He did not know which angel was Teluli, but he knew that Wyndle was the only angel left alive on this side of the portal.

"Do not feel sorrow for Teluli, for he is one with all of creation now," she explained to Tye. "It was through his bravery that we were able to return. He challenged the wavering leadership of the Proconsul and won. I linked with him and shared my memories of what the Globe of History revealed to us. He dismissed my sentence and we left for Sylvanor." She thought better than to go into the whole story of the Proconsul being her father, for it would only give rise to more questions she would rather not answer.

"I'm glad that you're back, Wynd," Tye confessed.

Ayku helped Aldara walk a horse over to the group. Although Wyndle had healed all of her physical wounds, losing her familiar left an unseen, bleeding scar on Aldara's emotions and on her soul itself.

Outoo placed his hand on her shoulder, "It will be some time before you will recover, I'm afraid."

"I'll live." Aldara wasn't sure if she believed her own words, but even after all she had been through, she could not bring herself to show any weakness to her companions. She gave Eldin a hard stare and he mirrored it back to her.

Tye knew from her response that she was anything but okay. He thought about engaging her in conversation; maybe, if he could get her to open up, she could begin the healing process. Realizing, however, that she would not want to discuss this openly, he used his caring eyes and warm smile to say everything he needed to say to her, at least for the time being.

The silence was broken when the remaining supports of a nearby building gave way with an echoing thud. Terrenal, the once shining jewel of Solaris Arbor, now lay in ruins.

"What do we do now?" Tye asked Outoo as he hopelessly surveyed the destruction.

Outoo took in a deep, thoughtful breath before he answered, "We use the information we have gathered and add it to our existing knowledge." The puzzled look on everyone's face was a signal to Outoo that he had better continue. "When I traveled down into Under Hollow, to the Queen's castle with the elders, we used a portal to travel to another realm that the Overlord referred to as 'Caliron'. I believe it to be the dragon realm. I believe more answers reside there. This is where you must travel next, my young friends. There must be another portal other than the one in the heart of the Queen's castle. You must find a way into that other realm to stop the Overlord from making more of these beasts."

"What do you mean 'you must find a way'?" Ayku asked

him. "Aren't you coming with us?"

"My dear, my journey ends here. I am getting far too old for all of this travel," said Outoo in surrender. It was a painful statement to make for someone who had spent his entire life traveling and fighting for the good of his people. "I will do what I can from here."

The sun was setting, bringing with it an end to a day that no one could have predicted. The last province of Sylvanor had fallen to the evil forces of the Overlord and those who were not enslaved in his dark empire were now merely hiding from its grasp.

Tye refused to believe that all was lost. *Perhaps the Circle of Thirteen still existed? Maybe they know how to get to the other realm,* he thought. He let out a sigh as the setting sun turned the sky a calming shade of pink. The only thing he knew for sure was that he and his friends were just at the beginning of their adventure and they were going to need all of the luck they could get.

Aldara looked at all of them in turn. "I won't be joining you, either."

"But Al, you can't—" started Tye.

"I must go. I have put you all in danger and it is because of me that all of this death and destruction happened." Never one for long, emotional goodbyes, Aldara climbed up onto the horse to escape any hug from Tye that might come her way. He was probably the only member of the group who would offer one.

"You know, the Queen didn't actually watch you fall," Ayku attempted to offer some hope to Aldara, "She may not even know you're alive."

"Is that a chance you'd like to take?" Aldara looked at her companions, "Would any of you?"

Eldin folded his arms and let his body language speak for itself. He had never liked Aldara and he had never trusted her. He was not sad to see her go; he only wished it had been sooner. In his eyes, she was the sole reason everyone in Sylvanor wasn't rejoicing over the Winged Angels' victory over all the Dracal.

"Where will you go, child?" asked Outoo.

"I don't know," she confessed, "but I've got to find a way to break this bond that I have with the Queen." She gave Tye a loving glance and they eyed each other in silence for moment. "I have wrapped up Ali-Mimi's body." She gently tapped on her shoulder bag. "I will give him a proper burial, one that he deserves." She then added in a lower tone, "I just wish we could have done the same for Gusseus." She gently kicked her horse, signaling that it was time to go.

Aldara slowly disappeared into the smoky haze of what was left of the Breathing Forest. She did not look back, but kept her eyes forward on the future...a future that was now more uncertain than ever.

Epilogue

The Future's Leader

"I am Valeria, Queen of Sylvanor," the Queen said proudly as she bowed on one knee in the Overlord's Circle of Identification in the middle of his throne room. "I am here to report on the battle of Solaris Arbor." The Queen waited a few moments for the magic circle to verify her identity. It pulsed with its usual green light, then after the flash of white light, it went dark. She was who she claimed to be.

"Rise, my Queen," the Overlord's voice echoed from his throne. "I can surmise from your new title that the battle went well?"

The Queen rose to her feet, and in the dim Caliron sunlight, the Overlord saw that she looked more beautiful than usual. In fact, she had taken extra time on her appearance before visiting him on this trip. "We are victorious, my love," she answered, taking a few steps closer to his throne. "The glory of your name was heard throughout the entire province of the light elves," she lied.

"Excellent! You have done well, Valeria." He admired her exceptional beauty once again. "Clearly, victory agrees with you."

Queen Valeria flashed him a seductive smile and stood before him in a silent flirtation. The Overlord had not seen her act this way in quite some time. Surely, winning the battle had returned his Queen to a mood not displayed to him for so long, he had almost forgotten about it.

The Overlord raised his hand in the air. "Guards," he ordered, "leave us."

On cue, two royal guards stepped out from the shadows and exited the throne room. From underneath his hood, the Overlord gave Valeria the nod to approach him. She wasted no time in moving around his desk and behind his chair, as she had several times in the past, to massage his shoulders. The Overlord's shoulders relaxed as he enjoyed the touch of his wife.

"And what about your half-breed puppet?" he asked her between his groans of pleasure.

"I killed her myself, as her usefulness to me had ended," she answered as she slid a knife out from under her sleeve, "just like yours." Her voice went cold and she plunged the knife into the Overlord's chest.

His body quivered uncontrollably and the Queen hugged him tight. He attempted to yell for his guards, but all that came out was a whimper. Valeria twisted the knife again and pushed it as deep as she could into his heart and the twitching stopped. He was dead.

The Queen threw back his hood and smiled at the face of her dead husband. She sighed, glad that she was finally free of him.

Just then, the throne's chamber door gently swung open and Fenrik hobbled through. As was customary, he kept his gaze to the floor while he made his way to the Circle of Identification. "Forgive the intrusion, my Overlord, but I believe it is time for you to make good on your promise made to me long ago," he stated, his eyes still to the floor.

The Queen watched him in disbelief—Fenrik had no clue what had just happened. She figured she had better act quickly, before he alerted the royal guards. She looked over at the throne room doors, and with a flick of her wrist, they slammed shut.

Fenrik raised his head to the throne and saw Queen Valeria standing next to the Overlord. She seemed to tower over his dead body. The Overlord's eyes looked on to eternity as the blood continued to trickle from his heart.

"What have you done?!" Fenrik gasped and assumed a defensive position.

"What I have been wanting for do for a long time, you old fool," she answered calmly.

Before Fenrik could act, she struck him with a few bolts of energy from her fingertips. They hit his chest and his neck, knocking him back to the floor and had him gasping for breath.

The Queen approached him quickly from around the throne and leaned down to him. Again, a smile came across her face as another one of her enemies had fallen. "No scream? No call for help?" she asked him. *Curious*, she thought. "At least give me the satisfaction of a duel. Fight back!" she demanded.

"You are still the foolish girl from all those years ago," Fenrik said to her, wincing in pain and coughing up blood.

"You lack the experience to hold onto the realm. You cannot win," he wheezed.

"My dear Fenrik," she leaned closer to him, "I already have."

The Queen stood up and conjured one final spell to destroy her opponent. "And now, Fenrik," she said coldly but with great satisfaction in her voice, "I revoke your existence."

A powerful ball of light appeared between her hands and she hurled it at Fenrik. It engulfed his body and lifted him off the floor. His body levitated in front of her for only a fraction of a second when the ball suddenly burst into a brilliant display of energy. The blast threw Fenrik's body against the wall with a loud boom. The energy shot in and out of his body. It poured from his mouth as he opened it to release his screams of agony and then his body fell to the floor. Fenrik no longer twitched and the Queen let out a sigh of relief at his demise.

"Guards!" She wasted no time on a cover story. The Overlord's elite guards burst into the room, ready to protect their master. They could not believe their eyes; their leader was dead on his throne. They raised their hands to Queen Valeria and she gestured at Fenrik's body. "He assassinated my husband before I had time to act," she lied. "Dispose of his body at once. Take his body to the Isle of Lost Souls," she paused, "but do not bury him with dark elfkind. Dump him with our enemies like the traitor he is." She thought back to the recent skirmish in her castle. "Bury him with the dwarf."

The royal guards looked at each other, not sure what to make of the situation, but they obeyed their Queen without question. They dragged Fenrik's body out of the throne room and shut the door behind them.

Laughter overcame the Queen and filled the royal chambers.

She walked to the large tinted windows behind the throne and looked down upon the strange realm of Caliron.

It was truly a sight to behold and the Queen took it in with great satisfaction. She was watching the conversion process from dragon to Dracal with great enthusiasm. Legions of Dracal stood in formation while the life force was sucked out of a giant red dragon. It was splintered apart in the large jewel the Overlord once referred to as 'The Dragon Heart' and could be shared between numerous humanoid creatures. Their features twisted and turned as they morphed into a new life form. Their cold black eyes suddenly sputtered to life with that familiar eerie yellow glow.

This was the secret to Under Hollow and although it had been discovered, it was much too late to matter—for Solaris Arbor had finally fallen to her.

"Everything is now mine," declared Queen Valeria of Sylvanor as she continued to look upon her dark forces. Her cold, calculating laughter filled the room and, it seemed, the realm itself.

www.ingramcontent.com/pod-product-compliance
Lightning Source LLC
Chambersburg PA
CBHW020927020726
47495CB00002B/379